To Kevin

Enjoy the history

Regards

Dave [illegible]

The Oyster Wars

A Novel

By

David Faulkner

ISBN 978-1-4507-2636-8

Printed in the United States of America.

Edited by: Rachel Faulkner

Map Art by: Carolyn Faulkner

Cover Art by: Rachel Faulkner

Published by: Pipe Creek Press
www.pipecreekpress.com

Distributed by: BookLocker.com, Inc.

The Oyster Wars

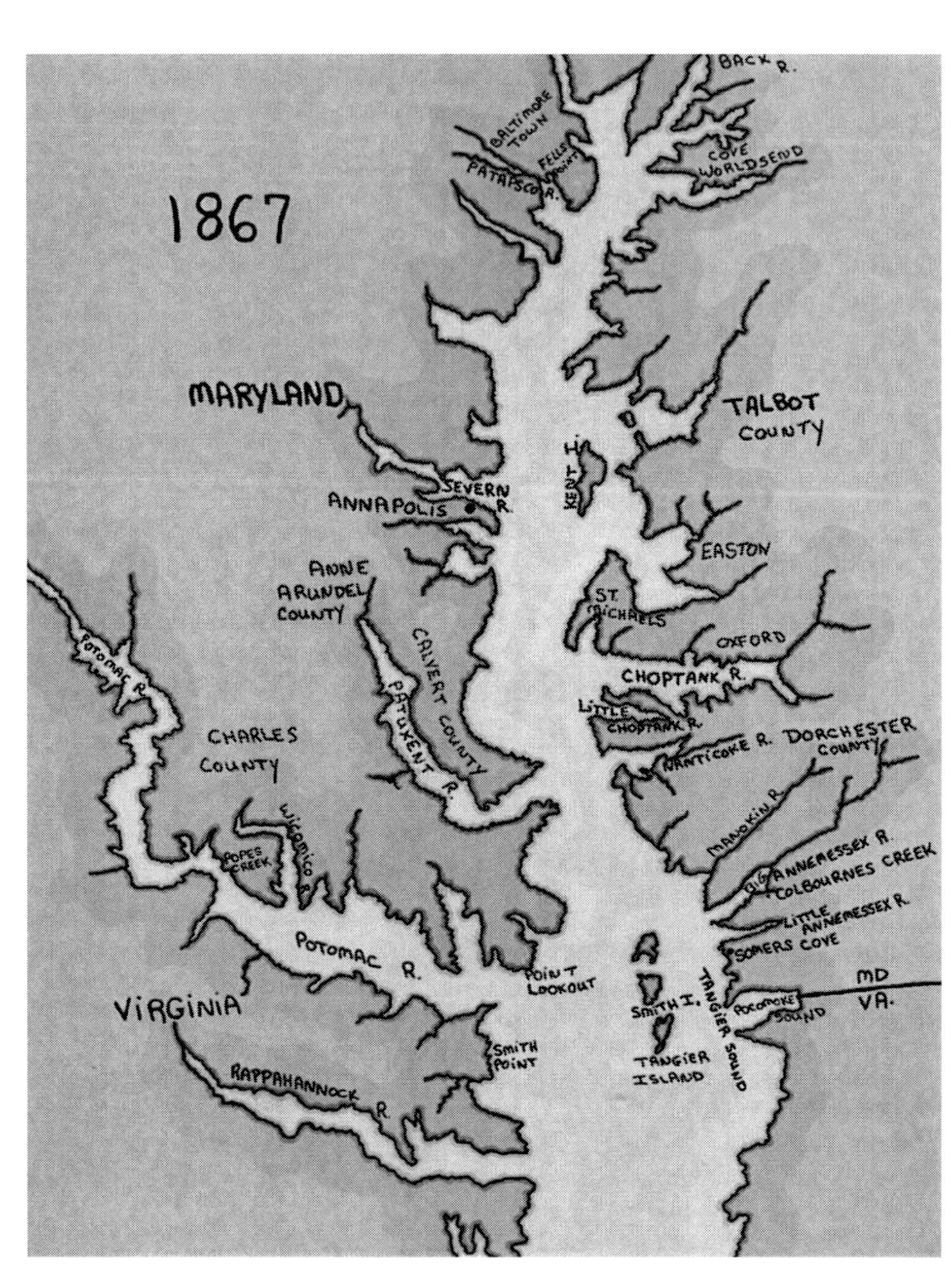
1867
BACK R.
BALTIMORE TOWN
FELLS POINT
PATAPSCO R.
COVE
WORLDSEND
MARYLAND
TALBOT COUNTY
KENT I.
SEVERN R.
ANNAPOLIS
EASTON
ANNE ARUNDEL COUNTY
ST. MICHAELS
POTOMAC R.
CALVERT COUNTY
OXFORD
CHOPTANK R.
PATUXENT R.
LITTLE CHOPTANK R.
CHARLES COUNTY
NANTICOKE R.
DORCHESTER COUNTY
MANOKIN R.
WICOMICO R.
POPES CREEK
BIG ANNEMESSEX R.
COLBOURNES CREEK
LITTLE ANNEMESSEX R.
SOMERS COVE
POTOMAC R.
POINT LOOKOUT
MD
VA.
VIRGINIA
SMITH I.
TANGIER SOUND
POCOMOKE SOUND
SMITH POINT
TANGIER ISLAND
RAPPAHANNOCK R.

For Carolyn:
Who makes all things possible

PREFACE

In the mid-nineteenth century, men began killing one another over chunks of yellow metal being wrested from streambeds near Sutter's Mill, in California. Meanwhile, across the country, other greedy men were killing each other over access to the equally rich oyster beds found in the waters of the Chesapeake Bay.

As the world began to savor the oyster, mountainous beds of this "white gold" shimmered beneath the surface of the Chesapeake's pristine waters. Watermen, battling over this treasure, spawned a deadly conflict, which the days' press termed "The Oyster Wars".

In 1868, the State of Maryland created a law enforcement resource intended to combat the sea going lawlessness, adding another dimension to these "wars" which endured for almost one hundred years.

1

Popes Creek, Maryland
August 1863

Corporal Haynie McKenna lay motionless among the sodden leaves, grass and tangled vines carpeting the forest floor. A few feet to his right lay a rutted wagon trail, flanked by the soldiers of his unit, the 1st Eastern Virginia Loyal Volunteers attached to General Sickles's command. Concealed and silent they waited in ambush for the notorious confederate coastal raider, Commander John Taylor Wood.

The trail, strewn with leaves and underbrush, snaked from the terminus of Popes Creek up the wooded hillside, disappearing over the crest to the north. Yesterday, Joe Phelps, a local hunter in the pay of the Union army, stumbled across the secret road while following his hound in pursuit of a lone rabbit. Phelps knew, as did everyone in the area, that the Union government was desperate to capture John Taylor Wood.

Wood's late night raids on shipping along the western shore of the Chesapeake Bay and its tributaries, principally the Potomac and Rappahannock rivers, wreaked havoc on the North's war effort in Maryland and Virginia. Haynie McKenna had heard it said that President Lincoln himself ordered General Sickles to do whatever it takes to stop Wood.

The growing legend of John Taylor Wood was familiar to McKenna and those Union forces under orders to rid the Chesapeake region of

Wood and his crew of rebel raiders. In April 1861, Wood, a grandson of U.S. President Zachary Taylor, and a nephew of the Confederate president, Jefferson Davis, resigned his commission in the United States Navy and left his position as an instructor at the naval academy in Annapolis, Maryland. Within weeks, he joined his uncle in the confederate cause and proceeded to revolutionize the rebel's approach to naval warfare.

In the fall of 1862, Wood and his raiders boarded a U.S. schooner, the *Frances Elmore*, anchored for the night in the Potomac at the mouth of Popes Creek. Meeting little resistance, Wood's raiders captured the crew and burned the ship with its cargo of hay destined for a Union cavalry division. Joe Phelps's discovery of this hidden wagon road supported the rumor that Wood had returned to the area of his first success.

In the year since that raid, John Taylor Wood had attained the dual rank of Commander in the Confederate Navy and Colonel in the Confederate Cavalry. Many of those competing with Wood for rank and favor in the confederate forces, grumbled that bestowing such rare, dual commissions was nepotism at its worst. At the same time, Wood's federal counterparts recognized him as a brilliant nemesis who had single handedly changed the rules of naval warfare.

Wood accomplished this remarkable feat by devising and building a wheeled naval attack force. He obtained three whaleboats each capable of carrying 18 men with weapons and supplies for a week. These he fitted to be quickly hauled from the water, lashed to wagons and carted overland to a nearby river or creek. Soon after a raid, Wood and his commandos would quickly be miles away in other waters, while Union forces vainly scoured the area around the point of attack. Wood's use of this tactic terrorized shipping around the Chesapeake Bay.

Joe Phelps believed that the hidden wagon trail signaled Wood's return to the waters around Popes Creek. The federals would pay good money to know this, and if his information led to the capture of Wood and his raiders, Phelps would soon be spending the large bounty offered by President Lincoln's government.

Phelps worried about those of his neighbors who were loyal to the South. The Potomac River no longer served as the border between two states. It now separated the United States of America, and its capitol city of Washington, D.C. from the Confederate States of America. At Popes Creek, the Potomac narrows to bring the shorelines of the two nations at their closest point along the river's length. This natural crossing amid so many rebel sympathizers resulted in the frequent smuggling of mail, businessmen, spies and weapons into the Confederacy.

Within two hours of his discovery, Phelps reported to the military commander at nearby Ledlow's Ferry. Orders were issued and Haynie McKenna's unit was on the march by three a.m. and concealed along the hidden wagon trail well before dawn.

Haynie secreted himself at the wide base of a leafy red maple, his long legs wedged under a gnarled tree limb long ago snapped off by a strong wind and now decaying where it fell. High overhead the sun's rays deflected among the broad green leaves, heating the still air. Though he could not position the sun through the overhang, Haynie knew that it was nearing its midday high point. It was not a piercing hunger that told him the time, for that had long been gnawing. More than ten hours ago, he hastily downed a skimpy breakfast of war coffee and three pieces of bacon fat, barely warmed over the campfire. The ersatz coffee, a mixture of boiled corn meal and coffee grounds, had tasted more of the corn meal than the coffee. A taste that lingered heavily in his mouth.

Haynie McKenna felt the time, more than reasoned it. Long days on the waters of the Chesapeake Bay and later, traversing the marshes, inlets and rivers near the small town of Somers Cove on Maryland's Eastern Shore, had nurtured an internal clock which was never more than ten minutes from the time kept by the wall clock at home.

Haynie lay on his stomach and peered up the wagon trail to a tall locust tree split apart in a recent storm. This was the point where Wood and his wagons would likely appear.

Mosquitoes attacked Haynie's face, neck and hands. Swarming skeeters had caused him to take up chewing tobacco, a habit widespread through the ranks. Chewing tobacco was cheap entertainment during the mind numbing boredom of camp life.

Some in the unit swore that rags dipped in tobacco juice and wrapped around wrists and ankles kept mosquitoes from attacking. On the eve of a field maneuver, each chewer who contributed spittle to a common pail was allowed to soak his rags in the bucket for use the next day.

Evenings, Haynie's camp split into tight knots of men. Soldiers gambled their pay playing cards; some played crude musical instruments and sang songs of pain and longing. Others gathered to spit tobacco juice at a campfire and swap stories.

Haynie valued his meager corporal's pay too much to risk it playing cards. After supper, he spent a little time chewing and talking, or listening to a fiddler, before heading back to his tent to read from one of the treasured books he lugged from campsite to campsite.

Listening to the camp music reminded Haynie of home. His father, standing in front of the fireplace, entertaining the family with songs from his fiddle. Some of the music he created as he played.

Tench McKenna was an oysterman. Sadly, years of handling icy lines and the thousand stinging cuts from oyster shells had produced a condition known to local watermen as "erster hands". Calloused palms and gnarled fingers forced him to give up his beloved music several months before his murder.

That Haynie McKenna read beyond a grade school level set him apart from most of the men in his unit and, likely, most men in the whole army. The fact that he actually enjoyed reading made him distinctive.

During his first weeks in the unit, men stopped by his tent to cajole him into a card game or drinking session. Without fail, one of them squatted trying to make out the title of the book Haynie held. After struggling with the words, lips moving all the while, the soldier looked to his pals and laughed. "What the hell is a Mus kat eer and why would a body want three of 'em?" Another, anxious to join the taunting said, "I ain't never see'd no city with a tail, let alone two cities."

Haynie explained that "A Tale of Two Cities" is a story about a civil war in the country of France. "It's history," he said, "just as this war will someday be written about in history books."

One of the soldiers said, "You must be a smart man, readin' books and such; maybe you can tell us why we're fighting this damn war, anyway. Who cares if the South keeps slaves? None of our business."

The flickering campfire reflected anxious faces as the men awaited a reply.

"I guess there's no single answer to that question," Haynie replied. "You'd get a lot of different answers from different folks. My answer is — that every man should care about the outcome of this war because the enslaving of human beings by other human beings is an affront to the dignity of all mankind."

The soldiers, embarrassed by their failure to understand, punched one another in the shoulder, called one another "a dumb shit" and stumbled away laughing too loud.

They were back the next night. Four of them crowded around glaring down at Haynie as he sat outside his tent reading *David Copperfield* by the flickering light of a kerosene lamp.

The tallest of the four, started it. “You reckon you’re smarter than us, don’tcha? ’Cause ya read them fancy books and use big words. Words folks like us cain’t understand.”

Haynie closed the book in his lap and scanned the faces looming above, stopping to hold the gaze of his tormentor. They were drunk and unconcerned by the fact that he out ranked them.

“No. I don’t think I am smarter than any other man.”

Another soldier moved closer, his leg brushing Haynie’s shoulder. “Well then,” he said, “Put down yer fancy damn book. Come along and have a drink with some real men.”

“No thanks. It’s late. I was just getting ready to go in to bed.”

The first tormentor nodded to his friends. “I told ya he was too good to have a drink with the likes of us.”

The second man reached over Haynie’s shoulder, snatched the book from his lap and stepped to the dying campfire.

“If’n we burn this here book,” he said with a smirk, “I reckon ya’ll come along then.”

Haynie sprang to his feet, fists clenched. “Don’t —”

Two of the tormentors gripped Haynie’s arms, shoving him back into his chair.

Haynie, eyes fixed on his cherished book, struggled to free himself. “Don’t —”

Instantly, the man and book were gone — yanked into the smoky darkness at the edge of the fire in the embrace of two huge arms.

“What the hell,” the tormentor cried out.

“Jesus,” said one of the men at Haynie’s side. The other tormentors released their grip and moved toward the fire, stopping abruptly.

Haynie jumped up and stood, awestruck. Emerging from the gloom was the most imposing man he had ever seen. Powerfully built and a head taller than Haynie, he toted the struggling tormentor effortlessly on his left hip. His right hand held the precious book, which he gave to Haynie.

The giant stopped beside Haynie and released the tormentor, who fell heavily to the ground.

The man scrambled to his feet and scurried to the protection of his cronies. The four of them stared at the giant, immobilized.

“You men, git,” Haynie barked. “And don’t come around again,” he called, as they stumbled into the night.

“Thanks for your help,” Haynie said, extending a hand. “I’m not much for fighting my own kind. I’d likely have lost the book. It means a lot to me.

"*Ja.*"

Haynie touched his chest. "My name's McKenna, Haynie McKenna."

"*Ja.*"

Haynie pointed an index finger. "What is your name, private?"

The man smiled, "*Ja. Prevat.*"

Gerhard Stein was the man's name. Stein loved to talk and the two men labored well into the night at communication.

At one point, Stein understood that Haynie wanted, in some way, to repay him for saving the book. Stein hesitated, then, after further prodding, pointed at Dickens's novel cradled in Haynie's arm.

Eventually, Haynie understood that the young Prussian wished Haynie to read aloud from the book. In that way, Stein hoped to learn the English language. Haynie agreed, though he doubted that listening to English fiction was the best way to survive in the ranks of the Union army.

With difficulty, Haynie learned that Stein had served in the Prussian army in the late 1840s, fighting against the Dutch during the revolutionary wars of 1848.

Haynie swept an arm toward the rest of the camp. "Why did you come to America — now?" he asked.

Stein shrugged, "*Nicht gut* wars in old country."

Stein had left Prussia and traveled extensively through Europe. He stayed for some months in Spain and France, with lesser time lived in Italy. In halting English, he described the Spanish countryside, lush with trees laden with olives and oranges, and bawdy times with several young ladies in Paris. Haynie, chagrined at the idea of intimacy with a woman of short acquaintance, somehow maintained his composure while listening to Stein's account of being with several women.

Haynie wondered about a man who trekked across Europe, deciding, largely on impulse, to cross the Atlantic Ocean and join this bloody war. Was he courageous, or unhinged?

Now, Haynie shifted his body and rubbed his head against his coat sleeve, wiping the perspiration from his eyes. The blue of his uniform coat contrasted starkly with the green grass and leaves surrounding him. Haynie lifted his head and spotted random patches of blue strewn along the slopping hillside in front of him.

Following their first skirmish with a confederate cavalry unit, Gerhard had complained to Haynie about the deep blue uniform coats they wore.

"In Prussian army – *mantel* —" Stein pulled at his coat sleeve.

"Coat," Haynie said touching his own jacket.

"Coat. *Ja*, coat. In Prussian army coat *farber* is *braun*. More better to *verbergen soldat."*

Haynie mulled Stein's words, associating them with his facial expression and other body language. "*Farber* must be color and *braun* is brown," Haynie reasoned, "But, I don't know what is *ver-ber-gen*."

Stein ducked his head and covered his face with his arms. "*Verbergen,"* he repeated.

Haynie thought a moment, "Oh. Brown coats would let us – soldiers – hide ourselves better than blue," he said pulling at his own coat sleeve."

"Ja, ja."

Following that exchange, Haynie wondered who in the government decided that their uniforms would be a deep blue. Probably no one who had ever had to wear one into battle through barren woods or across a grassy meadow.

Haynie rolled back and forth, swaying his body in a futile effort to deflect the pests swarming about him. When he stopped moving, they attacked through the thin socks and bit the back of his neck. The early and sudden departure this morning had meant there was no time to collect the tobacco juice. Now, Haynie lay on the damp ground with no juice rags to keep the skeeters away.

Wonder what old Watkins thinks about Sergeant Pruitt's words, today, he thought.

Private Watkins had joined The 1st East Virginia Loyal Volunteers straight from a life lived entirely on the streets of Philadelphia. It quickly became known that, though never having seen one, Watkins was deathly afraid of snakes – any kind of snake. One day while Watkins was away from camp, someone killed a huge black snake and coiled it, as if poised to strike, under Watkins's blanket. That night Watkins pulled back his cover and let out a chilling shriek heard throughout the camp.

When Haynie reached him, Watkins was out of his tent lurching about in tight circles, arms outstretched and flapping wildly. Watkins strained mightily, his face now a deep shade of red. His mouth, though agape, was silent, his stricken throat unable to produce a sound.

Sergeant Tub Pruitt, arriving simultaneously with Haynie, grabbed Watkins, pinning his arms to his side. Pruitt eventually quieted

Watkins and asked Haynie to sit with them while Pruitt spoke to the city boy about life in the country.

Haynie respected the Sergeant, and was pleased to be asked to stay.

"Look, son," Pruitt began, "I lived in the country all my life and never been bit by a snake. Corporal McKenna here, the same, though a lot younger than me."

Glancing at Haynie, Pruitt continued, "He's a progger. You know what that is?"

Watkins looked up slowly, the fear still evident in his eyes, and shrugged apologetically. He gazed down at his shaking hands and shook his head.

Pruitt touched Watkins's shoulder, "No reason you should. But a progger is a hunter and a trapper who walks the marshes and stream banks for miles and miles looking for all kind of animals to catch. He's been doing it for years." Giving Haynie a stern look, Pruitt concluded with, "And you've never been bit, have you corporal?"

Haynie did not need the warning look, for the truth is, he was never snake bit. "No, Sergeant," he said shaking his head.

Sergeant Pruitt squatted next to Watkins and motioned for Haynie to do the same. "Listen good to what I tell ya."

Watkins watched him closely.

"You know what a musketo is?"

Watkins nodded.

"Ever been bit by one?"

Watkins studied the sergeant, then said, "I reckon. Why 'course I have."

"What are you most afraid of son, snakes or musketos?"

Watkins blinked and looked at Haynie as if trying to understand the joke. He turned to Pruitt and, squaring his shoulders said, "I may be a city boy, but I ain't scared of no little bitty skeeter."

"That was not a joke, or an insult, private. Someday, if you last in this army, you will fret more about musketos than snakes. And that's a fact."

Watkins shrugged, "How can that be, sergeant?" he asked.

"If you meet a hunderd snakes and a hunderd musketos, the musketos will be more bother than the snakes, and they can be as deadly. It's true. A snake will warn you off and run away – if he can. They only want to be left alone, same as you would. But them musketos will keep pesterin' at you, bitin' an' drinkin' your blood all the while they maybe givin' you a real bad sicknesses."

Pruitt concluded with, "Snakes are the most misunderstood of God's creatures. You have to be real unlucky or real dumb to get bit by one."

Within a week of that conversation, the sergeant had ridden off with McClellan's forces. Haynie still felt the despair and sadness, which had overcome him when the men were told that Pruitt had been killed on the last day of battle at Gettysburg. The pain was as sharp and suffocating as that which he had experienced 10 years before when, at the age of 13, he learned that his father had been killed while tonging an oyster bed just off their Smith Island home in Tangier Sound of the Chesapeake Bay.

To Haynie, his father, Tench McKenna, and Sergeant Pruitt were very much alike. Both had little formal education and each man had devoted himself to a single calling, which had ended his life violently, at an early age.

Tench McKenna had worked the Chesapeake Bay from the age of 12, surviving early by selling a few fish he caught in the warm months and the occasional bushel of oysters he tonged from their beds during the cold ones. He had withstood harsh bay winters and brutal boat captains to become master of a log canoe, which he had crafted by hand.

Tub Pruitt had joined up with the U.S. Cavalry at the age of fifteen as a civilian paid to tend the horses and muck out their stalls. At seventeen, he went on the rolls of the military as a drummer. For much of the next thirty years he thrived on garrison life in the western frontier, surviving howling winter storms and numerous Indian wars. Pruitt seldom spoke of his role in these frontier battles, but on a rare evening he could be coaxed into describing, often in gory detail, the massacre of a lone settler's family or a wayward wagon train. As Haynie McKenna, Watkins, and the other young men listened, they felt wholly lacking as soldiers and always left these sessions in awe of the sergeant.

The single thing that most endeared Haynie to the old sergeant was that Pruitt, unlike many of Haynie's comrades, never rousted him or poked fun at him for being well spoken. Around others, Haynie had learned to choose his speech carefully, selecting the words and phrases common to the soldiers in his unit. One thing he refused to do was to corrupt the English language by ever using the word "ain't."

Haynie considered ain't, as profane as any word spoken. It was as offensive to his ears as any of the curse words he rarely used.

Haynie McKenna, like his older sister Mattie, and younger brother Caleb, had been born on Smith Island, a swampy wedge of land situated in the middle of the Chesapeake Bay at the Maryland, Virginia border. Three hundred souls who lived on the island were watermen and their families, variously clustered in small communities. Schooling on the island was rudimentary and spasmodic, conducted by a procession of locals with little or no teaching background. For a time, the parson read from the bible, later one of the mothers, with little schooling herself struggled with a few outdated textbooks.

The paucity of education was of little concern for most of the island families. Girls were needed at home to help their mothers sew the family's clothes, make soap and candles, smoke and cure meat, and preserve fruits and vegetables for the next winter season.

Watermen's sons much preferred spending their days progging the waters and marshes of their island home. Traditional watermen wanted their sons working with them and discouraged them from going to school. Winter was the time for tonging oysters and hunting game for fresh meat. The days were short.

Tench McKenna, saw his sons' futures differently. He wanted them to have the opportunity for a more comfortable and fulfilling life.

On icy mornings aboard his oyster boat, a log canoe he'd named "Miss Lettie" for Haynie's mother, Tench would stare down at his scarred and gnarled "erster hands". Many of these mornings, he spent painful minutes prying his fingers apart and gingerly rubbing feeling back into them. Each such day, he renewed his vow to see his sons off the bay and free of the perils posed by the work, the weather and often violent clashes over territorial rights to the rich oyster beds in Tangier Sound.

So Tench and Lettie McKenna dug deep into their resolve and found enough money to send eleven-year-old Haynie up the bay to Baltimore to receive proper schooling at the Chesapeake Academy, a small private school on the edge of Baltimore Town. They could only afford this luxury because their older daughter, Mattie, had married at age eighteen and fled the tedium of Smith Island for the excitement and comforts of city life.

During the school year, Haynie had lived with Mattie and her husband, Levin Tilghman, returning home for brief holidays and summer lulls.

Much to his surprise, Haynie had enjoyed the excitement of learning in a confined setting. His initial aching to tromp the bogs of Smith Island, track game over wooded acres, and fish the waterways ebbed as he became absorbed by the writings of classical authors and intrigued by the revelation of a world beyond Smith Island.

Now, lying motionless among the ferns and prickly brush at Popes Creek, he simultaneously reveled at the learning he'd acquired in less than two years at the academy while lamenting all that was yet unknown.

Haynie maintained a steadfast gaze to the top of the rise, frequently dabbing a piece of gray cloth at the sweat that stung his eyes and tickled his nose. He recalled, as he had many times in recent years, the sacrifice his father and mother had made so that he could have a better life than they.

The moment the Head Master approached his desk was still vivid. He was sitting in class having just finished reading aloud a passage from Charles Dickens's recent book, *David Copperfield*. The Master, ever solemn, wore a particularly grim expression as he approached. Haynie's stomach rolled while he frantically sought to understand what antic of his might be cause for such a forbidding visit from the Master, himself.

The Master leaned down and, with a gentleness belying his stern countenance, told Haynie that he needed to speak to him outside of the classroom. Haynie, head bowed and legs trembling followed the great man into the hallway. He could feel the eyes of those around him and knew that his present trouble was a source of joy to Sterling Wallis and the other *snots* that let him know, from his first day there, that he did not belong and would never be accepted as one of them.

Out in hall the Master laid a hand on Haynie's shoulder and said, "Son, I'm sorry to be the one to tell you, but your mother sent word that your father has been killed."

Haynie searched the Master's eyes for some hint that it wasn't true. He left school the next day for home and did not return. To this day, he had not wept for his father because his father would have forbid it.

Back home, on Smith Island, Haynie learned that his father had been shot and killed while working a small oyster bed along the Great Rocks Oyster Bar, near the Maryland, Virginia line. Haynie was convinced that those responsible were likely Virginia watermen who had crossed into Maryland waters or Maryland drudgers poaching on the shallow beds frequented by tongers.

Haynie knew that the hollowness he felt in his chest and the frequent night terrors tormenting him persisted because no one had been held accountable for his father's murder. No one had ever bothered to look for the killers.

In time, Haynie recognized that, because his father had been attacked on the open waters of Tangier Sound, it was impossible to know if he had been killed in Maryland or Virginia. Even more disturbing was the realization that there was no law enforcement agency with jurisdiction over these waters. Finally, he understood that even if jurisdiction were not at issue, there was little interest in resolving the death of one lone waterman, who, it was said, was likely poaching someone else's bed.

Tench McKenna was an independent oysterman, a tonger, whose death had no affect on the money flow streaming into the burgeoning oyster processors in Somers Cove or the large packinghouses strewn along the Pratt Street wharfs up in Baltimore Town.

Haynie's father worked from a log canoe, a small craft dug from logs and fitted with a sail. His tongs were an iron rake attached to handles long enough to reach the bar while showing above the waterline. Anchored over a shallow oyster bar, often so clear and shallow he could almost touch them; Tench worked the metal teeth into the bed until he felt sufficient resistance. Then he pulled up his catch and dumped it sprawling across the culling board.

Using a culling hammer, he separated the oysters of legal size from those too small. Tench McKenna, always scrupulously honest, tossed the smaller ones back to be taken another day. At day's end, he headed his boat farther into the bay to meet up with a buy boat and sell the day's catch.

The buy boat was a much larger bay schooner operated by a seafood-processing house that paid tongers for their catch and transported the oysters to the Baltimore docks for processing.

Drudgers were a different breed from the tonger. A large sailing ship was needed to drag the heavy iron baskets, called drudges, through the beds. Operation of the ship and drudge gear required a crew of five or more men who worked for a small percentage after expenses and profit was taken out for the owner and captain. It was common for ships captains and owners to cheat the crews out of their full share.

The work was backbreaking and treacherous, with the crews often away from port for weeks at a time. The result, not surprisingly, was a perpetual surliness among most crewmen.

Unlike the tongers who were local, independent owners of their boats and businesses, drudge boat crewmen were recruited from the larger port cities in the Chesapeake region. The crews were a motley mixture of immigrants, recently processed through Ellis Island and duped into signing on. They were pressed alongside homegrown ne'er-do-wells and good-for-nothings, likely avoiding the law or running from a debt or a woman. Such men quickly learned to despise the tongers, who went ashore each night to a home and family with a little money from the buy boat in their pocket.

Tench McKenna and his fellow tongers feared and despised the drudgers who regularly profaned their homeland and forcibly violated the sanctuary of their oyster beds. It is no wonder their encounters often ended in deadly violence.

Only recently did Haynie understand that his father had been a visionary among the hordes of watermen competing for the treasures littering the floor of Tangier Sound. The elder McKenna's eagerness to harvest the oysters was tempered by a stubborn conviction that care be shown in how the bounty was taken.

On the other hand, many drudge boat captains had no interest in preserving oyster beds for another harvest; their only thought was today's catch. They proceeded to wantonly drag their clumsy and cumbersome iron jaws across a bar, crushing oysters not taken and leaving the bed destroyed. They could not be bothered to cull their catch.

Haynie heard a sharp noise off to his rear left, the snapping of a fallen tree branch perhaps. By turning his head slightly and peering over his left shoulder, he saw a blue figure, bent low and moving nimbly from tree to tree.

Lieutenant Stewart. Likely checking our positions. He's a sittin' duck in that blue coat.

Haynie respected the lieutenant. Most of the good officers he had served with were the lieutenants and captains. Sadly, the ranks above, majors, lieutenant colonels and full colonels, along with all manner of generals, were replete with fools and idiots. Unfortunately, these were the men who made the life and death decisions.

He thought it a perversion that the political appointees and other incompetents were awarded the higher rank. The merchants and politicians joined up for the glory, or to escape a strong willed woman at home, or for the thrill of ordering other men to their death. They hung on as long they could until being found out.

Lieutenant Stewart, still in a crouch, paused alongside Haynie and patted him on the shoulder.

"Keep a sharp eye, Corporal," Stewart said in a hushed voice. "They could be coming down that hill any time now."

Haynie nodded as the lieutenant moved across the wagon road, disappearing behind a mossy chestnut tree.

Haynie scratched at his beard, now a sodden clump from the sweat, and inspected his Sharp's carbine resting on a tuft of grass in front of him. Next to the weapon's stock lay the leather bullet pouch within easy reach, its flap unsnapped and yawning open. Beside the pouch, his campaign hat had been precisely placed with the topside down. Inside the blue hat he had carefully set his rations of three hard tack biscuits and four pieces of the nearly raw bacon saved from breakfast, carefully wrapped within a piece of grey cotton cloth. Hunger gnawed, but Haynie knew that he may well be laying here for several more hours and disciplined himself to resist the pangs a while longer. To occupy his mind, he reflected on his life before the war.

Following Tench McKenna's funeral, Haynie's mother, Lettie McKenna, was fiercely determined to provide for her sons. Dispirited by her daughter Mattie's marriage and abrupt departure from Smith Island at eighteen, her "escape" as Mattie called it, Lettie would come to view her daughter's absence as a blessing.

"One less to fret about," she would say.

Mattie and her husband had come to the island from Baltimore to attend her father's funeral. Back at the house, Mattie hugged her mother, pressed thirty dollars into her hand and left by the next packet boat.

"She fled," Lettie told her neighbors afterward. "Couldn't wait to get off this island. They never visit."

For two years following her husband's death, Lettie and her sons struggled mightily to subsist. Haynie assumed command of his father's boat while Caleb had inherited the fiddle and rifle.

When the boys weren't hunting or fishing, they chopped firewood for cooking and heating, picked fruit and wild berries, tonged oysters and snared game and crabs in baited traps. Soon, the pain Haynie felt at missing school gave way to the sense of pride he and Caleb shared each night when their mother set the supper table with the food they had provided. After the meal, Caleb would take up their father's fiddle, trying to entertain them with music, much as Tench McKenna had done for so many years.

Now, Haynie decided, he viewed Caleb's efforts with bow and fiddle more kindly than he had when forced to sit and listen politely almost ten years before.

Lettie, too, had worked endlessly. She took in sewing, made quilts from odd bits of cloth and sold baked goods along with preserves and jams she put up. Occasionally, she hired out to do laundry and cleaning for folks that were too sick or too old. But, it was not enough.

Smith Island was twelve miles by boat from Somers Cove, Maryland, the nearest land based town. By necessity, families on Smith Island were self-reliant and none had any extra money to pay out for things they could do for themselves. A few neighbors bought her pies and preserves, others gave her some sewing to do, but mostly it was charity and could not be sustained.

In the spring of 1856, Lettie sold their home, along with her husband's boat and rifle and moved her family to the mainland. She found a dilapidated house on River Road, just north of Somers Cove. She dreamed of turning it into a stylish rooming house; her boys would finish school in a real school.

The house was massive compared to the four rooms and outbuildings of their Smith Island home. Before neglect set in, it was rather elegant, two full stories topped by dormer windows tucked beneath the overhang of a sloping mansard roof. A wide wooden porch enveloped the house, and porch posts, topped with baroque ginger brackets, buttressed the overhanging roof. Faded yellow cedar siding was split and mottled.

The first floor consisted of a dank sitting room to one side of the entryway while across the foyer two pieces of furniture, partially hidden by dusty covers, loomed sullenly in a musty parlor. A walk-in fireplace, black with soot and cold, took one wall. A carved heavy wooden mantelpiece hovered above the hearth. The remaining walls were finished in wainscoting capped with a wide chair rail. French doors of wood framed glass panes, opened into a large empty dinning room.

To the boys, the place was gloomy and foreboding. Lettie explained to them that the house had stood empty for years, but with their love and hard work it would become a showplace. She referred to it as her "Manor House".

Caleb maintained that the place was "spooky" and likely had ghosts, while Haynie began to understand the promise for their future that his mother had seen.

The first day, the three of them stood at the roadside as Lettie described their new home, her voiced tinged with an excitement Haynie could not recall having ever heard before.

"See those windows, up there," she said pointing up to the glass panes of two dormers, facing River Road. "See Caleb," she urged, "the one on the left is where you and your brother will sleep. Your own room. The one on the right is where I'll be."

Caleb glanced briefly in the direction his mother pointed, then dropped his head and glared at the ground. Gently she said, "Haynie will be right there with you and I'll be only just across the hall."

Caleb had responded by kicking the ground. "I don't need nobody lookin' after me," he said, "I ain't scared."

Haynie caught glimpses of Stewart's blue coat as the lieutenant worked his way up the sloping hill, encouraging each man as he went. The dampness of the forest floor grew steamy in the mid-day heat. Sweat tickled down Haynie's sides and ran along his spine.

Worst of all, perhaps, was the stench of his own body, rising in the heat and clinging to the clammy air around him.

Shifting to his left side, Haynie lifted his uniform cap and shook the ants from his rations. He set the cap back on the ground and kept a hard biscuit for himself.

I don't get to these 'fore the shootin' starts, the ants'll get 'em.

Haynie thought about the nights he lay awake in their dormer room, worrying that Caleb would again wake screaming. His reverie inevitably included his mother's late night visits to a room occupied by a visiting drummer on the floor below.

Three, sometimes four nights a week, long after the house was quiet, Haynie heard the creak of his mother's door and her light step as she moved toward the staircase. Presently a door on the lower floor would click shut. As he lay listening for her return, he pictured his mother in her woolen robe and crinoline nightgown and tried to imagine which of the drummers she had chosen.

As these nocturnal treks repeated, Haynie vowed not to judge his mother and never to mention a word to Caleb. It occurred to him that while they worked at restoring the house, Lettie often left for town in the wagon, sternly repulsing the boy's pleas to come along and help. She told Haynie that if it got too late she would stay in town and he would have to get supper for himself and Caleb. She invariably appeared by noon the next day with the materials or tools they needed to continue the work.

He reasoned that she was only doing what she had to. What any woman, struggling to survive, might do.

Suddenly, he heard it. The labored sounds of wagons and the horses pulling them. The birds who had resumed their song after the troop had settled in fell silent again. More intruders.

Haynie wolfed down another biscuit and a strip of bacon fat, and then took a quick drink from his canteen. He returned the remaining rations to his knapsack, shook out his cap, and settled it on his head. Instinctively, he sidled closer to the red maple, pulling his carbine and bullet pouch with him. He rested his weapon on the down limb, sighted along the barrel to the point atop the hill where the first Rebs would appear – and otherwise prepared himself to take the life of another human being.

2

Fell's Point
Baltimore, Maryland
October 1867

The port of Baltimore Town was singularly well located to profit from the vigorous trade burgeoning from a nation reunited in April of 1865. This, the western most deep-water port on the nation's east coast, abutted both the industrial North and the agricultural South. On any day of the week Baltimore's inner harbor was a forest of masted vessels.

Thousands of Europeans, particularly Irish and Germans, emigrated through the Port of Baltimore. Passenger ships, crammed with eager families, docked at the foot of Light Street affording their bewildered cargo a short walk to the Camden train station. There, many boarded a Baltimore and Ohio train for a trip overland to Chicago, St. Louis and the western frontier.

Those newcomers to America, who lingered near the waterfront anxious to find work on the docks, or to slack the thirst of a long sea voyage, often received a jarring welcome to their new country. Many became the targets of insult and ridicule; others were robbed and beaten, often left cringing in a grimy back alley, the smell of rotting fish and human urine strong in their bloodied noses. These were the lucky ones.

Most nights roving gangs of thugs prowled the dock areas hunting for fit young males to be subdued and sold to a ship's captain in need of crew for a lengthy sea voyage. Other men were rounded up, crammed into the fo'c'sle of a small fishing boat and transported down the Chesapeake Bay for a season of labor on an oyster boat. Five years after Lincoln's Emancipation Proclamation, and three years after a state constitutional amendment outlawed slavery in Maryland, a form of slavery thrived on the outskirts of the nation's capital.

Naive immigrants were the likely targets of this sea going slave trade; no passerby would understand their cries, and the authorities routinely ignored subsequent appeals for help by an immigrant family.

On rare occasions, a gang eager to fill an order mistakenly abducted a local man of standing. When the thugs, or more often the ship's captain, discovered the error, the citizen was quickly released with profuse apologies and a small payment for his trouble. Once, a young doctor making a late night house call near an isolated pier was taken. Another time, the son of a distinguished lawyer went missing for several hours. No one was ever charged but rumors persisted that in each of these cases the sea captains involved had set sail with one, or more, of the kidnappers in chains below deck.

In the spring of 1867, Colonel Silas Teackle Wallis moved his family into one of the finest homes in Fell's Point on the north shore of Baltimore's harbor. In an area of fine homes, the Wallis house stood out. Walls of dark red brick housed four stories of elegant glass, marble, mirrors and chandeliers. Sitting majestically on the crest of a sloping side street, a few blocks from the Fell's Point waterfront, the grounds were adorned with leafy shade trees and new gas street lamps. The building's front stoop, cut from a block of quarried marble, was kept scrubbed and gleaming by one of the house staff. The mistress of the house, Beverly Sterling Wallis, insisted that the domestic help be referred to as "staff" and not "servants". In her mind, it distinguished the Wallis family from the antebellum slave owners.

Silas and Beverly Wallis had three children, the eldest, a son, Sterling Teackle Wallis, the younger twins, Landon Crockett Wallis and Beth Harford Wallis. The children were doted on by their mother and largely ignored by their father. Sterling, having finished an apprenticeship in his father's seafood processing plant and allied shipping enterprises, was recently named to fill a sudden opening as a senior manager in the business. The man he replaced left abruptly after eight years of loyal service.

Landon and Beth were in their first year at a prestigious local liberal arts college, which allowed them to remain at home.

On All Hallows Eve, Landon Wallis sat brooding at a corner table in the Irish Eyes, a rowdy dockside tavern at the end of Broadway. Alone, and ignored by those wedged around him, he glared at his glass of hard cider and fingered the cloth mask jammed into the pocket of the thin jacket he wore.

"I should never have believed that bastard," he muttered banging his fist on the table.

Yesterday, at school, Asbury Boston had approached him. Landon's weak chin and whiny personality precluded his acquiring any true friends at school, especially not Asbury Boston. Boston's family was from old money, which assured him a leadership role in his own clique of friends. Landon had been thrilled when the other boy suggested that they meet the following evening for a night of hi-jinks.

"Some of us are going out and have some fun on Mischief Night," Asbury said.

Landon, desperate not to appear over eager, replied, "I don't know, I'm supposed to be at a party my parents are throwing. What are you going to do?"

Asbury shrugged, "That's the fun of it; we'll see where the night takes us. Tip over some privies; let some horses out, who knows. But, if you would rather stay home with mommy and daddy, that's okay with us."

"No. Never. I'll get out of it," Landon blurted. "It wasn't you that sunk that boat last year at the end of Thames St., was it?"

Asbury gave him a dark look. "What if it was?"

"Oh nothing," Landon replied. Fearing the invitation might be withdrawn, he added, "Sounds like fun."

Asbury eyed him momentarily, "Be at Irish Eyes at nine o'clock," he said. "We'll have a couple of glasses to fortify us against the night air and the goblins."

Boston laughed and turned away. "Oh. You know to bring a mask so no one will recognize you, right?" he asked over his shoulder.

The idea had not occurred to Landon at all. "Of course," he said. "And Asbury thanks."

Neither had it occurred to Landon that the Irish Eyes was a peculiar place for them to meet. The Eyes, frequented by sailors and other lowlifes, was usually avoided by young men of good breeding. The thought of going there on All Hallows Eve was especially disturbing. Though only a few blocks from his home, it was an entirely different world. One that was foreign and frightening, especially at night. Asbury had chosen The Eye, Landon convinced himself, because it was a perfect beginning to the evening they had planned.

If they don't show up, he thought, *at least I won't have to wear this stupid mask.* Fingering the material, he had an urge to take the mask out and fling it in the corner.

That morning he had begged Mrs. Hudson, the housekeeper, to make a mask for him. A plump matronly woman, she wore her grey hair pulled tight and held in a bun at the back of her head. Though she had only recently joined the Wallis staff, she had quickly grown fond of Landon.

"But I am in the middle of getting everything ready for tonight's party," she scolded. "I don't have the time."

"Anything you can do will be fine. It won't take long. You know I wouldn't ask if I didn't really need it," he pleaded. Landon had convinced himself Mrs. Hudson cared more for him than she did for Beth, his twin.

Mrs. Hudson could never bring herself to deny Landon anything, largely because she felt that he was in need of so much. Sputtering, she left, returning directly with a piece of satiny red cloth which she deftly turned into a mask to cover his face from the tip of his thin pointed nose to his eyebrows. It was secured by two strips of material to be tied at the back of his head.

Chagrined that he had considered casually discarding the mask he had begged her for, Landon gazed around the bar.

They might still show up and what would they think if I didn't have my mask?

It was now close to midnight and, despite the uproar, Landon was overcome by a feeling of desolation. He propelled his chair further into a corner, in an effort to distance himself from the drunken rabble.

The room was hot and stifling. The smoke of cigars, pipes and cigarettes brought from around the world moved in eddying clouds around him. Landon wished desperately that he had not been so haughty with his sister when she begged him to go to their parents' party.

If his argument with Beth had not become so shrill and bilious, he would have gone home hours ago. It would be no fun, but at least he would not be in this place.

Beth had spied the mask Mrs. Hudson was sewing and sought out Landon. She found him in the spacious kitchen preparing a snack of cold chicken.

"I saw what Mrs. Hudson is making," she said. "You know the Colonel doesn't like anyone to wear a homemade costume. Are trying to cause trouble?"

"I wouldn't worry about it, Miss Snot." He gave her a hard look, "And don't call him, 'Colonel'. That title is so very phony — just like everything else about him."

"He is too a real colonel. And somebody has to keep you from causing a scene," she said, her voice rising. "You'd wear that silly thing just to embarrass THE COLONEL."

Landon carried his plate over to the kitchen table and sat down. "I have something else to do. I'm going out with some friends."

Beth laughed, "I know that's a lie." Leaning close, she spoke directly at him, "Because you don't have any friends."

He glared at her spitting a piece of white meat as he spoke. "That shows how much you know, Miss Snot. Besides, what's the difference to you? You'll get all the attention – and be the belle of the ball – which is all you care about."

"I care about this family, which is more than you do," she shouted. "You won't mind telling me the name of this so called friend, will you – Mister Nose?"

Beth was instantly sorry that she had resorted to using that awful name. During the summer they were six, Landon began calling her, Miss Snot. Stung by the name, she had groped for a response most likely to return the pain. Knowing how sensitive he was about his long bony nose, she struck back with the name – Mister Nose.

As they grew older, it became apparent that Beth was going to become a beautiful woman, like her mother, with a slender, leggy grace and thick blonde hair touching her shoulders.

It was equally apparent that Landon was not to be an attractive man. Modeled after his father, he was shorter than Beth and retained his baby fat. His nose was more pronounced as it jutted from an angular face, sloping to a high forehead and capped by thin wisps of dirty, ash blonde hair. As their physical differences became more evident, Beth had all but stopped calling him Mister Nose, deciding that it was too cruel. But, sometimes it just came out.

"Well...I'm waiting," she said, arms folded across her chest.

Landon, furious at her for using that name, had lost his concentration.

"Waiting for what?" he snapped.

"The name of this imaginary friend."

Her brother drew himself up, sneering. "For your information, it is Mister Asbury Boston and a group of our friends. We're going to get drunk on cider and raise some hell. And don't wait up." He continued chewing as he spoke, "You and your Colonel may well have to come and bail me out of jail."

Beth issued what she hoped was a glaring look, ripe with warnings of dire consequences. "If it was up to me, I'd let you stay in jail," she snapped and stormed from the room.

Landon had laughed after her. Now, staring into his glass of cider, it did not seem at all funny.

The proprietor of the Irish Eyes, an Irishman named Brendan Doyle, loved All Hallows Eve second only to Saint Patrick's Day. He frequently reminded all in earshot that both celebrations were carried across the sea from Erin. Many in the crowd became even more boisterous, merrily contending that All Hallows Eve had actually originated with the witches in Salem, Massachusetts.

"This is an Irish bar," Doyle shouted in response. "Every day is an Irish holiday. Raise your glass." The crowd roared raising their glasses in salute.

The long evening of drinking and brooding in a room heavy with smoke and unrelenting noise had worn on Landon. He drained his glass, threw money on the table and elbowed his way to the door.

The Eye was located on a darkly narrow side street with shadowy doorways and assorted offensive odors. Once outside, Landon found the night eerily quiet and menacing. He considered returning to the bar, full of light and human sound. As he reached for the knob, the door jerked open and two burly men in heavy coats blocked his way. Their faces, weathered by long days at sea, glared down at him. Landon turned and, with head down, walked quickly away, clutching his thin jacket against the night air. The footsteps behind him echoed in the darkness and he hastened to cover the few paces to the wider, well lighted, avenue.

Just before stepping onto the avenue, Landon felt the fierce grip of strong, heavy hands on each arm. A panic seized him. Too limp to struggle, he slumped against the arms gripping him. A wet cloth was clamped hard over his face, and a sweet taste filled his mouth, rising through his nostrils. He gagged on the spew in his throat before sagging into insensibility.

Even though the last of their guests had not been ushered out of the house until after 1 a.m., Colonel Wallis was in his chair at the breakfast table precisely at 7:30 the following morning. He deemed it essential that family life be formally structured and behaved accordingly.

Nothing less was expected of those around him. Today, as every business day, he wore a dark frock coat over a matching waistcoat, concealing black suspenders.

He believed the combination of dark clothing helped conceal his bulk. Equally unsuccessful were efforts to hide the roll of flab that fell over the high starched collar and neatly tied cravat. Each morning, Wallis artfully brushed long, thin strands of graying hair from a fringe above his left ear, across his head, and ending just over the right ear. Each strand carefully positioned in a futile effort to conceal his pasty scalp.

Silas Wallis had been unable to believe his exceptional fortune when Abbie Sterling had accepted his proposal of marriage 28 years before. He never doubted his own promises to supply her with wealth, but was greatly sobered to find that such an exquisite woman believed in him equally. Many a morning, over the years, he reflected on his blessings as he enjoyed her loveliness across the table.

This was not one of those mornings. Face flushed, he glared around the room and drummed his fingers.

Abbie knew that her husband was still irate because Landon had ignored the family party and gone off with his friends. She was determined to avoid any further discussion of the matter until Landon was present to speak for himself.

"What a lovely affair, last night, don't you think, Silas dear?"

Before he could answer, Beth rushed in, brushed her father's cheek with a kiss and took her seat at the table. "Good morning parents," she said brightly.

"Where is your brother?" Colonel Wallis snapped.

Beth had come to understand that the question, "where is your brother", always referred to the location of her twin brother, Landon, never to her older brother, Sterling. Sterling's whereabouts were never in doubt. He was always where he was supposed to be.

She had rehearsed an answer designed to protect her twin and opened her mouth to reply when her older brother appeared in the doorway. His face was grey and he fell heavily into his chair.

Without a greeting, Sterling began to drink greedily from a water tumbler in front of him.

Silas glared first at Beth then at Sterling, before saying, "Am I to understand that Landon, after insulting the family, failed to come home at all?"

No one spoke.

"It's just as well the selfish boy did not return," he continued. "Failing to attend the party and then not coming home is entirely unacceptable. Such behavior violates several family rules making him liable for severe punishment."

"For God's sake, Silas," his wife cried. "He could be sick or hurt, laying somewhere in need of aid."

Sterling, always pleased to see his brother in trouble, raised his head focusing successfully on this father. "Or, maybe he is in jail. It would serve him right."

Abbie opened her mouth to protest.

Silas cut her off. "Being arrested would be an embarrassment to the family, otherwise I would agree with you."

Beth seeing the anguish in her mother's eyes could hold back no longer. She looked at her father. "Landon told me he was meeting Asbury Boston at some Irish saloon on the docks," she said.

Silas Wallis was enraged at what he viewed as Landon's insolence. It was a personal affront that a son of his would forgo a family function to carouse the waterfront even with a boy from such a fine family as the Bostons.

Beth continued, "I don't —"

Silas cut her off with a shout. "I won't have such behavior," he yelled, slamming the table with a flat hand.

Abbie spoke in a strong, forceful voice, a tone she seldom found necessary to invoke.

"I need to know that Landon is all right," she said fixing her gaze on her husband. "He would not act like this just to perturb us. Something has happened. You and Sterling must go out and look for him."

Silas Wallis correctly read the expression of fear and determination on his wife's face.

"Of course my dear. Immediately after breakfast."

Mrs. Hudson entered the room carrying a steaming plate of scrapple. The aroma of the fried breakfast meat came to Sterling who clamped a hand over his mouth and ran for the back door.

Silas strode briskly along the edge of Thames Street, a gnarled walking stick tapping out a rhythmic cadence as he and Sterling approached the area of the still shuttered waterfront stores and saloons.

Both men slowed their pace as they neared the narrow side street that housed a row of saloons. The Irish Eyes was at the far end. Silas had grudgingly agreed to his wife's demand for action because he had no other option. However, he had formulated no clear understanding of how he and his impaired older son were to proceed.

Now, approaching the only place they had to look he was gripped with despair. What were they expected to do? Unless Landon was lying in the street, there would be nothing to see. There was no one about at this early hour of whom to inquire. And, if there were, what would they ask? It is beyond reason to expect that anyone who might be about this early would have been here last night and in a position to see anything of assistance.

At least he could return home and report to Abbie that they found nothing. Maybe that would put her mind at ease. Highly unlikely. He had decided that after they found nothing here, he would dispatch Sterling to locate Master Asbury Boston and determine what time he and Landon had parted. If they were fortunate he might find that Landon had stayed with the Boston's, rather than try to negotiate his way home at such a late hour.

Silas hesitated at the mouth of the narrow alley and peered into the damp gloom in an effort to locate the Irish tavern. It was then that Sterling let out a cry and stooped to pick up a piece of red cloth from the alley.

"What is that?" Silas asked.

Sterling began to shake. "It's a devil's mask. See the holes for the eyes, nose and mouth. And the two ties to go behind the head."

Silas took it and turned it slowly in his trembling hand. "I fail to understand its significance," he said.

"Beth told me that Landon had begged Mrs. Hudson to make a mask for him for last night. She described this exactly."

3

Somewhere on the Chesapeake Bay
Friday, November 1, 1867

Landon Crockett Wallis awoke choking. The vomit in his mouth tasted sweet, while an acrid odor stung his nostrils. He tried to swallow but the chunks in his throat would not go down. The uncertainty of his whereabouts terrified him. He kept his eyes clamped shut as he groped for reality through his other senses.

Colored dots floated behind his eyelids; streaks of brilliant white flashed painfully through his head. His back was propped against something cold and hard, and his legs, stretching in front of him, rested in several inches of frigid water. He heard water slapping against the wall at his back while his prison rolled and tossed from side to side. He was unsure what had made him sick, the chloroform or the rough sea. He hated the sea.

Landon felt the front of his pants and found another wet spot, this one still warm. His neck and face heated as he understood that he had wet himself while unconscious.

Anger quickly replaced the embarrassment. "*You fool*," he scolded himself. "*You got a lot bigger worries than peein' your pants.*"

Now he sensed the warmth of human bodies pressing against him from either side. The air was smothering. He took a breath and his stomach reacted violently to the stench, but it had no more to give.

A voice at his right arm whispered, "Ya'll gonna be sick agin?"

Landon forced his eyes open. There was no light; he could still see nothing.

"I got nothing left," he said.

"That be good, that be damn good."

Landon turned his head to face the sound. "Who are you?" he asked.

"Luther."

Landon recognized the voice as that of a young, Negro boy.

"Luther what?"

"No one ever said two names to me. Luther is the only one I know."

Landon felt the boy shiver where their arms met. A chill penetrated his own body, which responded with a violent shudder.

"Any idea how long we been here?" he asked in a low voice.

"Hard to tell wif it bein' so dark. Seems like I was down here a good long time by masef, den they brought in the other two and after more time they brought you in, then we dun left out."

"Any idea where we are?"

"Naw. We been gone for some hours now, but even if I was up top with a spy glass I'd have no idee where we was. I's not from around here — you didn't tell me yo' name."

"Landon. Landon Wallis. Maybe you heard of my family."

"Nope. Like I says, not from around here."

"I know, but if you were around the Point – Fell's Point – for anytime you would have seen the name on our warehouses and other buildings along the waterfront."

"Cain't read."

Landon immediately regretted his patronizing words. Anxious to move on he asked, "Where do you come from?"

"I came up from Noth Carlina, lookin' for my ma. Afore the war, she was sold to a family up to Balimore. 'Course the war set her free but she never came to home. I could'n wait no more, so I came to fetch her to home."

"You came all that way by yourself?"

"Had to. No one else to come. I had a older bruther, but he was sold off to Missippi' an' we don't know where he be. Pa is ta cripple up an' my sisters are all ta young."

"You sound young. How old are you?

"I reckon I am, but I dunno years. Wish I did."

Landon realized that the boat had ceased tossing and was slowing. Though he hated the sea and everything about it, Landon knew something about boats. According to Luther, four of them were jammed into this cramped space. There had been no sound of an engine so they were traveling under sail. They were likely in the forepeake of a pungy, or brogan. Maybe a small schooner. Either way there was only two or three crewman up on deck. He knew immediately that any thought of rushing the crew and seizing the boat was a fantasy. They would likely be brought out of the hold one at a time, no other way it could be done. If it was daylight they wouldn't be able to see for several minutes; besides, they were too stiff and weakened to mount any fight against what are certain to be armed captors.

The boat struck something solid and stopped. There was movement on the deck above as men scurried around, undoubtedly to tie off the boat. Within moments, a deck hatch opened directly overhead and daylight flooded the hold. Landon struggled to stand, eyes blinking against the glare.

"Siddown 'til yer tole to move," a voice bellowed from overhead. "You try any tricks and you'll be floatin' away, dead as a mackerel." The voice waited until Landon had settled back into the icy water awash in the hold.

"You'll come out of there one at a time when you're tole to. See this here ladder?"

Landon shaded his eyes. Through the open hatch, he could make out a shack squatting several feet above the water on log pilings. Their boat was tied off, fore and aft, between two of the pilings. A ladder of rope and rough wood dangled from a trapdoor opening in the floor of the shack, ending a couple of feet above the boat deck.

The voice above snarled, "When I tell ya, come up on deck and climb up this here ladder. Oh, and welcome to the paddy shack." He cackled loudly and looked aft.

"Good 'un, Jake," a second voice said.

The one at the ladder abruptly stopped laughing and swung back to the men in the hold. "You, nigger boy, come on outta there and get up this ladder."

Luther stood on wobbly legs, climbed out of the hold and scurried to the ladder. As he started to climb, the one called Jake produced a wide strap of dark, worn leather and flailed the back of Luther's legs, tearing the thin pants he wore. Without a sound, Luther clamored up the ladder and disappeared through the trapdoor.

"Good 'un, Jake," the other repeated.

"They is used to it," Jake chortled. "If they don't get a whippin' everyday they don't guess ya luv 'em. Now, you – daddy's boy," he said shaking the leather strap toward Landon. "Get up here."

Landon grabbed the edge of the hatch to steady himself as he climbed onto the deck. He moved carefully to the ladder, fearing the sting of the strap across his own legs. Before reaching the rope ladder, he saw two men standing behind the one holding the whip. Each man was bearded and they looked related, displaying the same witless grins. Inbreeding immediately came to Landon's mind. Their obvious dimness was offset by the breech loading rifles they carried. Each wore a crumpled oilcloth hat and a ragged piece of canvas hanging from shoulders to knees.

Beyond the two armed guards, Landon glimpsed a wide swath of grey marsh grasses stretching to a stand of tall pines at the edge of dense woods. Overhead, a tern hesitated in mid-flight then dove out of sight behind the shack. Landon dared not look back, but was certain that they were in the midst of a great marsh and a considerable distance from dry land.

Landon reached the ladder, breathed deeply and turned to face Jake.

"You've made a mistake. Please contact my father, Colonel Silas Wallis of Fell's Point," he said, hoping the military title would somehow influence these violent men.

"He will pay a reward for my safe and immediate return." Landon almost shouted the words – 'safe–and–immediate'.

The one called Jake curled his lips revealing chipped teeth, darkly stained and uneven. He pushed his face at Landon until their noses joined.

"Yore daddy is gonna pay sure 'nuf, Mister Wallis. We gonna decide how – 'safe' – and how –'immediate'. Now, get that fat ass of yours up that ladder, 'fore I whip it just like I did the nigger."

"Good 'un, Jake."

Landon, eyes tearing with rage and humiliation, scaled the ladder and pulled himself through the opening in the log floor.

He found the shack to be one room devoid of furniture or any other necessities of a civilized existence. He crawled to an empty corner where he situated himself with his back against the wall, legs splayed in front of him. Only a couple of feet separated Landon from a white man huddled in a corner his head perched on drawn up knees, hugging his legs with boney arms. Landon looked to his left and saw that Luther had gathered himself into a third corner in a similar fashion.

Quickly, Jake prodded the two remaining captives through the door and stuck his head in after them. "Aw right, listen up 'cause I ain't chewing my cabbage twiced." He picked up a clay jug and held it in front of him. "This here is ya drinkin' water. It's all there is 'til mornin' when we bring yer grub. See that little hole in the floor?" He indicated a point between Landon and Luther where a square of light shown up through the floor.

"That there is for ya to do yer business. Course ya'll can shat in here if ya want." Landon heard loud giggles coming from the boat as Jake spoke.

"An' mind, ya'll now work for us'n. Don't go crazy and start killin' one 'nother, cause you is all a valable piece of propity. Our propity. An' we want ya' lookin' right smart when you get called to work." He shook his leather strap at Luther. "Hey, boy, you can tell 'em all 'bout how to be propity."

"Good 'un Jake," came from the boat as the trapdoor closed.

The windowless room grew dim and shadowy. Anemic rectangles of light leaked from small holes cut into the top log of each wall at the roofline. After sunset, their prison would become pitch black until sunrise the next morning.

The shack now held five men crowded into a space Landon judged to be no more than ten feet by ten feet and of equal height from floor to roof. Hastily constructed of rough-hewn logs packed with mud, light rays filtered through gaps where bits of dried mud had crumbled away.

Landon shifted slightly, affording himself a better view of his fellow prisoners. In the corner to his left, Luther sat facing him, his own eyes fixed on the floor. In the far corner, Landon strained to make out a form crouching in that dim recess. He recalled a fleeting glimpse as the other man had crawled through the open door. This man looked to be around Landon's age, reasonably well groomed, wearing clothes which, though rumpled, were precision tailored.

Landon's gaze continued along the far wall, resting on the fourth member from his prison voyage. Light trickled through one of the square holes and fell across the prisoner's head and shoulders. Landon took the lad to be a few years older than himself, likely in his mid twenties,; wearing the look and the clothes of someone newly arrived from the old country.

The fifth man, the white man Landon had glimpsed as he crawled to his corner, was watching the activity with dark eyes set deep in a bony skull. His gaunt look made it difficult to fix his age. Landon looked directly into those eyes and nodded. "Howdy," he said.

The eyes continued to watch Landon, then a raspy voice answered, "Howdy."

Landon saw more movement in the room and sensed that the others had taken an interest in their exchange. He asked, "How long you been in here?"

The other man cleared his throat and, when he spoke, his voice was stronger.

"'Cuse me, but Ah had no reason to talk for a while."

After swallowing, he continued. "Jake brings the slop and water ever mornin', just after sunup. Unhooks that trapped door and yells 'oink, oink', shoves the jars in here, cackles real loud and locks 'er up. Ah has counted sixteen of them mornin's. Hope Ah got it right, never had to count that much afore."

"Have you been alone, for all that time?"

"Naw. There's been others come through here. Most was gone in a day or two, a few stayed some longer."

"You have any idea why they are keeping — you?"

"It's likely 'cuz Ah'm a Reb. Jake and his brothers was guards at a Yankee prison camp. Ah was wearin' my uniform pants night they took me off the docks at Annapolis. My cousin Horton tole me and tole me I was askin' for trouble if'n Ah weared them to town. I knowed he was right, but they is the only town pants I got."

Landon paused before saying, "You have any notion of where the others we taken when they left here?"

"Not fer sure. When they come for 'em, Jake'd call out whatever name he'd given 'em, sayin' they was goin' sailin'. They was a few mornins' when Ah was in here alone, them ole boys would sit out there in that boat an' smoke an' talk. Smelt like they was smokin' cob pipes. Sure smelt good, but Ah never said nothing – knew it wouldn't do no good. Why shoot, some of them mornins' they didn't leave me no grub or water – it was for sure they wasn't gonna give me a smoke."

The prisoner paused, seemingly to catch his breath before continuing, "After they set there a good while Ah commenced to holler for 'em to give me' my grub. They'd just laugh an' holler back then bye n' bye they cast off and it got quiet. Then Ah knew they was gone."

"We must not be close to any roads or people, or they wouldn't have been so quick to let you holler out."

"For sure. The first days, when Ah knew they was gone, Ah'd sit in here an holler loud as Ah could 'til Ah couldn't hardly whisper. On days when they was others here with me, we'd all set ta holler'n, but nobody never come."

"What's your name?" Landon asked. The only response was labored gasps for breath coming from the corner. When the answer came, it was in a weak, raspy voice.

"Billy Ray. Billy Ray Washington. Sure good to have some company."

After more silence, he continued. "All this excitement's got me plumb tuckered."

A question came from the far corner. The voice, pinched and edgy. "Are you going to tell us what happened to the others or not?"

"No call to be short with me," Billy Ray replied. "Ain't no rush, we dun got all night. 'Sides, Ah only know what Ah heared from Jake and his kin. They is likely worse liars then them Yankee carpetbaggers down home."

Billy Ray waited to make certain that it was understood he would proceed at his own pace, then continued, "They was talkin' about sellin' one of the boys back to his kin folks for a lot of money. Other's they sell off to work on erster boats. Anyways, I heard 'em talkin' about how it weren't fair – them doin' all the work and someone up to Baltimore took most of the money they got fer sellin' us'n to some boat captain."

Landon studied the pitiful figure, then said, "Pardon me for speaking so bluntly – but it looks like they are starving you."

"I'm right hungry, sure nuf. Reckon Ah'm used to it, though. I was fourteen months in a Yankee prison camp. So far, this here ain't as painful as that were."

Landon was aware that he was, at least for the time being, better off than he had been roiling on the bay in the dark, cramped hold of that boat. The sweet taste of the chloroform was gone and he no longer felt the rumblings of nausea. In fact, the pains in his belly rose from hunger and not seasickness. "Any water in that jug, Billy Ray," he asked.

Billy Ray hesitated then handed the jug across to Landon. "Easy, now. It's all we got 'til mornin'."

The clay jug was damp to the touch. Landon sniffed at the opening before tilting it to his lips. The tepid water smelled of rotting vegetation and mold. He took in only enough to work between his teeth and flush the refuse from his mouth. Careful not to swallow any, he scooted himself over to the hole in the floor and spat it to the marsh below. The thought struck him that Jake and his half-wit kin probably dip the jug water right below this toilet hole, cackling the whole while. "Good 'un, Jake," he could hear the one saying.

A voice, thin and halting, came from the shadowy form sitting next to the man in the tailored clothing. "*Wasser, bitte.*" An arm emerged from the shadows, its fingers working as if gripping air.

"You want the water," Landon said and placed the jug in the grasping fingers. "Careful, that might make you sick."

Billy Ray said, “What’s yer name?”

“Landon. Landon Wallis.”

“Howdy, Landon. Sorry ta meet ya like this here.”

“Has the water made you sick?” Landon asked.

“It’s not bothered me none,” Billy Ray said. “But, ya see, ma belly ain’t like ever body’s. Ah lived through 14 months at Point Lookout. Now nuthin’ bothers ma belly.”

“The Union prison camp on the Potomac? You were there?”

“Ah was there from February ‘64 ‘til the end.”

Landon asked, “Was that where Jake and his idiot kin were guards?”

“Naw. Least ways I never seen ‘em there. They tole me how right proud they was of all the hurt they done us Rebs at the camp up to Elmira, New York.”

Darkness began to impose its will on those in the prison. Advancing relentlessly from the recesses of each corner until it controlled every inch. Staking a claim over the spirit of everyone in the little room.

A new voice spoke out and Landon peered into the far corner, unable to see the man he had earlier glimpsed wearing rumpled tailored clothing. The voice was deep, authoritative, someone used to being obeyed.

“Pass that jug along,” the voice ordered. An arm, sleeved in a black woolen sack coat, reached out impatiently. Landon saw movement in the gloom before him, as the jug was passed.

“I’m from Philadelphia,” the voice offered. “And we heard up there that, of all the prison camps, you Rebs got the best treatment at Point Lookout.”

Billy Ray hooted. “Mebbe. But, if that were the best, the worst must a bin real hell.”

“Point Lookout is smack on the water. I know your kind got to go swimming and had lots of fish and fresh vegetables from the farms. Must of had plenty of fresh water.”

“Yore Yankee newspaper sure ’nuf had a strange idea of a good time. Ya think they give us a pole an' a can of crawlers an' said, ‘take a boat out an' catch ya some fish for supper’? ‘Time vittles got to us’n they was rotted side meat and taters stinkin’ up a plate, or greens rottin’ in a bowl of lukewarm water. Only went to swim twiced. Ya’lls papers tell ya about the dead-line?” Billy Ray waited for an answer that was slow in coming.

“Could have, I guess. I might have missed it.”

“Point Lookout is a strip o’ land what sticks out where the Potomac joins up with the Chesapeake Bay. River is ten mile across an' the bay is

– well – the bay. Not likely a body could swim either one, but they wasn't takin' no chances. Yanks drove a row of pilings into the river bottom. Big un's that stuck up above the water. Called it the dead-line. Anybody that swum passed it could expect to get shot."

"Nothing wrong with that. Same as if you went beyond a fence on land."

"We had these negrah guards. Meaner'n snakes they was. 'Course they hated us'n. They would all the time get their face up real close, glare at us for a minute, then say 'Better watch it – boy, we on the top now.' The white guards was purty decent. Anyhow, soon as we got into the water, these negrahs would up an start a shootin' at 'us. Swore to the white officers that we was tryin' to excape. Got so it was worth your life to get a bath."

The voice from Philadelphia spoke with disdain. "I don't know — I never heard of anything like that. Hey, you, Landon you say your name was?"

The room was filled with the night now. There was nothing to do but talk or sit silently in the gloom and shiver with fear and cold.

"Yes — Landon. What is it you want?"

"Where you hail from?"

"Fell's Point, next to Baltimore Town."

"You ever hear of such goings on at Point Lookout?"

"Can't say as I have. But, I didn't pay much attention to war news. Stories about all the killing and suffering made me sad. I didn't want to hear about it. But, I'm not calling Billy Ray here, a liar. He says he was there and saw it. Why would he lie about it, it's over and done with."

Billy Ray spoke up, "That's not near the worst of it," he said. "They was more than twelve thousand of us jammed in there, some had tents most didn't. Even in the cole weather. Only the rags they come with." His voice softened, "Lots of them boys died just from bein' there. Good 'ole boys they was too." Now, the voice quickened, harder. "Landon, you axed me 'bout this here jug o' water. Reason it don't bother me, is they pumped our drinkin' water direct out of the river jus' next to the camp. It smelled an tasted worst than this here water. Lots a boys got real sick from it, sure 'nuf."

"He's lying. He must be lying." The words came from the dark area occupied by the man from Philadelphia. "And, you – Landon, don't ask why would he lie. He's a Reb. They all lie, that's where the darkies learned it."

Landon had little energy for an argument. He tried to keep his voice even, without rancor. "How are you called, other than Philadelphia?"

"The name is Arthur, Arthur Prescott. I come from a Mainline Philadelphia family. A long line of lawyers. Perhaps you know of the law firm Prescott & Bowles."

"Sorry, no."

"Would not think so," Prescott snorted.

"Betcha didn't get yore hands dirty fightin' in the war," Billy Ray said.

"I have studied law and am preparing for the bar. Please don't try to engage me in an argument or ethical discussion concerning the war. You will lose. Again."

The room became silent. The cold penetrated the floor, chilling Landon's legs and buttocks. He remembered the tattered, thin pants worn by Luther, concerned that the boy from North Carolina would languish through the cold night ahead.

"How about you, Luther, you thirsty?" Landon asked.

There was restless movement in the room before Luther answered.

"What you mean' Mister Landon? Mister Lincoln, God rest his soul, set us free, but didn't say that we could drink from the same jug as white folks."

"I'm certain that if he had lived, he would have seen to it," Landon said.

"This is Arthur Prescott. Your point regarding Mister Lincoln's intentions is moot, as the water jug is empty."

"You son-of-a-bitch," Landon cried.

4

Baltimore Town, Maryland
Friday, November 1, 1867

Haynie and Lila McKenna moved slowly down the gangway amid the throng of passengers disembarking the steamship, Bay Queen, at Baltimore's Light Street pier. Haynie carried his sleeping son, not yet two years old and named for the boy's late grandfather. Young Tench, so called by the family as if his given name were two words, was bundled against the damp chilling breeze of a late November afternoon.

Lila, still queasy from a slow choppy boat trip up the Chesapeake Bay, readily agreed to walk the eight blocks to the house of her sister-in-law rather than endure a jarring ride over the city's cobblestone streets.

With Haynie leading the way, they turned down Light Street toward Federal Hill, a hillock of note, rich in the history of the War of 1812, which rimmed the harbor's southern shore.

Haynie's sister, Mattie, and her husband, Levin, still lived in the small house on Fort Avenue where Haynie had stayed while attending the academy fifteen years before. The easy going Levin, not given to ambition, had maintained the same position during those years, that of a mid-level accounting clerk at Stringfellow Fisheries. Levin's wage, though steady, was marginally sufficient.

In recent years, while the local seafood industry prospered, Stringfellow Fisheries struggled. The decline was due initially to the neglect of its founder, Isaiah Stringfellow, followed by the lack of business sense of his young widow.

There was a short period when Levin Tilghman feared that the business might go under, taking his livelihood with it. In the fall of 1861, Isaiah Stringfellow perished during a cruise on the Chesapeake Bay. Late one night, after days of heavy drinking aboard one of Stringfellow's own passenger ships, he disappeared. His body was eventually located tangled among the spartinas and widgeon grass at the marshy edge of a small uninhabited island off the shipping lanes. Quickly, the local authorities determined the cause of death to be accidental drowning. They agreed that Stringfellow must have fallen overboard during a drunken turn around the deck.

Isaiah's widow, Grace, was years younger than her husband – at least twenty, gossiped many who knew them. On a Monday in April of 1861, Isaiah left Baltimore on a business trip to Richmond, returning on Friday married to Grace Mooney formerly of Staunton, Virginia. The Stringfellow's acquaintances – no one in their social circle qualified as friends – did little to hide their distaste for the new Mrs. Stringfellow. Just thirty-one at the time of their marriage, she wore the weathered comeliness of an aging libertine. Though physically delicate and outwardly demure, she smoked tailor-mades in a long ivory holder, often imposing her will with a blazing temper.

Following Isaiah's death, Grace knew what the local newsmongers were saying. Some were convinced that she had pushed her husband overboard to get his money; others believed that she pushed him overboard because he was a Yankee businessman and she was, at heart, a southern sympathizer. Inevitably, they all agreed on one thing, Grace and her so-called "brother" were responsible for the death of Isaiah Stringfellow.

Shortly after Grace settled in as mistress of the Stringfellow mansion, H. J. Mooney appeared in her company. Normally taciturn about anything relating to her past, Grace uncharacteristically made everyone aware that H. J. Mooney was her brother from Staunton, Virginia. She explained that he was afflicted with malaria, since before the war, and therefore could not have served in the Confederate army, as she knew some would suspect. She was quick to explain that poor Horace J. lived alone in the Stringfellow summer home on the Potomac River in Southern Maryland. Frequently, he experienced severe spells of chills and fever requiring her to leave Baltimore on short notice and spend days at a time ministering to him.

Most in Stringfellow's social circle paid little attention to her rambling, but the few that listened had trouble understanding why a man suffering from malaria would choose to spend a summer on the mosquito-infested banks of the Potomac.

Once in control of Isaiah's business, Grace launched a pitiless scheme of acquisition against smaller competitors who struggled for survival along the piers and wharves of the Baltimore harbor's southern shore. Some, who refused to sell at her set price, were beset by an early morning fire; others were attacked and beaten by thugs and left limp and in severe pain. No one in authority made a connection between this collection of seemingly random crimes and Stringfellow Fisheries' offers to purchase.

Haynie, though well conditioned, was glad to reach his sister's front door and hand Young Tench to Lila. He shook his right arm to restore circulation and rapped solidly on the door that opened almost at once. Mattie smiled warmly and motioned them inside.

The change in rhythm from his father's footstep to his mother's arms caused Young Tench to stir and begin to fuss. Mattie, eager to hold the nephew she had never seen, cradled him in her arms cooing softly while Haynie and Lila shed their coats and hats.

Haynie bent down for a quick kiss from his sister, then stepped back as the two women brushed cheeks.

On the trip up the bay, Haynie recalled the last time he had seen his sister. It was July of 1865 at home in Somers Cove. Mattie and Levin had traveled there for a party Haynie's mother had given to celebrate his homecoming from the war.

Mattie had become what he would describe as "more matronly" in recent years. She had added a little weight, but there was something else that he could not identify until Lila said to her, "Mattie, you've changed your hair."

Then he recognized that her hair was pulled back and pinned in a tight bun, giving her the look of someone's maiden aunt.

Mattie patted her hair with one hand. "Yes, thank you. It's much easier to take care of," she said, ignoring the fact that Lila's comment was not necessarily complimentary.

Mattie looked Haynie over. "The last time I saw you," she said, "you still had that awful beard from the war. When did it come off?"

Haynie nodded at Lila and smiled, "She let me keep it through last winter. I shaved it in the spring. It was getting itchy, anyway."

Mattie handed Young Tench back to his mother and motioned them to sit. "I'll get some coffee," she said and left the room.

Little about the house had changed in the years since he had lived there. The few pieces of furniture in the cramped living room appeared to be those that he knew from almost fifteen years ago. A worn sofa faced the fireplace that snapped with a hardwood fire. Mattie used a flowered patchwork quilt to cover the sofa's bare spots. A familiar chair had been re-upholstered.

The house sat in the middle of a block of similarly depressing homes. No grass separated neighbors as the families on either side shared a common wall. The walls facing the street were sided identically, while patches of cement hard dirt made up the front and back yards. Each about the size of a wagon bed. If anyone on the street made an effort to adorn their home with bushes or flowering plants it wasn't evident as winter approached.

"Do you take milk or sugar?" Mattie called out from the kitchen.

"Yes, please," Lila responded. "Both, if you have them."

Haynie recalled how small the kitchen was and speculated on how Mattie managed to prepare family dinners in such a confined area.

I reckon a person gets used to what they have.

A tiny dining room, squeezed between the kitchen and living room, filled out the first floor. A tight stairway, led from the entryway to three second floor sleeping rooms. Haynie amused himself with recollections of how the stairway walls seemed to close in as he had climbed up to bed. At times, he feared he would suffocate.

Haynie settled onto the sofa while Lila sat with Young Tench in a wing back rocker crammed between the sofa and wall. Mattie served the coffee with a plate of cinnamon wafers then took the third seat, a worn straight back chair of soft pine facing Lila.

"How are Kate and William?" Lila asked. "They must be near grown now."

Mattie sipped her coffee and smiled. "Kate is almost fifteen and William is twelve." She sighed. "Seems like yesterday they were just the size of Young Tench there."

Looking at Haynie she said, "I hear there are a lot of changes down East. I noticed that the letter you sent last Christmas was marked 'Crisfield'. I guess no one calls it Somers Cove any more."

"A few old ones insist on calling it The Cove. They say John Crisfield is a foreigner and the town shouldn't be named for him."

Lila looked up from feeding a cinnamon wafer to Young Tench. "Well, he is from Virginia," she said.

"True. But, look at all he's done for us," Haynie replied. "Run that railroad straight through town to the docks."

His gaze shifted to Mattie, "Now he's extendin' the railroad bed out into the bay so the trains will reach deep water. We got packing plants, three actual hardware stores – not just general stores selling keg nails – and all kind of businesses built on pilings and spreading out into the Little Annemessex."

Haynie beamed with pride, "Near twelve hundred people, just in town. It won't be long before Crisfield will be as big as Baltimore Town."

Lila scoffed, "You forgot to mention all the big city problems we have now that we never had before."

"What kind of problems?" Mattie asked.

Haynie turned his attention to his coffee and wafers while Lila welcomed an opportunity to speak her mind.

"Most of those new businesses your brother is referring to are saloons, honky tonks and gambling houses. It's getting like a frontier town out West. You've heard how cowboys, drivin' a herd of cows, or prospectors from the mines, will run over a town with their drinking and gambling," she stopped long enough to cover Young Tench's ears with her palms, "and be with loose women," she concluded.

Mattie tilted her head to indicate her understanding of such things. "Surely, it's not that bad," she said.

"It certainly is. Like he said, most of the town is sittin' on pilings, out over the water. What he didn't say is, that after the businesses close for the day, those horrible drudgers and other watermen, come from all over, raising the devil. Most of the warehouses along the waterfront re-open as honkey tonks. Why, they rope off a piece of floor and drunken men get inside the ropes and fight for a few dollars of prize money. Nearly kill each other while a bunch of other drunks bet money on who will still be alive when it's over."

Lila stopped to catch her breath.

Mattie said, "It doesn't sound at all like the quiet village we used to sail into comin' from the Island."

"Well, Mattie, that was near to twenty years ago," Haynie noted.

"And another thing," Lila said, again covering Young Tench's ears while Haynie rolled his eyes at the ceiling. "Where did all of those loose women come from? The town's full of 'em. Women like that were not raised in Somerset County. Every one of the men who own these dens of sin came from somewhere else – and – they brought their harlots with them. Instead of renaming the town Crisfield, they should've called it 'Sodom'. "

The room grew quiet, then Mattie offered more coffee, which was gratefully accepted by Haynie and declined by Lila.

Mattie raised her cup and studied her brother over the rim. "How is our mother," she asked.

Haynie wondered if her question had been prompted by Lila's condemnation of women of low morals. They had never discussed their mother's life style and he did not want a discussion of her morality in Lila's presence.

"Mother is well," Haynie said. "She asked that you think about coming for Christmas this year. It hurts that she has no part in your life, or the lives of her grandchildren."

"It was her doin'," Mattie said. "She never wanted me to marry Levin and leave the Island. When I did, she called me a cursed child and said I was lost to her forever. I've heard nothing to think she has changed her opinion of me."

"Please think about it," Haynie said. "I'll talk to her when we get home."

In a voice laden with sarcasm Mattie asked, "Is her Manor House doing well?"

Haynie ignored her tone. "With Somers — Crisfield becoming a boom town, the rooms are full most every night. Railroad men, drummers — lots of activity."

"Tell her about the reverend," Lila said.

"Oh, there's also the occasional itinerant preacher."

Mattie watched as Lila gave Haynie a dark look. "You know perfectly well what I mean — the Reverend Doctor Josiah Muse."

"Well, I don't think there is much to tell," he said. "The Reverend Muse is one of the itinerant preachers I just mentioned. Boards at the house a few days every month."

Lila handed her sleeping son to his father and said, "Haynie McKenna, how can you say such a thing? They're together just about every minute when he's in town."

She turned to Mattie, "He's got this small boat —"

"A bugeye canoe," Haynie offered. "Calls it *The Fisherman.*"

"— And when he's gone, he's all your mother talks about." Lila concluded.

"He travels the shore towns," Haynie added. "Rivers, creeks and even the marshlands preachin' the gospel to folks. Only in Crisfield a few days a month."

"In case you haven't noticed," Lila said, "every month he stays a few more days than he did the previous month."

"What faith is this Reverend Muse?" Mattie asked. "And where does he come from?"

Haynie said, "Believe he' a Methodist. Real strict. He claims to be a Deacon and a licensed Exhorter. Doesn't believe in having any fun and doesn't want anyone else to either."

"You say – 'he claims'. Do you doubt his word?"

With Haynie slow to reply, Lila said, "Doubt may be too strong. We're wondering. Your brother wants to have a chance to get to know Doctor Muse better. Lettie said something about us coming to dinner one evening next week – just the four of us – in the small dining room away from the boarders."

Mattie nodded. "I guess this reverend is from out of town, or he wouldn't need to stay in a boarding house. Do you know where he's from?"

Haynie shrugged and Lila said, "Seems like your mother told me he's from up in Delaware. Wilmington, I believe."

Mattie put down her cup. "I'm not surprised they get along so well; I hear that some of those preachers behave worse than sailors – keep a woman in every port," she said and turned to Haynie.

"What have you been up to," she asked. "The last I heard, you were thinking of reading law in the office of a local barrister."

Haynie nodded, "I talked to a solicitor," he said, "but it takes a long time to complete – and," he shifted in his seat, "it would be awful confining. It's not for me."

"That's a shame. You're a decent man – and smart. You'd be able to help people and they could trust you. You wouldn't cheat them."

Lila reached out and gave her husband a playful shove. "See," she said and looked at Mattie. "That's exactly what I told him — but he can't sit still that long."

Haynie spoke up quickly, "I've got a small boat and been tonging oysters, fishin', trappin'— beaver and marshrats mostly. Oh, and did some day work building the railroad."

Mattie studied him before asking, "Are you still trying to find out who shot father?"

"When I can."

He nodded to his wife and sleeping son. "I know I have to provide for them, but I have to keep searching. Mainly because no one else ever will."

"Have you learned anything about what happened that day?"

Haynie shook his head, “Very little. A few months ago, I found two tongers who were at Ape’s Hole when father was shot. It’s been a long time. They recollected some yelling, then the report of musket fire echoing over the water. By the time they located where the shots had come from, a boat with two men was under sail and high tailing it south. The Hole’s right at the Virginia state line.”

“Well you did your best. At least you tried.”

Haynie bristled, “I haven’t given up.”

Lila heaved a sigh, “He’s still obsessed with finding out who did it. Truth be told, I’m as afraid for him now as when he was in the war. At least then, a man was watchful, knew where the danger was comin’ from. Bein’ a waterman is awful risky in the best of times, now it’s much worse. And bein’ a tonger is worst of all.”

Mattie nodded. “The newspapers up here are saying there’s a war going on — an oyster war, they call it.”

Lila looked at her husband, “He won’t say it,” she said, “but that’s just what it is. Your father’s killing was the first shots of *this* war — like the Rebels firing on Fort Sumter. You didn’t hear of these killings during the war years, but it’s going on. Virginia and Maryland watermen killin’ each other over a few oysters, and —”

Haynie broke in, “Not just a few oysters. They’re bringing boat loads out of the sound and people are getting rich.”

Clearly vexed, Lila said, “I don’t know any tongers getting rich. Sure families like the Stringfellows, and other packinghouses, and railroad men like John Crisfield. Meanwhile the tongers – the McKenna’s – don’t get rich. If a tonger is lucky enough to get old, he’s got nothing to show for his years but knotted hands and a leaky boat.”

Haynie started to speak, “I wish you —”

Lila refused to be silenced. “Those awful drudgers are the worst,” she said. “They come sweeping into a bed with their big boats and crews of ruffians and thugs. They push the tongers, in their little boats, right off. They will sink you, drown you or shoot you; they don’t much care which.”

Haynie shook his head. “It’s not that bad,” he said.

“Not that bad?” Lila said, then looked at Mattie. “He doesn’t want me to worry. Thinks I don’t know what’s going on. Oh, I know all right. I know about the time that drudge boat went up the Wicomico River, all the way to Whitehall, and tried to storm the town.”

Now, in full frenzy, she continued, “If the local militia hadn’t driven them off with the town’s cannon, who knows what awful things they would have done.”

Lila drew a breath, "Why, a decent woman can't be out on the street after sundown in any shore town I know. Can't take the chance."

"Must be something that can be done," Mattie said. "Where's the sheriff while all this is going on?"

Haynie said, "That's the problem. No county sheriff has the men or boats to police the waters. If they did, they'd likely spend their time feuding over where the county waters ended, trying to show it was the next county's problem. I've been the only one looking for father's killers. Who is a tonger supposed to tell what happened to him? There's no federal or state force with authority on the water. A county sheriff will shrug and say he has to attend to the people on dry land. Everybody knows a tonger doesn't count for much, and fish don't vote. Bodies could come floating into waterfront towns, like Crisfield, every day and nothing would get done about it."

Haynie looked at Mattie. "You know who Horsey Towne is?"

"No," Mattie laughed. "Is it a person, place or thing?"

Haynie smiled and shook his head. "Course you wouldn't know him, you never lived in Somers Cove. Anyhow, Horsey is the town bailiff for Crisfield. Closest thing to a law man we got and still a long way from it."

Haynie slumped back. "It's hopeless. And, even if we had the lawmen, it wouldn't help if a Virginia waterman comes across the line and shoots somebody. He gets back across the state line and Virginia won't do anything to their own. That's exactly what I believe happened to father."

Mattie began collecting the coffee cups and stacking them on the serving tray. "That's awful," she said. "Seems like if folks raised enough of a fuss, the state would have to do something. Isn't that what our democracy is all about? The will of the people?"

"There's some talk about the legislature authorizing a marine police." Haynie shrugged, "But who knows how many more killings it's going to take before they act?"

Mattie said. "I recall reading something about that. The Oyster Navy, I believe the papers are calling it." She looked at Haynie, "Say, why don't you get involved in something like that?"

"What do you mean – involved?" Haynie questioned.

"Stand for sheriff at the next election, or agitate the House of Delegates for a marine police force, and, when we get one," Mattie called over her shoulder, "tell 'em you want to join."

Haynie looked at his wife. "I don't know. I hadn't thought about it," he said.

Lila was emphatic, “I would hope not,” she said. “It’s a dirty business and too dangerous.”

Mattie returned wiping her hands on a tea towel. “Would it be any worse than being a tonger?”

Lila was thoughtful. “You might be right about that.”

Mattie walked over and sat beside Haynie. She took his hands into hers and turned the palms up.

“There’s still time,” she said softly.

Looking up she asked, “Remember how awful father’s hands were? They gave him so much pain. So gnarled and coarse, I shrank from him when he came over to touch me.”

Glancing at Lila, she said, “You don’t want to be afraid to have him touch you.”

Suddenly, it seemed, the room was almost dark. Mattie patted Haynie’s hands then rose and began to light the lamps.

Haynie stood and added two pieces of split hardwood to the fire.

“Our brother sends his love,” he said.

Mattie paused, “Caleb said that?” she asked. “He used the word, love?”

Haynie laughed. “Well, not exactly.”

“Well what did he say, exactly? Did he say anything?”

“We haven’t seen him for some time,” Lila injected.

“But,” Haynie continued, “If we had seen him, and he had known we were coming to visit you, he would surely have felt it – even if he didn’t speak the words.”

“Not the Caleb I know,” Mattie said. “At least he’s still alive. Has he taken a job?”

Lila answered, “He’ll help your mother for a few days, then just disappear and we don’t see him for a week or two. Hates living under a roof – he’s a dyed in the wool progger. More so than Haynie ever was.”

“She’s right, there,” Haynie agreed. “Caleb knows that marsh a lot better than I do. When he comes back, he’ll have a couple of marshrats, maybe a ’possum, couple of otter pelts, or the shank of a big stag. Always something to put in the pot on mother’s cook stove.”

Mattie finished lighting the lamps and sat down. “How does our mother take to him being gone so much?”

“She worries about him, as you would guess,” said Lila.

Haynie said, “Mostly about his salvation, I expect.”

Mattie rose from her chair and went to answer a knock at the front door. She returned shortly and handled a sealed envelope to Haynie.

“A boy brought this telegram – it’s addressed to you.”

Haynie turned it over in his hand. It was plain white, of good stock with his name neatly printed in full.

"I can't imagine who would know that I was going to be here," he said.

"I don't think anyone did," Mattie said. "The boy was very polite and asked that I get this to you as soon as I could. His master needs to reach you but doesn't know how. Seemed to know we're related."

Haynie produced a small pocketknife, carefully slit the envelope, removed a folded sheet of paper and read in silence.

Lila studied his face. "What is it? Not bad news, I hope."

Haynie folded the note, returned it to the envelope and shook his head.

"It's very strange," he said. Looking from Lila to Mattie, he asked, "Do either of you recall me mentioning Sterling Wallis, a boy I went to school with up here?"

Both women shook their heads.

"We never got along, and I forgot about him as soon as I left school. Seems he and his father, Silas Wallis, are desperate to see me as soon as possible. I see by the signature that Sterling's father has taken to calling himself colonel since I knew them. They have an office just across the harbor in Fell's Point. I'll go in the morning."

5

Fell's Point, Maryland
Saturday, November 2, 1867

Saturday morning, Haynie took a short ferry ride across the city's harbor to Fell's Point. The telegram from Colonel Wallis requested to meet with Haynie McKenna on an urgent matter. He could not fathom how Wallis knew to reach him at Mattie's.

In the message, Wallis introduced himself by saying that Haynie was recommended by Wallis' son, Sterling. Haynie was not at all anxious to renew his acquaintance with Sterling Wallis, who had bullied him during his short stay at the Chesapeake Academy.

Haynie wore the same attire as yesterday, as these were his traveling clothes and the best he had. Lila smoothed the collar of his flannel shirt and tugged at the hem of his black waistcoat all the while assuring him that he looked as fine and handsome as any man she would see all day.

"That's not saying a whole lot," he replied. "Seeing as you'll be inside this house all day."

Once docked, Haynie quickly crossed Thames Street to a three-story frame building freshly painted a deep blue. He spent the ferry ride telling himself that it was they who needed him; he had not asked to be invited. Yet, as he approached the Wallis building, he resisted mightily an urge to re-board the ferry before it left the dock. Passing a show window, he touched his shirt collar buttoned at his throat, the best he could do in the absence of any suitable neckwear.

The Wallis building was fronted by vast plate glass windows. Displays of rusting anchors, ship's wheels and other treasures salvaged from the sea, decorated the area on either side of a polished mahogany door. Above the door, three wooden flagstaffs jutted from the building, their flags motionless in the still morning air. The Stars and Stripes, the flag of a reunited nation, dominated the middle pole. Two smaller flags filled poles on either side. One, a Maryland State flag, and the other a banner of colorful signal flags displayed on a bed of brilliant white satin. When read together, the signal flags spelled out
W A L L I S.

Above the flags, a large sign stretched the width of the building. Gold colored, wooden block letters proclaimed the building to be the home of Wallis & Sons Merchant Traders. At either end of the letters, a blue marlin, hand carved from the same wood, leapt toward the letters from a painted sea of deeper blue.

Inside, Haynie spotted a young woman seated at a small wooden desk in the dusky recesses of the high-ceilinged room. She looked up as he made his way between uneven stacks of sailcloth, piles of fish netting and tangles of anchor rope. Not all of the material was unused and he caught the stench of saltwater and seaweed.

The girl looked to be about 20. "May I help you?" she asked.

Haynie removed his cap, a treasured possession that Caleb had made from the fur of a large grey rabbit and proudly presented to Haynie on his return home from the war. He smoothed his hair with the palm of his right hand. "The name is Haynie McKenna," he announced, "I was asked to come and meet with mister – er, Colonel Wallis and his son Sterling."

She glanced at the far wall and eyed the stairway rising to the second floor. "They haven't come in yet. What time is your appointment?"

The front door opened and a handsomely dressed young man entered, moving with the assured grace of one with nothing to fear from his environment.

Though heavier than their school days, Haynie immediately recognized Sterling Wallis. No mistaking that retreating chin which seemed to disappear into his neck, and the receding hairline, revealing much more scalp than hair.

Sterling Wallis stopped and stared, his mouth working soundlessly as he gawked. Eventually, he moved forward and extended his hand. "Am I right? Is this Haynie McKenna?" he asked.

"It is," Haynie replied, taking the offered hand firmly in his grasp.

Sterling Wallis was befuddled. “But, I don’t understand. We just yesterday delivered the note to your sister. I recalled that you stayed with her during school and, as luck would have it, she is still in the same house.”

“You’re timing was perfect. I arrived late yesterday on the Bay Queen for a short visit.”

“Well no matter,” Sterling said, “the main thing is you are here.”

He pointed to an open stairway along the far wall.

“Let’s go up to the helm, as daddy likes to call his office. He’ll be along shortly.”

Sterling gave the girl at the desk a look that defined their respective stations in life as clearly as the spoken word. “Daddy and Major Hollins will be in shortly. Inform them that Mister McKenna and I are at the helm, and bring coffee for four.”

As Haynie followed Sterling on the long climb to the second floor, he thought how differently he was now being treated. In school, he had often received the same look Sterling had just given to the helpless, and obviously frightened, girl. Instilling fear in others always seemed to buoy Sterling’s spirits.

Of course, it was not sufficient for Sterling to glare in silence. In Haynie’s case, Sterling and his sycophants regularly taunted him in the schoolyard.

“Haynie’s a hinney,” they would jeer in unison. It was surprising to Haynie that, with the obvious rise in Wallis family wealth and power, Sterling still felt the need to dominate those he viewed as beneath him, which, currently, was pretty much everyone.

The second floor landing opened to a spacious alcove offering a view of the cluttered floor below. To their right, a long wall contained doors to several offices. Between each office door, a framed drawing of a vivid nautical theme hung on the wall. Haynie found one, a rendering of a masted schooner with billowing sails foundering in rough seas, particularly fascinating.

Sterling nodded to the drawings and said, “My sister, Beth, pestered The Colonel to let her help redecorate. She paid good money for these hideous pieces of — art.”

Sterling led the way into a spacious room with a vaulted ceiling and a polished hardwood floor. At the far end, floor to ceiling windows looked across Thames Street to the waterfront and a warehouse that extended into the harbor on pilings. Across the front of the warehouse, a great sign at eye level identified the building as part of the empire of Wallis & Sons Merchant Traders.

Haynie had not been in many offices, but the layout seemed strange. The furnishings were clustered along the front window. A captain's desk, dwarfed by the size of the room, sat at right angles to the window and the door. Three wooden chairs and a small sofa of worn, brown leather were grouped around the desk. No rugs or other adornments were visible, leaving the remainder of the room with a hollow, cavernous feel.

Sterling stopped in front of the middle window and gazed across the street, just in case Haynie had missed the Wallis company sign on that building. With his back to Haynie, Sterling said, "Glad to see you survived the war. I wanted to join," he swept an arm indicating all that was in view, "but, as you can see, I was needed here."

Haynie decided he wanted no more of Sterling Wallis, "Why am I here?" he asked. "We were never friends at school."

"The Colonel will explain when he arrives. As for school, that was kid stuff. All forgotten by now, certainly."

Haynie's response was interrupted when the door opened and two men entered. The first, short and round, wore a dark woolen cloak draped casually around his shoulders. In one hand, he carried a wool hat; the other held a burled walking stick. Certainly, this was Silas Wallis. The second man was tall, a little shorter than Haynie, and fit. He was dressed in a suit of polished cotton with a matching brown ascot knotted under a jutting chin. Mutton chop side-whiskers and a flowing handle bar moustache filled out his otherwise thin features.

The shorter man approached with a puzzled look and extended his hand. "I am given to understand, by Miss Hazlett, that this is Mister Haynie McKenna. But, how did you get here so quickly?"

Sterling quickly explained the fortunate timing and introduced the second man, "This is Major Southey Hollins, he's helping us with a family problem, which is also the reason you were asked to come."

The Major's look belied a friendly handshake.

Colonel Wallis moved to the chair behind the captain's desk, and the others took seats in a semi-circle in front of him.

He spoke first, "Mister McKenna, again, thank you for coming so promptly. We have a terrible situation and believe you can be of help."

Colonel Wallis inclined his head toward Major Hollins while keeping a steady gaze on Haynie. "The Major," Wallis said, "is a close family confidant, not without experience in these matters. We may speak freely in his presence with the utmost confidence in his discretion. I trust we can have your word that you will be equally circumspect."

Haynie said, "You have it."

Colonel Wallis smiled. "Your word is good with me, sir," he said. "Sterling here has told me how close you two were at the academy, though I must admit, I don't recollect seeing you at the house back in those days."

Haynie glanced at the profile of Sterling Wallis who maintained a fixed stare at the family sign across Thames Street.

Miss Hazlett appeared pushing a wheeled cart laden with an urn of coffee, patterned china cups and saucers, a small bowl of sugar along side a matching pitcher of milk, and a plate of assorted biscuits. The Colonel smiled pleasantly while she poured the coffee; Sterling fixed her with an unforgiving stare.

Silas Wallis sipped his coffee while the others were being served.

He remarked, "This is the finest coffee from South America. We bring it in on Wallis & Sons ships. It could not be any fresher."

As the girl pushed the cart toward the door, the elder Wallis lifted his cup and saucer and called, "Miss Hazlett, please bag up two pounds of these beans for our guests." The girl nodded and pushed her way through the door, closing it behind her.

Silas Wallis sat his cup and saucer carefully on the desk. He laced his fingers on top of the papers strewn about the desktop and said, "Now that we have the preliminaries out of the way, we can turn to serious business. May I call you 'Haynie'?"

"Of course."

"Thank you. It with a heavy heart that I tell you, two nights ago, on All Hallows Eve, my son Landon, Sterling's younger brother, disappeared without a trace. We believe that he was coming from a local saloon where he was to meet some friends for the evening. The saloon itself, Irish Eyes, is an unsavory place along the waterfront, a few streets over from here. Normally, Landon would never frequent such a place – certainly not alone – but we believe he thought he was to meet some friends and go on to a party with them."

Silas nodded and Sterling cleared his throat before saying, "I talked to Landon's friend, Asbury Boston, myself. He was vague, but I don't believe they ever intended to meet Landon. I think they were playing a trick on him."

"Or, this Boston was part of a kidnap plot," offered Major Hollins.

"Very doubtful," Sterling said. "The Boston's are a fine, old family. He's something of a bully – but I don't think him capable of intentionally harming Landon."

Colonel Wallis dismissed both men with an impatient wave of the hand.

"We are particularly concerned that we have not heard anything about ransom," he said. "This may sound overly dramatic, but it is literally killing Missus Wallis. She stays in her bed and takes no nourishment save a little soup or tea." His eyes became red rimmed as he twisted his napkin into tight little knots.

"We'll hear from them. They must want the money as badly as we want Landon returned." He looked at Haynie, "Don't you agree?"

Haynie saw a father distraught and fearful for his son's life.

"I'm afraid I've no experience in such matters, Colonel Wallis. I don't know what Sterling has told you to make you think I can be of help, but, I'm afraid you've been misled."

The Wallis men exchanged looks, but before they could reply Major Hollins said, "I agree with Mister McKenna. It might do more harm than good to have an amateur flailing about on his own. I feel certain you will receive a demand for payment soon, certainly within hours, and then things will happen very quickly." Sitting back, he muttered, "Too many cooks and all that."

"The Major is right," Haynie said. "The police are certainly more experienced at this sort of thing. You are very fortunate to have a police major to turn to."

Silas Wallis said, "Major Hollins is not present in any official capacity. He is a major, retired from the Army of the Confederacy, not a law officer, and serves only as a friend and advisor on this matter."

Haynie asked, "What are the police doing while waiting for a money demand?"

Hollins spoke up, "Colonel Wallis wisely agreed not to report the matter to the authorities."

Haynie looked from Hollins to Colonel Wallis. "Excuse me, sir, but why haven't the police been notified?"

"Landon is an adult," the colonel replied. "In the absence of any evidence indicating a crime has occurred, the authorities are powerless to act. No, I agreed with the major, this is the right approach. The kidnappers will issue their demand and, after taking proper safeguards to ensure Landon's return, I'll pay them. The police are often clumsy in delicate matters. I don't want those buffoons in blue stumbling around and further upsetting Abbie – Missus Wallis."

Silas Wallis dropped his gaze to his desktop and sighed deeply. When he spoke again his voice was low, agonized, "There'll be plenty of time for the police if the unthinkable happens."

"Don't even think that, Silas," Hollins said, "I'm not going to let that happen — by God, I'm not."

"Thank you, Southey."

The room was quiet, each man pensive.

At length Haynie said, "I'm sorry, but it's still not clear to me, why you asked me here."

Colonel Wallis stirred and gestured toward his son. "Sterling, please."

Sterling Wallis turned to Haynie, cleared his throat and spoke.

"Perhaps you have heard that, on occasion able bodied men are shanghaied from our piers. Men, who are then pressed into service on oyster boats in the bay or aboard a ship bound for ports throughout the world."

Haynie nodded.

An impatient Silas Wallis injected, "Haynie, I don't have to tell you how terrible the conditions are aboard oyster boats, especially during the winter months – virtually impossible for a captain to keep a full crew 'til spring. It takes too much time for a captain to return to port and scour the docks for a man or two every time he needs a new hand. He'll lose out to the captain who can stay out. They pay good money to anyone who can bring men right out to the oyster boat while they keep on working the beds."

Haynie said, "Are you now saying that you think Landon was dragged aboard one of these work boats?"

Silas shrugged, "Unfortunately, we don't know enough to rule out anything." Inclining his head toward Southey Hollins, he continued, "The major discounts that possibility entirely —"

"With all respect," Hollins replied, "to follow that theory is a waste of time and resources."

"If so, Southey," Silas replied, "they are my resources to waste. However, I don't consider any expenditure that might result in the safe return of my son as wasted. As for time, I will not sit idly by, while awaiting a money demand."

"Silas," Hollins quickly added, "it might be dangerous to have a greenhorn poking his nose into this. He could run onto them, by chance mind you, and spook 'em. No telling what might happen to your boy in that event."

Sterling Wallis spoke up, "Haynie McKenna is just the man for this job. He's one of the most experienced proggers on the Eastern Shore. Why his own father was killed on the bay and Haynie has been hunting the killers for years. Isn't that right?"

Where is all this coming from, Haynie wondered. *I haven't seen him since the day the Headmaster came for me. Moreover, I believe, if I were Hollins, I'd point out that it would be better to have someone who had actually tracked down a killer, rather than a man who has failed at it over several years.*

Before Haynie could speak, Colonel Wallis said, "Southey, I know you have the family's well being at heart, but I have given the idea a lot of thought since Sterling, here, brought Mister McKenna's name to my attention. I am siding with him on this one."

Colonel Wallis turned to Haynie, "Abbie needs something to cling to – some hope. Tonight, when she looks at me, crying and begging for some news, I'll be able to tell her that Mister McKenna – Haynie – is scouring the Bay and the Eastern Shore for her son — I will be able to tell her that, won't I, Haynie?"

"Well sir," Haynie said, "I want to see Landon returned to you as soon as possible, and, if there's some way I can help, I will do it. So far, I don't have a handle on what I can do."

Silas Wallis opened a desk drawer and removed a nautical chart of the Chesapeake Bay region, which he spread across the desktop.

The four men moved closer.

"If he was taken by scoundrels looking for a crewman," the colonel said, jabbing his finger at the Fell's Point area, "they would have sailed down the Patapsco, turning south when they got to the bay."

He looked at Haynie, "I doubt they went north; all the good beds down your way, in Tangier Sound."

Haynie nodded.

Wallis dragged a finger along the map, the length of the bay. "By now they could be clear to Pocomoke Sound, so we are dividing the bay and its shoreline into sectors – areas of responsibility – if you will. Two on the eastern shore and two on the western. Haynie, you'll be responsible for Sector 4 – running from Pocomoke Sound up to the Choptank River."

Haynie nodded.

"Sector 3 will continue north from the Choptank to the Patapsco."

Wallis shifted his finger across to the bay's western shore. "Sector 2 will cover from the south bank of the Potomac, north to the South River; Sector 1 from there north to Baltimore. Any questions?"

There being none, Silas Wallis folded the map and returned it to the desk drawer.

The men sat down and mulled what they had heard.

Colonel Wallis closed the drawer and looked over at Haynie.

"Due to our timely good fortune," he said, "yours is the first sector to be manned. Sterling is overseeing the two Eastern Shore sectors, and is working hard to find a good man for Sector 3. Southey will do the same for 1 & 2. He is also in the process of identifying someone to fill those jobs as quickly as possible. If you have any suggestions for manpower, please pass them on after we break up here."

The quick look Hollins cast in Haynie's direction clearly said, "Don't bother."

Haynie thought of the daunting task being asked of him. "There are thousands of acres of marshland, not to mention the islands, coves and rivers in my area, alone. I wouldn't know where to start looking."

"I'm not merely asking for your help — I'm begging for it." Silas Wallis jammed a finger into the desktop with each word. "I want you to start immediately and keep slogging until I tell you to stop. I want you to talk to every boat captain, hunter, waterman, saloonkeeper, dance hall girl, shopkeeper and town drunk you can find. You'll be well paid, and you'll be given extra funds to use as reward money for anyone who helps you."

"But, sir —"

"— If Landon has been shanghaied for work on an oyster boat, his captors are likely servicing drudgers in a particular region. They'll need to buy provisions in some town. If they're running in Tangier Sound, it's likely Crisfield. Am I right?"

"Yes..."

"These men are getting paid, and they're blowing it in saloons on cards, drink, women, and cock fights – some kind of entertainment. They're men of violence who are apt to take to brawling after a few drinks. Could be they've been jailed. They're likely braggarts. If they're sailing the bay vending human beings – somebody else knows about it – if —"

"– Sir," Haynie interrupted, "I'm sorry to be blunt, but before I can take any of your money, it must be clear that we both understand how little chance there is of finding him."

Colonel Wallis folded his arms across his stomach and studied Haynie.

"I appreciate your honesty. Look, I fully expect this to be resolved in the next few days, with a ransom paid and Landon safely back home. If not, I could not look Abbie in the eye if I didn't believe we had tried everything we could. I need someone who knows that area, and who knows it better than you?"

"My brother."

"Good!" Wallis cried. "It's settled then — you hire him, too."

The elder Wallis rose and extended his hand, "Thank you for coming so quickly. I meant it when I said hire your brother and any others that can help us in any way. Please go with Sterling. He will arrange the details of your relationship with Wallis and Sons, and provide an advance of funds.

Haynie shook the Colonel's hand. "I will do my best," he said, "and, that's all I can promise."

Colonel Wallis broke into a smile and pumped Haynie's hand.

Major Southey Hollins sat still and said nothing.

6

Fell's Point, Maryland
Sunday, November 3, 1867

Colonel Silas Wallis was seated at his desk, chewing on the stub of a cigar, as Sterling and Major Southey Hollins dashed into the room.

The offices of Wallis & Sons, closed for the Sabbath, were dark and chill when the Wallis men arrived a few minutes earlier. Sterling had returned to the front door to await the arrival of Major Hollins, while Silas busied himself illuminating the second floor hallway and his office.

Hollins dashed into the room ahead of Sterling and strode directly to a chair.

"You have news, Silas?" he asked.

The elder Wallis nodded solemnly and handed an envelope across the desk.

"This came last night – to my home, of all things."

Major Hollins removed a single sheet of paper from the envelope and read aloud, as if the others were hearing it for the first time.

> "We have your son. You want him back you deliver $75,000 in a carpetbag. A new bag with red flowers.
> Come alone with our money
> At 7:00 Monday night at the Pratt Street Steamship dock.
> Stand by the entry gate and

Face into the terminal. Carry the bag in your right hand. Keep
your left hand out of your pockets.
We got to see you got no gun.
When you feel somebody grab the bag – let go
DON'T TRY TO SEE WHO'S THERE.
You don't come with ALL the money as we are telling you.
Come back Tuesday night and watch your son float past."

Hollins set the paper on the desk and looked across. "You're going to pay, of course."

The Colonel picked up the paper, scanned it and said, "Of course. What choice do I have?"

Hollins nodded.

Sterling looked at his father, his voice shaking, "Who's going to deliver the money?"

7

Somerset County, Maryland
Monday, November 4, 1867

Letty McKenna's boarding house, her "Manor House" as she referred to it, was perched on a cut bank of the Little Annemessex River, at the north edge of the town once known as Somers Cove. For years, the village had languished on a low-lying peninsula fringed with a multitude of coves and thousands of acres of marshland. Here, the Little Annie, so called by the locals, emptied into Tangier Sound and hence the glorious Chesapeake Bay. Annemessex, an Algonquin Nation word, means "Bountiful Water". Whoever had, so long ago named the river, was indeed a sage.

In 1860, about the time John Woodland Crisfield was connecting the town of Somers Cove to the rest of the world by railroad, a man from Norfolk, Virginia arrived by boat and began instructing the local town folk in a method of shucking oysters more rapidly than they had ever imagined possible.

As the Civil War ended and the nation shifted its resources to a peacetime economy, the town, renamed Crisfield in honor of its railroad benefactor, prospered. The newly completed railroad allowed seafood, harvested from the surrounding waters, to be marketed to a world ravenous for Blue Points and Oysters Rockefeller. The town of Somers Cove was being transformed from a tranquil fishing village into the flourishing boomtown of Crisfield, already being hailed by many as "the seafood capital of the world".

Throughout the winter, the town's harbor teemed with boats bobbing restlessly as they waited for a berth at one of the oyster packinghouses lining the docks. Small, hand hewn log canoes manned by one or two tongers, wedged their way between much bigger bugeyes, brogans, or pungys and their ominous crews, as the tongers struggled to sell their comparatively meager load

At their peak, Crisfield oyster houses shipped 25,000 barrels of shell oysters and 300,000 gallons of shucked each season.

In the two years since the war ended, the railroad had been extended on pilings into offshore waters with the town following close behind. Crisfield grew hastily, with cavernous warehouses and flimsy frame store buildings springing up as quickly as foundation pilings could be driven into the riverbed. Downtown Crisfield soon extended into the river, wading out eagerly on thick wooden legs, to embrace the day's catch and the waterman's money.

Like boomtowns of every time, the lure of riches attracted entrepreneurs of all stripes, as surely as if someone had gone to the water's edge and shouted — GOLD. A variety of merchants and traders, along with a doctor, a couple of lawyers and a newspaper publisher, vied for the available space. Tradesmen contended for the few remaining dollars as the watermen tottered from the saloons, gambling houses and dance halls. After dark, when the packinghouses and other day businesses had shuttered, many warehouses were reborn as gambling dens, dance halls and prize fighting arenas.

Bare knuckle prize fighting was recently introduced to the town by John Blizzard when he erected a boxing ring in his dance hall and theater at the foot of Broad Street.

Ellie's Island, the largest and most popular bar along the Wharf, occupied a large corner building at the mouth of Goodsell's Alley, a noisy street of rundown saloons.

The Island offered stage shows, burlesque theater, prizefights, and rooms upstairs.

The bloodthirsty sport of bare knuckle prize fighting was a major source of amusement along the waterfront, attracting vulgar crowds clamoring for blood each night. Routinely, the bout in the ring spawned drunken brawls among the crowd, with the combatants flailing away at one another until they eventually tumbled out the front door onto the plank street. Anyone who picked their fight at the rear of these cavernous halls risked stumbling through one of the large loading doors along the back wall and plunging into the dark, rapidly moving waters of the Little Annie. Such a fate was not uncommon. In the month of December 1866, no less than six men drowned in this fashion while out on the town.

Gerhard Stein, having no particular place to go after the war, followed Haynie McKenna home to Crisfield. The town's rapid growth meant opportunity for a man willing to work. In particular, the oyster processing houses and the railroad sought strong men for their backbreaking labor. Gerhard Stein was easily the strongest man in the county, however, he had declined offers of full employment by both. It was not that he was lazy; on the contrary, Stein was always toiling at some job. He often said that he was never idle during daylight and he had never told a lie. Stein could have added that he was restless as well, after dark.

Haynie observed that his friend projected different personalities, depending on the company in which he found himself. Around females Gerhard was a polite, gentle man, always tipping his hat in passing or removing it in the presence of a lady. All were charmed by the deep timbre of his voice and thick Prussian accent when he spoke. Stein treated all females the same. He showed the bawdy women at Ellie's the same respect he gave to the parasoled wives of Crisfield's leading citizens.

In the company of men, Stein drank heavily and behaved as boorishly as any of them.

Gerhard Stein's workday depended on his mood. On a given morning, he might appear at one of the packinghouses and spend the day loading and unloading barrels of oysters. Another day he would show up at the railroad to unload freight cars or wrestle timbers into the sawmill to be cut for cross ties. Thursdays often found him at Haines & Company, the town's largest dry goods store, lugging bolts of cloth for ladies dresses, or cartons of men's ready-made shirts and pants from a covered supply wagon parked in back. Other times he disappeared for a day or two, to turn up on a boat hauling firewood into town from Deal Island or the banks of the Wicomico River.

Though industrious, Gerhard Stein accumulated no wealth. His money was quickly spent on drink, gambling and, occasionally, one of Ellie's rooms for two. Regardless of what he spent, Stein always had some extra for those in need.

There was the day he worked unloading farm wagons laden with cords of firewood only to give his wages to the family of a local waterman who had drowned days before. Though not a religious man, Stein saw to it that any money still in his pocket on Sunday morning went into a church poor box.

Given Stein's restlessness and wanton ways, it was natural that most nights he could be found in one of the saloons along Goodsell's Alley or among the crowd at the larger burlesque houses, Blizzard's or Ellie's Island.

Haynie McKenna had, on two occasions, given in to Stein's relentless pleas and accompanied him to that part of town, now branded "Dodge City" by some local cynics. On these evenings, he had stayed long enough to sip a beer at each of Stein's first two stops before leaving for home. Though Haynie had no interest in spending his money or time this way, he was glad that he had come along. Any concerns he had about his friend's ability to fit in were quickly dismissed.

It was Stein's ritual to begin each evening at The Schooner, a small bar at the head of Goodsell's Alley. After one or two beers, he proceeded to visit every drinking establishment in the two blocks leading to Ellie's.

Haynie was surprised by the crowd that descended upon them as they settled in at The Schooner. The owner, always tending bar, broke into a massive grin when Stein filled the doorway and two large frothy glasses of beer appeared before they were seated.

Grimy men pushed their way toward Gerhard Stein, each competing for the big man's attention and the right to pat his shoulder and speak directly to him.

"Hey Kaiser, I'm buying the next one," someone shouted.

Stein's first drink was invariably on the house, which he hoisted while returning the salute of other regulars, his loyal subjects. He then entertained them with heavily accented tales of Prussian royalty, Spanish senoritas and Parisian burlesque houses. The free drinks lined up at Stein's elbow and, when he reached for his money, he was shouted down by the crowd. When it was time to move on, Gerhard always left a few dollars on the bar.

Haynie was aware that in the weeks since they had visited Goodsell's Alley, Stein's routine had changed. Now, the Prussian stopped only briefly in The Schooner and one or two other Alley saloons, before going directly to Ellie's where he was paid to serve as a bouncer and, occasionally, a prize fighter. It was rare to find anyone deluded enough, or drunk enough, to get into the ring with Gerhard Stein; but when it happened, word spread quickly through the town. Alley bars emptied, gamblers left dice or cards and all rushed to pack Ellie's Island, clamoring for beer and blood.

Ellie put up prize money for anyone who could beat Stein – her fighter. She offered a substantial sum to tempt an opponent, and gave long odds to anyone willing to wager against the house. On a night when business was slow, she would occasionally agree to pay the cost of setting the challenger's broken bones or stitching up his face.

The road in front of Lettie McKenna's Manor House was overlaid with three inches of crushed oyster shells; brilliant white, and wide enough that two teams and wagons could pass with room to spare. River Road followed the bank of the Little Annemessex River into the center of Crisfield, where it became Main Street. Even on a moonless night, River Road was luminous under hoof or heel, serving as a lodestar for those making their way back to the Manor House after a late night on the wharf.

Today, the sky was deep blue, the air clear and crisp. Haynie McKenna sat in the buggy, reins held tight against the neck of the high-strung mare. Shielding his eyes against the glare of the roadbed, he gazed up River Road to the point where it disappeared into the tree line. Two images emerged from a grove of chestnut trees and proceeded on foot toward the Manor House.

Haynie had returned from Baltimore yesterday and now waited impatiently for his brother, Caleb, to come home. Squinting into the sun, he took the person he saw to be Caleb. The figure walked with Caleb's slouch and had the same ambling pace. Caleb always carried a hunting rifle, named Minnie after a girl he had liked. This figure carried a long gun balanced carelessly over his right shoulder, an arm draped casually along the barrel. It was very likely Caleb, but Haynie hesitated because an animal, about the size of a large dog, seemed to be following at the man's heels. It was not Caleb's way to take up with animals. He believed they were on earth to be shot by Man. On occasion, he had fired over the head of strays to shoo them away from the house, but usually he shot at them.

The figure grew closer and waved.

Haynie recognized the threadbare hunting coat and raccoon skin cap. Caleb had fashioned the cap for himself, choosing not to adorn it with the long tail, once so popular on the American frontier.

The figure was indeed his younger brother. The dog panted heavily, tongue hanging, and favored his right foreleg as he labored to keep pace with Caleb. The animal looked to be a mixed breed, some type of retriever with long flapping ears.

Caleb was considered by all to be a "good looking boy", always clean shaven even after days or weeks away progging the woods and marshes.

"Hey brother," he called across the open field.

Haynie waved back as he reflected on Caleb's moods.

It was always the same after they had been apart. Caleb's greetings were full of genuine good feeling toward his older brother, but after a few hours together, certainly no more than a day or two, Caleb turned snappish, impatient to be out on the prog. Away from family.

The one exception was Haynie's return from the war. Caleb hugged him and they enjoyed more than a week of each other's company until one night Caleb grew sullen during supper. Early the next morning he grabbed Minnie and left abruptly, taking only some bacon and coffee from the kitchen.

Caleb had returned, days later, walking casually into the kitchen of the Manor House, then dropping two rabbits and three muskrats onto the cutting table. His mood was jocular and that night he ate hungrily of the muskrat stew and readily shared amusing stories of his skirmishes with wild animals.

The first time Caleb acted strangely toward his older brother, came after their father was killed and Haynie had returned home from school in Baltimore. Haynie reproached Caleb for using off color words like "ain't".

"If you use such words it shows everyone that you are lazy and crude. Only uneducated people speak like that," Haynie scolded.

"You're a stupid oaf," Caleb yelled and ran into the bedroom, slamming the door behind him.

Haynie dismissed the action as childish behavior, quickly forgotten. Caleb's outbursts, directed solely at Haynie, became more frequent after the family moved from Smith Island to Somers Cove.

Once settled into the Manor House, Haynie went to his mother and asked her what he had done to make Caleb hate him so much.

"Caleb doesn't hate you," she replied. "He is jealous of you, but he docsn't hate you."

"I don't understand."

Lettie McKenna sighed. "When your father died, it was right that you, as the oldest, would take on some of his responsibilities. Caleb thought he too should be able to do more. Then, of course, we – I – couldn't afford to send him to a city school like we did for you. He feels that you got an advantage and he got cheated."

Looking about she dropped her voice. "Now, he realizes that he will never grow as tall as you and that bothers him. In his mind, he's always comin' up short compared to you."

"But none of that is my doing."

"Brothers were never meant to get along," Lettie reasoned. "It's just nature's way. Take the bible, right at the start one brother killed the other and they've had a tough go ever since."

Thinking over what she said, Haynie agreed that his mother was probably right about the inevitability of brothers being at odds, still he was determined to bring Caleb closer to him.

Haynie climbed down from the wagon and shook his brother's hand.

"This thing with you?" Haynie asked, pointing at the dog whose coat was covered with burrs, marsh mud and matted blood. A piece of filthy cloth trailed from the gimpy leg.

"He is now." Caleb propped his long gun against the spokes of a wagon wheel, then swung his bedroll from his shoulder and set it on the ground. Two plump doves and a cock pheasant were tied to the roll.

"Nice shooting," Haynie, said. "Left most of the meat for eating."

The dog stuck his nose out toward the dead birds and his body quivered. Caleb gave a deep-throated growl and the dog backed away and lay down, but remained alert if his quarry tried to take flight.

"How'd you come by him?"

Caleb looked fondly at the dog. "Found him layin' hurt up around Injun Crick about five days ago. Figure he tangled with wolves or mebbe a big ground hog. His leg was real chewed up and he had some gashes on his chest. I was takin' aim to send him on to his heaven, but he didn't cry – just lay there lookin' at me real pitiful. Since he didn't seem to be suffering, I figured it wouldn't do any harm to give it a day or two to see if he come around."

Haynie put a hand on Caleb's shoulder, "Couldn't do it could you, brother."

Caleb shook his head, "I don't know why. I killed plenty of animals, but something wouldn't let me pull that trigger. I can still shoot a bird," he added, kicking at the birds with one toe.

"You keeping him?"

"Might better ask him if he's keepin' me. You know how they are, I could come out one morning and he'd be gone."

Haynie nodded. "He got a name?"

Caleb hesitated. "Well, I've taken to callin' him Junior."

"Junior? Like Caleb Junior?"

Caleb studied the toe of his boot as it dug a line in the crushed shells of the road.

"It just came to me to call him, Junior."

"I've been back two days and need to talk to you," Haynie said. "Ride with me into town. I've got to send a telegram back to Baltimore."

Caleb studied his brother's face, then said, "Let me take these birds into mother and we'll go."

Haynie nodded. Caleb picked up his gun and his bedroll. Junior whimpered softly as he struggled to his feet, trailing Caleb to the house.

Caleb returned at a trot and climbed onto the wagon, settling himself next to Haynie. The mare snorted and moved away briskly under Haynie's touch. They had gone only a few feet when Caleb yelled for Haynie to stop.

"It's Junior." Caleb jumped from the wagon, the oyster shells crunching under his boots. "He won't let me leave him and he'll only hurt himself tryin' to keep up."

The dog's tail wagged in expectation as Caleb lifted him carefully into the back of the wagon. Junior ran his large wet tongue over Caleb's cheek in thanks, before flopping heavily in the wagon bed. Caleb pulled himself up onto the cushioned seat and the mare trotted for town.

Haynie spent several minutes detailing his trip to Baltimore. He mentioned seeing their sister but said nothing about her stubborn refusal to come home. He described the meeting with Colonel Wallis and Major Hollins, explaining why Wallis had sought his help.

Haynie answered Caleb's questions about the abduction, and they spoke of the likelihood that Landon Wallis would be found alive. Haynie admitted to being well paid by the Wallis family.

"When I told them you know the land around here better than I do, Colonel Wallis insisted that I get your help. Got cash money for you."

"You knew this Landon's brother from going to school up there, right?"

Haynie nodded.

Caleb said, "He's your friend, right?"

Haynie considered his answer. There was nothing to be gained by delving into the resentment and anger that had surfaced at seeing Sterling Wallis.

Caleb, mistaking Haynie's silence as agreement that he and Sterling were friends, said, "I always thought friends helped each other. So how come you're taking their money when they're in trouble?"

Haynie chose his words carefully. “Things are different in the big city than down here,” he said. “Mostly because the people there are different. We wouldn’t think of taking money from a neighbor to help him out. Here, everyone is your neighbor and likely always will be. In big cities, people aren’t real neighborly; they don’t stay put so much. The neighbor you helped out may well have moved away when you need him.

“Down here, a man’s word and a hand shake is good enough. City folks pay their big city lawyers lots of money to see that a man keeps his word. A hand shake‘s worth nothing.”

Caleb listened intently as his brother continued.

“A man’s worth is figured differently in the cities. Cash money is how they keep things straight. When they offered money to me, if I’d said, ‘no thanks, just give me a bushel of your oysters some time’, they’d a showed me out the door, figuring I can’t be worth much to them if that’s all I’m worth to myself.

“Here, people pay you with what they have. Some potatoes, a few ears of corn or a fresh caught fish. You don’t expect money because you know they don’t have any. The people we’re dealing with, the Wallis’s, have plenty of money. They’ll trade it to us for something we have that they don’t, and can’t get any other way.”

Caleb gave him a questioning look. “What might that be, brother?”

Haynie collected the reins in his left hand and made a sweeping gesture across the horizon with his right. “They’re paying for us knowing this land and the sound out there. Why not? They pay their lawyers for all the time they spent at college learning the law. It’s right that we get paid for all the time we spent progging these parts. What else we got to offer?”

Caleb sat in silence. He shifted his gaze from the gleaming road and scanned the Little Annemessex racing along its banks. In a race to town, he thought, the river beats this buggy every time.

Sensing that Caleb was unconvinced, Haynie began again.

“The point is there’s nothing wrong in taking a man’s money, if you can do what you promised to do and it’s not wrong to do in the first place.”

“I guess that’s why I’m havin’ trouble with this. I don’t understand what it is you promised we can do.”

“You heard stories about men getting shanghaied and being sold to oyster boat captains in need of crew?”

“I’ve heard ‘em. But don’t know if there’s any truth to ‘em.”

“Yesterday, I talked to Gerhard about helping us find Landon. The other night at Ellie’s, a waterman was talking about fellows getting shanghaied off the docks in towns like Annapolis and Baltimore. Sounds like they are grabbed and kept in a holding pen, like cattle–paddy shacks he says they call 'em–until a captain needs a crewman. Then the gang goes to the shack, fetches how many they got a call for, and hauls them out to the oyster boat."

Caleb shrugged. "Sounds like a ghost story somebody tells their kids so they'll behave. 'You be good or a pirate will take you away and pen you up.'"

Haynie chuckled, "Still —"

"Are you saying we're going to search the whole shore for these ghost shacks?"

"From what the guy told Gerhard, this shack is supposed to be in a marsh near a main waterway – river or deep cove. Could be around here."

"And?"

"That means we're going to look for such a place, and if Landon's being kept there, we'll get him back to his folks."

Caleb almost shouted, "Even if there is such a place, there's thousands of acres of salt marsh along the bay."

"What would you have me do, refuse to help these folks? They know very well how little hope we have of finding their boy."

"How about – no hope."

"Maybe. But when all is said and done, they want to know that everything that could have been done to find him was done. I expect to be able to look the Wallis family in the eye and tell them we did everything we could. In order to do that, I need your help. Are you with me, Caleb?

"And you and me are gonna find this Landon Wallis by ourselves."

"Not just us. Gerhard is helping; he knows a lot of watermen from working on the docks. We're not just tramping around and looking. We need to talk to people, proggers like us, who know creeks and marshes we don't. You must have run across a house or camp out there, or somebody to talk to."

Caleb shrugged, "I'm out tramping around woods and marshes, anyhow," he said, "might as well keep and eye out for one of these ghost shacks. ..I could ask Gumps, he might know somethin'."

"Who's Gumps?"

"He's an old timer. Got a shack up towards Jones Creek. I come across his place at dusk one evening a while back. He almost shot me for a bear." Caleb laughed. "Then he threatened to shoot me — just for bein' so close. I told him he was too far away to hit anything and I could be on him 'fore he could load 'er up again. After a while, he got tired of pointin' that old muzzleloader at me — Edith, he calls her. He put her down an' told me to come and have some supper with him. I wound up stayin' around a few days to help out. Cut some fire wood, shot a deer, helped him dig a new hole for his outhouse."

"How you figure he can help?"

"He's pretty old and real ornery, but nobody knows these marshes better than him."

"That where you been disappearing?" Haynie asked. "Mother says she has no idea where you go."

"I make it a point to look in on him ever so often, and I always stay a couple of days to help out. Gumps says he's near eighty and he sure looks it. He was living in these parts since right after the second war with England. If there's any of them shacks around here, likely he'll know somethin' about it."

"An old codger, living alone way out like that, should be real happy you are willing' to stay around and help out."

"It's not just me helpin' him." Caleb laughed, "We help each other. I thought I knew a lot about plants and animals, but I don't know nothin' next to him."

Caleb sat quiet for a minute. "Gump's got an old fiddle," he blurted out. "Had it since he was about my age. I been takin' father's fiddle up there. We play together."

Haynie could see the frame buildings on the edge of town. The road forked and he guided the mare to the left in the direction of the telegraph office.

"Least there's no one around to complain about the noise," he said. "Come to think of it, I haven't heard you playing around mother's house for a while now."

Caleb's voice was low, pained.

"She told me to stop playin' music. Said a fiddle is an instrument of the devil. Once I found her in my room lookin' for it."

He looked quickly at Haynie, his voice angry, "She was goin' to burn my fiddle. That and this old pocket watch is all I have of father's. And she was going to burn it."

Haynie reined in the mare, stopping in the middle of the street.

"I can't believe mother would do that," he said. "Not destroy one of the few things we have from him. She must remember those winter evenings when we'd be sittin' around the fireplace. Him standing in front of us, a big fire roaring behind him, and we all'd sing while he played that fiddle."

Caleb said, "Even though you live close by, there's a lot goes on at the Manor House you don't know about."

He shook his head, then continued, "One night, after supper, a few of the boarders were sittin' in the parlor and I walked passed 'em carryin' my fiddle. They asked me to play a song. So, tryin' to be obligin', I started a tune. Mother came in from the kitchen and stood there listening and kind of hummin' along. I figured she was thinkin' of those very same nights. After a couple of minutes, this preacher, Reverend Muse he calls himself, came bustin' into the room so mad he could hardly talk. His face was all blotched and twisted up angry. Soon as he came in, Mother got red in the face and yelled for me to stop blasphemin' at once, and ran back to the kitchen." Caleb looked up, "Is that even a word — blasphemin?"

Haynie cracked the buggy whip and the mare started forward. "I don't know," he replied, "but the reverend's probably got a lot of words I never heard of."

"It was the next day she came lookin' for father's fiddle. She must have only got started when I came in on her 'cause she hadn't found it. That's when she told me–to my face–that I needed to burn his fiddle or bring it for the reverend to burn. 'Said that's the only way I could be saved."

Haynie shook his head, "I didn't know that Muse fellow had such a hold over her."

"He's got her so scared of not goin' to heaven, that sometimes she don't seem in her right mind."

"Lila says mother's been talkin' like she's a born again."

"If you wanna know what I think," Caleb said, "I'll tell ya. But, I'd only be guessin'.

"Let's hear it."

"You know how Muse always wears that long black cut away coat and wide brim black hat. Makes you kind of forget that he's so short and fat. And, he watches you with little black eyes set back into that fat face. His lips, they're always puckered out like he's been eatin' a bad persimmon."

Haynie nodded.

"I figure the only chance he's got with a woman — even a plain lookin' woman like mother — is by preachin' salvation so hard he scares 'em 'til they're afraid not to do what he says. The other day he says to her that two of the drummers stayin' there were sinners and if she didn't get them out, he would leave, for God would not allow him to stay in that house."

"What did she do?"

"Well she threw 'em out of course. One was that Mister Hanson, been comin' there since before the war. Nice man, quiet, always polite. I think he was paying mother too much attention for the reverend's taste."

Haynie reined in the mare in front of the telegraph office and looked at Caleb. "How often does he leave the house?"

"Every few days he'll get in that little log canoe of his. Says he's got to go on his 'ministerial circuit' to tend to his 'flock'. You ask me, he's got other women, like mother, scattered around within a day's sail of town."

"What do you mean — like mother?"

Caleb took off his fur cap and studied it in his hand, smoothing out the fur with a finger. "For one thing, he won't let her give out his room to nobody while he's gone. Says it's his Rectory, that he has blessed it, so now it's sacred ground. He and mother go in there for services, as they call it. Lots of hollerin' and shoutin' out, comes through those walls; callin' out the Lord's name and such. I doubt it has much to do with prayin'."

Haynie handed the reins to Caleb and climbed down from the wagon. Looking up he said, "With Crisfield bein' a boom town, the Manor House is always full. It's pretty valuable property. What's to keep him from sayin' he had the whole house blessed and it's his manse?"

"Nuthin', I reckon. I tried to talk to her, but she won't listen to anything about the reverend. Say's we will all be doomed to eternal damnation. That's why I been stayin' away so much."

"I'm going to talk to her," Haynie said as he climbed the wooden steps leading to the telegraph office. "Then, I'm going to have a come to Jesus meeting with this Reverend Muse."

8

Somerset County, Maryland
Monday, November 4, 1867

As Haynie climbed back into the buggy, Caleb said, "You just sent a wire up to this colonel in Baltimore?"

Haynie nodded.

"What did you tell 'em you had done? I only found out about it this morning."

Haynie patted Junior's head and said, "I wasn't sitting around waiting for you to wander in. I've been busy. We got a good man on the docks, talking to all the watermen. Then I mentioned Gerhard's story about these paddy shacks – maybe in this area. Said you were getting in touch with an old timer who knows the marshes and rivers even better than you do. While we're here, we'll see Squire Towne. Unlikely, but he may know something."

Caleb grunted.

"And, I'm going to talk to a few others I can trust. We need to cover as much ground as fast as we can; still, we have to move carefully. This shanghaiing is being done by a gang and, for all we know, they could have somebody right here in Crisfield."

"You think you can trust Horsey Towne?" Caleb asked.

Haynie shrugged, "No reason not to, that I know of."

The town bailiff's desk was located in a cramped room over a lawyer's office. The town council occupied two larger rooms on the same floor. The attorney owned the building, and after being named to do the town's legal work, agreed to rent his upstairs rooms to the council.

The local jail was a boxcar that the New York & Pennsylvania Railroad had loaned to the town. It was inconveniently located on a rail siding at the edge of town.

A few nights after the car was converted into a jail, a switch engine mistakenly included it in a freight train headed for New York and Boston. The next morning the town's bailiff took some coffee and bread to the two drunks he had locked up the night before, only to find them and the jail car missing. The drunks were already north of Wilmington, Delaware, vowing sobriety if the jail would only slow down.

The railroad returned the jail car, braked the wheels and removed a section of track to prevent it from disappearing a second time. The incident was front-page news in the local weekly, the Somerset Times. The story included a tintype of the railroad car before it left town and the following paragraph,

When asked how the jail had disappeared right under his nose, a red-faced town bailiff, Squire Horsey Towne, shouted back that it was not any of his doing and he had been against the idea of having a jail on wheels from the start.

When Haynie McKenna stepped through the office door, Squire Towne was seated behind a scarred roll top desk, shuffling through some papers and struggling to keep his eyes open. Caleb, concerned about leaving Junior alone in the wagon, had carried him up the stairway and now sat him gently on the floor.

Horsey laid the papers on the desk and eyed both men coldly from beneath the wide brim hat he wore indoors and out to conceal his baldhead. A worn deer hide pouch rested near his right hand.

The disappearance of the jail had fueled talk around town questioning whether Squire Towne was up to keeping the peace. Fistfights and gunfire erupted more frequently in the section of Crisfield lately being dubbed 'Dodge City'. Names of younger men were being offered up for the bailiff's job. Men who had served in the war, were fit enough, and tough enough, to keep the peace.

Without his knowledge, Haynie McKenna had been mentioned as a leading candidate. While McKenna was unaware of this, Horsey Towne had heard the rumor.

The bailiff eased back into his chair and nodded. "McKenna," he said looking at each of them. Shifting his gaze to Junior, he said, "That a stray? You expect me to shoot 'em for ya?"

Caleb bristled. "That's my dog and you better not touch hi m."

Horsey shifted a wad of chewing tobacco to his cheek and grinned. "Well now, I don't see no license on him. If he is yourn, you damn sight better get him a license, or I will shoot him."

Caleb scooped Junior up and held him. "I don't guess the fact that you make something off of every license you sell has anything to do with it."

Horsey spat tobacco juice toward a chamber pot in a corner behind his desk. The dark brown spittle clung to the wall, well above the pot.

"'At don't matter. The law says ever dog in this town has got to have a license and that mutt is for damn sure, in this town. Now, what will it be?"

Haynie stepped forward. "Give us a license."

"Can't do that," Horsey laughed, "but I will *sell* ya one. That'll be fitty cents."

Haynie paid the money, handed the license to Caleb, and turned back to the bailiff. "Squire, I want to ask you about talk of shanghaiing said to be going' on in these parts."

"Here in the Cove? Who says such a thing? I ain't heard of nobody gettin' took."

"Not taken in Crisfield," Haynie said. "But there's a chance the shanghaiers may be keeping' those they took somewhere nearby."

"What crap. You think I got nuthin' better to do than listen to nonsense. You been drinking, McKenna?"

Haynie said, "You've heard nothing about this?"

The bailiff spit at the wall, then turned and glared at Caleb and Junior. "Get that mutt out' a here, afore he craps on my floor."

Turning to Haynie, he said, "You're talking about people stealing other people, that right?"

Caleb picked up Junior. "We'll be in the wagon," he said over his shoulder as he headed for the stairway.

"Stealing people," Haynie said. "Well, yes, that's one way to put it."

"Folks steal chickens and I might sleep right through it. But, folks stealing other folks, I believe I'd stay awake for that one."

"So, you're saying you've heard nothing about shanghaiing."

"What are you up to McKenna? Trying to make out I'm not doin' my job?"

Without taking his eyes from Haynie, Towne opened a desk drawer, grabbed up a handful of shredded tobacco and added it to the cud already working in his mouth.

Speaking around the bulging wad, the bailiff said, “Have you heard, down at the Cove, folks is bein’ stole right under the town bailiff's nose. And he don’t know nuthin’ about it. Reckon they need a new bailiff. That how it is, McKenna?”

Stunned, Haynie stared back. “What are you babbling about? If you’ve heard nothing just say so.”

“Might as well have it out in the open, that how you see it? I been hearing about you likely wanting this job, but it was just talk – gossip. Now, you come busting in here and tell me to my face, how it is. At least those old biddies on the council can’t deny it no more.”

Haynie took a step toward the desk. “Look here, I’ve no idea what you’re raving about. A young fellow was taken off the docks up in Baltimore and his family has asked me to hunt for him. Find him before anything happens. I was just asking for your help. But, if —”

Squire Towne moved forward, the front legs of his chair hitting the floor with a crack. “They’re payin’ you to find him, ain’t they? Like folks hire that Pinkerton fella?”

“Doesn’t matter. Only thing that matters is finding’ Landon, his name’s Landon Wallis, as quick as we can. You going to help or not?”

“What makes ya’ think he’d be around here?”

“Long as we don’t know where he is, he could be anywhere. Now, have you heard anything about shanghaiing?”

A sneer curled Squire Towne’s mouth. “I know what yer up ta. I help ya find him, then you end up with a big payday – and likely, my job.”

The two men glared across the desk.

Haynie pressed, “You going to help?”

“What’s in it for me?”

Haynie looked at him with disgust. “What’s in it for you?”

Horsey collected the papers from the desk and held them in front of him. “Well, Mister McKenna, the way I figger it, you, or someone like you, is gonna have this job real soon. I ain’t a gettin’ rich selling dog licenses, so if there’s any kinda reward for findin’ this boy, I want a piece of it.”

“If we find him alive,” Haynie said, “and you had a hand in it, I can get you some reward money. But, we have to move quickly or the boy might perish.”

“Haw,” Horsey chortled. “If you mean he could be dead soon, I know that.”

He studied the man standing across his desk, finally saying, "All right, from here out, I'm in for a share of any reward money."

Haynie nodded, "If you help get him back alive."

Horsey nodded his head toward the street, "There's a crewman off one of these oyster boats, comes into Ellie's place, tells anyone who will listen a story about bein' took off a dock up to Baltimore Town last year. Could be he was, or, could be the likker talkin'."

Haynie calculated that this was probably the same man Gerhard had mentioned. It wouldn't hurt to have both men looking for him. No point in telling the bailiff about Gerhard.

"If it is true, he might be of some help. See if you can find him." Haynie fixed the bailiff with a steady gaze, "Don't try any tricks," he said, "We talk to him together."

Horsey returned the stare. "I might say the same to you, McKenna. If I find him, I'll take you to him."

"Fair enough," Haynie said.

He took three two dollar bills from his pocket and laid them on the desk in front of Horsey. "This will buy drinks for the boys at Ellie's while you ask around."

Horsey grabbed them off the desk with greedy fingers. "This ain't comin' out o' my reward money, is it?"

Shaking his head in disgust, Haynie stalked out.

Squire Horsey Towne touched the fingers of his right hand to his hat in mock salute.

Caleb and Junior sat huddled together against the chill of a late November afternoon. The wind came off Tangier Sound, pushing roiling clouds ahead of it. Haynie studied the cloud formations, forecasting that they would get home ahead of the snow.

Caleb stood. "Look at that," he said, pointing to a horse and rider plodding down the middle of the street. Heading toward them was a boney, grey gelding about fourteen hands, as emaciated as the man in the saddle. The unshaven rider wore a grimy beaver hat, pulled low over his eyes. Slender wrists jutted from frayed cuffs, boney hands held the reins. The rider gazed ahead ignoring the clusters of people gathered along the street's edge, whispering and pointing as he passed.

"What's he wearin', tied with that bit of rope?" Caleb asked.

"Looks like an old piece of buffalo hide. He's cut a hole in it to poke his head through."

"They both look like they're starvin'," said Caleb.

Across the saddle, lay a large bored rifle with a barrel almost sixty inches long. The highly polished wood grain and shiny brass fittings were in stark contrast to the neglect apparent in horse and rider.

Caleb asked, “You ever see a long gun like that?”

“In the war,” Haynie said as he climbed into the wagon. “It’s a Prussian rifle, seventy-two caliber.”

“Whoever he is, he thinks more of that gun than he does of that horse, or himself, for that matter.”

As the horse passed within feet of the wagon, the rider’s hard look remained fixed on the road ahead, but Haynie was certain those eyes missed nothing.

“He’s real mean lookin’,” Caleb whispered. “You ever seen him before?”

Haynie shook his head and jiggled the reins.

His voice still low, Caleb said, “Looks like some kinda wild animal. Those little beady eyes and pointy face. Got them long scraggly whiskers growin’ under that boney nose. I’ll bet if he ever smiled, he’s got two big front teeth, just like a rat’s.”

Caleb wiggled his nose, drew back his upper lip and bared his front teeth. “Another thing,” he said, “did ya see the way he never looked around, just seemed to be starin’ way up the road ahead. And, what about that big gun, what do you think he hunts with that?”

“Men.”

Caleb jerked around to look at his brother, “Why do you say that?”

“That’s what a gun like that is made for. Could use it for buffalo or elephants. None of either one around here I know of.”

Caleb slapped his forehead. “I should of thought of that,” he said.

Haynie reined the mare in, maintaining the gap between them and the horse and rider. “Why you going so slow?” Caleb asked. “We can go around him. You’re not afraid of him are you? What’s he going to do, shoot us right here?”

“I’m as careful around him as I would be any other wild animal. Since he’s in front of us, I want to see where he goes.”

The two brothers hunkered down against the chill wind and followed the stranger in silence. Haynie kept a distance between them, hoping the man ahead could not hear the creaking of the wagon, nor the sound of its wheels on the oyster shells. Occasionally, Junior would yip at a passing buggy, while up ahead, both horse and rider seemed oblivious of the passing scene.

9

Crisfield, Maryland
Tuesday, November 5, 1867

Haynie McKenna stepped into his mother's kitchen, hat in hand. The breakfast meal was over and Callie, the young Negro girl who did most of the cooking and all of the cleaning, scrubbed dishes in a small wooden tub.

Lettie McKenna stood at her floor to ceiling larder, busily selecting items for that evening's supper. The Manor House did not serve a midday meal as the drummers were in town making their sales calls and any overnight travelers were gone.

"Morning, Mother."

"Sit at the table and Callie will fix you some breakfast," Lettie said without looking up, intent on her search.

"Thanks, but I'll just have coffee."

"You need some eggs and side meat. You don't eat enough."

Haynie laid his hat on a chair seat. "Lila feeds me," he said.

Lettie shrugged. "If you're lookin' for Caleb," she said, "he left hours ago."

"Did he say when he might get back?"

"You know him better than that. He took some coffee and biscuits and was gone long before sun up."

She turned and carefully sat a jar of peaches on the table.

"Why are you wearing that?" she asked, a shaking hand pointing to the Colt .44 revolver holstered at his side.

"It's my gun. Brought it home from the war."

"I know what it is, Haynie McKenna, and I don't want it in my house."

Callie set a cup of coffee in front of Haynie. "Thank you, Callie." He smiled, and then looked at his mother, "I'm on my way into town and I wanted to speak to Reverend Muse, if he's here."

Lettie, hands still shaking, folded her arms defiantly across her chest. "Well, he's not here. Won't be back 'til later. Doesn't matter," she continued glaring at the gun belt, "'cause he wouldn't talk to you as long as you're wearin' that tool of the devil. You know better — 'Thou shalt not kill'. Haynie McKenna, don't you want salvation?"

"Too late, I killed men in the war."

"Well, God will forgive you for that."

"Why? Seems to me, killing is killing," he said.

Callie wiped her hands and hurried from the room.

"You, you had no choice. You was ordered."

"The Rebs are the sinners, then?"

"Yes, of course. They were trying to kill you."

Haynie, leaving the coffee untouched, picked up his hat.

"The Rebs were under orders from someone else, same as me. How can God take sides? Seems like every soldier must be doomed, or every soldier must be saved."

Lettie put a hand to her mouth, "Oh, my," she said, "I wish the Reverend was here, he would know what to say —"

"You have to wait for the Reverend to tell you what you believe, is that it?"

Tears rimmed Lettie's eyes. "How can you be so cruel? I'm trying real hard to see that both you and Caleb get into Heaven. Him with that fiddle and, you lettin' Young Tench get this old without being baptized, and now with that awful gun."

"Are you saying that a man playing a fiddle is as sinful as a man who kills another human being?"

Lettie lifted her apron and dabbed at her eyes.

"I think that Josiah – Doctor Muse – would say that neither man will be accepted into Heaven."

"What do *you* say?"

"It's not what I say that matters; it's the word of God."

"It's the word of God, according to some man, in this case, Josiah Muse. How do you know that God's word is not just whatever Muse wants it to be at the time?"

Lettie pulled a chair away from the table and sank into it. She looked up at her son eyes brimming with tears.

"Oh, mercy, please don't blaspheme. The Reverend Muse is a man of God, a good man, who, like Jesus, has devoted his whole life to helping us – his flock – find our way."

"Who says that burning father's fiddle will save Caleb's soul, Muse or Jesus?"

Lettie reached out to him, "None of us understand, son," she said. "That's why we are so fortunate to have Reverend Muse to guide us. You should talk to him; he'll help you to see the light."

She stood, excitement in her voice, "I have a splendid idea. When he gets home, you come for dinner and have a nice chat with him. Bring Lila and Young Tench, of course." Her words tumbled out, fast enough she hoped, to keep Haynie from protesting.

"It'll be a good time to talk about Young Tench's baptism, which we believe is long overdue."

Haynie was furious. "Back home? How long has this house been *his* home, mother? And, when Young Tench is baptized is up to Lila and me, not the Reverend Doctor Muse"

Lettie's neck reddened, from the lace atop her high neck dress to her ears. "I uh – didn't — uh —"

"It's my understanding that *Doctor* Muse is from up in Delaware, around Wilmington. He very likely has another home up there, along with a wife and children." He glared down at her. "Maybe you need to worry about your own salvation, Mother," he warned, then turned on his heel and left.

Once in Crisfield, Haynie stuck his head in the front door of the telegraph office, surprised to find a telegram waiting for him.

Wes Moore, the town's sole Western Union agent, called Haynie in. "Saved me a long ride out to yer house," he said, and handed the envelope across the counter.

"Thanks, Wes."

Haynie studied the envelope as he left the office. He took a seat on a nearby bench and saw that it was a message from Colonel Wallis.

Fell's Point, Maryland
Tuesday November 5, 1867
Telegram

Mister McKenna,
I feel that you are due a briefing on the current situation. At 7:00 last evening, Major Hollins, acting as emissary for the Wallis family, delivered a carpetbag containing $75,000 in U.S. currency to the kidnappers as demanded by them. We even met their demand that the bag have a pattern of large red roses. Major Hollins informed me that this was to enable the scoundrels to identify our bag from all the others to be found moving in and out of the Pratt Street terminal.
We anxiously await Landon's return, as promised. This nasty business will be over soon and we will all be able to get back to what passes for a normal life around here.
The Wallis family thanks you for your efforts. Please, do not return any of the remaining advance funds.

Regards,

Colonel Silas Wallis

After finishing the telegram, Haynie returned to the Western Union office.

"Can you take a return wire for, me?"

"Certainly, Mister McKenna. Some serious business, eh?"

When the agent was ready, Haynie dictated this message:

Very pleased to hear that all has ended well.
I would appreciate a short message telling me that Landon is safely home.

Haynie McKenna

Haynie paid for the telegram and headed off to look for Gerhard. *Even if Landon does get home*, he thought, *this shanghai business isn't over*.

Haynie crisscrossed the town trying to locate Gerhard Stein. A little after noon, he saw Squire Towne coming out of the Horn O' Plenty, a small restaurant popular with local businessmen and town officials. Towne worked a toothpick through his teeth, the deer skin bag holding his Sharp's four shot pepperbox pistol dangled from his left wrist.

The bailiff started across Broad Street toward Goodsell's Alley. It was well known in Crisfield that Horsey Towne reveled in being addressed as Squire, though no one could recall how he had come to acquire the appellation. While Haynie thought the title silly, he needed the man's help and saw no reason to anger him.

"Squire, you have a minute?" he called out.

Horsey turned, "Oh, it's you McKenna. Come on, I got to get up to the train station to meet the twelve-forty from Philadelphia and Wilmington. That's one of my responsibilities — have ta meet every train that comes to town. Any news?"

"I'm looking for Gerhard Stein. You wouldn't happen to know where he is working today?"

"Believe he's down at Bay Fisheries unloadin' oyster boats." The bailiff's eyes narrowed. "Hold on, is that furriner gonna get some of my reeward?"

"Take it easy, Squire. You'll get what's due you."

"I damn sure better," the Bailiff grumbled as he turned into Goodsell's Alley.

Gerhard Stein was stacking bushel baskets of oysters in a dank warehouse. The space was cold enough that he exhaled a cloud as he worked; yet he wore only a thin undershirt above his work pants. He stepped away from the stacks as Haynie approached.

Gerhard wrapped his friend in a brief bear hug. "*Guden Tag, mein freund*," he said.

"*Bitte,*" Haynie replied. "Let's speak English, my German is *nicht gud.*"

"*Ya* – yes. You want know what I hear about shanghai business. Is right?"

Haynie nodded.

Gerhard shrugged, "Only little."

The big man seemed embarrassed that he didn't have more to report.

"I talk around to many men on docks and in Ellie's place. Not some know — um — *wahrheit* — sorry — what is?"

Haynie listened intently, "Not many know — the truth — the facts?"

Gerhard nodded vigorously, "Ya, ya, that it. I hear one who comes to Ellie's, speaks about he been a shanghai. But, he gone and not here for —" Gerhard paused and counted in silence as he raised the correct number of fingers, "*veir* — four night."

"That must be the same one Squire Towne talked about," Haynie said. "Gerhard, it's very important that we talk to him. He may be able to help us."

“Yes, yes, I know. I wait every night for him to come to drink and be with — *freundin* — girl friend.”

“The next time he comes in, you send for me at once.”

Haynie touched his right eyelid. “Watch him. If he goes upstairs with a girl, let him alone, but don’t let him leave Ellie’s. Tell him he’ll be paid to talk to me. I’ll get there as quick as I can.” Haynie watched him carefully. “Do you understand?”

Stein nodded, “*Ya, ya.* He not go, until you come.” The Prussian’s size and harsh guttural manner of speaking convinced most folks to do as he asked. Haynie touched Stein’s arm and turned to leave.

“Is another,” Stein said.

Haynie stopped, “Another? Another man?”

“*Ya.* I speak to oysterman when unload boat. He tells of bad man who sails around bay to take men to big boats for work. These men not want to go — one jumps into water and tries to swim away, but he die.”

“How?”

Stein shrugged. “Can no swim, or too *kalte*, I not know. Oysterman say bad man swears at man in water.”

“The oysterman you spoke to, saw this himself?”

“*Ya.*”

“Does he know the man’s name, or the name of his boat?”

“Oyster man heard bad man called something – maybe – Jock.” Stein shrugged. “He said boat was dirty. Not know name on boat.”

“Where did he see this and how many days ago?”

Stein grinned and touched his forehead. “I know to ask that,” he said. “Waterman was at Hazard Cove. See dirty boat at mouth of Man-o-kin River.”

Gerhard Stein held up two fingers. “*Zwei* days ago.”

“Good work,” Haynie said. “*Sehr gud.*”

Gerhard smiled.

Haynie found Horsey Towne on Main Street, heading toward his office. Squire’s breathing was labored and he seemed grateful for a reason to stop. Though the afternoon was chilly, he wiped beads of sweat from his face and neck as he waited.

Horsey said, “I sweat even in the winter. Summer’s like livin’ in hell.”

“Squire,” Haynie asked, “have you heard anything about a man being drowned up around Hazard Cove, in the last day or two?”

Horsey studied the inside of his hat as he wiped the band with a small cloth.

"Not a thing. Unless he was from Somers — damn I can't get used to the new name — from Crisfield, no reason I would. Hazard Cove's the county sheriff's territory. You think our boy drowned?"

"I just heard that a man was seen jumping from a small boat, at the mouth of the Manokin, and he drowned before he could reach shore. Thought I better check it out. Can you send a wire up to the sheriff and ask him about it?"

"I can do it. But, if it's him don't forget I helped ya find out about him. We still gonna get some reward?"

Haynie's eyes narrowed and Squire Towne shifted uneasily under the other man's gaze.

"I only want what's due me," he said. "I got to look out for myself."

Horsey settled his hat on his head and added, "Especially, if I'm not keepin' this job."

"Listen to me, Squire. If you help us find that boy, you get your damn money, either way we find him. But, every time I come to talk to you, I don't want to have to listen to you whining about it. Understand?"

Horsey turned abruptly and started down the alley. "I should have an answer tomorrow 'bout this time," he said without looking back.

10

Crisfield, Maryland
Tuesday Afternoon, November 5, 1867

Haynie heard shouting behind him, and turned to see three men racing up Main Street from the docks. As they came closer, it was apparent that two of the men were chasing a third, who was screaming for help. Bystanders watching the spectacle, made no move to help and the man appealed directly to Haynie, as his pursuers gained on him.

"Help me! Please, help me!," he gasped. "I was kidnapped. They'll kill me."

They were within thirty feet of Haynie when one of the pursuers, smaller and faster than the other, leapt on the man's back and both crashed heavily to the street. The slower man reached them and directed vicious kicks at the two men rolling on the oyster shell surface.

"Goddamn it, Jake," the smaller pursuer yelled from the ground, "Yore kickin' me as much as him, stop it."

Haynie McKenna drew his gun and fired a single shot into the air, as he ran toward them. He pointed the gun at the pursuer who was intently aiming another kick at the men grappling on the ground.

"Back away," Haynie ordered.

"Mind yer own damn bizness," the man growled, though he did as ordered.

The two men stopped rolling at the sound of gunfire and, still clutching one another, stared up at Haynie.

"You two, get up and stand still." Haynie said, stepping back to have all three men in view without turning his head. As the two men struggled to stand, the smaller pursuer drove his fist into the other man's jaw.

"That was a good one, huh, Jake?" he laughed, and quickly moved behind the man he called Jake.

"Jesus, Rod, don't be tellin' my name."

Jake turned and glared at Haynie. "You the law?"

"He's not," Horsey Towne gasped, "but I am."

Horsey moved beside Haynie, his chest heaving. He pointed his Sharp's four-barrel pepperbox pistol at the three men. "What's going on here?" he challenged.

The third man rose slowly holding his jaw and shaking his head. "They kidnapped me. I'll tell you all of it," he said, "but you got to promise not to leave me with them. They'll kill me for sure."

The smaller pursuer stopped brushing pieces of oyster shell from his clothes and pointed a finger, "He's a damn liar. We was just tryin' to get our own propity back."

The one called Jake turned and slapped his comrade hard across the face.

"Jesus, Rod, Jesus. Shut it and keep it shut."

The smaller man, embarrassed at being publicly shamed, turned away rubbing the sting from his face.

"That's enough," Horsey said, "You better take yer own advice and keep it shut, 'til I tell you different."

Haynie leaned his head close to Horsey's ear, "We better split them up until we get this sorted out."

"That's what I was thinkin'," Horsey said. "You stickin' around 'til this is finished?"

"Of course," Haynie answered, without taking his eyes from the scene in front of him. "Good chance they can tell us where to look for the Wallis boy."

Horsey turned back to the three men. "What's your names?"

The two pursuers stared at the ground.

"I'm Milo Porter," the other man said, "from Annapolis."

Horsey took a step toward the two pursuers. "Let's have yer names."

Rod peered around Jake. "We're brothers," he said proudly.

Jake drew back his fist, "Jesus, Rod —"

"That's enough," the bailiff barked. "We're takin' the three of you to the jail. Then—"

"For God's sake," Porter bawled, "you can't leave me with them. I'm begging you."

"Dammit, Porter," Horsey said, "If you listen instead of talkin' you'll know what's gonna happen. We're marchin' all three of you to our jail."

He waved his small pistol at the other two. "After these two are locked away, we'll bring you down to the office and you can tell us your story. If I don't like what I hear, then you'll be back in with them."

Small knots of town's folk watched with amused curiosity as the three men trudged through the streets, followed closely by the Town Bailiff and Haynie McKenna, guns leveled at their prisoner's backs. Each group cheered as the parade passed them.

"Hurrah for Squire, Show 'em Squire."

Horsey Towne smiled and tipped his hat at each hurrah.

When they reached the rail jail, Horsey climbed the wooden steps, unlocked the heavy door and slid it open. Timbers being cheaper than iron on Maryland's Eastern Shore, the walls to the two cells within the car were fashioned from thick locust posts secured floor to ceiling. A small, barred window set in each door allowed the jailer to check on a prisoner without unlocking the door.

Darting eyes and a dirty grey beard appeared at the door of the first cell as they passed.

"That you, Squire? When 'm I gettin' out of here?"

"What ya wanna leave fer, Cecil; I just brought ya some company."

"Dammit, Horsey that ain't funny. I've sobered up. Let me outta here."

They stopped in front of the second cell and Haynie waited with the prisoners as Horsey unlocked the iron padlock and pulled the door open.

"You two, inside," the bailiff said.

After Jake and Rodney had moved to the middle of the cell, he closed and locked the door. Squire looked into the cell and said, "We'll be back later to talk to you fellas."

"You better hurry," Jake cackled, "because we ain't stayin' long."

Milo Porter sat in a wooden chair in front of Squire Towne's desk. One hand held a tin cup filled with freshly made coffee, the other clutched the torn edges of a baggy trouser leg, shredded by jagged pieces of Main Street's oyster shell surface.

Haynie looked on as the man, in obvious pain, studied his injuries. Milo looked to be about thirty years old, slightly built with the natural pallor of a man who spends his days indoors, behind a desk or a sales counter. His brown wool suit jacket had separated along one seam, exposing a yellow lining.

Haynie sat his coffee cup on the bailiff's desk and pulled over a chair for himself.

"How's that leg?" he asked. Milo released his hold on the cloth and peered at his lacerated knee. His voice quavered.

"It's still bleeding some."

Squire Towne sat heavily behind the desk. He withdrew a tin cup and a bottle of whiskey from one of the drawers. The cup, sometimes used as a spittoon, was mostly empty. Horsey poured a liberal amount of whiskey in it and smiled at his visitors.

"Good thing about this whiskey, it'll kill anything nasty it lands on."

He offered the bottle to Milo Porter. "Pour some in yer cup, pour a little on that knee and then give it to Haynie there. Mind ya, don't waste much on that knee."

Milo hesitated, looking from Haynie to the bailiff.

"I'm still feeling poorly from being on that boat — and I'm not used to drinking hard liquor."

"Take it," Haynie said. "Splash a little on your leg and just drink your coffee for now."

Milo took a piece of cloth from his pocket, soaked it with whiskey and laid it gingerly on his knee. He winced from the stinging pain and gulped the coffee to keep from crying aloud.

Horsey Towne chuckled at the man's discomfort and grabbed the whiskey bottle.

"When you feel like talking," Haynie said, "tell us how you came to be with these men."

Milo shuddered, "I was visiting in the town of Easton. As it was my first visit, I wandered around and happened along the docks when someone grabbed me from behind. When I came around I could see I was stuffed in a dark space on that horrid little boat."

He dabbed at his wounds. "It was like living in a coffin."

Haynie asked, "Anyone else with you?"

Porter shook his head.

"When did this happen?"

"Seems an eternity, but it was just last evening. Who would have thought to be afraid in a little country town like that?"

Milo looked into his cup then held it toward the bailiff.

"If you mixed a little of that whiskey with some more coffee, I guess it wouldn't be too terrible."

Squire hesitated, "Hold the damn thing steady," he said.

Milo squeezed the cup with both hands as the bailiff splashed a small dash of liquor into the coffee. Horsey Towne looked at Haynie as he poured a hearty dollop in his own cup, “I ain’t wasting good whiskey on him. Let’s see if he pukes it up first.”

Haynie turned away, “Its okay. Go on,” he said to Milo.

“Well sir, we had been at your dock here, for some time. I didn’t hear nobody moving on the floor above.”

Horsey scoffed into his cup, but said nothing.

“So I shoved against the door, hopin’ to be able to see a little somethin —”

“Jesus,” Horsey Towne roared, his face flush from the alcohol. “On a boat it ain’t a floor — it’s a deck — and, it ain’t a goddamn door, it’s a hatch.”

“Dammit, Squire.”

Horsey shrugged, “Just tryin’ to be helpful,” he said. “No need for the boy to go through life embarrassing himself ever time he tells it.”

Haynie looked at Porter, “Tell it the best you can,” he said.

Milo nodded.

“Well, sir, when I shoved that door – hatch – it flew open with a bang. I jumped up and, seeing nary a soul, I stumbled up on the deck and made for the dock.”

Milo, swigged the laced coffee, then wiped his mouth with a ragged coat sleeve.

“I didn’t look back,” he continued. “I reckon there was a man in the cabin — maybe sleepin’— anyhow, I was on the dock runnin’ as best I could when I heard someone shout out behind me.”

Porter’s voice trailed off, “I was a-scared, so I just kept runnin’.”

“Speak up, dammit,” the bailiff snapped and poured more whiskey into his own cup.

Haynie reached out and moved the bottle to the far corner of the desk. Horsey leaned over, dragged the bottle back and closed it in a desk drawer.

Haynie asked, “Did they keep you on the boat the entire time?”

“Yes. I heard them talking about getting provisions here before going on to someplace they called some kind a shack. I guess that’s where they were going to keep me.”

Milo gulped his drink, coughed and grimaced, “Ick,” he said.

Horsey laughed. “Another snort?” he asked as Porter pulled back on his cup.

Milo studied his injury. “Anyhow, just as I got to the end of the dock I seen those two comin’ at me, so I started yellin’ for someone to help me, and kept on runnin’.”

Haynie said, "I want you to show us where that boat is tied up."

Milo shuddered inside his suit. "I — don't want to go back there."

Milo limped along, struggling to keep up with his two rescuers. He was comforted by their bulk, their determined strides and the guns they carried. Once on the dock, he slowed, carefully scanning the boats tied off ahead.

"I thought it was right there," Milo said, pointing a shaking hand at an empty spot. "Right behind that big boat with all the winches."

Haynie surveyed the inlet leading into Tangier Sound.

"It probably was," he said. "The one aboard, he likely saw the ruckus and hightailed it. Going to be hell to pay for letting you get loose and those two getting jailed."

Horsey shielded his eyes against the setting sun, scanning the boats riding at anchor in the middle of the Little Annemessex River.

"He's likely sittin' out there waitin' to see if them two comes back," Horsey said.

Milo spoke up. "The one called Jake, that's locked up in your jail. He's real mean. Likely the one on the boat would be scared to stay and just as scared to run off and leave him."

The three men stood at the river's edge studying the bobbing boats.

"There's one or two could be it," Milo said, "but I can't be sure from here."

Haynie put a hand on Milo's shoulder. "Well, Mister Porter, I expect you got some folks who are worried about you. The bailiff here will help you send off a wire and get you a place to sleep for the night."

Horsey scowled but said nothing.

Milo's knee had stiffened in the evening air, his limp more pronounced, as they left the dock. After a few paces, he stopped and bent down to rub the injured area.

"I been feelin' sorry for myself and clean forgot to thank you gentlemen for saving me from those men. My folks will send me money to get home on and I want to give you both a small reward."

Haynie said, "That's not —"

"How small?" Horsey interrupted.

"Well — I don't know —"

"You work that out with the bailiff," Haynie said. "After all, he's the one going to see that you get fed tonight and have a place to bed down."

Facing Horsey, he said, "I'm going to send a wire to Baltimore, about this."

Horsey jerked his head toward Milo, "What do they care about this here guy?" he grumbled.

"They ain't gonna pay nothin' for him."

Haynie held his temper, "Milo said they were stopping here for provisions."

Porter nodded in agreement, "That's what they said."

"Which likely means their paddy shack is nearby. It narrows our search for Landon considerably."

Horsey frowned.

"You know, Squire," Haynie said, "it may be that Crisfield is the home port for this shanghai gang."

11

Somerset County, Maryland
Early morning, Tuesday, November 5, 1867

Jeremy Coates repeatedly drew the large, bone handled Bowie knife carefully over the small whetstone he held in his left hand. This he did ritualistically every morning, waiting for the campfire to boil his coffee. The great knife gleamed in his hand, always sharp enough to cleave a hair from a man's head in one motion.

"Never can be too sharp," he said to no one.

Jeremy stuck the razor thin knifepoint into his palm and smiled at the blood oozing from the wound. This too was part of his daily ritual. He liked to be reminded of the pain he and his knife rapturously inflicted on others. The sight of his own blood slaked his needs until he could draw someone else's. After wiping the blade with an oiled cloth, he settled the Bowie into a sheath strung on a leather belt under his buffalo robe coat.

The coffee pot sat on a flat rock, heated by the breakfast fire. Jeremy poured a cupful and drank noisily, anxious to complete his ritual. Next, he unfolded the Indian blanket lying beside him, removed the large bore Prussian Musket and laid it across his lap. As always, Jeremy was seduced by the beauty and precision of the weapon. He stroked the blonde wood stock gently with a piece of soft cloth. The ceremony continued as he burnished the brass fittings and long iron barrel that made the .72 caliber gun so distinctive.

When fired, the weapon's jarring recoil was like that of a shoulder-fired cannon. Jeremy Coates enjoyed the pain, believing it gave him a kinship with his target, who, at the same time would be dying a horrible death mere yards away. He cared more for that gun than anything else in his life. Certainly more than any feeling he had for his mother and father.

They had named him Jeremy, and he hated them for it. At age twelve, he decided they were of no further use to anyone and cut their throats while they slept. After setting fire to the house, he had worked up real tears for the neighbors who arrived, too late to save the house or its occupants. Homeless, Jeremy left Virginia's Eastern Shore for a brief stay with a spindly, maiden aunt in Roanoke. With only weeks left in the school year, she insisted he enroll in a nearby grade school. At home, he had achieved little in the way of formal education, here he was in a classroom of children much younger and smaller than himself. Initially, Jeremy enthralled his classmates with stories of his own bravery and daring, so that he actually enjoyed his few days at the school.

One chilly morning, a crowd had gathered in the schoolyard to hear Jeremy describe, in gory detail, how his parents were hacked to death and scalped by savages while he barely escaped with his own hair. The next day a classmate disrupted another of Jeremy's tales, shouting out that the new boy was a liar. It was a fact, the other boy yelled, that there hadn't been any savages in Virginia for a hundred years.

Jeremy erupted in a rage, hitting the smaller boy so hard the lad squealed in pain as blood gushed from his nose and mouth. Following that incident, the other children kept their distance, whispering that Jeremy was a "liar" and "the rat face boy".

On a night in early June, Jeremy quietly left his aunt's house and returned to the amicable surroundings of the Eastern Shore. He had given considerable thought to killing her and burning her house down, but decided it was too much trouble.

Back on familiar ground, he built a small lean-to near the mouth of Messongo Creek, just below the Maryland state line. There he spent his teenage years roaming the forest, living by cunning and guile.

What Jeremy couldn't get by hunting, fishing, and trapping, he stole. He avoided other people, always careful to make sure no one was around when he helped himself to a blanket, a frying pan, or a pair of boots.

Jeremy considered himself a frontiersman. Now, as he buffed the barrel of his long gun, he scoffed at the thought of those men along the bay's Eastern shore, who prided themselves on being accomplished proggers. He had lived a decidedly more rugged existence than a mere progger.

"A progger ain't nuthin' more than a momma's boy," he'd argue to himself.

"Spends a couple a days out in the woods huntin' and thinks he's done somethin'. If he gets cold or hungry he can always crawl home to his momma."

Jeremy looked at his spavined horse nibbling at weeds and grass.

"Meantime, a real frontiersman lives by his wits, 'cause he's got no momma to run to."

Jeremy spent most of the autumn of 1861 avoiding the federal patrols who scoured the region for able-bodied men to be pressed into the service of the Union army. One morning, while moving quickly to evade a cavalry troop, he stumbled into a clearing, in the middle of which sat a log cabin. A wisp of grey smoke curled above the chimney, signaling that someone was likely at home. He had no choice but to try for the cabin. Anyone inside would have to be silenced before they could cry out.

Jeremy drew his hunting knife with his right hand as he hit the cabin's door with his left shoulder. The door was unlatched and banged hard against the wall before hurtling back into Jeremy. He slammed into a small wooden table, sending a bucket of water crashing to the floor.

Jeremy scrambled to his feet, crouched low, his knife in front of him to fend off any attack. Quickly, he realized he was alone in the one room cabin and sheathed the knife.

He heard shouting as horses and riders emerged from the woods and galloped toward the cabin. Glancing around, Jeremy was satisfied there was no point in trying to conceal himself under the cot against the far wall. The wisps of smoke he had seen were the remnants of a cooking fire smoldering in the fireplace.

With two strides he was at the fireplace, looking up into the rough sooty stone interior. With the fire below dying, the chimney was barely warm. Grabbing protruding stones on either side, he hunched his shoulders, pulling himself up into the chimney. He bent both legs and jammed his knees into the wall he faced, while digging boot heels into the wall at his back.

Within moments he heard soldiers enter the cabin. They cursed and began smashing everything in the room.

"You think this is a Reb hideout, Sarge?" One of them grunted to the sound of dishes being smashed.

"I doubt it. I don't think even a Reb would live like this," said a second voice.

"Let's burn her anyway," said a third.

Jeremy recalled how the chimney was the only thing standing after the flames consumed the rest of his own house. He wondered how hot these stones would get if those damn blue bellies set fire to the tiny cabin. It was in his favor that the house was small and tinder dry. It would burn quickly, affording little time to heat the stones around him. With clenched teeth, he determined to hold out until the pain became unbearable.

"We're not burnin' the damn house," said the sergeant's voice. "We got to round us up some reeecruits, 'fore we can get supper."

Army boots stomped to the door and the cabin became quiet. It would be another seven months before the Union army learned that young men all along the Eastern shore of the Chesapeake Bay had taken to their chimneys to avoid conscription.

After several minutes of quiet, Jeremy lowered himself onto the grey ashes and stepped back into the room. He waited until well after dark, and then headed south, deeper into the Confederacy; eventually joining up with an artillery unit at Blacksburg, Virginia.

Within weeks of his enlistment, it was apparent to anyone who encountered Jeremy Coates, that he was ill suited for the structured discipline of an organized military.

One morning he was approached by his sergeant and a captain he did not recognize. The captain stood to one side while the sergeant spoke.

"Private Jeremy Coates, you are ordered to head west to Kansas and join up with Quantrill's Raiders. If you choose to remain in this unit, you will be court-martialed and likely sent to the stockade."

The exploits of William Quantrill and his raiders were cheered throughout the Confederacy. Jeremy could not believe his good fortune at being asked to join them. The idea of being a force in the wanton destruction of others thrilled him. He left immediately for Kansas by horseback; wanting neither to wait for a westbound train nor put up with the humanity he would encounter in a crowded passenger car.

It was while riding through Tennessee that Jeremy secured his beloved Prussian rifle.

He emerged from a copse of small trees onto a sprawling meadow, thick with smoke and the acrid smell of a recent battle. The land was littered to the rise ahead with the lifeless remains of horses, and men clad in uniform remnants, both blue and grey. The sounds of battle moved to the south as he guided his horse between the dead and dying at his feet.

Along the hill line to his left, men in grey uniforms loaded stretchers. On the horizon to his right, blue uniforms did the same. Jeremy knew that, even if he was seen, those moving about were too busy to concern themselves with a lone rider. He was in no hurry to pass into the woods across the meadow. It pleased him to gaze down upon these fallen men and revel in the thought that he was a better man than any of them. He was, after all, still alive.

About half way across the field, Jeremy came upon a young soldier lying on his back. Bright red blood spurted from a hole in his chest, soaking his grey uniform jacket. The boy's eyes were cloudy, almost lifeless, his mouth moved silently. Cradled in the boys arms and running the length of his body, was the most magnificent long gun Jeremy had ever seen. The young soldier desperately gripped the barrel with both hands.

Jeremy dismounted and squatted down next to the boy.

"Don't expect you'll be needin' this anymore," he said taking hold of the rifle barrel and giving a tug. The boy tightened his grip, his head turned toward the sound of Jeremy's voice.

A soft, "No," his only response as he mustered his remaining strength to resist the efforts to take his beloved weapon.

"Look boy, you're good as dead – give it up. 'Sides it didn't do you no good anyways. Likely too much gun for ya." Jeremy yanked the gun while the boy hung on.

Quickly scanning the battlefield, Jeremy drew his hunting knife. "You were a tough little shit, I'll give you that much," he said, slitting the boy's throat in one motion.

Jeremy set the rifle aside while he went through the boy's pockets. Finding a few Confederate dollars, he jammed them into his own pocket. Grinning, he held up a nearly full bottle of laudanum. He took a swig of the drug, corked the bottle and secured it in his jacket.

"Now, ain't that a fine howdy do," he laughed. "Wish that old lady of a sergeant was here, so I could wave this under his nose."

Being caught stealing laudanum from a medical unit was one of the reasons Jeremy was riding to join Quantrill.

"Better yet, if he was here, I'd lay him out right next to that dead soldier boy there."

Jeremy mounted his horse and laid his new gun across the saddle in front of him. His eyes shone, "You'll be a real beaut as soon as I can get ya cleaned up," he said aloud.

Now, drinking his breakfast coffee, he remembered his days with Quantrill as the best of his life.

Jeremy had caught up with the fabled raider near Joplin, Missouri, making a splendid entrance, according to his plan. After proving himself to the outriders securing Quantrill's headquarters, Jeremy rode slowly into camp, ahead of his escort. He held the great gun upright with his right hand, the butt of the weapon resting on his right thigh. Sitting ramrod straight in the saddle, he passed knots of hard looking men who interrupted their duties to follow him with menacing looks.

Jeremy felt their eyes on him and imagined them filled with envy when they saw the great gun. Later, he learned that among those who witnessed his arrival, stood young Jesse James and his brother Frank, along side Cole Younger. When Coates eventually met these legendary men face to face, he was not going to tell them his name was Jeremy. "You can call me, Rat," he would say.

Over the months with Quantrill, Jeremy and his gun gained the respect of those with whom he rode. Many of these men were deadly with a six-shooter, quickly drawn and fired from the hip, but none could match his marksmanship at a distance. He soon became the one Quantrill called upon to bring down a Yankee officer, or Kansas lawman, from long range. What he aimed at – he hit – and what he hit, died. He proudly recalled the raiders' praising his marksmanship.

"Good shootin' Rat", or, "Rat, you sure emptied some Yankee saddles, this mornin'."

Today, as he finished polishing the great gun, he grew more sullen than usual, realizing that he would never again have the admiration of such great men. By the war's end, Quantrill's raiders were scattered from Missouri to Texas. It seemed to Jeremy that one night they were all together, then suddenly, the others were gone and he was alone again.

After the war, Jeremy drifted aimlessly over the countryside. At a saloon in Kentucky, he found himself standing next to an ex-Reb captain who admired the great gun leaning against the bar.

The captain laughed, "Gun's almost as tall as you," he said. "You hit anything with it?"

"Only, whatever I aim at," Jeremy grunted.

"What're you drinkin'?"

"What're you buyin'?"

"Name your poison."

Jeremy smiled for the first time all day. "Whiskey — the good stuff."

The captain bought a bottle, grabbed two glasses and nodded to an empty table in the corner. "Might as well sit while we drink. Bring your field piece, there," he added.

Jeremy grabbed the gun. "Don't go nowhere without it," he said.

Once settled at the table with glasses filled, the captain raised his own glass in salute. "Here's to Jeff Davis and Robert E. Lee, may God bless 'em."

Jeremy took a long pull at his glass. *Long as he's buyin', he can drink to any damn fool he wants to,* he thought.

The captain raised his glass to eye level, "And here's to makin' some damn good money for ourselves," he said, draining it in one motion.

Jeremy agreed that he would like to make some "damn good money". Did the captain have anything in mind?

"I might," he said, and asked a lot of questions about Jeremy's background.

Jeremy was wary of talking too much about himself, particularly the years before the war. But, as the other man poured drinks, he reasoned that it would do no harm to let the man know that he was drinkin' with one of Quantrill's top men. After all, they had both fought the same enemy.

Jeremy slouched in his chair, tilted the beaver hat back on his head and bragged at length about having been an orphan, forced to survive as a frontiersman in the forests along the eastern shore of the Chesapeake Bay.

Jeremy made no mention of setting fire to his own home, and the two men laughed heartily as he told of a Union patrol searching in vain while he hid inches from them, in a chimney.

He touched the great gun standing sentinel at his side. "If I'd a had 'General Jackson' back then, I wouldn't had to hide out."

"You must admire the late Stonewall Jackson."

"Where I come from, ever body has a name for their long gun. I thought on namin' it after Will Quantrill, but far as I know he's still alive."

The captain listened absently while Jeremy bragged of being Quantrill's right hand man. He poured generous drinks and pressed for more detail of Jeremy's life on the Eastern Shore of the Chesapeake Bay.

"I'm from Virginia, myself," he said. "Down around Richmond though. Never spent any time up to the bay."

Jeremy gulped his whiskey without comment.

The captain wondered if this man would be a nasty drunk and tried again.

“You heading back home?”

“Guess you wasn’t listening. Home is wherever I drop my bedroll.”

Jeremy emptied his glass and shoved it across the table for a refill.

The captain tilted the bottle, pouring only enough to cover the bottom of the glass.

Jeremy pushed his glass closer to the bottle. “What the hell’s that?” he asked.

The captain splashed more whiskey into the glass, and then filled his own.

“Being from the Chesapeake Bay area,” he said, “you must a heard about the killings over oysters goin’ on back there, same as I have.”

Jeremy dragged his glass back across the table and eyed the other man with mistrust.

“What bizness is that of yours? You the law?”

“Just curious.”

Jeremy shrugged. “I reckon any body who lives there knows that there’s been some shootin’ going on. Ain’t heard nuthin’ since I left for the war.”

“I hear from folks back there. They say now this war’s over, it’s getting fired back up.”

The captain sat back, studying Jeremy as he sipped slowly from his glass. “I’m also told that a man can make good money, if he’s working’ for the right side — and a man’s not too picky about what he does.”

Jeremy thrust his face closer, “Do I strike you as a picky man?” he said.

“No. No you don’t.”

“Well then, tell me who’s doin’ the payin’ an’ I’ll go see ‘em, straight away.”

The captain pulled a piece of paper and the stub of a pencil from his pocket, “I’m gonna write down the name and where to find him. You can read can’t you?”

“Well, course I can, but you better say the name, easy for that little bitty piece o’ paper to get lost.”

Jeremy swirled the remaining whiskey in the bottom of his glass. When he looked up the other man was watching him.

“I can read pictures — good as any man — I have some trouble with writin’ though.” The captain wrote a name and the town where the man could be found.

"I'm gonna send a wire, tell 'em someone's on the way. What's your name?"

Jeremy held his glass high in salute. "Tell 'em — Rat's a comin'," he said and emptied his glass.

The captain smiled at how much the man resembled the epithet and read the name on the paper aloud.

Jeremy finished caressing the great gun and set it aside, then pulled a laudanum bottle from his shirt pocket. He poured a generous dose into the remaining coffee in his cup and gulped it down.

He sat quietly, waiting for the drug to deaden the persistent pain in his back. Gazing at the nearly empty bottle, he realized that it took an increasing amount of the opiate for him to get through each day. *Reckon I need to quit sleepin' on this cold ground. Should find me an old woman to stay with 'til spring.*

Eventually, he forced himself to his feet, poured the coffee pot dregs over the fire and began saddling his horse.

The work was easy enough. So easy it made him long, even more, for the days with Quantrill. So far, there had been no one to kill.

His orders were to make sure nobody found the old stockade where his employer's brought shanghaied men. Hidden in a secluded marshy area, the prison was well away from any deep water. No danger of it being spotted from a passing boat. Only fellow likely to come across the prison would be a progger out 'tarpenin', for Jeremy had seen some big turtles in the marshy area around the building. And it wasn't likely anyone could escape it.

When he was shown the paddy shack, Jeremy was told he could shoot anyone who might escape, and scare off anyone who stumbled onto it.

"With that long gun, you can hide in the woods and they won't know where it's coming from. Aim just close enough to scare 'em off."

Not likely. I don't miss what I shoot at.

"Now, in the unlikely event anyone could get free of the place, you need to kill 'em."

Jeremy sulked that no chance for killing had presented itself.

He grabbed up the great gun and swung himself into the saddle. Laying the rifle across the saddle, he pointed the horse toward Crisfield.

Jeremy was in no hurry to get anywhere he would encounter other people and allowed the horse to set a leisurely pace while he dozed in the saddle. He used a soldier's trick of lapsing into a sleep like state on long, tedious marches, while maintaining an awareness of his surroundings. At this pace, it would take close to an hour to reach Crisfield.

Jeremy Coates had just finished stuffing his saddlebags with provisions from Blades's General Store when he heard yelling nearby followed by a single pistol shot. He untied his horse and led it around the corner, stopping at the edge of the crowd converging in the middle of the street.

It was impossible for him to see the action, so he mounted his horse and sat in the saddle.

What he saw did not surprise him; it did however enrage him. Jake and Rodney Drumm being led off to jail at gun point by two men. A third man limped along beside the lawmen.

"Now look what those two fool brothers went and done. Dumb brothers' is a good name for 'em," he grumbled.

Realizing that on horseback he stood out above the crowd, Jeremy dismounted and followed along on foot. "I didn't hire on to baby sit the Dumb brothers. Those two sit in jail and one of 'em, likely that idiot Rodney, will blab fer sure."

Jeremy watched from a distance as the fat lawman unlocked the jail car and the Drumm brothers disappeared inside.

"I'm gonna have to do something about this. And it's gonna cost 'em extra."

12

Crisfield, Maryland
Tuesday Evening, November 5, 1867

The Reverend Doctor Josiah Muse gave no indication that he was, in any way, cowed by Haynie McKenna's size. The two men along with Haynie's wife and mother were finishing dinner in the small dining room behind the kitchen of the Manor House. When they gathered for the meal, the round little man in the cut away coat seated himself at the head of the table, to Haynie's obvious displeasure.

Haynie and Lila sat side by side, across the table from Lettie. Young Tench McKenna fussed as his father bounced him gently on one knee. For years, following the death of their father, Haynie and Caleb were seated across the table from their mother, while their father's chair had remained empty. Now, this itinerant minister, this stranger, was comfortably seated in that place of honor, prattling on about the work of his traveling ministry.

Haynie observed that, while Josiah Muse wore severe, black clothing, in keeping with his religious teachings, his trousers, vest and cut away coat were richly tailored from the finest wool. Yet, Haynie's mother had stopped wearing lip rouge, thus her face was drained of color, a reflection of the lifeless grey dress she wore. Of late, Lettie McKenna's life seemed devoid of any color or cheer. Haynie could not remember the last time his mother had laughed or even smiled. She lived in fear. Fear that a word or deed would offend Reverend Muse, and the God for whom he claimed to speak, thus denying Lettie, and those she loved, a place in His eternal paradise.

Before dinner, Lettie had pulled Haynie out of hearing of the bustling little man of God and spoke of how pleased she was that Haynie was not wearing that horrible gun. He did not bother to explain that he had not forsaken the gun.

She glanced around the room before asking about Caleb.

"Do you know where he sleeps when he's not here?"

"Don't worry about Caleb, Mother, he can take of himself."

"Oh, I do hope he's not playing that fiddle. Caleb must understand that he won't be able to join us in the hereafter, if he doesn't stop."

She looked up, her eyes filled with dread, "I'm sorry, but it is an instrument of the devil."

"Are you saying that father is rotting in hell because he enjoyed playing that fiddle for us?"

"Please don't be upset. Your father did not know that he was sinning and he has been forgiven. Sinning in ignorance is not a sin. But, Caleb does know, both the Reverend and I have told him. He must stop."

Lila walked toward them, holding Young Tench at arms length. She looked from her husband to his mother and decided she would wait to find the reason for his distraught look.

"This boy wears me out," she said, and walked away.

The Reverend Muse had seated himself at the table, waiting impatiently to be served.

"Let's all sit down," Lettie said, "so that the Reverend can say grace."

Reverend Muse scraped the last crumbs of apple pie from his plate and settled back in his chair. "Wonderful meal, as always," he said, casting his eyes to heaven.

"Yes, Mother, thank you for the delicious meal," Haynie said.

Lettie McKenna gave a small nod and a smile that quickly faded when Josiah Muse spoke.

"False pride, Sister McKenna," he scolded, "false pride." Pointing to the heavens, Muse added, "All good things come from Him."

Turning to Haynie, Muse said, "Saul's pride started small when he took credit unjustly for his son's efforts. That sin destroyed his whole family."

Throughout the meal, Josiah Muse had deftly sprinkled the conversation with short sermons on the need for salvation, the holy sacrament of baptism, and the requirement that one forsake music and all other secular pleasures.

Both women maintained an uncomfortable silence throughout.

Haynie had responded politely, but now his anger and frustration, suppressed through the meal, were overwhelming.

This stranger was changing Haynie's world and there seemed little he could do about it. The woman who bore him was no longer his mother, but rather, Sister Lettie, an apostle of The Reverend Muse. She served as his disciple, willing to destroy the fiddle that was Tench McKenna's legacy to his son. She risked driving her youngest away, rather than offend Muse. Besides assuming his father's seat at her table, Haynie was certain this man had taken his father's place in her bed.

As far as Haynie knew, no one had confirmed that Muse was indeed an ordained minister, yet all who heard him accepted his word as gospel.

Muse's personal belongings, a weathered bible, books of religious teachings and a small writing desk, were prominently displayed in the small library. Caleb had mentioned that the Reverend Muse often referred to the house itself, as his parsonage.

It was time.

Haynie looked steadily at the reverend. "Mister Muse," he said, "if the ladies will excuse us, I think you and I should talk."

The Reverend Muse, a man whose existence depended on the goodwill of others, thrived on his ability to read their faces. Haynie did not hide his feelings well.

Muse worked his own face into a disarming smile. "I look forward to it, my boy. Sister, we'll have coffee in my rectory."

Haynie unfolded from his chair to tower above the little preacher.

Muse touched Haynie's arm, leading him from the room, as if he were a stranger to the house.

"Please, call me Doctor Muse," he said.

Haynie seethed as they crossed the dining room. *The little son-of-a-bitch is sure of himself* he fumed inwardly. Somewhere, in all the anger, he began to reason. *The man is confident that if he can force Mother to choose between us, she will go with him. He already has her willing to destroy father's fiddle and abandon Caleb. If he can drive me away, this will all be his.*

In the library, now Muse's rectory, Haynie sat stiffly in a wing back chair facing the crackling log fire, while Muse seated himself at his writing desk.

Haynie decided that if he were to have any hope of besting Muse, he would need to keep a cool head and be able to read Muse at least as well as Muse read him. Wishing now that he had played some poker in the army, he settled into the chair, forcing a relaxed and genial expression.

Lila came through the open door carrying a serving tray laden with a pot of coffee, cups, spoons, a pitcher of cream, a bowl of sugar and a plate of molasses cookies, Haynie's favorite. There was also a small bowl filled with wisps of whipped cream that she placed directly in front of Muse.

Josiah Muse smiled as he spooned dollops of the fluffy cream to float atop the coffee in his cup.

"A little sinful pleasure I allow myself on rare occasions," he said. In a second cup, he poured milk from a small pitcher, added sugar and offered it to Haynie.

Haynie set the cup on a small table beside his chair. *The man doesn't even bother to ask how I like my coffee.*

Lila rolled her eyes at her husband.

As she turned to leave the room Haynie said, "Lila, ask Mother to pour me a glass of port from that bottle she keeps on the side board. Thank you."

Muse wagged a finger at them, "No, no, no," he scolded. "This is a Christian home. Alcohol is forbidden."

Lila shrugged and closed the door behind her.

Haynie glared at Muse. "I'm not a particularly religious man," he said, "but I believe Jesus offered wine to his disciples at the Last Supper."

Without waiting for a response, Haynie continued.

"Speaking of homes, Mister Muse, you're from Delaware, if I'm not mistaken. Do you have a church up there? Some family? Is that where you go when you leave here?"

Muse was up quickly, emotion flickered across his eyes. Was it anger or fear, Haynie could not be certain. The little man began to pace, hands clamped in the small of his back.

"I have no control over where I go," he said.

"It's God's will. There are so many lambs of His flock to be fed and I am only one man. Many preach the gospel, while so few of us speak the Word.

"When I leave here I climb into my little boat, The Fisherman, and scour the streams, rivers, coves and marshes of the Annamessex Circuit." He stopped and smiled. "We have a similar calling, you boys and I. We cover much the same territory. You both forage for game, while I forage for souls."

Muse looked for a reaction, perhaps a softening. Seeing none, he resumed pacing.

"Sister Lettie has been saved, and prays everyday that her sons will join her on the road to salvation. Will you be in the company?"

Haynie understood how this encounter would go. Muse would answer no questions directly and deflect unwelcome inquiries with pointed questions of his own.

"Is yours the only road that leads there?" he asked.

"If you had been to over twenty years of Sunday services, church meetings, camp meetings and prayer meetings – as I have – and seen the thousands of sinners collapse, sobbing and shouting the Lord's praises when they found Him – as I have – you wouldn't need to ask such a question.

"I started down that glorious road at a camp meeting in Easton, Maryland. The Reverend Joshua Thomas was in his prime. Oh, glory, he had the harness on that day and we were all mesmerized by his words. Suddenly, I began to tremble like Belshazzar when he saw the handwriting on the wall. I couldn't stop myself. I rushed forward and fell to my knees at the mourner's bench begging for salvation."

Muse's voice quaked, "That is the blessed day that I joined the Army of Immanuel."

His gaze softened. "Please forgive me," he said his voice steady. "As you can imagine it recalls a very moving time for me."

He's watching to see if I'm falling for this, Haynie thought. *Sounds rehearsed. If that's his best, it's not good enough.*

Haynie said, "I understand that my mother has been heard to shout and cry out in your room at all hours of the night. Is that some sort of prayer meeting?"

Muse turned away and quickened his pace.

"As their Shepherd, my door is always open to any member of my flock. I'm ready to minister to their needs at any hour. True believers are not ashamed to rejoice and sing His praises whenever we feel the urge. It is a testament to my teaching that Sister Lettie feels the need frequently."

"Why does Mother believe that my brother, Caleb, is doomed to hell because he plays our father's fiddle? How can making music be sinful?"

"The salvation of her son's souls is of great concern to Sister Lettie. She has shed many tears over the moral wilderness roamed by you and your brother. You must understand the consequences of resisting salvation. Those who do not believe the Word; those who fail to swear eternal love and devotion to the All Mighty; and most surely, those who lead lives of sin — all shall perish."

Muse paced steadily, head down, speaking now in stentorian tones.

"Dancing and frolicking are sinful in God's eyes."

He stopped abruptly and stared at Haynie.

"Praise the Lord," he sang out and resumed pacing. "Fiddles, banjos, all evil. False idols that have no place in a Christian home. Brother McKenna, all mankind is evil. So many sinners to be saved. I pray everyday for the strength to go on. Even those I have led to His pasture are in danger of backsliding. Old and young alike, they begin to feel wicked. The devil also forages for souls."

Muse stopped in front of Haynie's chair, dark eyes flashing, his face hard set.

"It's not too late for you and yours, Brother. Sister Lettie spoke to me about your young son. She is terrified — that's not too strong a word — she is terrified that his soul be taken before I can baptize him in the one, true faith. Praise the Lord!"

Muse moved to the fireplace, thrust a hand inside his jacket and stared into the fire.

Is he trying to look like Napoleon or is that a trait of every madman?

Haynie said nothing, but imagined many folks, like his mother, uncertain and fearful about an after-life, unable to resist the powerful words and fierce countenance of this man.

The Reverend Muse has frightened these people. Afraid to risk the wrath of his God, they listen only to him. The True Word. Muse is selling himself as the only hope, to those he has convinced are otherwise doomed.

Muse plunged on, red faced, consumed with energy, his voice growing shrill.

"Brother, there is only one path to salvation. The Lord has sent me to lead the way. Other religions are doomed for the hypocrites they are. They allow their flock to play music, drink spirits and cavort wildly all week, then tell them that it is enough to attend Sunday services, offer repentance, and God will forgive them.

"Pray for their souls, Brother, pray long and loud, for the Lord has told me that he will destroy these hypocrites as surely as he destroyed the sinners of Sodom."

Muse stopped suddenly, turning his face upward. "Lord, I am your instrument of destruction," he roared. Muse continued to shout, eyes flashing wildly about the room.

"Believe me, Brother, I know sinners and they are everywhere. I have exhorted them at camp meetings and tabernacles from the Susquehanna to Norfolk. I can tell you of the terrible consequences visited upon those who turned their back to Him and, having heard the Word of God, continued to live in sin. Entire families, infants and young children, all smote by disease, or plague, or violent death because the man of the family refused to allow these innocents to follow me into His house."

Clearly, Muse intended his words to be heard in the adjacent rooms. Certainly by Haynie's mother, and Lila too, if she had not taken Young Tench home to bed.

In contrast, Haynie spoke softly, keeping emotion from his voice through great effort.

"Are you saying that your God kills guiltless women and children, to retaliate against an errant husband and father?"

"'Vengeance is mine' sayeth the Lord. Praise the Lord."

"I knew many men in the war, from both sides, who died never knowing your God. They were just scared, young boys. Sounds like they are doomed to eternal damnation. Do I have that right?"

Muse stopped in front of Haynie's chair, his eyes scolding. "Sir, you would be better served to concern yourself with your own redemption and that of your family. If you do not heed the Word, you are doomed to remain in Egypt with the Pharaoh."

Muse moved to a rug in front of the fireplace and fell to his knees, eyes shut.

"Shout with me, Brother; let Him hear your voice."

Muse's chant resounded throughout the house. "Tell Him you're ready to be saved."

Haynie sat motionless, stricken by the little preacher's antics.

As a boy, he had once attended a small church where the minister had rushed from the pulpit to leap upon the mourner's bench directly in front of the pew occupied by Haynie and his family. Dressed in ministerial black, that pastor strode the length of the plank bench, calling out to his parishioners as he moved.

The minister, as Haynie recalled him, had a fringe of black hair just above his neck, was rail thin, and bellowed with boundless energy about 'A trembling Felix', 'Elijah's mantle', ' Wielding the sword' and 'The Lord of Hosts'. The congregation had responded with appropriate cries of 'True', 'First rate' and 'Hallelujah', sprinkled with murmurs of Amen'.

Initially frightened by the waving arms, thrusting hands and shouts of agony around him, Haynie, the boy, slowly comprehended that the minister's behavior was appropriate, even harmonious, within the crowded church. Soon his young eyes had become riveted to the performance and, swaying with the chorus around him, he heard himself moaning an 'Amen' and 'Hallelujah'.

Here, in his mother's house, Haynie, the man, found nothing inspiring in the antics of Reverend Muse. Indeed, he was embarrassed for himself and for the little man kneeling before him.

Eyes shut tight, arms flung about, Josiah Muse shouted to the ceiling.

Though Muse would likely say he was speaking in tongues, it was all gibberish to Haynie. He gripped the chair, wondering how long this would go on while resisting an impulse to flee the room.

Abruptly, Muse grew silent and dropped his arms. Rising slowly to his feet, he gazed about the room as if trying to understand his whereabouts. His face flushed, breathing labored, Muse spoke, his voice lower, now under control.

"Brother, did you ask the Almighty for his forgiveness? Did He show you that you must forsake the handgun – just as your brother must forsake the fiddle – before you can walk with Him. Did you ask for His blessing?"

Haynie sprang to his feet. "Please excuse me, Mister Muse," he said, and moved toward the door.

Before Haynie reached the doorway, Muse exploded in a rage. Voice shaking with anger, he shrieked. "Until you and your brother come to me seeking forgiveness and salvation; until you see the light, and have that child baptized, by me, you are not welcome in this Christian home! Amen."

Haynie threw open the door and strode through the dark and quiet rooms, finding his mother seated at the small table in her kitchen, a lone candle burning next to the bible open before her. With eyes closed, and hands folded in prayer, she gave no sign of recognizing her son.

Thankfully, Lila had taken Young Tench home, away from the bellicose roars from the study.

"Your pastor has ordered me banned from this house, Mother. From your home."

Lettie's eyes remained closed, her lips moving silently.

"Is that your wish as well?"

Haynie waited another moment, and getting no response, stormed from the house.

13

Crisfield, Maryland
Wednesday November 6, 1867

Day broke behind them as Jeremy Coates moved his horse through the shadows cast by the darkened buildings along Cove Street. The animal plodded, ears drooping, head down, past the frame cottages, the crunch of hooves on oyster shells muffled by the new fallen snow. Jake and Rodney Drumm trailed behind, Jake muttering about walking in the snow while Coates rode.

From their first meeting, Jeremy Coates hated the Drumm brothers, and they him. Jake Drumm particularly resented having to take orders from Jeremy Coates, a newcomer to the outfit and a former Reb to boot.

Jake, though dull, possessed enough animal wiles to avoid a showdown with the man who bragged about being called Rat.

"We'd a won the war if more blue coats was as dumb as you two," Coates would say, riling Jake.

Once, Jake and Rodney had come across Rat sitting under a tree stroking his Bowie knife across a small whetstone. Rat peered out from under his filthy beaver hat, his tiny pointed eyes laughing at them.

"I need me a practice killin," he said, waving the knife.

"Been awhile. Maybe I'll slit ole Rodney's throat to keep my hand in. No body's payin' me to kill him. It's not likely anyone would miss him."

Rodney swallowed hard and stepped closer to Jake, who glared at Rat but said nothing.

Now, Jake spoke out, "Whyn't you fetch horses for me and Rod, when you come to get us out?"

Coates turned sharply in the saddle and shot Jake a withering look which failed to penetrate the early morning shadows.

"Dammit," he hissed, "I tole you Dumb brothers to keep shut, leastways 'til we get away from these buildings. Folks might hear you."

The Drumm brothers trudged along in silence, eyes following the clean imprint of the horse's hooves.

Jake had quickly tired of taking orders from this former Reb who never made it to sergeant, which Jake had. More than likely, this Rat fella was thrown out of the Reb army for a troublemaker. *And,* Jake thought, *we got nuthin' but his own say so, that he rode with Quantrill. Nuthin' at all.*

Another fifty feet and they would be past the houses, entering the marshland edging the town. If he waited to speak, Jake would appear cowed by Coates, which he was, but he wasn't going to be shown up again in front of his brother.

"Roy come and got ya, didn't he," Jake said.

Rat dug his heels into the horse's boney hide; the animal lifted his head and trotted feebly for a few paces.

Jake quickened his step and cursed his brother to move it.

After a few minutes of struggling, Rodney complained, "This ain't right, Jake. I can't keep up. Let him go on, if he's gonna be that way."

Jake Drumm cuffed his brother at the back of the head, knocking Rodney's knit cap into the snow.

"Jesus, Rod, Jesus," he growled. "How we gonna find Roy and the boat without him? *You* gonna take us?"

Rodney stooped to pick up his cap, and went sprawling in the snow as Jake shoved him again.

Jeremy halted his horse to watch the fun, laughing as Rodney Drumm struggled to his feet, knocking the snow from his pants.

Rodney gingerly tested the bleeding cuts on his knees and palms.

"Damn you, Jake," he said, "what'd you go and do that for? Them oyster shells cuts."

"Rod, stop yer damn blubberin' if front of this Reb."

Emboldened by his attack on his brother, Jake turned to Coates. "You gonna sit there, or ya gonna take us to our boat?"

Jeremy held Jake's gaze for a full minute then, with a laugh, prodded his horse to movement.

"As fer yer whinnin' about horses," he said without looking back, "I didn't git ya no horses cause I didn't have no time. 'Sides it wouldn't look right if somebody seen one rider with three horses headin' to that boxcar this town calls a jail."

Coates turned in the saddle and looked back. The truth was he had other reasons for making them walk behind him. It pleased him to be able to look down on the former blue coats. If he could, he would have the horse crap on them.

"The people up ta Balimer tell you to kill that old bailiff?" Jake asked.

Rat slowed his horse and answered, "Didn't have time to wait on them. Had to get you out before you two sisters blabbed something."

Jake was adamant. "There's nuthin' that fat ole bailiff could a did to make me or Rodney talk. We wouldn't a said nuthin'."

"It wasn't the bailiff, worried me," Coates said, "it was the other one."

Without raising his eyes, Rodney said, "We ain't sisters; we're brothers, right Jake?"

Still gazing at the ground, he continued. "They are too gonna be fierce at you for killin' a law man. So, there," he finished by sticking his tongue out at Jeremy's back.

Coates wheeled his horse around, resting the butt of the Prussian Musket on one thigh as he faced them.

"As usual you dumb sisters don't know what you're talkin' about. They don't give a hoot about some old lawman out here in the marshland. The best part is, it was so easy, I ain't gonna charge 'em extra," he lied.

"Rod's right they're gonna be right fierce at you and you don't know why. Who's the dumb one now?"

"All right, let's hear what you got to say."

Jake knew he had gone too far to back down. If he didn't speak up, Rat would force it out of him.

"Yesterday we was just a couple of roustabouts who had a set to with some city drummer. It weren't nuthin. Be forgot in a couple of days. Now, we're gonna get blamed for a killin' we didn't do, nor want done. They'll never stop lookin' for us, meantime, nobody even knows about you —" Jake's mouth hung open as it dawned on him why he and Rodney were walking.

Coates studied Jake's face, "You got some else to say, let's hear it – now."

Jake looked at his brother. “We’re walkin’ because if anyone saw us ride off they would figger we had help. This way they see our tracks walkin’ away, everbody’s gonna believe we done it alone.”

Rat tightened the grip on his musket and showed a toothy sneer.

“Well now, Jake, boy — heard you was the village idiot where you come from. Maybe I heard wrong.”

Coates lowered the long musket, leveling it at Jake’s forehead, and then swung it over, the end of the barrel resting at the tip of Rodney’s nose.

“You boys listen here. When you get caught, and I’m bettin’ you do, you better never say nuthin’ about me. Cause then you’ll be dead.”

He swung the barrel back to Jake’s forehead. “And when I come for ya, don’t ’spect you can say ‘why it weren’t me, Rat, it were Rodney who told.’ ’Cause I’m gonna kill both of you anyhow. ’Sides it wouldn’t make no never mind what the folks in Baltimore Town said. I killed that fat tub because I felt like it. That’s the only reason I need.”

Jeremy Coates wheeled the horse again and headed for the marsh in a trot.

“Wait up,” Jake called, “You got to show us where Roy is waitin’ with our boat.”

Without looking back, Jeremy said, “I got no idea where your other Dumb brother is. Ain’t seen him.”

14

Crisfield, Maryland
Wednesday, November 6, 1867

Haynie McKenna had risen early, eaten a quick morning meal and was buckling on his gun belt when Lila appeared in the kitchen doorway rubbing sleep from her eyes.

"Where are you off to so early?"

"Squire and I are going to talk to those two men we put in jail yesterday. I'm certain they know where Landon is being held."

"Why would they want to help you?"

Haynie shrugged. "Won't know that until we talk to them. A night in jail may get them talking. At least one – and that's all I need. Or —" Haynie was interrupted by frantic pounding on the front door. Lila retreated into the bedroom and closed the door.

"Mister McKenna, it's me, Tawes Butler. Hurry, sothin' awful has happened."

Haynie jerked open the door. A skinny lad stood before him, clutching a leather cap, face grey, his breathing heavy and uneven. A lathered pony stood behind him pawing the small yard for blades of grass.

"Tawes boy, what is it?"

"Oh it's awful, Mister McKenna," he said, his head wagging from side to side. "Worst thing ever to happen in the Cove. Why —"

"Tawes. Stop. Take a deep breath and tell me why you're here."

"Somebody has killed our bailiff, Squire Towne at the rail jail. And some prisoners was excaped from the jail-car – oh, it's awful. I was told to fetch you straightaway. You must come, Mister McKenna."

"Of course. I'll saddle up. You tell them I'm right behind you."

Haynie raced along River Road at full gallop. Turning down Somers Avenue, his horse kicked chunks of the oyster shell road onto the plank sidewalk. A drummer jumped from the spray, his sample case crashing to the ground.

"Where's the damn fire," he yelled.

Haynie did not look back as he followed the iron tracks into the rail yard.

George Noch, a member of the Town Council, waved him over to a group of men huddled around a prone figure covered with a thin army blanket. Tawes Butler stood to one side, holding his pony by the halter. Noch, wearing a bowler hat, vested suit and broadcloth necktie, stood out from the others, all clad in the grimy work clothes of railroad day laborers.

Haynie worked the bit against the back of his horse's mouth, reining him to a shuddering stop. He dismounted and nodded a greeting to Noch. The others watched closely.

"McKenna." Noch said, "Thanks for coming so quickly."

Haynie gestured toward the blanket. "That Squire?" he asked.

George Noch nodded. "Nothin' like this has ever happened here."

Haynie stopped at the edge of the blanket and knelt down.

"You gonna look at him?" Noch asked, turning his head away. Some in the group followed Noch's lead, others craned to get a closer look as Haynie pulled back the blanket.

Squire Towne laid face down, the dirt under him dark and wet, saturated with blood from a deep gash running from ear to ear across his throat.

A stooped old man wearing frayed clothing several sizes too large for his brittle body stepped from the crowd of onlookers. He stood as straight as age would allow and spoke.

"With respect sir. I found him, Mister Haynie."

Haynie McKenna looked up to see one of the town drunks, the one called Bozo, standing beside the blanket. Bozo had removed his hat and, with head bowed, several large liver spots were visible beneath thin strands of white hair. Bozo had been a drunk for as long as anyone could recall. His consensus age was past seventy, but no one could be certain. Bozo's chronological age, along with his family name, had long ago lost any meaning.

"Is this the way you found him?"

"With respect, yes, sir. I never touched him. On days they is prisoners in the jail-car, Squire comes early in the morning to bring them coffee and some bread. I always come around to help him pass out the breakfast, maybe sweep up. I know he always brought extra so there'd be some little bit left over for me. He's – he was a good man." Bozo grew quiet, head still bowed.

George Noch stepped toward Bozo. "Get on with it," he snapped and moved back to the edge of the crowd.

Bozo swallowed hard and nodded.

"With respect sir. I'm sorry Mister Noch and Mister Haynie sirs, but I wasn't 'spectin' nothing like this. It has unnerved me, and me without nuthin' to drink.

"It's all right, Bozo," Haynie smiled, "you're doing just fine."

Bozo pointed toward the open door of the jail-car, as the crowd gave way, affording Haynie a clear view to the boxcar not ten feet away.

"I knew right off that he, Squire, was gone, you know, dead. Then I see the door was wide open, with the big cell at the far end empty. So I ran," Bozo gave a quick laugh, "much as I can run anymore – to fetch somebody and found Mister Noch."

Noch nodded and stepped forward.

"I came right away," Noch said, "and immediately took charge."

He paused, removed his hat and held it in both hands. Tilting his head toward the jail car, he continued. "Word is that you helped Squire – God rest his soul – arrest those men yesterday. Hope you don't mind, I sent the boy there to fetch you. I didn't know what else to do...." his voice trailed off.

Haynie carefully replaced the blanket and stood. "Looks like they stabbed him in the back and then cut his throat. Big knife, very sharp."

Bozo stepped forward again. "With respect, Mister Haynie, sir. Squire's big ring of keys is missing and that leather bag what he aw ways carried that little bitty gun in, is gone too."

Haynie knelt again and the crowd shuddered as he examined Horsey's left arm that splayed away from the body. "You're right Bozo, thanks for pointing that out."

Bozo turned his head and beamed proudly to the bystanders, until he caught George Noch's glare and quickly returned his gaze to the ground.

"There's some small cuts on his wrist and back of the hand," Haynie noted. "Looks like the killer cut the leather thong to get the bag. They likely came at him from behind. Squire never had a chance to get his gun out."

Bozo shifted to his left a few steps, effectively removing George Noch from his vision. He swallowed hard and summoned the courage to speak again.

"With respect sir," he said to Haynie, "it probably don't mean nothin', but Squire always brought the coffee in a covered pail, the bread was wrapped in a red checkered cloth and carried in a small wooden box. Them are gone too."

Noch stepped forward. "You're right Bozo," he scolded, "it means nothing. Now stop botherin' us with your drivel."

Haynie put a hand on Bozo's arm and spoke to the crowd.

"It's too early to tell what might be important. If any of you saw something, or heard something, that could help to know who killed our bailiff, you need to tell Mister Noch here, or whoever is put in charge of finding the killers and those men that escaped. Now, I'm going inside the jail-car to see if there's anything in there that will help. It won't do any good to have a crowd in there, so I'm asking you all to stay out here."

As Haynie moved to the open jail-car door, George Noch left the crowd and stopped him at the steps.

"I need to talk to you, privately," Noch said. "Can I join you just inside the car? I won't go further and I won't disturb anything."

"Of course," Haynie replied, and climbed through the open doorway with Noch close behind.

"What's goin' on?" a voice thick with sleep and drink yelled out from the cell immediately to the left of the jail-car door. "That you, Squire? Where's my damn breffast?"

"Dammit Cecil," Noch called, "go back to sleep. You'll get breakfast when you get it."

"Who's that talkin'? Don't sound like Squire — and I want my damn breffast now."

Haynie stepped to the small barred window in the cell door allowing the man inside to see his face.

"Cecil, its Haynie McKenna. There's been some trouble. If you will go sit on your cot, I will come and talk to you in a few minutes. Just settle down."

Haynie did not want Cecil to know that without a key to the cell door, no coffee was coming in and Cecil wasn't coming out anytime soon.

"Long as it's you, Mister McKenna, I'll do 'er," Cecil muttered and returned to his cot.

Haynie turned back to the doorway. "Yes, George?"

Noch motioned Haynie away from the muttering man in the cell, and backed carefully along the wall to the right of the open doorway.

Noch said, "It seems pretty clear that whoever killed Squire broke those two men out of our jail. I saw him last evening and he told me about you asking for his help in finding the men who shanghaied your friend up in Baltimore. And how you helped him bring in those two.

"Many business owners, and those of us who are town officials, are fed up with all the drinkin', and brawlin', and whorin' going on in this town — and now this," he waved a hand toward the open door.

"Lord knows I'm not one to speak ill of the dead, but the job had got to be too much for him. He couldn't handle it."

Noch waited for a response, getting none he continued, "Some on the Council have been saying that we needed to ask Squire to quit."

Noch's voice wavered. "If we had just gone ahead, and faced up to it and let Squire go when we should have, he wouldn't be laying dead out there."

"Maybe," Haynie said, "but somebody else would be laying there, getting just as cold. The killers wanted those two out of jail."

Noch shook his head, "But maybe a younger man, a stronger man... In the name of the Town of Crisfield, I'm asking you to accept the position of town bailiff and lead our efforts to find Squire's killer."

Haynie was silent for a moment, his mind racing.

Noch looked away, twisting the brim of his hat with both hands.

"How can you speak for the Council?" Haynie asked. "This just happened."

"Truth is, we've been talking about someone else taking the job, for some time. Several names been said, your name being said the loudest. Seems important that we act quickly to catch the bastards that killed poor Squire. I have every confidence the Council will agree with my decision to ask you now."

Haynie removed his hat and ran his fingers through his hair. He recalled Squire's comment about Haynie getting his job. The bailiff, though not popular in town, had one or two friends in the inner circle. One of them must have said something about the talk of him being replaced.

"This is completely unexpected, George, more so, under these circumstances. I'll need to talk it over with Lila, before I can give you an answer."

Noch nodded.

Haynie settled his hat on the back of his head and said, “Long as I’m already here, I’ll work on it the rest of the day, talk to her tonight, and give you an answer tomorrow.”

George Noch gripped Haynie’s hand.

“We need you, McKenna. The town needs you. Come down to the office when you’re finished here.”

Haynie nodded.

Noch climbed down the steps. Looking back into the car, he said, “Can we take Squire with us?”

“Of course.”

“He’ll be at Davidson’s,” Noch called without looking back.

The pale November sun was now well above the tree line, and filtered into the jail-car, yielding a faint square of light through the open door. The rest of the car was cast in deep shadows. Haynie lifted a lamp from a wall peg, lit the wick and, holding it high, walked slowly toward the rear cell, watching the floor in front of him as he moved.

He found it difficult to focus on the job at hand. His mind raced across a spectrum of thoughts as he deliberated Noch’s offer. He held a thought only briefly before it slipped from his mental grasp splintering into other, related thoughts.

The offer excited him, but did he really want to be thrust into the job – and the politics that came with it? Was he up to it? He knew little about the law and legal matters. The idea of bringing lawbreakers to justice and peace to the town intrigued him. Could the job help in his efforts to find his father’s killers?

To be honest, until today, the job of town bailiff was pretty routine. The bailiff attended public meetings, maintained the town fire engine, met trains and steamboats, lit the streetlights, and sold dog licenses to those citizens that bothered to license their animals.

Haynie readily admitted that there was no future in the life he was now leading. Foraging woods and marsh for hides and pelts had become drudgery. Tonging oysters for a living was hellish. He had kept at it in hopes of finding someone who knew about Tench McKenna’s murder. And, he would not go to work on the hated drudge boats.

As for any danger attached to the bailiff’s job, Haynie believed that it was safer than working the icy decks of an oyster boat. A month didn’t go by that you didn’t hear of an oysterman slipping overboard in the dark, or a fishing boat that capsized in rough water. If he decided he really wanted to be bailiff, he would have to assemble such arguments to use on Lila.

It suddenly occurred to Haynie that he was standing at the open cell door with no idea of what he had seen along the way. Clearing his head with a vigorous shake, he forced himself to focus both his eyes and mind on the floor's surface.

He noticed, for the first time, a faint set of muddy boot tracks among the packed dirt of the floor. The tracks formed a trail from the jail-car door to the open cell.

Haynie squatted to get a closer look, swinging the lamp back and forth, inches above the floor.

Heavy, dark marsh mud had not yet begun to cake. His progger's instinct told him this was the spoor of Horsey's killer. His excitement at the discovery was quickly tempered by doubts.

"Likely they're the killer's tracks," he muttered, "but they are also meaningless. All I can do is study them and hope that I might know 'em if I ever see them again. Even if I am sure they're the same, whoever made them can say I'm wrong. Likely, there's many boots make a track like that."

About three feet out from the cell door, where a man would stand as it swung open, Haynie spotted a clump of short, brown hairs beside a muddy track.

"Now how in blazes did those hairs get there?" he asked himself. *Did the killer have a dog with him? I don't see any fresh dog tracks. It's possible they been here for a while and have nothing to do with the killing."*

Haynie took a long look at the tracks and hairs and it occurred to him that he could learn when the hairs were left on the floor. He set the lamp down beside the footprints, and then lowered his head bringing the tracks and hairs to eye level.

With the brighter light and different angle, he discovered three small hairs lying atop the spoor. He smiled, pleased with himself for realizing that by finding the hairs resting atop the track, he had shown that the hair had fallen this morning, after the track was made, not before. The killer had been the only one there at the time, so the hair had come from him or an animal with him. *"Maybe I have a knack for this kind of work, after all,"* he thought, still smiling.

Haynie straightened. From a coat pocket, he pulled out the telegram from Colonel Wallis, took the message from the envelope and stuffed it back into his coat. Carefully, he collected the hairs from the muddy floor and placed them inside the envelope, which he then folded and pocketed.

The acting bailiff retraced his steps to the first cell and looked in. Cecil was curled under a blanket, snoring lightly.

Haynie extinguished the lamp and returned it to the wooden peg. Through the open doorway he saw Bozo, the sole remaining bystander, his felt hat crushed on top of his head. The crowd had moved on, most likely with the departure of Squire's body.

Bozo watched Haynie descend from the jail-car. "With respect, sir," he said licking his lips, "I stayed to see if there was anything I can do to help. Squire treated me real good ever time he had to lock me up."

Haynie knew that the sot was looking for a hand out. A cup of coffee – maybe some spare change – or, if he was really lucky – enough for a shot of whiskey.

"Are we going over to the bailiff's office?" Bozo asked, "I can show ya the way."

Haynie slid the rail car door closed and faced the little man whose body quivered with expectation.

"Thank you, but I know the way to the Town offices."

"Course ya do, course ya do," Bozo mumbled, eyes downcast.

"But, Squire and I could use your help right here."

Bozo looked up, an anxious smile on his face.

"It won't be an easy job – and it's important. You can't let us down. Don't go off looking for a drink when you feel a thirst. You take care of this for me and we'll get you something to eat, maybe a drink."

Tears filled Bozo's rheumy eyes. "With respect sir, I don't mean to blubber but Squire was the only one in the whole town who didn't yell at me to get away, and would give me a job of work sometimes. Wasn't much, but he knew it meant a lot to me. Now, you sayin' you believe I could help you and — him." He took a deep breath and shuddered. "Sir, I never let him down and I won't let you down, so help me God."

Haynie gave Bozo his orders, then mounted his horse and rode to the Crisfield Town Offices.

Haynie McKenna stepped into the open doorway to the town council's meeting room and removed his hat. George Noch was seated with the other council members at the far end of a long wooden table.

Noch waved him into the room and all four councilmen stood, unsmiling, faces grim.

Haynie nodded at George Noch and shook hands with the others. Quentin Tyler, owner of the hardware store; Luther Blades, owner of the general store; and Asbury Carter-Haines, the founder and publisher of the town's newspaper. Each nodded in turn.

Haynie noted that Tyler, who never appeared in public without a suit coat, faced him wearing a cuffed shirt, buttoned vest and cravat. Seemingly, so distraught he had forgotten his coat.

Quentin Tyler spoke first. “Poor Squire. How could this happen right here in Crisfield? This foul deed must not go unpunished.” He opened his mouth to say more, but no words formed and he abruptly sat down.

Luther Blades spoke with equal conviction. “I say it’s that riff-raff from them bawdy houses along Goodsell’s Alley. Couple of them likely got drunk and went off to break those other drunks outta jail. We need to close down that whole place.”

Blades looked for signs of agreement from the other council members. Seeing none, he grumbled, “You’ll see. You’ll see,” and sat down.

George Noch said, “Let’s hear from Haynie McKenna.” He and Asbury Carter-Haines took their seats. The four councilmen watched Haynie, hoping desperately for some comforting words, some miracle answer to this horror.

This is not really about Squire, Haynie thought. *They’re terrified for themselves. None of them was in the war and it’s likely this is as near as any of them has been to violent death.*

This is now a much different job than each of them accepted. Suddenly, it’s not going to be enough to smile and tip your hat to the ladies as you strut around town. Hard decisions are called for and you don’t know what to do. Like Squire, you’re beginning to doubt yourselves. Might be getting close to panic because of it. If the whole town gets panicky, a vigilante mob could be near.

Haynie, conscious of the fact that he was the only one present wearing a gun, unbuckled his gun belt and laid it on the bare floor next to his chair. Once seated, he set his hat on the table and plowed deep furrows in his hair with the fingers of one hand.

Luther Blades drummed the tabletop with both hands. “Squire’s killer and those two drunks he broke out are most likely sittin’ in one of those saloons in the Alley, at this very time.”

He shook a finger at Haynie. “You go down there right now and arrest them. We’ll take care of hanging ‘em. Get this over with.” He looked at the men on either side of him. Quentin Tyler stared at the wall and George Noch occupied himself by wiping at an imaginary spot on the gleaming tabletop.

Asbury Carter-Haines said, “I’d like to at least hear from Mister McKenna before I run off and hang anybody.”

Noch and Tyler nodded.

Haynie looked at each of the four men. “Gentlemen. I’m not a town official and I know little about what happened to Squire, but you asked me to speak and I’m going to tell you what I think. Do with it what you will.

“A terrible thing has happened and the town’s people are going to be afraid. They’ll think maybe they, or theirs, are next. They’ll look to you for strength and the grit to get through it. You need to watch what you say and do. Mister Carter-Haines is going to have to be careful what gets printed in his paper...”

“Be good for circulation, though won’t it?” Luther Blades grumbled.

Haynie continued, “It would be best if you four would agree on what to say and stick to that. For God ’s sake, don’t be spreading any rumors or gossip. There’ll be plenty without any of you contributing to it.”

He looked hard at Blades. “Like I said, I don’t know what happened, but, I can tell you this: those men, and the killer who freed them, are not drunks to be easily found in a local saloon. They’re part of a gang who shanghai innocent men and the killing was done by someone who came to free them. Wanted them out before they could say anything.”

“Whoever it was came awful quick,” George Noch pointed out.

Haynie nodded, “Killer was already in the area. Could be they have their hideout around here. There’s more of ‘em – we have to be real careful.”

Luther Blades moved to protest, looked around and sunk back in his chair. “Still need to clean up the Alley,” he mumbled.

Asbury Carter-Haines spoke up. “Hanging a couple of drunks for this could appeal to some people. A mob. Mister McKenna’s right about watching what we say. I swear by the All Mighty, before this company, that no gossip or words to enflame will be seen in the Times.”

He glared at Luther Blades. “Circulation, be damned.”

Haynie McKenna asked, “Are we all agreed that no one in this room will say anything about this until he’s spoken to the others?”

Noch, Tyler and Asbury Carter-Haines nodded agreement and looked at Blades.

“Does that mean I gotta check with you before I can talk to my wife?” he snapped. “Oh, stop yer gawking, ya don’t have to worry about me.”

Haynie continued, “Mister Noch here asked me if I would take the job as Town Bailiff. Before I consider it, I need to know if he spoke for each of you.”

Quentin Tyler cleared his throat. "Mister McKenna, if you say yes, you will have our full support. We realize you'd be in an awful position and this council will not be a hindrance."

Tyler nodded at Blades, seated next to him, "Why, even Luther here, who is against just about every thing, will support you."

Carter-Haines said, "We have to have something to tell the townsfolk. Something we can all agree on." His gaze settled on Haynie, "I know it just happened, but do you have any ideas about catching the devils who did this?"

George Noch held up one hand and said, "Before we hear from McKenna on that, I have a question. Do we have a duty to send a wire to the High Sheriff up in Princess Anne about our bailiff being killed?"

Haynie waited as the four councilmen talked among themselves.

"Seems like we should," said Carter-Haines.

"What good would it do?" said Luther Blades. "He's a damn politician. I doubt that him or anyone he sent would know anymore what to do, than —" he looked around the table "— than McKenna here. Or even one of us for that matter."

The room grew silent, each man reflecting on the question. Finally, George Noch cleared his throat and said, "Seems to me we ought to see what McKenna here thinks about it. We're all hoping he'll be the bailiff, and he's not said no."

"If I decide to take the job," Haynie said, "I will do what I can to catch the man who killed Squire and get to the bottom of this shanghai business. I can't have other folks stomping around and mucking it up; especially not some politician from out of town."

The councilmen nodded in agreement.

Haynie continued, "There's something else needs to be said. There's some talk that this shanghai gang is running out of these parts. If it's true, they been doin' it for a while now — and without our sheriff getting in their way. That seems another reason not to be talking loose about what we're doin'. We don't know who we can trust."

The councilmen began to grasp the import of what had been said, and looked at one another in silence.

Haynie addressed Noch, "As for your question about catching the killers; I've got some ideas where to look. Whether it's me or someone else does the lookin', you need to understand — it's not going to get done over night."

15

Crisfield, Maryland
Thursday, November 7, 1867

Haynie McKenna sat at the desk of the town bailiff. It was his desk now.

By arrangement, he had met with the council at 7:30 that morning and told them of his decision. They were visibly relieved when he agreed to accept the bailiff's job, staying at least until Squire's killers were punished.

Haynie was immediately sworn in by George Noch and signed on as a town employee at an annual salary of $400 plus a portion of each dog license he sold.

Each councilman vigorously shook Haynie's hand, voiced support in every way possible, and then left the room. Even to a political novice it was evident the council was relieved to have someone else upon whom to deflect the public outcry sure to follow.

Lila had offered less resistance than he had expected. Last night, when they spoke, she questioned him at length. He explained his belief that Squire's killer, and the men freed from the jail car, were part of the gang that kidnapped Landon Wallis. It was growing more likely this gang made their base here in Somerset County.

Once convinced that her husband would have no peace until these men were caught, she kissed him, then reminded him that Young Tench needed his father.

Though Haynie had not recently mentioned his failure to find his own father's killer, she knew it weighed on him. In her heart, she believed that her husband was the best man for the job.

At the end of their discussion, Caleb appeared at the front door, wearing a wide grin.

"I hear that you were banished from Reverend Muse's parish house. I came to see if you have a forked tail."

Haynie stood in the open door. "We've got a lot to talk about," he said.

The brothers sat in the small living room, as Haynie told him of the young man fleeing for his life up the center of Main Street, followed by the arrest and jailing of the two men chasing him. Caleb stiffened at the particulars of Squire Towne's murder and the jailbreak.

Haynie talked of his decision to become the town bailiff and finished by saying, "I need your help."

Caleb slumped against the back of the chair. "What in bejesus are you getting us into," he said.

Haynie hurried to the coat rack in the front hall, returning with the wrinkled envelope that he handed to his brother.

"Can you tell me what animal these hairs came from?"

Caleb picked two hairs from the bottom of the envelope and rubbed them lightly between a thumb and forefinger.

"Where'd you get 'em?"

"Found 'em on the floor of the jail-car, next to the open cell door. They were lying on top of the muddy tracks, so I know they came with the killer."

Caleb looked up, "Impressive, big brother. Sounds like you might just know what the hell yer doin'."

"We'll see."

"Curly and kinda coarse." Caleb shook his head. "One thing for sure though," he said returning the hairs to the envelope, "they're not from any animal I ever seen."

"I was afraid of that," Haynie said and reached for the envelope.

Caleb pulled back. "Let me shows these to Gumps. If anybody around here will know, it's him."

"Well — okay. Be careful. They're the only ones we got. Don't know what they mean, yet, but they can't be replaced."

"I understand."

Caleb straightened. "I near forgot. Gumps says that about two year ago, he run across the ruins of an old fort next to a marshy creek off the Manokin or, maybe at Jericho Marshes, he's not certain. Thinks it was put up by the Redcoats back during the war of 1812. You ever heard of such?"

Haynie shook his head. "Wouldn't surprise me though. I know they were all over the bay durin' those years. Smith Island, Deal, too. Set up around here for a run at Baltimore and Fort McHenry."

"He didn't think nuthin' of it at the time. Came trampin' through there early one morn'. Still a mist layin' over the marsh. 'Said the timbers for the outer wall was mostly rotted away and overgrown with vines and them wild roses. Inside walls the same. He 'members a breeze kicked up and lifted the mist." Caleb laughed and his face reddened. "'Like a woman pickin' up her skirt,' Gumps says. For a minute, he could see the whole place then she dropped her skirt. Sittin' out in the marsh grass was a little house built on pilings. And the walls was in good shape, not rottin' or nuthin'."

After a moment, Haynie said, "Likely a sentry post at one corner of the old fort. Could be hunter's fixed it up as a shootin' blind. Still—"

"Gumps thinks he can find it. I'm goin' back to our camp tomorrow. Next day we'll likely head up there to have a look around."

"You stayin' with Gumps most of the time now?"

Caleb nodded. "When I leave in the mornin', I'm takin' everything I got, which ain't – sorry – isn't, much. I can't stay in that house no more."

"You tell mother?"

Caleb shook his head; tangles of dark hair fell across his face.

"She'll know in the morning though. She told me about your run in with her preacher. It was by way of warnin' me not to make the same mistake. Says the preacher will be back 'home' tomorrow and I should talk to him about bein' saved. Means I gotta let them burn father's fiddle."

"And you're not staying around for the meeting."

"Nope, leavin' at first light. I'd never give up that fiddle. Me and Gumps sound pretty good." Caleb rubbed his fingers together. "Ol' Gumps says he believes I could some day play for a barn dance, or maybe at a county fair."

He stood to leave and smiled. "I believe I'd like to do that. I reckon the girls like a fella can play music."

Haynie stood with him. "I expect they do. Maybe Lila and I could come listen sometime."

Caleb nodded and stuck the envelope in his coat pocket.

Haynie opened the front door, "Where's your hound?"

Caleb shrugged. "Gone – I guess. One day I threw him a big leg bone from a deer, he growled at me and slunk out of camp draggin' the bone with him. Hasn't come back in. Once or twice I glimpsed him through the trees. Sometimes, at night, me and Gumps are sittin' around the fire playing our fiddles and I hear a growlin' out there and see his eyes shinin' back at me. Least I believe it's him."

"Sounds like he's sick. Be careful of him."

"I know. That's what Gumps figures. The other day I found where he's sleeping and I leave food there. Next time I go out there, it's gone. Hope it's him that's gettin' it."

The murder of Squire Towne was an epochal event in the short history of the village now called Crisfield. Though nothing was said, Haynie McKenna knew instinctively that he needed a written report, some kind of historical record. Especially if things did not go well.

He could figure to get a little glory if he found the killer and all the blame if he did not.

Haynie knew from the war that field commanders had entered the battlefield cloaked in a nimbus of victory, only to leave shrouded in a pall of defeat. This was often a result of events over which they had no influence. Such men had relied heavily on their own written account of these battles, to salvage an otherwise doomed career.

Haynie found writing materials in the desk, poured himself a cup of coffee and settled in to prepare a summary of the events surrounding Squire's murder, beginning with Tawes Butler pounding on his door just over twenty-four hours before.

Next, he recounted the scene at the rail yard. He listed the names of those faces in the crowd he could recall and made a note to talk with them about what they had seen, and who else was there that he didn't know. Someone with information may have left before he arrived.

He described Squire's wounds and listed the missing gun bag and breakfast utensils. Following this was his conversation with George Noch and the offer of the bailiff's job.

In some detail, he told of his search of the jail-car floor and discovery of the fresh muddy boot tracks leading to the cell door, the animal hairs, and the reasoning for his conclusions as to the significance of each finding. Haynie labored as he wrote this section, concerned that it made him sound too prideful. In the end, he struck all references to himself simply reporting what had been found.

Haynie put down his pencil and worried over how to explain his decision to leave Bozo, a known drunk, in charge of the jail-car. What had seemed trivial at the time, now made him cringe. It was a stupid thing to do. Besides not being in the best interest of the town, it was unfair to Bozo. The little man lacked the authority and respect required to enforce Haynie's decree banning everyone from the jail-car.

Any gawkers or busy bodies, who insisted on a look inside, would only be the more insistent after being forbidden by the town drunk. Someone, likely Bozo, could have been hurt in the aftermath.

Haynie decided that it was not necessary to mention Bozo's name other than to say that he had found Squire's body.

The next entry recounted Haynie's meeting with the four councilmen, noting that each one agreed with Noch's offer of the bailiff's job to Haynie.

Finally, he recorded his return to the jail-car, bringing along Art Hastings from the hardware store. While Hastings worked to free the bellowing Cecil from his cell, Haynie examined the ground around the jail-car, without success. Hastings then secured the outer door with a heavy iron padlock, giving the only keys to Haynie.

The bailiff's desk was a scarred roll top of heavy unfinished oak. With the top rolled up, Haynie sat looking at several odd sized drawers and pigeonholes, each stuffed with paper. He opened the drawer just above the kneehole, laid his notes and writing materials inside and closed it.

Haynie was considering which crevice to sort through first, when a man strode briskly through the door, stopping in front of the desk. He was big, at least as tall as Haynie, and fit. His face sported mutton chop side burns; a neatly trimmed goatee and pencil moustache surrounded a small mouth. A wool felt hat sat cocked over the left side of his head, a woolen great coat, in matching gray, hung unbuttoned over his shoulders. A black silk neck cloth was neatly knotted at the collar. Dark hair, flecked with gray at the temples, was slicked back below the hat. In the left hand, he held a mahogany walking stick tipped with ivory at each end. The stick was carried to be easily swung as a weapon.

Haynie eyed him carefully. *If this man is at least as important as he thinks he is, this should be very interesting.*

"I'm Jonathan Gastineau, the High Sheriff of this County. Who am I addressing, sir?" As he spoke, the visitor grasped his cane with both hands, holding it parallel to the floor.

"I'm Haynie McKenna. Excuse me, Mister Gastineau, do you have something to prove that you are who you say?"

Gastineau snorted and yanked open his greatcoat revealing a gold star pinned to his vest. The star was engraved–Sheriff, Somerset County.

"That good enough for you?"

"Yes."

"You the town bailiff?"

Haynie nodded.

"You got something to prove it?"

Haynie sipped his coffee. "You're standing in my office. Now, what can I do for you?"

"I heard the other one, what was his name, Horsey, got himself stabbed dead."

"Squire Horsey Towne was killed yesterday."

"I'm the sheriff of this county – the whole county. How come I didn't get a telegram about the killing of a law officer? Had to hear about it from one of my deputies who was told by a drummer passing through on his way to Salisbury."

"This is my first day; you'd have to ask one of the town council."

"Of course, of course," Gastineau said. "You're as green as a new apple, got no training or experience in these matters. You need my help. We need to work together for good of the folks around here.

"Sticky, real sticky this one. Feel sorry for ya. This'll be a real quagmire. You're not real careful it'll suck you right down in it. Us lawmen got to look out for one another. Tell you what, how about I have my top deputy ride down to see you get it right. "

More likely to keep an eye on me, Haynie thought. *This is the perfect situation for him. People all worried about a killer running around loose, lots of chance to get his name in the newspapers. We work together, and if the killer gets caught, he'll shove me aside and take the credit. If they get away, I'm the rube who messed things up for this great lawman. Still, it can't seem like I'm refusing his help.*

Haynie smiled, "That's real good of you, Sheriff," he said. "Right now there's nothing to work on. Be a waste of his time, man like that must be in demand around such a big county."

"Well course he is, but the killing of a lawman naturally comes first."

"Glad to hear it. Why don't you give me a few days to get settled in? I'll send a wire when I'm ready."

Gastineau huffed, "Wouldn't be a good idea to put me off," he said.

"I'll remember."

Gastineau swung the walking stick to his right shoulder where it rested, held loosely by one hand. "Any witnesses?" he asked.

"Not so far. Still looking."

"Anyone come to mind, who might have done it?"

"Nope."

"Heard there was some prisoners who were freed. What do you know about them?"

"Nobody seems to know who they were. There's talk that they're a couple of drunks from the Alley. Maybe some other drunks broke them out."

Gastineau's smile was gone, his words hard edged. "Too bad. Since it was you that caused 'em to be locked up, I figured you would know something."

That was stupid. I need to be more careful.

Haynie shrugged, "Neither one would give a name, or tell why they were chasing a stranger through town in the middle of the day."

"What did the stranger tell you about it?"

"It wasn't my place to talk to him. Likely, Squire didn't bother to ask. He wasn't one for any extra work."

Haynie felt terrible speaking ill of the dead. But, it was better if the sheriff believed he knew of no connection between the escaped prisoners and the shanghaiing business. Gastineau would easily believe that Squire was lazy.

Gastineau scowled. "Damn shame," he said, wagging his head from side to side. "Squire, eh? Heard he wasn't much of a law man."

Gastineau walked to the desk and extended his hand. "I got to move on," he said, "other pressing business in the county".

Haynie put down his coffee cup and shook the hand. Gastineau walked back to the open door then turned, as if a thought had suddenly occurred to him.

"I'll expect written reports – regular like."

"A written report. Good idea. Trouble is, I'm not much for writin'. Still, I'll try my best."

"You try real hard, son. I need to know what's going on."

Haynie nodded.

"It'd be good for your career to work with me." Gastineau waved his walking stick and strode through the doorway.

Haynie mulled his visit from the county sheriff, as George Noch walked in the room.

"Heard Gastineau in here, what'd he want?"

"To run this office."

Noch paused then said, "Well, we can't have that. However, he is the high sheriff. Important man in the county."

Haynie grabbed some loose papers from a pigeonhole in the great desk.

"That man should be selling snakebite medicine out of the back of a gypsy wagon."

George Noch opened his mouth to protest, then left the room.

Haynie sorted through the loose papers pulled from various pigeonholes. Finding nothing of interest, he replaced them and then pulled out a slender leather bound book snugly archived in a narrow opening at the back of the desk.

It was a journal, embossed in thin gold leaf on the worn cover.

Inside the front cover, the words "Bailiff Journal–Town of Crisfield January 1867 to " had been penned in a heavy hand.

Leafing through the pages, Haynie found hand written entries by day and month, with names and money amounts listed beside each. Some of the names he recognized as local townsfolk and the amount entered next to these names was consistent, undoubtedly recording the purchase of a dog license.

Other names were followed by a single descriptive word; Drunk, Thief, or Tramp with one or two designated as Scoundrel. The money entries after these names were likely a record of the amount Squire spent to feed each prisoner during his stay. Haynie was told that as bailiff he was expected to feed prisoners, as he saw fit, and submit a monthly expense sheet to the town for payment.

Haynie saw entries for Cecil and Bozo, identifying each as a Drunk. Both men had more entries during cold weather than when the weather was warm. The same was true of a few other familiar names, with the word Tramp next to them.

Haynie concentrated on the names of those men identified as Thief or Scoundrel, especially those with more than one entry.

The crime committed by a Thief was evident; however, he was uncertain what activity qualified a man as a Scoundrel.

March was a particularly busy month for Squire, with multiple entries for several days around the middle of the month.

"Ah, the Ides of March," Haynie said aloud, "I'll have to remember that."

Two men arrested on the 16th, were labeled as Scoundrels. Rodney Drumm and Jake Drumm had been fed until the 19th. Haynie studied the item with particular interest. He recalled that the men he and Squire took to jail called each other by those same first names.

Haynie took a drink of now cold coffee and made a face. He rose slowly, moving absently toward the pot bellied stove across the room. After stoking the fire from a pile of split locust, he filled his cup, wishing that Squire had been more detailed.

Those two are definitely scoundrels, but it would help to know what they had done to get themselves arrested.

Seated again at the desk, Haynie located a brown envelope among a sheaf of papers in one of the larger cubbyholes. Pulling back the loose flap, he spilled the contents onto the desk. The desktop was littered with tintype photographs, two by three inches, each one of a man full face to the camera.

He selected two from those scattered across the desktop. Though the tintypes were grainy and shadowed, there was no doubt in Haynie's mind that he was looking at photos of Jake and Rodney Drumm.

16

Somerset County, Maryland
Thursday, November 7, 1867

Landon Wallis had his belt off, using the metal prong to etch another mark into the floor between his legs. This was the sixth mark he had dug into the rough planks. He was pretty certain that he had been here five days with the sixth dawning.

No one had come with food or water for two days. If no one came today, he wondered if he was strong enough to make it through another long day and cold night.

Following Prescott's greed with the water jug, Landon took charge of rationing the victuals. Prescott had whimpered, but was too preoccupied with the diarrhea, to offer any serious objection. He spent the first night and much of the next day, squatted over the privy hole alternately crying out in anguish and lashing out at those around him. When the others saw that Landon was sharing the provisions evenly, they said nothing. By acclamation, he assumed domain over the daily rations and leadership of his fellow captives.

Landon turned first to Billy Washington. "Billy, please eat something. We're all going to need our strength, to survive this place."

Billy replied, "What are we havin' ta day?"

Striving to sound cheerful, Landon said, "On our menu today, we have – dried deer meat and hard tack."

Billy gave a weak wave of his hand, "Ya'll go on ahead," he said. "Just give me a taste from thet water jug." He rose up and swallowed some water before settling back on the floor.

Next, Landon set the pail and jug in front of Luther who selected 2 pieces of the deer jerky and a biscuit followed by a short drink from the jug. The immigrant, after watching Luther closely, did the same for himself. Landon then took out his share before setting the rations in front of Prescott.

"Sir, may I remind you that I am a Prescott. It is insulting that I should be served after a foreigner, AND I am certainly not going to drink from the same vessel as some field hand."

"That's your decision," Landon said, pulling the pail and jug back into his corner.

"You — you can't treat me this way. Your family name is Wallis, isn't that right? When I get home, I'll have my family firm sue your family. You'll be left with nothing. We'll see how you like living like this all the time."

Landon took a bite of hard tack and shook his head. "I don't know the law, but I doubt that you can collect much on the grounds that you are an arrogant boor."

The morning that Prescott left, the bolt on the trapdoor slid back and the door fell away. The prisoners stirred as Jake's head poked through the opening, a cruel sneer on his lips. He conducted his morning's ritual with the usual evil look and hate filled voice.

"Mornin' Mister Reb," he said, touching the bill of his cap in mock salute.

"Mornin', Mister Mama's Boy; Mornin' Mister Nigger; Mornin' Mister Feriner; Mornin' to you, Mister Fancy Pants Lawyer."

Jake finished his taunt with, "I got some good news for you fellas."

He watched each face waiting for a flicker of hope to appear, "We're takin' stinky pants here with us. Ought to stink better in here with him gone."

Prescott rose up on all fours, "Thank you, Jake, thank you," he cried, scuttling toward the opening "You're freeing me from hell. You won't be sorry."

"I' know I won't — but you might," Jake chortled.

Prescott stopped, frozen in place. He looked from Jake to his fellow prisoners, then back to Jake, as if trying to decide the lesser of two evils.

It was not, Landon recalled, as if Arthur Prescott had a choice.

Jake cackled, then gazed into the corner where Billy Washington loomed as a pile of discarded rags.

"You, Johnny Reb, I know this ain't fancy grub a fine southern gentleman like you is used to, but, goddammit, I tole you to eat and you ain't eatin'. You're no damn good if ya cain't work. Now eat."

With no sound or movement from the corner, Landon thought Billy might have died in the night.

"If'n you don't get strong enough to work, I'm gonna haul you out o' here and dump your bony ass in the marsh and drown ya."

Jake whirled on Arthur Prescott, "Get your own fat ass down this ladder," he said, as his head disappeared below the floor.

"Wonder what they's gonna do wif him?" Luther had asked. "Ya'll think they'll kill him?"

"I doubt it," Landon said.

"How come?"

Landon shrugged. "Way I see it," he said, "none of us is worth anything to them dead. They are either gonna sell us to some fishing boat captain, or see if they can get some ransom."

"What's a ransom?" Luther asked.

"Well, they get a hold of a man's family and tell the family they can have him back if they hand over some money or jewels or such valuables."

Luther sighed and shook his head, "Looks like I'm gonna get sold back into slavery."

With Prescott gone, the atmosphere in the shack improved.

Landon deciphered that the immigrant was called Christian. Whether it was his given or family name could not be determined. In any case, Christian was clearly bewildered about his fate within days of having arrived in America.

And Luther became more talkative.

"You know, Mister Landon, I been thinkin' on this fix we're in."

"How's that, Luther?"

"Even though you and me are in the very exact same place, I 'spect it's a lot harder on you than it be on me."

"I don't see how, but tell me."

"Oh, Lordy, where does I start? First off, we is hungry."

Landon nodded.

"I'm used to it, but you not. And I've eat and drunk worse than this here slop to keep myself alive. You've not."

Luther nodded to the privy hole between them. "Doubt that you spent any time squattin' over such a hole, with others lookin' on. And no arse paper to boot. As for me, I squatted out in the fields and shat with little girls and old women, no kin to me, all about. Fer what its worth, tobacco leaves dun burn back there."

"What you say is all true," Landon replied. "I never expected to be having such fond reminiscences about Gayetty's Medicated Paper, as I have these past days."

"There's more, if you want to hear it."

"I have no more appointments for today."

"Huh?"

"Just trying to add some humor," Landon said. "Go ahead on."

"First off," Luther said, "I want to thank ya for listenin'. Nobody has never minded what I was sayin', before. Maybe 'cause I never said nothing worth minding. Truth be told, this is the first time I ever wasn't too tired or too scared to just think about things. When I'm done with my tellin', I'd ask you to tell me if I should ever try it again."

"I will," Landon said, "but it makes no difference what others think. Everyone, no matter who they are, has something to say. And anyone given the chance should listen."

Luther shifted, alternating the spots where the nodes in the log wall jabbed his back.

"Here's what I'm thinkin' is the biggest difference between us – 'sides our color. Ever since I can recollect, the whole world was just two short roads, dirt paths really. The only one I ever traveled ran from our shanty into the tobacco field come sunup, and back again in the evenin. The other one went straight up the hill to the Master's big house. I never set foot on it. It was worth a good hiding if I was to get caught on the hill.

"Mister Landon, I hope ya won't think bad of me when I say it —"

"Go on,"

"—But my onlyest dream was that someday one of the house niggers would run off, or get hung for somethin', and I could walk straight up that hill and spend my days in that glorious house. Be shut of the fields for good. Why, the house niggers had they own privy, with walls and a door.

"I heard tell that the white folks up there had a big two-holer. Made from new wood and good smellin'. You'd know — what's the other hole for? Do white folks like some company whilst they're sitting in there?"

Landon said, "None that I know of," then stood and moved in a tight circle, stomping as he went.

"Don't mind me, just trying to get warm, circulate the blood."

Luther remained quiet so Landon spoke, "Of course we're different, you and me, but if that's all there is to the story, I don't see what it has to do with it."

"Sorry 'bout that. I got to figgurin' on why folks would want a two-holer and lost my thinkin'. 'Member I said this was about us bein' different though we in the same fix."

Landon nodded, "I remember."

"Okay. Anyways, it weren't until I left home and begun trekkin' up here, searching for my momma, that I saw there was lots more roads to this world than them two bitty ones. There's so many, it'd be real easy for a body to lose his way, and not know he's on the wrong road till he gets to the end. Then it might be too late.

"What that means is, I'm sitting on this floor thinkin' on the wrong turns I took which got me here. I don't think I want to try any more roads so I'll just sit here quiet like and wait.

"Now you. You've been knowin' about the roads since you could walk and you learned to miss a lot of the wrong turns. So, you'd be itching to get shut of this place and back on your roads which ain't near as bumpy as mine."

"I must of taken the same wrong turn as you, we both wound up here."

Luther watched Landon as he paced. "I said I wasn't used to thinkin'. Now that I've tried it, I believe I'll keep at it a while longer."

One night they had a long discussion about how they could escape from the shack.

Billy Ray's voice filtered through the darkness. "Ya'll are wasting your time," he said.

Luther shot back with, "What else we gonna do with it?"

After that, Billy laid quiet while the others tested every inch of the walls, roof and trap door without finding a weakness in the fortress.

The four remaining prisoners realized that they would be warmer at night by huddling together while they slept. They agreed to alternate positions, laying inside the huddle one night and on the outside edge the next.

Tuesday morning, after Billy again refused food, Landon crawled over and felt his forehead. "You don't seem to have a fever," he said. "Do you feel sick?"

Billy shook his head. “I’m not exactly sick,” he replied. “Ya’ll don’t need to be fussin’ over me.”

Landon smiled, “You’re wastin’ away to nothing. And, by the looks, you weren’t much to start with.”

“It’s God’s will, I reckon.”

“Maybe so, but in the meantime, your bones are stickin’ me in the night.”

“I’m sorry ‘bout that, but it’s my plan.”

Landon laughed. “It’s your plan to have your bones stickin’ me while I’m trying to sleep?”

Billy gave a short laugh and wagged his head slowly from side to side.

“Naw — well, hell, Ah mights well tell ya. I’ve heard enough talk ’tween that Jake and the other two, to know that if we don’t get sold, they don’t get paid. And worse fer them, their bosses, whoever they is, don’t get no money. Then Jake and them gets into a lot of trouble. You heard him threaten to drown me if’n ah don’t eat. I know he’d never do it; he’s too scared of his masters. It’s the only way he knows to talk to a body.”

Landon passed the water jug, waited while Billy Ray wet his lips, and took it back.

“Well, sir,” Billy continued, “I’ve been doin’ a lot of figurin’ ‘bout this. Nuthin’ else to do. Way I see it; I ain’t had nuthin but bad luck and misery since the war. Just can’t seem to find no place where I can fit in. No, don’t say nuthin ’cause ma mind’s done made up.”

Billy closed his eyes and lay quiet waiting for his strength to return. Finally, he said, “There’s nuthin’ I can do about bein’ in this place. But I’m never gonna work for no jailer, ‘specially a Yankee. The only thing I know ta do to get right with Jake and them is to let my self go on off. They won’t get no money out of me and they will likely have hell to pay with their bosses for lettin’ me get away.”

Landon studied Billy’s face. “That seems like a real drastic step to take, to get even with someone.”

Billy shrugged, “Maybe so. You all looked real hard and couldn’t find no way out of this place. Well sir, I found one.”

Landon looked across the small room. He could still make out Luther and Christian in the gathering darkness of the November afternoon. Luther’s eyes were wide as he stared at Billy, but said nothing.

Christian seemed to be praying, eyes closed, hands clasped together in his lap. Did he understand what Billy was saying, or was it just his way of dealing with this place?

Landon said, “Luther, what do you think about what Billy has decided to do?”

“Not for me to say ’bout what another man does. ’Specially a white man.”

He thought a minute and then continued. “My mama always says it’s up to God when a man goes over. Our preacher sayed that God looked at a black man same as a white man. ‘Course he got whipped for sayin’ it. He would preach to us that God takes care of all of us’n. Black and white. So, if’n Mister Billy is gonna do that, it may be God sayin’ it’s his time, sure enough.”

Billy turned his head toward Luther. “God bless you, suh.”

Landon said, “I haven’t been to church as much as I should have, I guess, but I know they say it’s a sin to not try and live as long as you can. Lord knows, he’ll come for you soon enough.”

Billy closed his eyes again; when he spoke his voice was barely above a whisper. Luther crawled over by him and Landon bent down to hear his words.

“I know they say that, but I ’spect that is true only for folks with some hope left. I got none. I was in some fierce battles, Chickamauga, The Wilderness and more. We was fightin’ to save our homes and farms. Seemed to us like the Yankees was just out to deestroy ever thing they come upon. Anyways, a lot of good ole boys was kilt and we still lost ever thing. After the war, Yankees came pourin’ into the South and took what little we had left.

“Now, the only way I can earn my keep is by workin’ as a slave for some Yankee. I ain’t gonna do that.”

Billy grew silent and ran his tongue over parched lips. Landon moved to hand over the water jug, but Billy waved him to away.

“Hell, I dunno anymore what right is. Them carpet baggers treat us no better’n slaves.”

He looked up at Luther. “Mebbe we is gettin’ what’s due us, for the way we did yore people.”

Billy Ray closed his eyes, “Ah’m tired now,” he said, ending the discussion.

Luther started to speak but stopped when he saw Landon shaking his head through the shadows.

They watched Billy for a moment before Landon said, “I’m leaving the water jug right here next to you.” Billy nodded and they moved away.

Now Landon finished gouging his mark in the floor and threaded his belt back through the loops in his trousers. Billy was snoring softly in his corner and Luther was moaning, likely a bad dream. A dim light forced the darkness into the corners.

Just as he was again fretting about getting through another day without any provisions, Landon heard the voices and felt the bump against the pilings. The trapdoor fell away and Jake's head emerged through the opening. He was clearly in no mood for even his sardonic greeting.

"Hey, Johnny Reb."

Billy remained quiet.

"Godammit, you better not have gone and died on me."

Glaring at Landon, Jake yelled. "Mama's boy. Is the Reb dead or not?"

"I'm still here," Billy said.

Jake set the pail and jug on the floor and Landon crawled over to retrieve them before the jailer could change his mind.

Jake looked at Luther. "Mister Nigger, I'm holding you responsible to see that this Reb, here, eats. It's real easy for you to unnerstand. If the Reb dies, you die." Jake cackled. "Seems fittin' that a slave should tend to his master."

Landon started to protest and Jake shot him a fierce look.

"It's none of yer concern, Mama's boy. Put some jerky and a biscuit in yer pocket, yer comin' with us."

17

Popes Creek, Maryland
Thursday, November 7, 1867

Grace Stringfellow held tightly to the arm of H. J. Mooney as they strolled along the high bluff overlooking the Potomac River. Even here, far away from the competition and sniping from Baltimore matrons, she chose to dress formally, wearing a high necked dress with puffy sleeves of a gray, stripe patterned material. Her hair arranged low in the back and mounted on a pleated velvet ribbon of deep purple.

A chill breeze swept off the Potomac and over the bluff, tugging at the parasol she twirled in her right hand. Mooney's presence always aroused Grace, especially his mien when clad in the uniform of a Confederate officer. With a full head of wavy black hair and a neatly trimmed moustache and goatee, commonly known as a soldier's beard, he was easily the handsomest man she had ever encountered. Today, he wore the dress uniform of a Confederate Colonel, with polished leather and a glistening saber secured at his side. She always a southern belle, he an officer of the Confederacy.

Grace looked up. "Don't you want your great coat?"

"I'm fine, my dear. Don't fuss over me." Both reverted to a thick southern drawl when away from Baltimore society.

They stopped at the edge of the bluff and she rested her head against his powerful arm.

"I love to fuss over you," she said.

A sky of bloated clouds sagged overhead. Far below a United States Navy gunboat navigated the choppy river on its way to the Chesapeake Bay.

Horace Mooney bent down and said softly, “It’s sad that we don’t have a 12 inch Dahlgren mounted up here. We could blow that Yankee boat out of the water and they’d never know where it came from.”

Grace nodded, “It’s a disgrace,” she said, “the manner in which Robert E. Lee truckled at Appomattox Court House. Shameful. And right in our own state of Virginia.”

Horace Mooney rested a hand on the handle of his saber as he scanned the heights down to the river.

“Magnolia Bluff is indeed, good ground. We could control all the traffic on the Potomac from here. It’d take the entire Union army to remove us.”

When Grace inherited the property on which they stood, she and Mooney had decreed between them that it was an extension of The Commonwealth of Virginia. The large clapboard house sat on twenty five acres. Hardly a real plantation, but they imagined it as such, naming it Magnolia Bluff.

Following her marriage to Isaiah Stringfellow, Grace snuggled up to her new husband. While tracing the inside of his thigh with an index finger, she persuaded him to allow her ailing brother to move into their summer home on the Potomac while recovering from another attack of malaria.

Soon, she began visiting Popes Creek to minister to her ailing kin. When Isaiah voiced concern about her traveling so far without him, she pointed out that Pearl, her personal servant, would be with her. When that failed to soothe him, Grace shed real tears while wailing how terrible it is for her to be away from him, the only man she would ever love. If it were anyone but her own kin, she couldn’t think of it. Isaiah had puffed himself up, patted her on the arm assuring her that he too would be in pain while they were apart.

Grace found it amusing that Isaiah was oblivious to the lust she felt for Mooney, though she made little effort to conceal it. Isaiah, hopelessly smitten by Grace’s physical appearance, merely nodded knowingly at her explanation; she and her brother came from a very affectionate and demonstrative family.

Isaiah’s perspective was distorted by the chagrin and envy he imagined coming from the other husbands in their social set. He fancied their looks of rapture as they gazed at Grace. Looks quickly turning to disgust when they returned to the bitter crones at their side.

Isaiah Stringfellow begged Grace to agree to a big wedding at the Maryland Club in Baltimore. The better to show her off. She, under direct orders, cried that she could wait no longer to become Mrs. Isaiah Stringfellow. Her performance convincing, the ceremony was held in her hometown of Staunton, Virginia.

H. J. Mooney attended the nuptials, wrapped in a heavy blanket, and coughing periodically into a square of cloth.

At some point during each of Grace's visits to the Popes Creek house, Mooney would interrogate her for details concerning her intimacies with Isaiah.

"I can't stand the thought of that old bastard laying in the same bed with you."

Grace pulled him close. "Darlin', you know it means nothing. Besides, he's a rum hound. Most nights he crawls into bed in his cups, and before he can figure out how to get me out of my nightgown, he's passed out."

She laughed and said, "You should see the old sot puffing himself up in the morning, when I bat my eyes and speak of what a stallion he is."

Mooney scoffed at the notion that Isaiah Stringfellow was ever enough man to deal with a woman like Grace.

"Still," she said, "I must be careful not to rile him. In a snit, he might strike me from his will."

"One of the reasons he was selected, was because there was no one else he might leave it to. He hates that son of his."

"We didn't account for his ego. In a drunken stupor he might decide to leave it to some school, or hospital. Anyplace that agrees to name a building after him."

Grace had reached up and stroked Mooney's cheek. "Soon my dear. Soon."

Now, she stepped toward the river. "The real shame," she said, "is that no one would listen to you when you described this ground to Richmond. The 'Battle of Magnolia Bluff' would have been as big as Gettysburg or Antietam."

Mooney nodded. "We could have marched right up the Potomac and into Lincoln's bedroom. But, those asses in Richmond decided we were more useful as spies. Any damn fool can be a spy.

"They said it was the best site on the river. Vital for passing intelligence and smuggling arms and people."

Mooney moved closer and looked into her face. "We're just too damn good at what we do, my dear."

Just to their right, the bluff sloped sharply away to the lowland and Popes Creek.

Mooney drew his saber and gestured toward the river. "When I reminded them that it was also the best location for our army to ford the river, they said, 'we'll consider it'. Never heard another word about it."

She patted his arm and tried to cheer him. "Your work here, was —"

"Our work, dear," he interrupted.

"— Of course, dear," she smiled.

Grace pointed in the direction of Popes Creek. "Remember how those Yankees laid just down there in those woods, waiting to catch Colonel Taylor Woods?"

He nodded vigorously, as if this was their first discussion of that day.

The navy gunboat disappeared into the low hanging clouds. They turned and strolled toward the house. He sensed her eyes admiring him and straightened just a bit.

Grace noticed the movement and smiled, "I swear," she said, "the biggest mistake of the whole war was Lee naming Thomas Jackson to command the second corps, instead of you."

She continued to ignore the fact that, at the time, Jackson outranked Mooney by two grades and it was unlikely anyone in Lee's headquarters had even heard of Captain Mooney.

Though he and Grace had played out this same scenario countless times, Horace Mooney never tired of hearing her say her part.

She continued, "Stonewall Jackson, indeed. After his embarrassing performance in North Carolina, then the fool goes and gets himself killed by his own men."

On cue, Mooney spoke out, "It's well known that Jackson wasn't shot by accident. He was hated by his troops."

"It's so sad that history will likely treat him as a hero, a great man, while no one may ever hear of the brave deeds of Colonel Horace J. Mooney."

Mooney smiled. "I wouldn't rush to judgment, my dear," he said. "It's not over."

Pearl held the front door open as they climbed the porch steps.

Bowing slightly she said, "Colonel, suh, Ma'am."

Grace ordered two hot buttered rums as she handed her wrap and parasol to Pearl. The light-skinned Negress nodded and carried her mistress's things into the other room.

Grace stood warming her hands before the walk-in fireplace as her husband hung his saber and uniform hat on wooden pegs in the entryway.

Suddenly, Grace grimaced, emitting an anguished cry as she slumped onto a wingback chair in front of the fire. "It's all so sad," she wailed.

Mooney knew that she was on the verge of one of her spells.

Grace began experiencing mood swings soon after her marriage to Isaiah Stringfellow. She would arrive at the Popes Creek house, for one of their trysts, either ebullient or sadly morose.

Recently, these changes in temperament had begun more suddenly, were more violent, and of a longer duration. He remained mystified about the onset of such incidents. Were they set off by an external provocation, something he did, or failed to do? Or, was it wholly internal, something inside her, something of which even she was unaware?

It was during one of these episodes that Isaiah Stringfellow had died. Grace had been giddy as she helped Mooney hoist the drunken Isaiah over the ship's rail, giggling uncontrollably as Isaiah's bulk sank into the bay. Then, grabbing Horace's hand, she pulled him back to her cabin where she insisted that he make violent love to her.

As these spells worsened, Mooney suggested that she might be suffering from black bile and recommended that she see a physician. Grace sneered at the notion that she was ill, saying she had always been an emotional person. Of late, his efforts at ministering to her always received a harsh rebuke.

Pearl appeared and set the steaming mugs in front of them, cast a sidelong glance at Mooney and hurried from the room.

Horace and Grace had been together for many years. They shared a deep passion for Virginia and were bonded by their own particular vision of the Rebellion. She had been an enthusiastic partner in his efforts to fund the resurrection of their cause. Today, as always, he would deal patiently with this episode. Still, he was uncertain how long he could endure what he termed, her fits of dementia.

Mooney reached to pat her arm. She withdrew, her eyes closed.

"Where is our money?" she said. "Your Major Hollins should have been here by now."

"There's no cause for alarm, my dear," he consoled. "I'm certain it went smoothly."

"That's just it. The money was to be passed on Monday. This is Thursday, isn't it?"

Eyes still closed, she continued without seeing his slight nod, "We should have the bag, yet we haven't even heard from him."

Mooney, sounding buoyant, said, "If you recall, we discussed that it would not be a good idea for him to disappear for two or three days immediately after the money was passed. We agreed he would wait until the boy had returned home and everything was calm; only then was he to bring the money to us."

Grace raised her mug and swallowed.

Perhaps the alcohol contributes to her condition, he thought.

Grace clutched her drink. "I have never trusted him. Fifty thousand dollars would tempt a saint, and he's a long ways from a saint. How could you promote him to major?"

"Friends in high places, my dear. It is crucial that we have intelligence sources in Annapolis. As for his not reporting in, may I remind you how circumspect we must be with out communications?"

Grace glared until he said, "In the morning I'll ride up to Port Tobacco and see if there are any reports."

18

Tangier Sound, Chesapeake Bay
Thursday, November 7, 1867

Landon Wallis preceded Jake down the rope ladder and glimpsed two other men grinning as he landed on the deck.

Jake yelled after him, "Jesus, Rod, Jesus. Don't let him stand around gapin', get him below deck. I got to do every damn thing?"

Rodney rushed Landon, seizing him at the nape of the neck with one hand, while grabbing his left arm with the other.

"You heard him," Rodney said, "get your ass down there fore I break yer damn neck."

Landon, shoved head first through the open hatch, flung his free arm out to break his fall.

Jake cursed overhead and Landon heard a punch being landed, then the sound of a body hitting the deck. "Jesus, Rod, Jesus. How'd you get to be so stupid?"

"Dammit, Jake," the other howled, "I just done what you tole me to."

"Yer lucky ya didn't break nuthin on him. Then he couldn't work. Wouldn't be worth nuthin', and we might as well just dump him overboard."

Rodney crawled across the deck and peered into the hatch, blood flowing over his mouth, splattering the ladder rungs below.

"Hey, mamma's boy, anything on you broked?"

Landon worked his right arm back and forth, then glared up through the hatch. Finally, he shook his head.

Rodney pulled his head back, started to stand, thought better of it and remained on the deck.

"He's okay. Why'd ya hit me before findin' out if he was broke?"

"I hit ya fer doin' somethin' so dumb. If he'd been broke, I'd a heaved him overboard and you right after him."

"But–but, Jake, you know I cain't swim."

Jake laughed. "Then you best mind what I tell ya."

The hatch cover closed over head and the small boat slid away from the prison platform. Landon found that he was alone and groped in vain for a dry place to sit. After lowering himself into the brackish bilge water, he rubbed his shoulder and his mind churned, anxious over what was to come.

Landon Wallis believed it when Jake said that he was worth nothing to them dead. Still, these men had proven themselves as stupid as they were cruel. A dangerous mixture. A belief that, at this moment, they did not intend to kill him was of little comfort.

It suddenly occurred to him that, somehow, the kidnappers had contacted his family who had paid for his release. Jake's threats about keeping Landon fit for work were likely evidence of his ornery nature. There was no work. He was going home.

As quickly, Landon sagged back, overcome with guilt. In his haste to flee the shack, he had not said a word of goodbye to the others. Until this moment, he had given no thought to their fate. Like Arthur Prescott before him, Landon was going home because his family had money, while Billy Ray and Luther were staying, likely to be worked to death.

"When I get home," he vowed, "I'm going to get help and come back. We'll find them — in time."

He nodded and slapped his fist into a palm. "We'll be in time."

Landon judged that they had been underway about twenty or thirty minutes when the boat began to toss on rough water, waves slapping against the bow.

We must have just entered the bay, he thought. *So – their prison is 20 to 30 minutes up river from open water. But which river? There must be hundreds.*

Landon searched his memory, dredging up everything he could about the trip from Fell's Point to the prison. He could picture nothing, and then he recalled that he had been unconscious for all but the last few minutes of the voyage.

Next came images from the fleeting looks he'd had of the terrain on which the prison tower sat. *It seems like there was more to it than just that tower. What though? Sections of some kind of log fence. Like a stockade. Old. Rotting away. Maybe an old fort? That might help. If it was an old fort, somebody should know where it is. Can't be too many of them near the bay.*

His captors' faces and voices surfaced in his mind.

Must remember their names. Jake and now, Rodney. As if, I would ever forget those two.

Landon strained to remember anything said in the prison tower that might help. Especially, comments made by Billy Ray, who had been held the longest.

What had he said — something about – it being funny that their prison was almost directly across the bay from Point Lookout, where he'd been in the Yankee prison camp — didn't think to ask him how he knew that.

The slapping of the waves and the rhythmic motion of the boat intruded on Landon's thoughts. His mind drifted — *How long we been out now? Not sure —*

The boat bumped against a hard object, voices on the deck above him. The hatch over head opened and the face of a third kidnapper peered down. His lips parted in a sneer, revealing two rows of black stumps instead of teeth. "G,g, get up here, boy," he stammered, "we, we, we found you a real n, n, nice home."

Overhead, Rodney Drumm shouted, "Good'un Roy. Hey, Jake," he cackled, "Roy tole the rich boy, we found him a nice home."

"Jesus, Rod, Jesus, can't ya see I'm doin' bizness with Captain Jack? Idiot."

Landon's head was clearing the hatch when Rodney cursed, "Dammit, Roy, get that rich bastard out of there. Jake's doin' bizness."

Roy Drumm swore under his breath, grabbed a handful of Landon's hair, yanking hard in an effort to drag him clear of the hatch.

"D, d, damn you," he stammered, "We ain't g,g, got all day. J,J, Jake's d,d, doin' bizness." Landon swatted at the arm pulling his hair, and scrambled from the hold.

Once on deck, he saw they were tied off to a much larger boat. A two masted sailing vessel, like many he had seen moored at wharves around Fell's Point. Landon recognized it as a log canoe about sixty feet in length. A powerful boat was needed to drag the iron jawed dredge through an oyster bed. The shallow draft was requisite for working the river mouths and shoreline of the East Bay. Landon knew it to be an oyster dredge boat.

Two years before, following protracted and bitter debate, the Maryland General Assembly passed a law limiting dredgers to open water. Rivers, creeks and the Eastern Bay were reserved to tongers. Dredging was illegal in those waters, yet, at any given time, there were between four and six thousand armed dredgers roaming the bay.

The crew that got the biggest catch to the buy boat, the most often, made the most money. Dredge boats out manned, and out gunned, the much smaller boats used by tongers in these waters.

Many captains, and the crews they commanded, scorned the law, plundering the richest beds wherever they found them.

Landon had read articles in the Baltimore Sun about dredge crews keeping tongers cowed with rifle fire off the port bow, while other crewmen winched aboard dredges teeming with oysters, on the starboard side. Landon's father privately described dredgers as depraved scoundrels who came from the vilest parts of the city. Yet, he owned two of the buy boats who hauled the loot from these raiding parties to the Wallis processing plant in Fell's Point.

As Landon climbed aboard the bigger ship, he observed it to be equipped with oarlocks, muffled for quiet movement at night. The mark of poachers. It was well known that these oyster pirates operated without fear of the law.

The legislature passed the law restricting drudgers to the open waters of the bay, without bothering to fund an agency to enforce it. Other than a county sheriff, there was no place to report crimes occurring on the Chesapeake Bay; no agency existed, with the resources or authority, to take action. And the dredgers knew it.

Harper's Weekly had labeled the situation as, "a recipe for war".

Landon held little hope that anyone was searching for him. Once onboard the drudge boat, he understood that he was not going home. He was very likely going to be in the war, on the wrong side. Landon was resigned to the truth – there would be no rescue.

If I am to leave this boat alive, it will have to be my own doing.

Across the deck, four men lolled near the main mast, glaring. Landon clutched the rail, rigid with fear. His right shoulder ached, but he resisted the urge to rub it and stood shivering, his face drawn with the cold. Landon stepped away from the rail and stood, alone and shaking.

This is going to be a different kind of hell, but hell, nevertheless.

Jake Drumm, his business complete, looked at Landon and laughed

"Ya likely thought you'd never see the day when you wished ya was back in the shack. Well, today's the day."

Jake climbed over the rail, the other two cast off the lines and the small boat bobbed away on a worsening sea.

When Landon turned back, he was face to face with one of the crew. Though of equal height, the other man showed a hard jaw and muscular build. Heavy eyebrows merged above a nose, seemingly, no more than a ridgeline of bone.

On Landon's left, Captain Jack moved into his field of vision. The old seaman took a wide stance; steady as if rooted in the ground, arms akimbo.

"Mister Greeley, welcome our newest crewman."

The movement was but a blur before Landon felt the of the mate's backhand slap across his face.

Landon threw up both arms. "What the hell —"

"Stand at attention."

Landon's hand twitched toward a sympathetic touch of his jaw, then his arms fell to his side and he assumed the civilian equivalent of the military stance.

"We don't give a damn who you was or where you come from, Slick. Hear?"

Still glaring at Landon, Greeley flung an arm out, pointing at the three crewmen behind him.

"Every one of them is better than you. Hear?"

Greeley stepped closer and Landon feared the pounding of his own heart could be heard around the deck

"Look around," Greeley ordered. "Damn you, I gave you an order."

Wary of taking his eyes from Greeley, Landon glanced across the deck.

"Not at them. Look behind you."

Deciding the better choice was to do as he was told, Landon's eyes swept the empty horizon beyond the rail.

"Now you know," Greeley said. "This boat is yer whole world — and you're the least person in it. Hear?"

Teeth clenched, lips taut, Landon nodded.

Greeley cocked a fist. "Speak up, dammit, or you'll get another."

"Yes. I hear."

Captain Jack moved closer, Landon felt hot breath on his neck. “You’ll be giving Mister Greeley, the respect that this ship’s mate deserves. You understand?”

Landon was never so alone. “I-I-I understand.”

Again, Greeley roared into his face, the stink of his breath, nauseating, “I understand – SIR.”

Captain Jack crossed in front of Landon, stopping next to Greeley.

He was shorter than the mate, almost stumpy, with a full beard, like the others in the crew. Landon judged him to be at least fifty years of age, most of them undoubtedly spent at sea.

Captain Jack’s lack in height was compensated by a muscled body, ropy arms and penetrating deep black eyes, set in a small head.

Landon started to speak only to be silenced by Captain Jack’s glare. “Mind what I’m about to tell you. Mind it real good. Did you understand what Mister Greeley said about this ship being your whole world?”

Landon stammered, “Yes — but.”

Greeley leaned forward, fist balled, eyes glaring.

“I mean – yes, sir, but —”

“You a religious man, Slick?”

“Yes – sir – sort of.”

“As the captain of this ship, I’m your new god. I didn’t give you life, but I can sure take it away. Understand?”

Landon nodded, then quickly said, “Yes, sir.”

The ship’s captain raised a clenched fist above his head. “You get any ideas about jumping ship, remember: life or death,” he shook the fist. “Right in this hand.”

Captain Jack looked hard at Landon and then said, “Oyster season doesn’t last an eternity, it only seems like it does. You work hard and behave yourself, you’ll see next summer. Look back on this time as a sort of education.”

Captain Jack turned on his heel, “We need to get underway. Mister Greeley, tell Slick, here what he will be doin’ while a member of this crew.”

19

Somerset County, MD
Thursday, November 7, 1867

Jeremy Coates guided his horse carefully through the stand of hackberry trees, the reins tight in his left hand. A few shriveled sugarberries clung to the otherwise bare branches as he passed. His right hand held the long rifle at the stock. The gun butt rested on his right thigh, the barrel pointing upward, into the trees.

About thirty yards ahead, a golden hawk, perched on the limb of a gum tree, eyed the approach of horse and rider. Jeremy reined the horse in and brought the long gun up to his shoulder, sighting along the barrel at the huge bird.

"Bang," he yelled and chortled to himself.

The hawk blinked at the intrusion, before lifting off in a flurry of wings, retreating deeper into the woods.

Jeremy nudged the horse forward and they began moving up a gentle incline to the crest of a knoll. Once atop the hillock, he was satisfied he could see and hear anyone approaching through the naked trees. Jeremy had no timepiece, but instinct told him that it was at least thirty minutes ahead of the meeting hour. The meetings were scheduled every Thursday at three in the afternoon. They'd begun in August, when the woods were thick with foliage, flying pests and heat, the ground a tangle of weeds, ivy and wild roses.

He was led to this spot by Mister Brown. They had sat, biding their time, on lathered horses and sweltered in the clammy heat until Mister Green arrived.

Me and that fellow Brown wipin' off rivers of sweat, 'til I could hardly keep a hold on General Jackson here. Well sir, this Green comes a sashayin' in, all clean and dry, same as if he was inside an icehouse. I hated that he knew all about me, called me Jeremy right to my face, knew I had rid with Quantrill. Knew all of it.

The son-of-a-bitch even know'd about my trouble with that Reb sergeant. I still don't know nuthin' of him, 'cept he's a real dandy who fancies himself better'n ever body else. Calls hisself – Mister Green. Mister Green, mah ass.

This spot, about a mile from the main road, was remote, secluded.

Must say that it's a good meetin' place. Ain't nobody gonna sneak up on us here, be it summer or winter.

Mister Brown introduced Jeremy to Mister Green. Following that first meeting, Mister Brown instructed Jeremy to leave and return to the spot, from a different direction.

"Being careful," Brown had said. "So's you can find it again, without worrying a path."

Might as well a called me a idiot to my face. Said he wanted to make sure I could find the place, 'cause I wouldn't see him no more. Knowed all about me, except what a first rate frontiersman I am.

Before Mister Brown rode away, he said Jeremy was to be at this same spot every Thursday at three o'clock. If Mister Green didn't show up in an hour, Jeremy was to leave and come back to the spot the next Thursday, and the next, until Mister Green did show up.

More'n one damn day I set here like a dern fool, amongst all the bugs and sweat, and Mister Fancy Britches never showed. He better have my damn pay today, fer doin' my job on that old lawman. If he don't, I might just go ahead and shoot him. If he's got my money, I might kill him anyways. See how Mister Fancy Britches likes bleedin' to death on this cold woods floor. He smiled at the image. *It'd sure mess up them fancy clothes he wears.*

Jeremy reached inside his coat and felt the Sharp's four-barrel pepperbox that he'd taken from Squire Towne's body. *After all, I ought to see how this here baby gun shoots in case I need it for real. 'Sides, I'd like to have that carved walkin' stick he's always wavin' in my face. Yes sir, I'd like that a heap.*

Jeremy backed the scrawny horse up so that his left side was protected by a large hackberry tree. He lowered the long gun, resting it across the saddle and sat still, listening for the sound of someone approaching, watching for any movement through the trees.

This ain't so bad in the cold weather, but sittin' here during the hot months is like sittin' in hell. Them musquitos liked to bleed me dry. I finally had to kill me a skunk and rub it on myself whenever I come out here.

Jeremy laughed at the thought. *It was fun to be all skunked up and go into the general store. Move right up next to some man's wife who was dressed up real purty and see her face all scrunch up and her move off in a puff. The store man took care of me first off, just to get rid of me. Good thing I don't have to skunk myself up now, 'cause I took my winter bath back in October. I wouldn't even be able to stand myself 'til next Spring.*

"May I ask what you find so amusing, Jeremy?"

Coates swung around in his saddle and leveled his long gun in the direction of the voice.

"That you, Green?" he asked. "Show yer damn self or I'm gonna let go with this here big gun."

Mister Green stepped out from behind a large chestnut tree at the far rim of the hillock.

"No need for anger, Jeremy. Why don't you dismount and give that poor animal a rest."

"The name's Rat, damn you. How long you been back there anyways? What you doin' – spyin' on me?"

Green stepped closer to horse and rider, his carved walking stick resting on his right shoulder, clutched in his fist.

"I've been watching your back trail. Need to make certain we are alone."

Jeremy Coates stared hard, not bothering to conceal his hate for the other man.

Betcha that greatcoat would fit me just dandy. Don't care much for that fine silk cloth around his neck. Could use it as a nose rag, though.

"You got my money?"

"You've been paid, up to date."

"Not since I cut that old lawman's throat and got them two idiot brothers out from that there jail-car. You was standin' right here when Brown told me I'd get two hundred dollars for every killin' I had to do. You 'member that, don'tcha?"

Green took the walking stick from his shoulder and motioned toward the ground.

“We have some things to discuss. Climb down and let’s get comfortable.”

“I’m just fine up here. Give me my damn money; then we’ll talk about what ever ya like.”

Green returned the walking stick to his shoulder and stepped back from horse and rider. His eyes narrowed as he studied the man who demanded to be called, Rat.

“You apparently misunderstood your orders,” Green said. “You will get two hundred dollars for every person you are *told* to kill. And you have not been *told* to kill anyone, most especially not any lawman.”

“That’s a damn lie. Brown said I was to see that none of them boys ya’ll keep in that old fort gets loose. I’m to kill’ em if they did. Sorta like the warden of a prison, he said. And, I’m to see that nobody finds out about it. That’s the first thing them Drumms would a tole – about that shack – right after that, they’d a tole about me.”

Green took a step forward, as he spoke, “Now, Jeremy, you were never authorized to make any decisions, merely carry out instructions passed on to you by me.”

One or two steps and he would be close enough to bring the burled stick smashing down on Jeremy’s right wrist.

Rat stiffened in the saddle, his right fist tightened on the stock of the long gun. “What the hell’s goin’ on here? It had to be done, and I done it. Got those Dumb brothers out afore they could ruin ever thing. You and your rich friends welchin’ on two hundred dollars?”

Green eyed the long gun.

A beautiful weapon. One day it’ll be mine. Lots of folks have seen him on that spavined horse, struttin’ through town showin’ it off. Won’t matter; no one’s going to be sad over him getting killed.

Green said, “We have worked hard. There’s a lot of money to be made, plenty for everyone. It can be quickly ruined by rash acts.”

Jeremy eyed Green’s hand tightening on the walking stick. Shifting the great rifle to his left hand, he eased his right hand inside a gap in the buffalo robe.

“Oh yeah.” Jeremy said, “How was you gonna get them two out, before they blabbed, ’sides killin’ that jailer?”

Green lowered his cane and held it easily in both hands.

“I share your concern about the Drumms,” he said. “That’s why they, like yourself, are told very little of our activities. We have a vast network of associates. People in high positions who can influence such things.” His voice tightened, “The Drumms would have been released in due course. If you hadn’t acted so rashly, it would all be over and forgotten by now. As it is, everyone is looking for them for the killing. Now, when they're caught, they will spill everything."

He smiled up at Jeremy. "Especially about how it was you that did the actual killing."

Jeremy Coates gripped the Sharps under the heavy robe and glowered.

I could kill him easy with this baby gun from here. Be quicker than tryin' to swing the long gun around on him.

"Seems like yer tellin' me I got to kill them brothers. All three of 'em."

Green stepped back and Jeremy relaxed his grip on the Sharps.

"That's one solution," Green said, "but not the one we want – at this time. We believe one killing will better serve our needs."

"Who is it you want dead?"

"It's by way of cleaning up the mess you caused when you killed that old bailiff. The new man—name's McKenna. He's a crusader. Bound to be trouble."

Jeremy, uncertain what a crusader did, quickly decided it didn't matter.

Green was saying, "— Lives along River Road. Got a wife and baby, there."

"Be more for them."

"We're not interested in them."

"Kill them first, sure get his attention."

Green shrugged, "We're not paying for them."

Jeremy Coates thought for a moment, and then said, "Yer tellin' me to kill this McKenna."

Green nodded.

"I think I should get more for him — three hundred."

"Sounds like you are afraid to face him."

Jeremy stiffened in the saddle. "I ain't scared of no man. 'Sides, who said I was gonna be facin' him?"

"Oh, one more thing. You got to get a hold of Jake Drumm and —"

"I ain't gettin' paid to mind the Drumms. Last time I saw them, Jake and that idiot brother of his was rolling around in the snow at the edge of town."

Green was impatient. "Just find them as soon as you can. They got a young fella name of Landon Wallis in the paddy shack. Tell them to take him to dry land across the bay and put him ashore – and he better be healthy enough to make it home."

Jeremy smirked. “I know what you big shots are doing. You’re selling the rich ones back to their kin. Can get more for ’em than selling them to a drudger.”

“It’s business. None of your concern.”

“I’ll tell ’em, whenever I see ’em. But you better for damn sure have all my money next time.”

“I’ll speak to them about the money —”

“Looks like ya ain’t as smart as ya let on. If I hadn’t got them boys out, they’d still be in that rail jail and couldn’t get up to the paddy shack to let this rich snot out.”

Coates maintained his glare, thoroughly enjoying his imagined mastery over Green and the others who so enraged him.

“Damn sure I ain’t showing my face to them at the paddy shack. They already seen the three idiots, so it don’t matter.”

Jeremy Coates worked the reins and jerked the horse away from the tree. “Just so we’re clear. It’ll cost ya three hundred for McKenna and the two hundred you owe me for the old guy.”

Green shook his head. “You’re in no position to make demands.”

“Looky here — Mister Green —” Jeremy snarled. “Or whoever the hell ya are. You get on back to them folks who’s payin’ fer this, and tell ’em Rat wants his damn money. Come a week, McKenna will be dead and I’ll be here for my money. All of it.”

Jeremy spurred the bony horse and started down the path. He jerked the old horse’s head back and turned in the saddle.

“Don’t think you can back shoot me neither,” he smirked, “it’ll just get you killed.”

20

Crisfield, Maryland
Thursday, Afternoon November 7, 1867

Wes Moore appeared in the doorway to the bailiff's office waving an envelope in his left hand. He displayed the weak mouth and shifting eyes of a man easily cowed.

Haynie looked up from his desk and motioned the agent into the room.

"I'm sorry to disturb you, Mister McKenna," he said, "but this here wire come for you. It's addressed to you and not Squire Towne. Come all the way from up to Baltimore, yes sir."

Haynie reached for the envelope

"Wes, we live in an amazing time," he said, as he sliced it open with a pocketknife.

Moore bit his lip and shrugged.

"I'm thinking back to the days of early Rome, the Crusades. Men struggled to put down the written word – only a few could put pen to parchment – now any man can send his words flying across most of this nation, over your telegraph wires. A man can know in hours, instead of days or weeks that his message has been read, and even get an answer the same day. At the same time, the recent great war was fought by men on foot, led by men on horseback, same as the Roman Legions, and Crusaders."

Moore nodded, pleased that he now understood the bailiff's meaning.

"Never thought of it like that, but o'course yer right about it, Mister McKenna."

As Haynie focused on the message, the agent said, "I hope it was okay for me to bring this to you. Thought it could be important. It being from a Colonel in Baltimore and all."

Haynie nodded, "That's fine, Wes, thanks."

"Long as I'm here, I might as well ask you how you want things done."

Haynie laid the paper down. "I'm sorry," he said, "I don't know what you mean."

"See, Squire Towne — we had a arrangement. He would stop over to the office – oncest in the mornin' an' oncest in the afternoon – when he could. If he wasn't there by 3:00 o'clock, I was to bring any wires over here and leave them on his desk. That's what I was doin' now, only you was here."

"What happened to the telegrams, if Squire was gone for a couple of days? Did they just lay here, unopened?"

Moore lifted his black billed agent cap and scratched the top of his head vigorously with his free hand. "Not sure," he said, replacing the cap. "Some times they set there for a couple o' days, other times one of the town council would collect them, usually Mister Noch."

"Would Mister Noch open them, or just hold them for Squire?

The agent shrugged. "Dunno. Guess he could read 'em if he was of a mind to. Them bein' town business and all."

"And, if you were asked to hold them for me, where would you keep them?"

"Oh, we got that big heavy safe behind the counter. With a dial lock and all. They'd go in there."

Haynie said, "You were in the war."

Moore nodded. "Wore blue same as you."

"What kind of unit were you in?"

Wes Moore drew himself to attention. "Signal Corpse, sir. That's where I learned Mister Morse's codes and such."

"And you learned how important it is to keep the words in those messages away from our enemy and their spies, didn't you?"

"Oh, yes sir," Wes said, his voice betraying doubt about the question. The bailiff was getting him confused again, and that was worrisome.

Haynie paused, the silence seemed endless to Moore.

When he could stand the quiet no longer, the agent shifted his weight and said, "The war is done over, Mister McKenna. What enemy are we talkin' about?"

Haynie motioned to the chair across the desk. "Have a seat, Wes."

Moore nodded and quickly seated himself on the chair's edge, tense, his back straight.

The bailiff said, "While it is true the war is over, we'll always have enemies, just different ones. For now, the enemy is whoever killed Squire Towne; the enemy is whoever took Landon Wallis and all those other men; the enemy is the poachers coming into our waters and stealing our oysters."

Wes Moore nodded his understanding. "But wait," he said, "none of those enemies wears a uniform. How we gonna know who they is?"

Haynie leaned forward, elbows resting on the desk. "That's a very good question, Wes."

Moore grinned.

Haynie said, "Even during the war, the enemy didn't all wear a gray uniform. It's the same now; our job is to figure out who they are, and stop them."

Moore was pleased the bailiff included him in this fight, even if he was uncertain who it was they were fighting.

Haynie went on, "Until we figure out who they are, we don't let anyone know what we know."

Wes pulled at his cap and scratched his scalp. "Er, do we know sumpon, Mister McKenna?"

"We know a little and we're learning. For now, keep any telegrams for me, or this office, locked up in that safe until I come for them. If anybody says I sent them for 'em, they'll be a liar."

Wes Moore clapped his cap on his head as he stood. "Mister McKenna, no one's gonna see them but you. That's fer dead sure."

"Oh, Wes, before you go, I'd like you to take a wire and see that it gets to Wilmington, up in Delaware, today."

The agent pulled a book of blank telegram forms from his back pocket and waved them. "Always keep a book with me. Folks fer ever stoppin' me on the street to take a wire fer 'em."

The agent resumed his seat on the edge of the chair, laid his book on the corner of the desk and, taking a pencil from his pocket, said "Let 'er rip, Mister McKenna."

Wes Moore wrote down the words as the bailiff spoke. Once, he stopped printing to ask how to spell the person's name. "Is he an enemy?" Moore asked.

"That's one of the things we have to find out."

When they finished, Moore stood, touched the bill of his cap in salute and left the office.

Haynie turned his attention to the telegram lying on his desk. He was stunned by its contents.

Fell's Point, Maryland
November 7, 1867

McKenna

It is with deep sadness and a heavy heart that I tell you, Landon has not yet returned to us.

As I told you on Monday, we followed the kidnappers' instructions and a carpetbag holding seventy-five thousand dollars was delivered to them by our good friend Major Hollins. He stood at the site described, at the specified time and was shortly relieved of the bag by a person he could not see as he was approached from behind and told not to turn around.

The Major was treated very roughly and it all happened very quickly.

I implore you to resume your efforts on Landon's behalf.

Sincerely,

Colonel Silas Wallis.

Haynie stared at the paper.

I shouldn't be surprised. How can you take the word of someone who steals another person? Fortunately, Caleb and Gerhard are still looking; I've had no time to tell them otherwise.

Haynie stood and felt a rumbling in his belly. He was surprised to see that it was already after three. Breakfast was hours ago, before daylight, and he was ravenous. He found it hard to believe he was sworn in as bailiff only this morning.

Haynie pulled open the lower desk and reached for his gun belt then hesitated. Earlier, on the ride into town, he had reflected on what kind of bailiff, what kind of town citizen, he would be. Most lawmen he had seen carried a handgun openly, in a gun belt, similar to his rig. But, they had been in big cities like Baltimore and Annapolis. This was Crisfield, a small town. How did he want to be seen by the townspeople? What kind of leader?

Squire Towne had not worn a gun belt; rather, he toted a small gun in the bag at his wrist. It was hard to imagine Squire giving any thought to his public image when he chose to carry a weapon such. Some joked that the late bailiff carried the gun on his wrist because he would never be able to find it among the rolls of fat at his waist. Would Horsey Towne be alive, had his weapon been handier to draw?

Haynie concluded that as bailiff, he would not wear a rig when about town on routine business and closed the drawer.

I don't believe a man needs a gun to go across the street to eat a meal in the middle of the day.

Haynie left the office and started down the stairs when the front door burst open and a man rushed in. Haynie stopped, unable to identify the intruder in the dim, unlit entry below.

"McKenna – it's Kenny Sipes. Yer misses sent me for ya. She can't find Young Tench – She's just crying and crying. You better come on home."

Haynie knew it would do no good to ask foolish questions for which Sipes would have no answers.

He said, "I got to get my rig and saddle my horse. You head on back and tell her I'll be along directly."

Haynie pulled hard on the reins, sawing the bit across the horse's mouth as he came to a sliding stop in front of the house. Lila was on the porch sobbing in the arms of Kate Sipes.

"Kenny and a couple of men are out lookin for him," Kate said.

Haynie ran up the front steps, looking from Lila to Kate, neither spoke.

"For God's sake," he cried, "tell me what happened."

Kate patted Lila rhythmically on the back and looked away. Lila slowly turned her face to him, tears streaming into the cloth she held to her mouth. Her body shuddered.

She sighed, then straightened and said, "I put him to bed for his nap and then went into our room to lay down. I was feeling poorly."

Taking a deep breath, she experienced another shudder and continued. "You know how I am, sometimes given to breathe heavy when I sleep. I was afraid it might wake him – so I closed the doors between us and...."

She searched her husband's face for some sign that he might forgive this dreadful thing that she had done. Swallowing her sobs, she said, "I must have dozed off, then something woke me – a sound – I thought it was him fussing. I went to look in on him and the bed was empty; he was gone. Oh God, oh God — you'll get him back – you must."

Haynie pulled Lila gently from Kate's arms and held her tight.

"We'll get him back," he said. "Whatever it takes, Young Tench is coming home."

He stepped back, returned her to Kate's care and said, "Does mother know what has happened?"

Lila shook her head. "I looked everywhere, then I ran to the Manor House for help, but no one was there. I searched along the way for him." Her voice trailed and she returned to sobbing into the cloth.

The McKenna's home was modest, four rooms in the front with a kitchen and summer porch in the back. It was covered with a tin roof and weathered shingle siding. The front door opened from a short, covered porch to a cramped sitting room. Haynie stepped through the door and scanned the room. He tried to imagine what the kidnapper had seen, what he had felt.

Once inside, the intruder had but a few steps to his left where Young Tench's door was closed, but unlocked. On the other side of the room was the door to their bedroom where Lila lay napping.

Haynie pushed open the door and examined Young Tench's tiny bedroom. The window was shut tightly. The blanket missing from his son's bed.

At least he had the decency to wrap the boy against the chill.

During the dash for home, it had occurred to Haynie that the taking of Young Tench might be an act of revenge by the ruthless men that he and Squire had jailed – a warning of some sort. Those two clearly had help escaping from jail.

Men so craven as to murder poor Squire could be vengeful enough to steal an innocent babe.

The image this idea carried terrified him, and he fought to put it out of his mind. Now, as he closed the door to his son's room, he imagined these men invading his home – his wife and small son defenseless – at their mercy. Lila asleep just behind the other door –

Oh, God. It could have been even more horrible if they had opened that door.

As he moved through the dining room into the kitchen, he could smell them.

A fetid animal stench grew strong in his nose and throat.

Finding nothing disturbed in the kitchen, he continued out the unlocked back door.

Haynie slowly circled the house, head low scouring the ground for strange boot prints under a window, or near the back door. Such men were unlikely to have come in a buggy or wagon, but he found no marks of a shod hoof in the yard or the dirt lane that ran in front of his place.

Haynie held out little hope for his effort, but knew that it had to be done. He sensed that what he knew so far did not fit. Something was wrong and it made him uneasy.

Night frosts and chilly days had left the ground firm, but pliable. More than once, he knelt to examine a crushed leaf, but if a sign was present, he could not read it. At the back of his yard, he found one set of faint boot impressions circling the privy and woodshed. Haynie looked in both buildings, without expectation, before backtracking this trail across an empty lot. The boot marks had looked familiar so he was not surprised when they led him to the Sipes's back stoop.

Kenny, too had searched here for Young Tench.

Haynie returned to his back door, paused, and took a last look around the yard before entering. Kate was boiling water for tea.

"Lila's lying down," she said, with a toss of her head.

Haynie nodded and moved toward their bedroom. At the door, he hesitated before entering. It suddenly occurred to him what was missing from his re-creation of the event. He was no longer uneasy.

Lila sat up quickly. Haynie saw a fleeting look of hope, gone the instant she saw that he was alone.

"I thought it was Kate with the tea," she said without conviction and slumped back.

Haynie sat beside her and gently laid a hand over hers. "You have to be strong," he said, "we both do."

"I'm trying. But, how can I be strong when I'm only half a person. I won't be whole again until my — until our son is home." She put one arm across her face as if to shut him out, "You didn't find anything, did you."

Haynie pulled her arm away from her eyes, forcing her to face him.

"You need to concentrate on what I'm going to ask you."

Lila propped herself on one elbow. "What? What is it?"

"You said you had fallen asleep – that you thought you heard something. Maybe the baby fussing."

She nodded.

He pointed to the bedroom door. "Could it have been someone opening this door?"

Lila shook her head. "It didn't sound like that. I lay still a minute or so after I woke, then I went to look in on him. I didn't hear anyone moving around."

Haynie got up, went to the door and gripped the knob. The lock gave a sharp click as he twisted; the hinges creaked as the door swung open.

"Do you think you would have heard that if someone had opened this door?"

She nodded. "Yes. I wasn't in a deep sleep. But, what does it mean?" Suddenly, tears were coursing down her cheeks and she drew a hand to her mouth.

"You are saying it's my fault – that I should have heard them — Oh, God."

Haynie ran back to the bed, grabbed her up in his arms, and shook her gently.

"Listen to me. Listen. That's not what I'm saying at all."

She stopped sobbing and looked at him, "It isn't?"

"Of course not. Think about it – you would have heard if anyone opened this door —" She nodded. "So that means they didn't look in here."

"I, I still don't understand."

"You weren't asleep very long —"

Lila nodded.

"They couldn't have been inside the house, but a very few minutes -"

"Not long at all."

"They didn't even look in here, but went right in and took Young Tench."

Lila fell back and began sobbing into the pillow. "And – they still have him," she cried.

"They never looked in here — how did they know which room he was in?"

"Maybe they just happened to look in that room, first. If they didn't find him, then they would have looked in here."

Haynie dismissed the notion. "They would know that a baby is not here alone. It's a small house. They would have to expect to be seen — unless they knew you were asleep. How could they know that?"

Kate Sipes cried out from beyond the closed door. "They found him. Young Tench is back."

Haynie reached the bedroom door just ahead of Lila and yanked it open. Kate set a cup of steaming tea on a small table and pointed through the window.

"There. See."

Lettie McKenna's covered buggy stood at the edge of the road. A glass enclosed Rockaway Coupe, drawn by one grey mare. Behind the glass, Young Tench was perched on his grandmother's lap. The Reverend Muse sat next to her holding the reins. All three were bundled under a down quilt.

Haynie, Lila and Kate ran onto the front porch. Kate stopped while Haynie and Lila continued on to the buggy. Lila, crying and laughing, opened the glass door and grabbed up her son.

"Oh, thank God," she cried, squeezing him tightly. "Thank, God – you're home."

Haynie held the buggy door open, smiling broadly. "Thank you, Mother," he said and nodded to Reverend Muse.

"Where did you find him?"

Muse glanced at Lettie and waited.

Lettie said, "What do you mean – find him – dear?"

"I mean – he had vanished from his bed – someone took him – where was he?"

Lettie looked bewildered. "He was with us, of course."

Haynie stepped back, looking from his mother to Josiah Muse, his face ashen. The joy he felt at the safe return of his son gave way to a throttling rage.

"Are you saying that you came into our house and carried our son out without a word to his mother?"

"Why, dear there was no time. Besides, we didn't wish to disturb her."

"No time for what?"

Lettie looked from Haynie to Lila and then back to her own son.

Lila glared at her mother-in-law.

Lettie removed the comforter from her lap and slid toward the carriage door.

"Dear, it's chilly out here, lets go inside," she said.

Haynie blocked her way. "No time for what?" he repeated.

Lettie McKenna eased back and pulled the down comforter up around her shoulders.

"I see that you're upset, dear, but I don't understand. After all, he is my own grandson."

Haynie shook his head. "I want to know what was so urgent that you and — this man — walked into our home and took our son."

Lettie glanced at Muse who sat unyielding, staring through the glass. She turned back to Haynie and Lila reaching to them with out stretched arms.

"We have given you both a great gift today. Hallelujah."

Lila tightened her hold on her son and turned her back. "I'm taking him in," she said.

"Dammit, Mother"

The Reverend Muse released the reins and wagged a finger at Haynie. “Here now, there’s no need to blaspheme, young man.”

Lettie patted Muse’s arm.

“Forgive him, dear. It will be all right after I tell him what a joyous thing has happened.”

Facing Haynie, her voice excited, Lettie said, “Lila had brought Young Tench to the manse shortly after noon dinner. The reverend was in his study reading the gospel. Just after they left – she said they were coming home to lay down – the reverend, God bless him, rushed out to tell me about a vision he had.”

Muse nodded encouragement and Lettie’s voice got stronger.

“He had been visited by an angel named Matthew, I think.”

Muse cut her off. “You must pay better attention, my dear.” He nodded to Haynie, “It was John The Baptist.”

“Sorry, my dear. John told the reverend that Young Tench must be baptized immediately, or risk losing his soul forever. Naturally, we were frightened and rushed out do John’s bidding.”

“Careful, my dear,” Muse admonished. “Saint John, The Baptist.”

Haynie looked from one to the other, grappling to comprehend what he was hearing.

“You two baptized our son without his mother and I, without bothering to tell anyone what you were doing?”

Lettie nodded, smiling. “It was no bother. We just took him down to the river.”

She pointed back down River Road. “You were taking ever so long to get it done. Now he is saved for all eternity.”

Haynie’s face was mottled with anger. “You immersed a baby in the Annemessex, in November? What the hell were you thinking?”

Muse looked askance while Lettie chose to ignore the curse word.

“Young Tench is blessed. Nothing can happen to him.”

Haynie reached across this mother, grabbed the Reverend Muse by the lapels, and wrenched him sprawling across Lettie’s lap. Haynie jerked the terrified minister, until their faces met.

“Hear me good, you son-of-a-bitch. If you ever touch my son again, even God will not be able to recognize you and the wolves won’t bother with the little that’s left.”

Muse twisted and pulled in a futile effort to free himself from Haynie’s awful grasp. After a moment, Haynie released his grip, shoving the stricken man back into his seat. Muse immediately grabbed the reins and pulled the horse around in a desperate effort to flee.

“Oh my, oh my,” Lettie repeated softly, her face ashen.

21

Tangier Sound, Chesapeake Bay
Friday, November 8, 1867

Two men, without face or form, struck him repeatedly with rifle butts. Landon Wallis opened his mouth to cry out, but made no sound. Searing pain stabbed at his back and thighs, while he struggled to cover his face and head with his arms.

Curses echoed through the swathe of sleep behind his eyes

"Get yer ass up, city boy."

Landon understood that he had been dreaming. The assault by two faceless men with rifle butts was in reality the ship's cook jabbing him repeatedly with the tines of a long handled oyster rake.

Around midnight, Landon had crawled behind a forward bulkhead in an effort to escape the sounds and smell of foul bodies sleeping in a confined space. While the captain and cook were housed in the warmth of the aft cabin, the rest of the crew slept below deck, on crude bunk beds built into the side of the ship. There were four bunks and five crewmen, so Landon had been told to find a place to sleep the best he could. He had stretched out on the hewn pine logs that formed the hull bottom, but exhausted as he was, his mind had quickened, alive with recollection of the day's terrors.

That morning, after Captain Jack had strode from the deck, Landon, afraid to move, stood trembling from fear and cold. The day was raw and heavily overcast, offering little hope of seeing a warming sun. A steady wind came out of the Northeast, stinging Landon with a salty mist collected from white caps along its path.

Greeley faced the other men. “You heard the captain, get that anchor up and hoist the main sail.” Turning back to Landon, he said, “Slick, you help Nails with the anchor.”

Landon remained in place, shaking.

“Get movin’,” said Greeley.

Landon, stiff with cold, fell to his knees as he tried to move across the pitching deck. The crewmembers hooted as they headed to their workstations. Greeley ignored the struggling Landon and moved aft along the rail with ease.

One of the crew, a skinny red headed lad, came to Landon’s side and helped him up. “You’ll be okay, soon as you get your sea legs. I’m Nails. We’d better get that anchor up before that sail gets full.”

Once underway, Nails identified the other crewmembers as Stick and Buckets. Each crewman wore a knitted cap pulled low to keep in the warmth.

Stick’s beard was a rich silky black, while Buckets, obviously the oldest of the three, showed streaks of gray competing with the brown. Nails’s own beard, a shade of rust, grew sparse and scraggly, doing little to mask deeply pock marked cheeks.

After securing the anchor, Landon followed Nails below deck where it was drier, though only a little warmer. He tried, unsuccessfully, to control another body tremor.

“I can’t seem to stop this shaking,” Landon apologized. “Is there an old coat, or something, I could wear? Anything at all would help.”

Nails shrugged. “We all wear everything we got,” he said.

Landon was afraid he would cry.

“Hold on.” Nails peeled off foul weather gear until he reached a bulky grey sweater.

“It’s got a coupla holes,” he said, as he pulled the sweater off, “but it’ll help.”

Landon tugged the sweater down over his thin jacket. “I won’t forget this, Nails. Thanks. Any gloves or mittens laying around?”

Nails shook his head. “Sorry.”

Buckets descended the bulkhead ladder and dropped into a bunk.

“You two get up on deck,” he said, flopping a forearm over his eyes.

“Aye, sir,” Nails replied, leading Landon up the ladder and onto the deck.

“What do we do now?” Landon asked.

"The captain's got the helm," Nails said, looking aft. "Stick is seeing to the dredging gear and Mister Greeley is likely in the cabin drinking coffee. So we need to be ready to man the rigging if captain needs us."

Nails nodded toward the stern. "Stick don't talk like us. Captain says he's a Polish. I'm not sure what that is, but Captain couldn't say his name exactly, so we call him Stick. "

Landon watched the low scudding clouds contesting with one another for dominance as they scurried along.

"Where we headed?"

Nails pointed off the starboard bow, indicating an irregular black line edging the horizon. "There. I 'spect we're headed to the north end of Tangier Sound. Real rich beds."

Landon scanned the deck, then leaning close to Nails said, "How long you been on this boat?"

Nails led Landon to the rail where they could both hold on as the boat pitched against the white capped swells.

"I was brought here same as you, by Jake Drumm."

He studied the look of surprise on Landon's face. "Been aboard since March."

Landon's stomach turned. "You mean, in all those months you couldn't get away?"

"Don't want to."

"What? Why?"

Nails rested his elbows on the rail and watched as the boat sheared through the leaden waves generating a trough of mist and foam.

"At first it was real tough, what with the cold and hard work. I thought about getting away, but they keep a real close eye on anyone they get from ole Drumm. Anytime we got close to a port, I was locked below. I never gave 'em no trouble, and now I'm sorta like one of them."

Landon asked, "So, now you can come and go as you please?"

"Not 'xactly. One day the captain come to me and says that I was one of the crew. Long as I behaved myself, I could go ashore, always with one or two of the others. Then he got his face right up into mine an' he says, 'Boy, you try to run away, or bring in the law, and I'll be obliged to kill you.' Voice real low and quiet, but I knew he fer damn sure meant it."

Nails watched Landon for a reaction, then turned back to the sea.

"By that time I'd been aboard a coupla months. It was gettin' warm and we had stopped oysterin'. Through the summer, we fish and catch them blue crabs. Why people pay good money for them ugly creatures is beyond me. Anyhow, the work was easier. And on a hot summer night, why nothin' beats sleeping up here on deck with only a big moon and all them stars fer covers."

"How can you let Jake Drumm get away with selling you to Captain Jack – like – like a damn Negra slave?"

Nails pushed back at arms length from the rail. "How old do you think I am?"

Landon looked him up and down, "I'd say, about my age, twenty or twenty one. But what difference –?"

"Just sixteen. I didn't get no cake with candles on my birthday from this crew. But, then I don't recollect a year when I got cake."

Landon turned his palms up and shrugged.

"What I'm tellin' you is, I'm better off on this boat than before I got took."

"It must have been real bad."

Nails nodded. "I come from just across the Rappahannock in Virginny. Like most folks there, the war took ever thing we had. Pa was killed at Shiloh and Ma just give up. After she passed, I moved around livin' off the land. Why, when them Drumm boys took me I was sittin' on a river bank tryin' to catch some supper with a piece a string and a bent nail."

Nails smiled, "Truth is, if they'd promised me some vittles I'd a followed 'em like a puppy. They couldn't have shooed me away."

Landon looked aft, at Captain Jack manning the helm. "He's a mean one. Is it 'cause I'm just a damn slave, or is it his way?"

"Near as I can figure," Nails said, "Captain Jack don't like nobody and don't trust nobody, 'cept maybe old Stew, the cook. You look under that slicker an' he's got a revolver stuck in his belt."

"A gun. Where does he keep it?

"On him."

"All the time?"

Nails nodded. "Sleeps with it. I told you, he doesn't trust nobody. Wouldn't be the first time a crew had broke into a captain's quarters, middle of the night, slit his throat and tossed him overboard. Why, just last month they found a forty foot erster boat aground up to Drum Point, at the mouth of the Patuxent. Boat stripped of anything worth a plug and the crew gone. A week later they found the captain's body floated ashore on Hog Island."

"Why don't any of you jump ship?"

"Where'd a body go? We don't know nothin' else. 'Sides, they're all the same out here."

He looked at Landon, "Better the devil ya know than one ya don't."

"This boat got a name?"

"*Fish Hawk.*"

"Say, anybody on board, besides us, sold to Captain Jack by Jake Drumm?

Nails dropped his head between his arms and studied the heaving deck.

Finally, Landon said, "Did you hear me? I said —"

"I heard ya. Nobody like that on board — now."

"But there was?"

Nails lifted his head and watched a seagull dive at the swells, then skim along the whitecaps before pulling up and veering toward the shoreline.

"It's not fair," he said. "A man is supposed to be smarter than a stupid old seagull, or a rock fish. Either one of them can get away from this boat, easy as you please, yet here we are two full growed men trapped on this floating jailhouse. Too scared to leave."

Landon shook his head. "But, you just said —"

Nails turned away, "I know what I said. I'm still scared. It's just that you and me – we're scared of different things."

Landon pressed on, "Which of the others did the Drumms bring out?"

"It wasn't none of these that I knows of. He was gone before I come aboard." Nails shrugged, "Dunno, maybe I took his place."

"Did they let him go or did he escape somehow?"

"They say, he drowned one night."

Landon waited.

"Even though a body is took by force and don't want to be here, there's a kind of unwritten rule, law of the sea, you might say. At the end of the oyster season, the captain is supposed to pay ya off and put ya ashore. Not ever body makes it to shore alive."

Landon paled.

"You wanted to hear it."

"Go ahead."

"It was the night before he was to get paid off —"

"What was his name?"

"I heard he was called Worm. I only know what Buckets told me. It was near morning, Worm was on deck, had the watch. Buckets said the deck was real slick and Worm wasn't payin' attention to the boom. It swung around, caught him full in the chest, and just slid him across the deck and over the side. Buckets, he laughs and says, 'Out here we call that, 'gettin' paid off at the boom.'"

Nails studied Landon's expression. "You see what that means," he said. "Not seen or heard of again."

"Didn't they try to save him?"

Nails shrugged.

Landon said, "Look here, that could just be a story they tell to a new man to scare him. Like you're doing me right now."

"That's what I thought, at first," Nails said, shaking his head. "Not now."

Landon thought for a minute, then said, "If they got a name for that kind of killin', it's been going on for a while."

Nails glanced aft, nodding to the captain at the helm, "I heard him telling Greeley that it's Drumm's doin' when a fella hasta get paid off at the boom."

"What's that mean?"

"He's saying that if a man that Drumm brings us don't earn his keep, then captain can't afford to pay Drumm and then pay the man off at the end."

"Doesn't give him the right to drown a man without cause. That's murder and – it's a sin."

"That's nuthin'," Nails said. "They's some ruthless captains and crews out here. Why, one captain had a couple of his men to sign on with another crew. They waited 'til the new boat was about full of catch, then the captain, he brought his boat alongside, likely in the night when one of his gang had the watch. Rest o' his crew stormed aboard, killed the other crew, stash 'em below, and sailed that boat on over to the buy boat. Sold the load and, after collectin' the money, they sail the new boat out into the bay, strip it and sink her along with her dead crew."

Landon stared. "That can't be true. It can't. Why, why that's out and out piracy. If it were true, somebody would be after these murders — these pirates. For one thing, why'd they sink a sound dredge boat. It's worth a lot of money. For another, men who got paid off and lived – got back ashore – those captains got to be afraid they will go straight to the law?"

Nails glanced around the deck, worried that Landon's words had carried on the wind. "Like I said, the captain is the law out here – the only law. You heard stories about the Wild West and how some sheriff or judge is the only law for miles — and runs ever thing? On the water, that's how the captain is."

"I know, but to think that they answer to no man is —"

"Boys, like you, sold to a captain, won't tell 'cause their glad to be done with it. Don't want no more trouble – maybe they're scared, or ashamed."

"But —"

"Suppose a body did go to the law, some small town along the shore, even Annapolis or Baltimore, and tell what was done to him."

Nails flung one hand toward the sea. "No land lawman can do nothin' out here. 'Sides, if one did come out here and ask what happened, you think any crew is gonna up an' say 'Oh yeah, that's what we done all right.'"

Landon opened his mouth, but Nails cut him off.

"As for pirates sinking a boat, well keepin' a stole boat is a good way to get caught. One o' these captains kept the boat he pirated. Him and his crew sailed around in both boats — like an admiral with his fleet in tow, ya might say. One day he sails both boats into a port over to Mobjack Bay. Well, sure as yer born that was the home port of the boat they stole. By then some of the crew had started floatin' into shore up north a ways, and word had got down to the families that the boat had likely sunk. Well, you can imagine the ruckus when that boat come sailing up to the pier with a whole different crew."

"What happened?"

"Well, them pirates excaped in their old boat while the townfolks was waitin' for the sheriff to come. The point is, the only way pirates is gonna be caught is to do something stupid like that. If they keep nothin' from the ship or crew, and stick to friendly ports, nobody'll stop them."

Landon was about to speak, when Nails called out.

"Look," he said, pointing toward the burgeoning shoreline. The boat was passing a large island just off the port bow headed toward an estuary protected by spits of land jutting into Tangier Sound.

"This cove is right at the mouth of the Nanticoke River," Nails said. Then waved a hand to starboard. "The Wicomico River branches off that away, just over there. We're headed to a rich oyster bed where both rivers pour in."

Captain Jack took one hand from the helm and yanked vigorously on a bell rope. The ensuing clanging brought the other crewmembers scrambling across the deck.

"Come on," Nails said.

Nails led Landon aft past the helm. Greeley was closing the cabin door as they neared the cabin.

"You two look sharp and man the drudge."

Without a backward glance, he moved toward the bow, shouting an order to lower the sails.

Nails stopped when they reached a wooden post set through the deck. Attached to the pole, about five feet above the deck was a u-shaped piece of iron, two feet wide. Between the iron points, a heavy wooden spool stood mounted on an iron axle. Coiled around the spool was a length of thick hemp, with one end secured to an oyster dredge resting on the deck.

Each end of the axle formed a long handled crank. Landon, familiar with the cruel looking mechanism, eyed it with fear and loathing. He had seen them on the oyster boats moored at his family's processing plant. He imagined a hand dragging the jagged iron spikes over his body, like some medieval torture device. Or, becoming tangled in the hemp-netting bag, struggling futilely at the bottom of the bay, pinned under the crushing weight of the iron dredge.

"Pay attention," Nails was saying, "or one of us could get hurt."

"Sorry."

"I was saying it takes two of us to heave this drudge overboard. Look out that you don't get tangled up in it or you'll go over with it. Then mind ya don't get caught up in the rope as it plays out over the side. Once it hits bottom, them jaws'll scrape up the ersters into that there rope sack. We wind 'er back up, dump 'em, and put 'er back down. "

Nails grabbed one end of the long handled crank.

"Mind this crank. If the drudge catches on somethin' while we're a crankin', that handle'll get yanked out o' yer hand and smash your arm before ya can blink."

Landon looked down at his hands, already stiff and red from the cold, and cursed under his breath. He could think of nothing to protect them from the icy water as they pulled the drudge aboard.

"How come one of them with gloves don't do this?" Landon asked.

"Bein' the newest, we get the worst job."

"What happens now?"

Nails said, "First, we wait for Captain Jack. He'll call out when he wants us to heave 'er over."

"What'll the others be doing while I'm freezing my hands off? Standin' by a hot stove drinking coffee?"

Nails pointed up, "See them clouds movin'. We got a off shore wind, so Captain Jack'll take her in as close to shore as we can get. Mister Greeley'll be at the bowsprit watchin' over the side for erster beds and markin' the depth. See there, the other boys are lowerin' the sails now. When Mister Greeley gives a shout, Captain will bring her about, hard. When she gets pointed back out to sea, the sails get hoisted and we heave the drudge overboard. It takes a powerful pullin' to drag this iron monster through them beds and come up with a full catch. Then we turn around and do 'er all again."

Landon studied the shoreline. The *Fish Hawk* had entered a sheltered inlet; fast approaching the mouth of the river Nails had called the Nanticoke. Up ahead, a hook of land poked into the cove, shielding the smaller Wicomico River from the open water. On every side, the terrain was a fusion of sprawling marshland, marked by its bounty of cordgrass and reeds leading to a tree line of loblolly pine.

Not a soul. No place to get help, even if I made it to shore. Anyone fool enough to be out in this God forsaken land, is more'n likely another waterman who'd keep me for himself, or sell me to someone else.

Landon was startled by a shout from the bow. The mate waved his arms, while the captain clanged the bell and spun the wheel as the *Fish Hawk* began coming about.

Nails said, "Grab hold here and get ready to heave this thing over the side."

They hunched over the dredge, awaiting the order from the captain, as the sails billowed.

Suddenly, Greeley whooped, pointing dead ahead. About one hundred yards out, two single masted log canoes maneuvered directly into the lane taken by the *Fish Hawk*.

Immediately, the crew began striking the sails to slow the boat.

"Belay that," bellowed Captain Jack. "Run 'em all the way up."

He glared at Nails and Landon. "You two — get over here."

Nails released his hold on the dredge and rushed to stand at attention before the captain, Landon close behind.

"Listen up lads, I want you holdin' that dredge, ready to pitch it over when I tell you. Likely, there'll be one of them tonger canoes alongside when you do."

Captain Jack looked hard at each man. "You do it exactly when I say, damn you, or I'll have you for mutiny. You know what that means. Now git."

They rushed across the deck to hunch down beside the dredge.

"Where'd they come from?" Landon asked. "They must of seen us go past and paddled out a purpose to get us to stop drudging here."

"I reckon."

"You know what happens, if we drop this dredge into one of those canoes, don't you?" Landon asked.

Nails gave a nod. “She’ll sink and them tongers’ll get drowned. But,” he added quickly, “mind, if them boys got a musket or shot gun. They might could shoot us before we get that monster up over the side.”

“Would you blame them?”

Nails peered over the side at the two canoes sitting mere yards ahead. “Oh, lordy, lordy I don’t want to kill nobody and I sure don’t want ta get shot, but, if we don’t do what the captain says, he’ll hang us. Oh, lordy, lordy.”

Landon shook Nails’s arm.

“Listen to me,” he said, “Captain Jack didn’t tell us to kill anyone, or even sink one of the canoes, so he can’t claim we’re mutineers if we don’t do it. He’s a smart one, if the law ever asked any questions, he could say he didn’t order us to kill anyone, as a matter of fact he warned us that a canoe might be alongside when we threw out the dredge.”

“I don’t know —”

“Here’s what we’re going to do. We’re back here almost to the stern. *Fish Hawk’s* running at a pretty good clip. If we don’t ram those canoes, they’ll only be alongside for a couple of seconds. We can stall, struggle with the dredge, even drop it once while lifting it up; you can blame me for that. When we get her up, we balance her on the top of the sideboards, and once past those canoes, we let her go. We follow orders and no one’s gonna get hurt.”

Captain Jack was shouting and gesturing, his back to the dredge. The off shore breeze took his words to the bow. Nails looked stricken until he realized that the Captain’s orders were directed at the crew on the starboard side. Landon left the dredge and ran to that side, Nails could not move.

Two of the crewmen tugged at the anchor rope, playing it out to lie loosely coiled on the deck. Greeley stood at the rail, next to the ponderous iron anchor tied off to the railing with a thick hemp rope.

The anchor was an iron shank, tall as a man, with a shaped crosspiece at the bottom and an iron handle welded near the top. The bottom piece curved up and away from the shaft on two sides, narrowing to form barbed, pointed ends, designed to gouge out a hold on the ocean floor.

With sails full, the *Fish Hawk* plunged forward, closing quickly on the canoes just ahead. Landon quaked at the thought of what was to happen. Two men were standing in the small boat, looking up and shaking their fists at the drudge boat looming over them.

Landon waved his arms frantically, and shouted in a vain effort to warn them off. Even if they heard him, it was too late for them.

Captain Jack swung the wheel hard to starboard and, as the *Fish Hawk* collided violently with the tonger's canoe on the starboard side, Greeley leaned over the side, cursing the two men, as he freed the anchor rope.

Landon gripped the rail and cried out, "No — please, God no," as the anchor fell away striking both men on its way to the bottom. One man had turned to shield his head and a barbed point dug into his back. It tore at him as would an iron spike driven with full force, before taking the canoe, and the two tongers, to the bottom.

Nails ran to the rail just as the banner on the canoe's mast disappeared below the water. He screamed, "What happened? Did we hit one of them?"

Landon turned to him, tears brimming in his eyes.

"The captain and mate of this ship, murdered those men —"

"What? Oh, lordy, no —"

"No different than if they had shot them in the back."

The ship shuddered and slowed as the anchor, and its burden, settled on the bottom. Now, Captain Jack cursed as he ran toward the bow.

"Come on," Nails yelled as he left the rail, "maybe we can help."

As they joined the others at the starboard bow, Captain Jack was yelling,

"Dammit, Greeley, what have ya done now?"

"Dropping anchor, Captain, as you ordered. Guess you was afraid we'd hit one of them boats."

Captain Jack looked around ensuring the entire crew was within hearing.

"Did I order you to sink that tonger tub?" All eyes fixed on Greeley.

"No, sir. Them little bitty boats are real hard to see. I didn't know it was there 'til it was too late."

Nails nodded, his expression confirmed that he was satisfied.

Landon wanted to shout out that the mate was a damn liar. Greeley had been looking straight into the faces of those men as they cursed him and the crew of the *Fish Hawk*.

Captain Jack looked to each crewman, his gaze staying on Landon. "Any man of you see it any different than what the mate said?"

Landon wanted to speak out, but he knew that it would change nothing, and, it was important that he not provoke the captain and crew.

When no one spoke out, Captain Jack continued. "Accidents happen. Nuthin' can be done about it. 'Sides, ever one knows that being a tonger in these times is real risky. Real risky." Then he turned to Greeley. "I am real het up if you ruined that anchor. It was nearly new."

"Aye Captain."

Captain Jack's attention was now drawn to the other tonger boat that had capsized in the *Fish Hawk's* wake. Two tongers propelled the craft toward the shoreline, their legs churning as they held on to the bobbing hull. They cursed the *Fish Hawk* and her crew as they floated off toward the shore, perhaps two hundred yards away.

Captain Jack glanced at Greeley. "What do you think, mate?"

Greeley shook his head. "They couldn't a seen nuthin'. 'Sides, it's us against them. And, there's more of us. "

"Their own fault," Buckets said, "damn fools was in our lane, a purpose."

Greeley watched the struggling men. "Don't sound like they want our help," he said.

"This is done then," Captain Jack said. "Mister Greeley, let's get underway."

That night, Landon had crawled behind a forward bulkhead, hoping for sleep and relief from the visions tormenting him. Now, as he fought off the oyster rake prodding him awake, he recalled that his last thought before falling asleep was — to trust no one on board the *Fish Hawk*. No one.

22

Port Tobacco, Maryland
Friday, November 8, 1867

H. J. Mooney sat astride Raider in front of the Port Tobacco telegraph office. Raider, an American Saddlebred with a sorrel coat and elegantly arched neck, stood sixteen hands. To trusted acquaintances, Mooney suggested that the name, Raider, honored their many forays together in the recent war.

The envelopes he held were addressed to Mister White. Both would be from Hollins as he was the only one who knew what name and telegraph office Mooney currently used. The requirement that he travel to Port Tobacco for his telegrams was nettlesome, but the need for security was paramount. And, the ride from Popes Creek offered time to imagine additional heroic deeds for he and Raider.

The first wire had been sent on Wednesday. It appeared to be a continuation of the cryptic message he received from Major Hollins on Monday, informing him that his inheritance would be available on the next day, Tuesday.

The wire he now held confirmed that the money had arrived, however, Hollins regretted that he could not make the trip to join him as planned.

Tragically, the son of a close friend is missing and has not returned home. I feel obliged to remain with the family until the matter is satisfactorily resolved. Will advise.

Brown

The second message was more disquieting than the first.

Events on the Eastern Shore have taken a decided downturn. Immediate action was required on a very serious matter and I was forced to make some strategic decisions in your stead.

I am dispatching a rider with a detailed account of the situation. He should reach you during the morning hours on Friday the 8th.

If, after reading the report, you agree that we should meet, I implore you to return to Baltimore, forthwith, as I am not free to leave at this time.

M. Brown

The message was distressing for several reasons. First, no mention was made of the ransom money. The whereabouts of that bag of money is the first thing Grace will demand to know.

Secondly, Hollins gave no hint as to the nature of the urgent matter on the Eastern Shore. Having no facts to work with, Mooney's imagination could run wild.

And it did.

Most distressing, was the likelihood that the rider from Baltimore would reach Magnolia Bluff ahead of his return. Grace would immediately open the pouch and be waiting with a flurry of questions and accusations he was unprepared to answer.

Raider summoned his remaining stamina as they crested the bluff to home. He veered sharply into the lane, galloped up the path and jerked to a stop at the veranda.

Once in the house, Mooney found Grace sitting ramrod straight in one of the wingback chairs. The contents of a mail pouch strewn across the low, wooden table in front of her. She grabbed up a single sheet of paper and waved it at him.

"What the hell is going on?"

"Perhaps you should take your medicine, dear, while I read what you have already read, then we can discuss it."

Grace moved to pick up her glass; next to it sat a half-empty wine bottle.

"This is all the medicine I need," she said, putting the glass to her lips.

Horace took a seat on the couch and reached for the papers.

She snatched them up, "Looks like your man, Hollins, has made a real mess of things," she challenged, withholding the documents from his outstretched hand. "Along with some bullshit excuse why he can't give us our money."

Mooney had vowed to remain under control whenever she lapsed into these humors, yet each recurrence required more effort on his part.

He withdrew his hand and, indicating the bottle, said, "Be a dear and fetch me a glass." Smiling, he added, "I too have had a hard day."

Grace stood and flung the papers at him. "Not as hard as you're going to have, I'll wager," she said, striding to the mahogany sideboard.

Mooney plucked the sheets from the air as they fluttered around him. There was a telegram from Mister Green on the Eastern Shore, another from Mister Black in Richmond and a two-page report from Hollins.

The message from Black was routine intelligence regarding political machinations in Virginia's state capitol. Hollins was the rebellion's man in Annapolis, but as Maryland's General Assembly was not in session, there was little need for him in the state capital.

Mooney read Green's telegram. If he deciphered it accurately, one of their enlisted men had killed a town lawman and freed two of their soldiers from jail. He smiled. This was the first skirmish in the second war of Southern rebellion.

Green mentioned having met with the new bailiff, describing the man as "devious" and "mulish" and recommended strong measures be taken, to deal with the problem before it got "out of hand".

Grace set a glass on the table, then turned her back, forcing him to retrieve the bottle and pour his own drink.

Mooney tasted the wine, found it an acceptable Cabernet and focused on Hollins's report. It supported Green's assessment of Crisfield's new bailiff.

Sir:

The escalation of action in the Tangier Sound campaign area is not necessarily to our advantage.

The new bailiff, McKenna, is coincidently the man that Wallis brought in to help find his son. He is a man who won't give up on a commitment. After all, he was in the Union army and saw first hand how one can prevail after experiencing years of calamity. Worse, he strikes me as an honest man and, therefore, untrustworthy.

This McKenna, already on a quest to learn who killed his father back in the '50s, now has the additional motivation of tracking down his predecessor's killers and finding the Wallis boy.

It was this McKenna who assisted in the capture of two of our troops in Crisfield. Couple this series of extraordinary events with the fact that McKenna now has the standing to pursue these matters with legal authority, and it is my judgment that he poses an immediate threat to our offensive in the Tangier Sound region.

It is in this context that I ordered Major Green to have this impediment removed, forthwith. To equivocate on this is to risk exposure of our entire network in that area.

The arrest of our soldiers and their subsequent rescue by our agent, has delayed getting orders to them for the immediate release of the Wallis boy. Until he is home, I must stay at the father's side to protect our interests.

Wallis is very appreciative of my efforts and has indicated that, after this is over, he will prevail on his many contacts in the state government, and submit my name for consideration as commander of that Oyster Navy being discussed in Annapolis. Such an appointment would be invaluable to our cause.

As to the ransom, I will turn it over to you at our next meeting.

Respectfully,
Major Brown

Mooney drained his glass, reached for the wine bottle and poured a generous drink.

Grace grabbed the bottle and studied the remainder with disgust. Putting the bottle to her lips, she emptied it.

"Pearl," she bellowed, "need another bottle in here."

Grace paced impatiently in front of the fireplace, awaiting her wine.

She said to Mooney, "What the hell do you plan to do about this mess?"

Pearl hurried toward her with an open bottle. "Don't be niggardly with this stuff," Grace sniffed, "it's manna in these troubled times."

A tight smile crossed Pearl's face, as Grace snatched the bottle from her hand.

"I insist," Grace said, refilling her glass, "that we leave at once, return to Baltimore and get our money before that scoundrel runs off with it."

She sat back in her chair, glaring across the table. "We are needed there. Why did you drag me down here anyway at this time of the year?"

Mooney was constrained from telling her the truth. He had always hated living in Baltimore. The house on Charles Street recalled to mind a clammy mausoleum, replete with vestiges of the late Isaiah Stringfellow.

Attending their circle's social events was added torture. Grace never refused an invitation to a gala evening, where she gleefully received compliments from gentlemen while their wives glared from off to one side.

Mooney saw the dark looks being exchanged and sensed that he was in danger of being unmasked. He was only comfortable during the formal balls he and Grace hosted at Magnolia Bluff, where all the men were officers of the rebellion and every woman kept to her place.

The increasing frequency and duration of Grace's mood swings, dictated that she was unable to function socially. At a recent soiree, she had gotten physical with their hostess for whom she had a particular dislike.

Of late, Mooney could never be certain what Grace might blurt out after some champagne. He enlisted Pearl's assistance in intercepting any envelopes coming to the house on Charles Street likely bearing an invitation to one of these potentially disastrous evenings.

Mooney saw to it that they spent more time here at Magnolia Bluff and less at their Baltimore mansion.

"In the first place," Mooney answered, "Hollins alerted us to the fact that it was young Wallis our men had captured. It was his idea to cash in by demanding a ransom. How can you not trust him?"

"Really. If Wallis relies so much on Hollins, how did he come to take on this McKenna, when your major was so opposed to it?"

Mooney felt his neck getting warm and fixed his attention on the report he held.

Grace's laugh was wicked. "I think you and Hollins spent too much time in the same tent," she said. "Perhaps, in the same cot."

23

Crisfield, Maryland
Friday, November 8, 1867

Haynie left the bailiff's office and proceeded down the stairs. Once outside, he paused to button his coat against the chill wind coming off the Little Annemessex River. At the foot of Goodsell's Alley, he stepped into Ellie's Island. At ten in the morning, the saloon was just opening for business. Mort, the bartender, gazed at the moose head over the door as he ran a bar rag over a row of beer glasses in front of him.

"Mort, you know where Gerhard is working today?" Haynie asked, disturbing the man's reverie.

The saloon's gas lamps were black and cold. Mort peered through the dim morning light trying to focus on the figure framed in the doorway.

"Oh, it's you, Bailiff. You lookin' for Stein?"

Haynie nodded.

"What day is it?"

"Friday, Mort. It's been Friday for several hours now."

"Oh, that's easy for you to say. Likely, you didn't work past two in the dark mornin' and told to be here at nine o'clock in the light mornin'. Well, I showed 'em," Mort said, slapping the rag hard against the bar, "I didn't get here 'til 'most nine-thirty."

Mort set his jaw, daring anyone to take issue with that statement.

Haynie waited patiently.

After a moment, Mort shook his head, shamefaced. “What was it you asked me about?”

“I need to find Stein. It’s important.”

Mort leaned his left hand on the bar and poked the air with the index finger of his right hand, his lips moved silently.

Looking at Haynie, Mort said, “These days all kind of run together, ya know. If I got this right, he was in here last night. Said he’d been out on one of them wood boats, all day. You know the ones haul cords of firewood in to town in the winter time?”

Haynie nodded.

“You know it gets real loud in here of a night and I was workin’ an......”

A woman’s voice hollered from somewhere in the back. “Who ever ya are, close the damn door. Ya born in a barn?”

Haynie stepped into the saloon and shut the door.

Mort rolled his head searching for the source of the shouting.

“Mort, what did he say about today?”

The bartender swung around with a blank look. “Who?–Oh, ya mean Gerhard, don’t ya?”

“Yes Mort.”

Mort resumed study of the moose, and then nodded with understanding. “Believe he said he would be workin’ over to Blades’s, unloadin’ freight wagons. Yes sir, Blades. ”

Haynie tipped his hat and turned to leave, “Thanks, Mort.”

“Bailiff,” Mort called.

Haynie stopped, his hand on the doorknob.

“If this is Friday, it’s gonna get real loud in here tonight.”

Haynie stepped out and closed the door. Crossing the plank street, he could hear the river lapping against the pilings beneath his feet.

As Haynie approached the general store, he recognized a horse tied to the store’s hitching post. He and Caleb had followed the same spavined grey plug out of town on Monday. At that moment, the door opened and the horse’s rider emerged from the store, wiping his mouth on a shirtsleeve. One hand held a brown glass medicine bottle; the other gripped the stock of the great Prussian rifle.

The narrow eyes stared straight ahead, never wavering. As he brushed past, an energy passed between them. Without the need for a look or a word, the stranger communicated a sense of menace to everyone in his presence.

In Haynie's mind, it was not a coincidence that Squire Towne was murdered after this man came to town. This was a dangerous man, a threat to the town; someone he would soon have to deal with.

The vast building, deep and narrow, was poorly lit. Once inside, Haynie headed toward the rear of the store, passing wooden barrels stood on end, sprouting axe handles and shovels. Shelves displayed men's work shirts and pants; others offered women's dresses and bonnets. Wooden tables bore tin plates, coffee pots and iron skillets.

Luther Blades stood at the back counter gingerly shoving chunks of split oak firewood into the pot-bellied stove that provided only enough heat to take some of the chill out of the air. The scarred counter top to Luther's right supported glass front cases displaying an array of ribbon, needles, threads and assorted sewing needs for those women who made their families clothes from the bolts of material arrayed along the back wall.

Approaching Blades, Haynie passed a display of wide mouth glass jars jammed with sticks of licorice, peppermint and assorted hard candy. He hesitated, moved past, grinned sheepishly at the storekeeper and stopped. He turned and plucked two peppermint sticks from their jar.

"For later," Haynie laughed, and set a two-cent coin on the counter. "Good for the digestion."

Luther Blades's appearance never changed. He seemed to possess only one set of clothes; baggy black britches, loosely hung from black suspenders, a collarless white shirt buttoned at the throat and a black vest, never buttoned. Out of doors, he added a black brimmed hat with a flat crown, his shoulders draped with a black cloak.

Blades's frame was sparse, all bones and neck leading to a narrow face and bald, bony skull, barren above the eyebrows. His high waisted britches ended several inches above his shoe tops. He scooped Haynie's coin into a palm and slid it into the cash drawer.

"Luther, you know that fella leaving when I came through the front door?"

Luther shook his head, "Can't say as I know him. He ain't much of a talker. Scary lookin'. Comes in couple times a week for tincture of opium, little coffee and tobacco."

"Laudanum. He in pain?"

Blades shrugged. "Hard to tell. Could be he has that 'soldiers disease.' Maybe got wounded in the war, they give him opium and now he just likes it."

"Anything else odd about him?"

Blades pulled on his chin, making his face seem longer. “Seems like there is sumthin — yep. Daggone if I know how I forgot it. Guess, ’cause it’s been a while. Anyways, when he first come around, said he’d be stayin’ in the area and would need bullets for that damn big gun he’s always totin’. Well, sir, he asked, no, more like – ordered – me to get some. Never seen him without that big gun. Shows it off to anyone in the store. Doesn’t threaten with it, sure sets folks back though. ’Specially the women.”

Luther began setting spools of ribbon on the counter while he talked.

“Seventy-two caliber. No call for that big a bullet around here, ’cept from him. Ordered two boxes. Got real angry like when I told him he’d hafta pay ahead, it bein’ a special order and all. I got a little fidgety, what with him glarin’ at me and wavin’ that thing around. Just to be talkin’, I asked him what he was gonna do with ’em. I didn’t mean nuthin’ by it. He kept glarin’ at me with them wicked eyes ’til I was sorry I asked, then he said, ‘huntin’. Threw the money on the counter and walked out. Just like that, ‘huntin’, and walked out.”

Luther looked up from his work, “Can’t figure what he’d be huntin’ around here, ya know. Be nuthing left of a dove, er rabbit er pheasant, gets hit by one o’ them damn big bullets. Don’t need nuthin’ near that big even for deer. You any idea what he might be hunting?”

“Hard to say.”

“Claims he shot the buffalo used to make that ratty old hide robe he wears. Brought it down at more’n a hunnert yards, says he, with one shot from that gun. Say, ya don’t suppose he thinks there’ s buffalo around here, do ya?”

Haynie ignored the question. “Did he say where he’s stayin’ or how long he’s gonna be around?”

Luther shook his head. “Like I said, not much of a talker, ’cept about that long gun and what a crack shot he is. From the provisions he gets, I’d say he’s livin’ out in the woods somewheres. He wanted for somethin’?”

“Don’t know — yet.” Haynie nodded toward a door leading to the stockroom. “Gerhard back there?”

“Yep. Go on back and see if you can get him to stop a minute. Man’s a working fool. Works like them perpetual machines are supposed to. Never stops.”

Haynie stepped through the doorway as Gerhard Stein came from the back alley carrying three large cartons. Though a chill breeze swept through the unheated storeroom, Stein was clad in light work pants and a thin, collarless white shirt.

"This like summer in Prussia," Stein always responded to comments about him "catching his death" or "sure to get the grippe." Haynie shivered inside his coat and motioned Stein to stop.

Stein smiled warmly, "*Guten tag, meine freund*," he said hurrying over as Haynie braced himself against the inevitable bear hug.

Hands at his sides, Haynie offered no resistance as Stein wrapped him in massive arms and lifted him clear of the floor. After returning Haynie gently to a standing position, Stein stepped back, his smile fading.

"You are troubled, yes?"

Haynie walked to a wooden crate labeled "Implements". Satisfied that it would hold his weight, he perched himself on it with one leg resting on the floor. Stein towered over Haynie, making him uncomfortable.

"Gerhard, please, sit."

Stein glanced at the closed door.

"*Is gut.*" Haynie said. "It's allowed for you to sit. Luther thinks you work too hard anyway."

Stein's body language said he did not agree as he slumped onto an adjoining crate.

"Is about the two men killed *gestern* – yesterday – on the *wasser,* yes?"

Haynie shook his head. "No. I want to hear about that, but first I want to know if you have found the man who was in Ellie's talking about being a shanghai."

"*Nein*. Sorry."

"You keep watching for him. It's still important. Now, tell me about the men. Where did it happen?"

Gerhard held out two fingers, "You not know about *zwei* tongers who are died at mouth of nanny goat river? But, you *polizeichef*."

"I have no authority out there. Only in the town – *stadt* – of Crisfield," Haynie waved his hand, "not in the county."

Suppressing a smile, Haynie added, "And, Gerhard, it's the Nan-ti-coke, Nanticoke River, not nanny goat."

Stein nodded.

"What happened?"

"Yesterday I work on wood boat. We at Ellis Bay, where Wi-co-mi-co," he paused.

"Wicomico River. *Sehr gut*."

Gerhard continued, "Wi-co-mi-co and Nan-ti-coke come out."

"Go on."

"Boat loaded. We going close near the land, heading for this *stadt*."

"Crisfield."

"We see *zwei* – two – men try for land. Boat go over," Stein flailed about with both arms, "two men fighting."

Haynie balled his fists and made short jabbing motions,

"The two men were fighting each other?"

Gerhard shook his head emphatically, "*Nein*. Fighting *wasser*."

"They were struggling —"

"Ya – struggle with *wasser."*

"To keep from drowning."

Gerhard nodded, "*Klieder* — clothes – heavy – wet. *Wasser sehr kalt."*

"Yes, very cold. What happened to their boat?"

"Boat go over." Stein made a flip-flop motion with one hand. "They try push it, but mast get caught on bottom."

Haynie nodded.

"We pull them on our boat. They *sehr* mad. Yelling and waving arms at big boat sailing out to big *wasser*." Stein shielded his eyes, "We can only see big boat. Almost gone."

"Into the sound."

"Two mens in one small boat to get oyster, other two men in small boat do same," Stein smashed a huge fist into the palm of his other hand, "when big boat sails into them. They say big boat *anker* fall into other small boat and two men go under *wasser*."

"Go on."

"After we get two mens onto our boat, we go out to where they say and see men who died lay on *wasser* —"

"Floating."

Stein held up one hand flat palm down "Ya, floating. We get them on boat." Gerhard held up four fingers, "and take all men to house."

Gerhard sat in silence while Haynie pondered what had he had just learned.

"Sounds like a drudge boat poaching in tonger beds," he said. "Did they see a name on the big boat?"

"*Ja — Fish Hawk."*

24

Crisfield, Maryland
Friday, November 8, 1867

Haynie McKenna stood on the porch of the Manor House, rooted in place by despair. His mother's fanatical devotion to the Reverend Muse coupled with Muse's religious ranting, had driven Caleb from the house. More recently, she had taken Young Tench from Haynie's home, and assisted, *no, enabled,* this spurious clergyman to perform a dubious religious rite on his son. All without a whit of remorse. When they drove away, she had nothing to offer except "Oh my."

With little expectation that what he was about to tell her would change her mind, Haynie knew he would always regret saying nothing. If this didn't work, he had one other recourse.

He had considered getting Muse alone; telling the *little bastard* what he now knew, then demand that Muse leave his mother and the Manor House forthwith. The report from Delaware, offered little hope that this tack would work. Muse was described as "an experienced confidence man" who had "victimized numerous women" as far away as New York City, leaving only when he had drained them of their assets.

As far as Haynie knew, his mother still controlled the deed to this house and the property within. She had, however, been easily convinced to dispose of his father's fiddle; would it take much more for her to give up her home?

That the fiddle was cherished by Tench McKenna, and now Caleb, counted for nothing in the face of Muse's unction. Haynie feared that soon, maybe very soon, his mother, unable resist to Muse, would give up everything to support his specious ministry.

"This man," the Wilmington authorities reported, "has been known as, Doctor Muse, Reverend Bishop, Colonel Johnson and Doctor Bishop Johnson. He has appeared in the uniform of either a Confederate or Union army officer when necessary for his scheme. Bishop/Johnson/Muse is quite accomplished at convincing his victims that he is either, a former army officer who now uses his meager savings to proselytize among the American Indians, a medical doctor battling the plague, or other ominous illness in Mexico or Africa, a missionary minister saving souls far and wide.

To date only one of his known victims has brought charges, making New York City unavailable to him. Of the remaining women, one wept as she told how bravely the doctor had died of the plague in a far off land; another shuddered when she related that Colonel Johnson had been 'scalped by Indians.' Those women to whom Bishop/Johnson/Muse did not have himself reported dead, believe he is off devoting himself to whichever cause he spun to them and that he will, in the end, return so that they may live happily ever after."

Haynie was certain that, to Muse, Lettie McKenna provided a safe haven while he convinced her to make the Manor House his pastoral manse.

Haynie felt compelled to knock before entering.

This was my home for many years and I'm damned if I'll knock, he thought and opened the door.

The late November afternoon left the interior of the house dim and chilled, giving it the look and feel of abandonment. Muse's puritanical ravings had driven away the last of the borders, leaving him to continue his seduction unfettered.

The rhythmical ticking of the big grandfather clock in the next room was disquieting in the emptiness. He found his mother seated at the table, in the small dining room, a lone candle barely penetrating the gloom around her. She seemed so tiny, huddled deep into a down comforter stripped from one of the empty beds upstairs. A book lay open on the table next to the candle.

As she turned a page Haynie said, "Mother, why are you trying to read in this dismal light? It will ruin your eyes."

Her head turned and she peered over her reading glasses. "Haynie. Is that you?" Her voice was flat, without feeling.

"Yes, Mother. I want to talk with you. I'll ask Callie to bring us some tea."

Lettie returned her attention to the book, a bible larger and not so worn as their old family bible.

She said. "Callie's gone."

He understood that his mother could no longer afford to keep Callie on. Still, the Negress had been like part of their family for as long as he could remember, it must have pained his mother deeply to see her leave.

"I didn't know. Where did she go?

"She has family in one of the Carolinas." Lettie looked at him and said, "You know, she wasn't a very good Christian."

"Why don't you light another candle and I'll start a fire in the stove and make us some tea."

"It is surely a sin to be wasteful."

"It may be, but —"

"Why should I burn two candles, when I can get by with one? Wasteful. Proverbs teaches us that the diligent make wise use of their resources; the lazy waste them."

Haynie moved closer, "What about some hot tea, Mother."

Lettie shook her head. "I know you don't abide tea and offer it solely for my pleasure. I don't deserve to be indulged. Besides, I would rather share what I have with the reverend."

Haynie pulled out a chair and sat across the corner of the table from her.

She asked, "Did you know he wouldn't be here? Is that why you came now?"

"I know his boat is not moored at the dock."

She smiled. "He is out 'foraging for souls' as he likes to say. Won't be home for a few days."

Haynie leaned toward her, fingers tightly interlocked, arms resting on the table.

"I hate having to do this, but, there are things you should know about Muse's past."

Lettie brought a frail hand from beneath the comforter and rested it on her son's clenched fingers. "We are both prepared to forgive you. It is not your fault. It is the demons."

Haynie could think of nothing to say.

"Of course, you don't know because you haven't been listening to the reverend. Demons are fallen angels who aide Satan in his revolt against

God. These evil spirits tempt people to sin. You and Caleb are both possessed; your sins are evidence of the demon's influence."

"Which sins is that, mother?"

"Oh my, there are so many."

Haynie, curious as to what she now considered a sin said, "How can I repent if I don't know how I have sinned?"

She patted his arm. "Of course. I'm so pleased you see it that way." Turning her eyes to the ceiling, she intoned "Hallelujah."

Facing her son again she said, "You must talk to the reverend for redemption, he has a complete list. I know it includes your blasphemy; your lust for violence and killing of other men; drinking of alcohol; worship of false idols; your life style. Dancing and frolicking are sinful.

"As for Caleb, he is younger, and living like he does, is not as tempted as you; still his demons are at work. His love for that evil fiddle is evidence of that. "

Haynie, resisting the impulse to mount an argument against each sin said, "Mother, do you know a Reverend Bishop?" She shook her head and he continued, "How about a Doctor Bishop Johnson, or Colonel Johnson?"

"I'm afraid not. Should I?"

"These are all names your reverend used when he victimized other women, much like you. Women he has fleeced of their savings and then left to cry alone. I'm sorry, but he's not an ordained minister, or a doctor; he's a confidence man."

Lettie McKenna showed no anger; instead, compassion for her misguided son was evident. "Men like Reverend Muse have been persecuted and hounded for their beliefs since the time of Jesus. Jesus, himself, said to them, 'and everyone will hate you for your allegiance to me.' And it has come to pass."

She removed her hand and, turning her palms up, continued. "Even if what you say were true, it's meaningless. The doctor has accepted Jesus Christ and lives only to spread the Good News about our salvation through Him, and His return. We have all sinned, it is only important that we seek salvation through Christ. It is not enough to know of Jesus, or even believe that he is the Son of God, you must also have the faith to follow and obey him. This, Doctor Muse has done and his sins have been forgiven, just as your sins and Caleb's can be forgiven as soon as you both see the light. You must act at once."

Haynie stirred, anger and frustration replacing rationality.

"You keep saying that," he snapped. "Couldn't wait to baptize Young Tench; Caleb and I must act quickly. What's the rush?"

"The Second coming is near. We must be prepared."

"How —?"

"The signs. They are all around us. The Bible says that before the Second Coming, The Good News must be preached in all lands. The Reverend Muse and other missionaries are doing just that. 'Brother will betray brother to the death and fathers will betray their own children.' We saw this in that awful war. 'Children will rise against their own parents'." She looked up, "You and Caleb. You both resist me."

She nodded her head. "Demons. You must be thankful that we have saved Young Tench. It was the demons that kept you from seeing the light."

She looked into the gloom. "It's true, just as he said. I should never have doubted. I was a Doubting Thomas. It is a terrible thing."

"What are you saying, mother?"

"The Reverend prophesied that Satan would send a messenger to me with a tale of lies, and I doubted him. What he failed to tell me was that Satan's messenger would be my own son."

25

Ape Hole Creek
Somerset County, Maryland
Saturday, November 9, 1867

Jake Drumm slammed his whiskey glass on the table sloshing precious drops in the process.

"Damn it, Roy, damnit, now see what you made me do," he snarled, swiping a finger through the liquid, then licking it dry.

Rodney Drumm glanced hastily around the cramped cabin. "You drunk or somethin'? I'm the only one here; you sent Roy into town 'cause you and me can't show our faces. That's why we laid up in this creek."

Jake reached for the bottle and filled his glass. "No, I ain't drunk, you idiot. But, it's Roy's fault I spilt my whiskey. If he'd got hisself back here like he was told, I wouldn't had to go and do that."

Rodney studied that for a moment then shrugged and said, "I reckon you'll see to it that he's sorry about it when he does come in."

"Damn straight."

Jake took a long drink and smacked his lips.

Rodney said, "It's been a long time since Roy's been to town. Likely he's had trouble finding ever thing you tole him to get."

Jake straightened, giving his brother a hard look. "I didn't tell him to take the whole damn day, now, did I?"

Rodney looked into his own drink and shook his head.

"Now, Rod you know what happens when you argue with me."

Rodney Drumm nodded without looking up.

Jake went on, "I have to take time away from my drinkin' to knock you down. If I have to put my glass down to whip you, it takes all the fun out of it."

"Sorry Jake."

"'Sides, we should be talkin' about how we're gonna get rich."

Rodney raised his glass in salute and swallowed a mouthful of whiskey.

Jake smiled. "Then we'll buy us a nigger to do all our chores and fetch us our whiskey," he said.

"I don't think they is for sale anymore, Jake."

Jake scowled.

Rodney brightened. "If I had my say, I'd get me another pair of britches."

"Jesus Rod, Jesus. You're thinkin' small, boy. Small. When we hit it big, we'll all get new britches with plenty left over for the nigger."

Rodney hesitated, deciding if he was supposed to already know the answer, "What are we hittin' big, Jake?"

Jake leaned back in his chair carefully pulling his glass across the table toward him. "Pearls," he said.

"Pearls?"

"You heard me right, Rod. Pearls. You know what they is, don'tcha?"

"Course I do. They's them little stones rich women wear on a string around theys necks."

"Stones! They ain't stones. Fer Chrissake, Rod. You even know where they come from?"

Rodney Drumm thought a minute, shrugged and said. "I never studied on it. I guess theys laying around – amongst the other stones."

Jake leaned his chair back on two legs, tilted his head back and roared. "Jesus, Rod, Jesus, how'd you get so stupid?"

Rodney felt his face and neck heating up, but thought better of saying anything that Jake might take as sass. "Sorry Jake."

"If you went out on deck and looked over the side there's likely a bunch of 'em on the bottom of this here creek bed."

Rodney stared at Jake, "How come this is the first I heard about these here pearls, if theys been right there all along?"

"'Cause it's a secret. Most folks don't know about it. The bastards who sell 'em, want a body to believe they come from far away – over to Jap an, such places as that. That a way they can make the rich bitches pay more."

"But, they really come from right here?"

Jake nodded. “Ever so many of these oysters which get dragged off the bottom has one of these pearls inside it. No tellin’ how many of ’em they is in a boat load.”

“How come it is that these tongers around here keep so poorly, if ever boat load has enough of these here pearls to make ’em rich?”

“They’re dumb is why. Years ago, the tongers who first found these pearls hidin’ inside an eryster, tried sellin’ up to Baltimore. Well sir, the city boys was too smart for ’em. Told ’em that their pearls weren’t worth nuthin’. And, the tongers, they believed it.”

Rodney sat motionless, dumfounded by what he was hearing. “How come you know about it?”

Jake motioned him to pay close attention.

Rodney, figuring Jake wanted him closer for easier slapping, busied himself pouring a drink.

Jake said, “Another captain who sails regular to Baltimore Towne told me that all these packin’ houses has got secret rooms where the pearl oysters get took to. Shuckers who work in these rooms are sworn to never tell no one, on penalty of death. These rooms are run by real rough looking men, men like me, to see that no pearls fall into a shucker’s pocket but get turned in to the company.”

Rodney nodded. “So, you and me and Roy is gonna get hired into one of them rooms and steal the pearls from the shuckers. Right Jake?”

“Jesus, Rod, Jesus. There ya go thinkin’ small again. We can’t get rich stealin’ a few pearls from some fool oyster shuckers. Damn good thing you ain’t in charge of us, we’d be done fer sure.”

Rodney gritted his teeth, grabbed the whiskey bottle off the table and put it to his lips. The heat from the alcohol radiated through his chest and back, quickly reaching his neck and flushing his face.

“And you doin’ such a real good job of it,” he growled. “They’s huntin’ us for a murder we didn’t do, nor want done, and we daren’t go near town.”

Jake jammed a thumb in his own chest. “That weren’t my doin’,” he shot back. “That was that damn Reb, Rat.”

Jake eased back and took a quick drink. “Look here, Rod, we three Drumms are all we got. We’re family and family sticks together.”

Jake poked a finger in the air. “We stick together and follow my plan, we can hit ’er big. Then we’ll head off, somewheres nobody knows us.”

“Now that there is a plan, Jake. A damn good one. I want shut of this place. How ’bout we leave as soon as Roy gets back.”

Jake was silent, his head shaking slowly as he stared at Rodney. The smile faded from Rodney's face and he diverted his eyes to the table, then the floor.

Rodney, unable to endure the silence, blurted out, "What'd I do now? I said it were a good plan."

"Jesus, Rod, Jesus. That weren't the plan at all. It were just the idea. Don't you know the difference between a idea and a plan? The plan is how a body gets to the idea. Our idea is to get rich and leave, the plan is how we do, it. We can't run off when Roy gets back 'cause we ain't rich yet. You unnerstand?"

"'Course I do, now. If you'd put it thataway in the first place, I'd a knowd right off. Tell me the plan."

"We need to get our hands on a mess of them pearls and real quick too. I reckoned we could catch our own batch, but we don't have the tools fer it and this here tub is too small to hold enough to get us rich. 'Sides it's a lot of work — that's not our style."

Rodney nodded.

"So, we have to take someone's load and get the pearls out of it."

"How we gonna do that, Jake?"

Jake chortled and swallowed some whiskey. "This is where the plan starts," he said, then paused a long moment for effect. "We wait around a oyster bed at the mouth of one of the big rivers, maybe the Big Annie, pretendin' to be tongers ourselves. About the time when one of them tongers is fixin to leave with a full load of pearls, we come along side, hit him in his head and take the boat."

"Sometimes, there's two of 'em in one boat. Did you think about that?"

"'Course I did, you idiot. We hit 'em both in the head."

"What happens when them tongers wake up?"

"Jesus, Rod, Jesus. We dump 'em over the side. If they wake up 'fore they are drowned, they'll have to swim for it."

Rodney looked stricken. "Chrissakes, Jake. If they drown that would be murder. We'd be killers."

"They already got us down for killin' that lawman. They can only hang us once, Rod."

Rodney jumped up, his chair skittering into the cabin wall. "They can't hang us, Jake." he cried. "We didn't do that one. It were Rat. We're not killers. I didn't even shoot nobody in the war — that I know of. If I did, it were on an accident."

"Face it Rod, ever body knows we was there 'fore that fat lawman was kilt, and we was gone, afterwards. Nobody – but us – knows Rat was there. Oh they catch us, they's gonna hang us all right. That's why we gotta follow the plan and then get outta here. We got no time to fret over a couple of tongers who might get in our way."

Rodney sat heavily, hands shaking, his right leg trembling hard against the table leg.

Jake grabbed the wobbling whiskey bottle. "Watch, you don't be spilling this juice."

"If'n we only hit 'em in the head, and they is still alive when we leave out o' there, then what happens to them after we're gone, ain't no fault of ours. Is it, Jake? Then we ain't killers, right Jake?"

"'Course we ain't killers, Rod. We just run on a spell of bad luck, is all. We get to a new place, maybe out west sommers, our luck'll change, for sure. I hear Californy is nice. Would you like to see, Californy, Rod?"

Rodney fidgeted in his chair, then looked straight at his brother.

"After we get this load of oysters," he said, "who's gonna get them pearls out? Likely that's what you got me and Roy along for."

"You don't give me no credit for nuthin', do ya? I got that took care of too."

"I'm listenin'."

"I know a couple of negra boys up along the Big Anny, we'll get them to open up them erysters and we'll be right there to make sure they don't help themselves to our pearls."

"What's in it for them?"

"They can have the damn oysters for themselves; we sure as hell ain't takin' ''em with us."

Jake laughed. "Ya know them boys'll think they died and gone on to white man's heaven, havin' all them oysters to eat. Personal, it's the same to me as eatin' snot."

Rodney tried to laugh along with Jake, but failed. "When do you figure we're gonna do 'er, Jake?"

"The sooner, the better."

26

Somerset County, Maryland
Saturday, November 9, 1867

Neither George Noch nor any other member of the town council had given Haynie instruction as to the number of hours of the day, or week, he was required to devote to his job. He had no idea at what hour Squire Towne took a seat at his desk, or when he ended his day. It had occurred to him that Cecil would likely know, but he reckoned asking a town drunk to set his hours was unseemly.

Haynie reasoned that the position of town bailiff could have no fixed schedule. He might be needed at any time of the day or night. Squire had been killed in the early morning taking some breakfast to prisoners. Cecil, the drunk, had likely been arrested late the night before. Though, with Cecil, it could have been much earlier in the day. One man could not be available every night to light the street lamps and quell fights, and every day to meet the trains and sell dog licenses. He was also needed at home.

Haynie had posted a schedule of office hours for Tuesday mornings and Thursday afternoons, when he would be available to sell licenses and listen to folks' troubles. He published nothing about his night hours, so as not to inform trouble makers when he would *not* be in their midst.

Historically, Friday and Saturday nights saw the streets and alleys of Crisfield overrun with watermen, proggers, gandy dancers, loggers and farm hands, each in a frenzy to obscure the past week and fend off the one coming. They elbowed their way among the saloons and dance halls along Goodsell's Alley, and into the sprawling waterfront warehouses for prizefights and brawling. Most of these men were even-tempered enough, interested only in their particular version of a good time. Very few wanted any trouble, but often that's all it took to stir up some.

Haynie had decided that on those two days, Friday and Saturday, he would be home until the early afternoon and walking the streets of Crisfield late into the night.

Consequently, he was in the parlor playing peek-a-boo with Young Tench on Saturday morning when someone rapped timidly on the front door. Haynie opened the door and there stood a sunken, old man, bare headed and shivering. Above a thin fringe of white hair, protruded a boney skull the color of watery white wash, in sharp contrast to the cordovan color of the weathered face below. The old man held a crumpled hat in clenched fists, cold tears stung his eyes as he looked up at Haynie.

"Oh, Mister Haynie. I'm real sorry to say it. There's no other way," he mumbled. "— Young Caleb's layin' dead over to the marsh around Colbourn Crick."

Haynie stared, legs quivering. Gripping the front door for support, he staggered to a ladder-back chair nearby. After sinking onto the chair, he cradled his head in his hands and stared at the floor, groaning softly.

The old man hesitated at the open doorway, anguish deeply etched about the eyes.

Young Tench crawled toward his father, fussing as he worked his way across the bare floor.

Lila McKenna appeared in the entryway of the dining room, drying her hands on a small towel.

"Where is that cold air coming from?" she asked before seeing the form through the open door. Her eyes moved from the man's face to her husband slumped in the chair, hands cradling his head.

"What's happened?" she asked as she scooped Young Tench from the drafty floor.

Neither man spoke. Haynie appeared not to have heard, while the old man dropped his gaze to the porch floor and shuffled his feet.

Lila gestured through the doorway. "Sir, please come in so we can close this door."

The stranger stepped hesitantly into the room, both hands furiously working the hat they held. "Thank ya, ma'am. I've not had the pleasure."

Both looked to Haynie who had not heard their words.

"I'm Lila McKenna."

"Yes, ma'am. The name's Gumps."

Lila studied his face. Dried tears smeared the dirt in the hollows around his eyes and down his cheeks. His body shuddered.

She said, "Though we've not met, I know the name."

She took a deep breath and asked, "Has something happened to Caleb?"

Haynie raised his head, his voice booming loudly in the small room, "He's dead. Caleb's dead," then dropped his face into his hands.

Lila looked quickly at Gumps who nodded silently. "Forgive me, Mister Gumps —"

"Just Gumps, Missus. Everyone calls me Gumps."

Lila nodded and tilted her head toward the next room. "Please go sit down at the dining table. I'll put Young Tench in his bed and fetch some coffee. Painful as it is, we must know every detail of what happened."

Gumps nodded and crossed into the cramped dining area where he hesitated to be the first seated. Living outdoors as he did, Gumps was always ill at ease inside a home, particularly in the dining room with all of its inherent social graces. The mister always had a special chair, and Gumps wasn't going to chance picking it. He waited for the missus to show him where to sit.

Lila appeared in the doorway carrying a wooden tray laden with saucers, cups, biscuits, a pitcher of cream and a sugar bowl. She set the tray in the center of the dining table as Haynie shambled to the table and slumped heavily into a chair.

Lila nodded toward a chair, "Please sit and I'll be right back with the coffee."

"Yes'um," Gumps said, settling awkwardly into the chair opposite Haynie.

Gumps waited timorously as Lila returned and poured coffee into each cup. Then he grabbed two biscuits from the plate, broke one in half and sloshed it in his drink. His face hovered just above the steaming mug as he guided the dripping pastry into his mouth, careful not to lose so much as a crumb in the process. Gumps looked up to see Lila watching him as she sipped her coffee.

"Sorry ma'am. Hope you'll forgive an old progger, but these biscuits are mighty good and that hot coffee sure hits the spot." Gumps hung his head, "I ain't et nuthin' since yestiddy, else —"

"You are family, here," Lila said. "No reason to feel abashed."

Gumps smiled, revealing but three yellowing teeth set into red, inflamed gums. Though ignorant of her meaning, he was comforted by her smile and warm tone of voice.

Lila laid a hand gently on her husband's arm and spoke softly. Haynie stirred in his chair, looked at the mug of coffee in front of him and raised it to his mouth. He drank deeply of the hot coffee, sweetened with honey, just the way he liked it. Setting the mug down, Haynie shook his head and gazed around before focusing on Gumps, as if realizing for the first time that the old man was in the room.

"I'm ready to hear it now," he said.

Gumps shoved the rest of the biscuit in his mouth and reached for the mug with shaking hands. Hot coffee slopped down the sides, staining the tablecloth. He mumbled an apology and proceeded to get the mug to his lips, ignoring the steam as he slurped the strong liquid.

After returning the mug to the table, Gumps pulled a ragged sleeve across his mouth, cleared his throat, and said, "First off, what happened weren't my fault. I loved that boy like kin, and I already wished a thousand times that it was me layin' there instead."

Gumps looked up, as if to the sky, "It weren't meant to be."

Lila nodded and reached out to pat his hand. Haynie waited.

The old woodsman looked Haynie in the eyes as he spoke, palpably searching for someone with whom to share the blame for what he was about to say.

"The boy had been a pesterin' me to get out and look for an old fort I had seed a while back, but couldn't 'member where t'was. He kept sayin' how it could be real important to you; that we might find some folks that had been shanghaied, or some such." Gumps paused as he peered into his nearly empty coffee mug, nodding as Lila refilled it from the pot in front of her.

Gumps raised the mug, "The boy near worshiped you," he said. "Believe he figured if he could find that prison place, you'd be as proud of him as he was of you. Said you was a war hero, and now, a real lawman. I don't know if you did anything special in the war. But that don't matter, bein' in it and fighting all those battles makes you a hero as I see it, so he got no argument from me."

Haynie shifted uncomfortably in his chair, his jaws grinding under drawn cheeks.

Gumps continued. "Like I was sayin', I couldn't rightly recollect where this old fort was. Didn't think nuthin' of it at the time I run on it. So me and him, we'd head out early ever morning, takin' a different tack the next day than we done the day before."

He paused, then satisfied they understood, continued. "We was scouting along the South bank of the Big Anney clear to Colbourne Crick. We followed the crick to its head and a strange feelin' come over me. The boy was some ahead, just getting set to break out o' the woods when I says, 'This looks real familiar.' Just then, through the trees, I seed what could a been the skeleton of a log wall from an old fort. It was mebbe two hunnert of yards ahead, into the marsh. Caleb, he sees where I'm pointin' and strikes out for it."

Gumps picked at a broken finger nail, his voice quavering, "The boy cleared the woods into open ground. He's real excited, but tryin' not to show it in case it's a bust, don't ya see.

"All this trudgin' and lookin' was a wearin' on me so I was lagging some behind — him being younger and all. I begun to step out of the woods when Caleb turned and waved me to stop. He was sayin' for me to rest while he looked. 'No sense both of us chasing a wild goose' he yelled back, with that big grin of his — funny thing to say. Well, sir, he took a couple more paces and was hit right square between the shoulders with a mighty big round. It took out the whole middle of his back —"

Lila cried out, stricken, her face drained of color.

Haynie's grip on his coffee mug tightened.

"I'm real sorry," Gumps cried. "I guess I'm tellin' it bad, but, there's no good way to say it."

"Tell it," Haynie said. "Tell it all, every detail."

Gumps nodded, then hesitated, looking at Lila. "You want to leave, ma'am?"

Lila shook her head and gripped her husband's hand. "Thank you, no. I cannot leave him to hear this alone."

"It wasn't 'til after he fell, that I heard the report. Big caliber gun, a good distance off – mebbe three hunnert feet. Right after that, I hear a dog growlin', across the way, real ferocious like."

Gumps took a drink of coffee then looked up at the husband and wife, his eyes beseeching them for understanding.

"Uh," Haynie grunted as the coffee mug shattered in his fist. His eyes remained fixed on Gumps, ignoring the trickle of blood coloring the table cloth.

Gumps said, “I been a livin’ with mother nature for a long time – long time. So, you must believe me when I tell ya’ that there was nuthin’ I could a done, anybody could a done for him.”

Gumps rubbed his hands together, hard, as if he could scrub away the very thing he was telling. “If you think I was a scared, you’d be dead right.” He looked up quickly, “Sorry, I didn’t mean nuthin — Anyways, I figure next thing the killer would set that vicious dog on me. But, scared as I was, I wouldn’t a left him, if there’d a been anything —”

Haynie spoke, his words a whisper, “We’re not blaming you,” he said. “Caleb loved being in the woods. ’Said you taught him a lot.”

The old man broke down sobbing, trying to bury his face in Haynie’s good hand as he kissed the palm. “Oh, thank you, Mister McKenna, thank you, sir, for those words.”

Haynie gently freed his hand from Gumps’s grasp, as Lila laid a small towel next to the old man. Gumps grabbed it up and rubbed his eyes.

Lila said, “Do you think this was a hunter, who mistook Caleb for some animal? You said it was a long distance – early morning. Perhaps a deer or even a bear.”

When Haynie said nothing, Gumps spoke up. “No, ma’am. Was a real poltroon shot that boy.”

Gumps shook his head and looked at Haynie. “I believe he was one of them sharp-shooters. You know, Mister McKenna, from the wa —”

“Enough,” Haynie roared. His chair clattered against the wall as he stood.

“It is my fault Caleb is dead. He was doing my bidding.”

Lila wiped the shards of crockery from his hand while Gumps shook with fright.

“We’ve got to get up there soon as we can,” Haynie said. “You up to showing the way?”

Gumps straightened. “Yes sir, Mister McKenna, wouldn’t think of not going.”

“I don’t want varmints getting to Caleb. We’ll need something to bring him back in. What’s the fastest way there — boat or wagon?”

Gumps scratched at the scraggly hairs around his chin. “Hard to say,” he shrugged. “Not sure how far we was from the water. All looks the same in them marshes grass. Still, that woods is pretty thick, be real hard to get a wagon close. If ya got a flat boat, I reckon we could pole through that grass and get closer than comin’ through them woods.”

Haynie said, “I can get a boat in town, but that’s no good, we’d have to sail out to the sound, up to the Big Annie, then back over to the creek. It’d take ’til this time tomorrow to get there.”

Lila came in carrying a pan of water and clean cloths. She pushed her husband back into his chair, and began bathing the cuts.

“Well,” Haynie said, “We’ll get as close as we can with a wagon.”

Gumps looked up, “There’s a feller named Maddox, lives over to Jones Creek. Caleb’s — where we need to go — is not an hour by water from his place. Got hisself one o’ them Sharpie boats, about thirty foot. He’s real particular about that boat, but I believe he’d take us, seein’ what’s happened. I’ll bring him a possum, or marsh rat. His wife makes a desirable marsh rat stew.”

Haynie winced as Lila dug out a sliver. “What if he’s not home?”

Gumps shrugged. “Can’t hurt nuthin’ to look in on him. We’d pass near there anyways on the wagon road.”

Haynie nodded in agreement. “You sit here and rest,” he said. “Finish your breakfast while I get this hand wrapped and hitch up the wagon.”

Gumps reached for the remaining biscuits.

Buster Maddox and Haynie were positioned at the stern of Buster’s Sharpie, each working a thick pole to propel the flat boat through the marshy creek.

Gumps hunched himself over the boat’s prow, studying the turbid water ahead, a .58 caliber Springfield Musket cradled in his arms. Maddox had charged Gumps with shouting out if he spotted a marsh tump or other obstructions in their path.

After turning upstream, they had hugged the shore of the Big Annie until reaching the mouth of Colbourne Creek. With one oar, Buster easily swung the boat into the creek then returned to the stern where he and Haynie proceeded to ply the craft into the thickening marsh grass.

Though the sky was overcast, Haynie judged that they had at close to 2 hours of daylight lcft and savagely dug his pole into the muddy creek bottom, willing the boat forward. His efforts were uneven and often at odds with Buster’s rhythmic movements, causing the boat to jerk about spasmodically. In frustration, Haynie jammed his pole into the mud with a force that simultaneously pushed the craft ahead while sucking the pole from his grasp leaving it sticking above the water behind them.

Buster grabbed up the oar and maneuvered the boat back to the jutting pole where Haynie jerked it free of the mucky bottom.

"McKenna, we'll get there quicker if you and me work together, like marching in step, in the army."

Haynie judged Buster to be near fifty with muscled arms and flowing salt and pepper whiskers, so full and long that they effectively covered his squat frame to the waist. When he spoke, the beard flapped about seemingly independent of his chin.

Haynie nodded and studied the boat captain's actions, counting a cadence to himself.

Once their movements were in harmony, he asked, "Captain, you ever hear of this fort that Gump's is talking about?"

Maddox scanned the marsh ahead, the boat making its own channel as it pushed aside the cattails and celery grass. If they encountered eel grass, they would be nearing the shoreline.

"Can't say as I have, but that don't mean nothin'. I spend my days out in the sound. Can't recall the last time I was this side of Jones Creek."

Gumps waved a hand to get their attention. "Water's getting real skinny," he said. "Might be just about to the end."

Haynie felt the boat slowing as it encountered more resistance. He and Maddox struggled to move it along and the hull screeched as their route became as much grass as water.

Haynie was the only one of the three tall enough to see above the expanse of waving grass. Standing on the balls of his feet, straining to scan the horizon, he glimpsed a sawed log roof seemingly resting atop the marsh grass ahead. Haynie got the attention of both men and motioned in the direction of the log roof.

Buster Maddox picked up a paddle and veered the bow, putting the boat on its new course. Holding the paddle over the starboard side, he used it to measure the water's depth. He gripped the paddle at the waterline and held it up for Haynie to see. Mere inches of water beneath them now, as the boat strained and groaned to push forward.

The reeds and grasses parted before the boat's prow, revealing a windowless log shelter perched atop pilings.

Haynie's heart pounded. "Watch yourselves," he said quietly, as he drew his sidearm. Gumps shifted around, bringing his musket forward, resting the barrel on the prow.

Maddox pulled his shotgun closer while steadying the craft with one hand.

Haynie knew they were seeing at least one of the prisons the kidnappers used to house their prey. The hut, constructed of newly sawed logs, sat perched about fifteen feet above the marsh floor atop four weathered pilings, long ago anchored into the marshy creek bed below.

Other weathered and rotting logs of varying girth extended out from the pilings at right angles to form the relic wall of a decaying fort, abandoned years before.

Haynie motioned for quiet as Maddox steered the boat directly between the platform's pilings. A rope ladder dangled from the hut floor, the bottom rung scraping the deck as Maddox deftly guided the boat to a stop.

The three men gathered at the ladder, studying the underside of the hut floor about fifteen feet overhead. The rope ladder had been nailed into the floor next to a dark stained trap door secured by a heavy iron bolt seated in U shaped straps of rough wrought iron. Clearly, the intent of the locking mechanism was to keep prisoner anyone inside, not to prevent entry from the outside.

Haynie holstered his pistol, bent lower and said quietly, "I'm going up and see what we have here. I know you all can't see beyond this marsh grass, but keep an eye out just the same. Once I get above the grass, I'll take a look around. If I don't see anything, I'll keep going. If something should happen, back out of here as fast as you can and go for the sheriff."

With nothing to say, Gumps and Maddox stood silently as Haynie began his climb.

About six feet above the deck, Haynie stopped and scanned the area. Ahead, was the shoreline where the waves of eel grass, cattails and sedge ceased, and the weeds and brush of dry land continued to the darkness of the forest. Behind him, cord and widgeon grasses competed with reeds and bulrushes for dominance until they merged into the unbroken grayness of the November sky.

Confident that any trouble would come from the woods, Haynie turned back to scan that horizon as he made his way to the top. Several vultures flew listless circuits above the trees and he suppressed an urge to cry out for them to leave his brother alone. Turning back to the immediate task, he drew a deep breath and angrily threw back the bolt letting the trap door fall open in front of him.

The trap door swung heavily away and Haynie recoiled with a cry, clutching the rope ladder with one arm. A hand slapped his face as it fell through the opening, and blood, darkened by hours of exposure to the air, cascaded from the hole, splashing over his head and arms.

"What the hell –" Maddox cried, jumping back as the blood splattered the deck at his feet.

Gumps realized too late what was raining down on him. "Damn!" he cried, stumbling backwards over a coiled rope, hitting the deck hard.

Using his weight, Haynie swung himself away from the opening and clutched a support piling. With one arm around the piling, he rubbed his face along a dry section of shirtsleeve to clear his eyes of the blood. Looking down, he saw Maddox helping Gumps stand, the two men holding one another upright as they stepped gingerly away from the slick pool of blood spreading across the deck.

The blood pouring from the prison became a trickle and finally droplets. Haynie released his grip, shifted his weight and returned the rope ladder to its position under the door.

The thundering in Haynie's ears and pounding in his chest quieted. With one hand, he moved the swaying arm aside, grim and fearful of what he would find.

27

Colbourne Creek
Somerset County, Maryland
Saturday, November 9, 1867

Haynie poked his head through the trapdoor into the gloom of the prison room. He identified three lifeless forms in the shadows. The arm that had fallen through the trap door was attached to the body of a man in his mid twenties, his clothing unfamiliar, a foreign cut. The other bodies were that of a young Negro boy, and, in the far corner, a gaunt frame clad in rebel uniform pants.

Though Haynie did not know Landon Wallis by sight, it was evident he was not among them.

Haynie withdrew his head and started back down the ladder. “Buster, you got an oil lamp aboard?” he asked.

“Aye. I’ll get it; it’s bad isn’t?”

“Bad enough.”

“How many are there?”

“Three.”

Gumps leaned over the side, rinsing the blood from his face with water scooped from the marsh. “The boy you’re lookin’ for in there?” he asked.

Haynie shook his head as he reached the deck. He proceeded to wash the blood from this head and neck, drying off with a piece of toweling Buster handed him along with the oil lamp.

Haynie checked the oil level in the lamp and said, “I’ll need some dry matches.”

Buster nodded and dug a handful of stick matches from his shirt pocket.

With the lamp hanging from his left elbow, Haynie ascended the rope ladder. Once his upper torso was inside the prison hut, he lit the lamp wick. Standing on the second rung of the ladder, he held the lamp high over his head and examined the interior of the room.

In front of him, a hole in the floor had been plugged with a wadded flannel shirt, causing the blood to pool at the trapped door.

The son-of-a-bitch did that on purpose, so that whoever opened up would get drenched in their blood.

Haynie leaned in to the extent he could without crawling onto the blood soaked floor. Each man’s throat had been cut deep and cleanly, by one thrust from a very sharp blade.

Looks like the same cut that did in Squire.

The body next to the trap door was fair skinned with blonde hair. Probably German. The blue eyes wide open, retaining the terror of that moment. The Negro boy was curled into the corner, one arm covering his eyes the other jammed at his side, pinned to the floor by his body. The one in the Reb pants was reposed, almost serene, hands folded across his chest.

Haynie theorized that the German, being closest to the trapdoor had seen the danger first and tried to fight off his killer. He was the first to die. The darky likely drew himself into the corner, terrified, maybe hoping to be obscured in the gloom by his skin color. He was the second to die. Reb pants, so emaciated he was already near death, appeared to have slept through his killing.

Praise be if he had.

Initially, Haynie suspected the boy had died before the attack, and then realized that if the heart had stopped beating, he would have bled little when his throat was cut.

Haynie shone the light over the floor and into each corner. Satisfied that he had overlooked nothing of importance, he sat the lamp on the floor and took out a pocketknife. He cut a section of dry cloth from the shirt of the German lad, then twisted the cloth tightly, forming a wick. He soaked it with coal oil from the lamp and emptied the remainder of the oil in a corner, saturating an otherwise dry area of floor.

After piling the wooden matches on the floor, Haynie carefully laid out the wick he had fashioned to connect the matches to the oil soaked wood. He paused and looked at each man.

"I'm sorry to have to do this. You all deserve better, but it can't be helped."

Striking one of the matches with a thumbnail, he ignited the piled matches and the wick. They flared, with the flame eating its way along the wick toward the coal oil pooled in the corner.

Haynie collected the lamp and started down the rope ladder.

Gumps and Buster watched as he descended from the hut.

Once on deck Haynie said, "Let's shove off, Captain."

Gumps pointed a gnarled finger toward the hut. "What about them poor souls up there?" he asked. Buster spotted the empty lamp in Haynie's hand. "I 'spect you set fire to the place with them in there."

Haynie pushed the boat away from the pilings. "We need to go now," he directed, pointing east, toward the woods. "Damn carrion birds are getting at my brother."

Neither Gumps nor Buster moved. Haynie looked from one to the other.

"He's my brother. I need to get him home and start lookin' for his killer. I'm real sorry about those boys, but we don't have time to tend to them and Caleb too. Say some words for them, if you like, I'm not of a mind to be real religious right now. "

"Seems cold," Buster said as he turned the boat away from the hut, towards the shore. "But, I'm afraid he's right. We'll be lucky to be out of here by dark. Their folks'll never know what become of 'em. They'll be cryin' for a long time."

"No different than if we took them with us," Haynie said. "They'd have to go into the ground before we could ever find any kin."

Gumps faced the hut, head bowed and lips moving soundlessly. When he looked up black smoke was escaping from the space just below the roofline.

"She caught, sure 'nuf, Mister McKenna," he said.

Haynie dug his pole into the marsh bottom without looking back.

After maneuvering the boat as far as the marsh would allow, Haynie figured they were about two hundred feet from where Caleb lay. They sloshed ashore, Gumps and Haynie leading the way, Buster close behind. Once out of the tall grass and marsh reeds, the ground was a landscape of brush and weed patches to the tree line. Gumps paused to get his bearings, pointed about ten degrees to the right, and they struck out in that direction.

Shortly, Haynie noticed movement in the weeds straight ahead. He signaled a halt, drew his sidearm and fired two rapid shots into the air. About seventy-five feet to the front, four vultures erupted in a flurry of thrashing wings and raucous calls. Haynie quickened the pace; the others had difficulty matching his long strides.

As they approached Caleb's body, Haynie removed his hat and stood motionless for a moment. Gumps and Buster followed his lead.

Caleb McKenna lay face down in the weeds, a gaping hole in his back, exposing fluids, bone and organs mixed with shreds of clothing.

Haynie, fearful of being overwhelmed by emotion when finally confronted with the body of his younger brother, was unprepared to feel nothing. The cold emptiness he was now experiencing.

Haynie returned his hat to his head, signaling that it was time to do what they had come for. He pointed alongside Caleb, "What do you make of that?" he asked.

Gumps voice cracked. "It's Junior. Looks like he crawled up and died next to the boy. Broken heart, I reckon."

Haynie circled the two forms, intently studying the terrain around them. Then he squatted and studied the dog's body.

"Junior was slit open; he bled out from his gut."

Haynie turned and pointed at an area of flattened weeds, stained dark, trailing off to toward the tree line.

"Looks like he was cut back there," he said, pointing toward a thickset sweet gum tree at the edge of the woods. "He must of crawled here to die with Caleb."

Gumps' eyes followed the trail of matted weeds to the base of the gum tree.

"Near couple hundred of feet. Maybe more."

The dog's mouth was agape, evidence of the struggle required for him to reach Caleb's side. Haynie closely examined the bared teeth. "Look at this," he said, pointing to a few hairs clinging to a small piece of hide wedged between the dogs upper incisors.

Looking at Gumps he asked, "Does that look like human skin?"

Gumps, unable to squat lower, leaned forward, squinting where Haynie pointed. "Hard to say what it is. Not from a man, though."

Haynie stood and spoke to Buster. "Captain, we're losing light and I need you to do something, so we can be clear of this marsh by dark."

Buster Maddox pulled at his beard and smirked at Gumps. "This started out as a little boat ride. Yer runnin' up quite a bill, Mister Gumps, already worth more than one little ol' marshrat."

Gumps looked at Haynie who said, "It's not his bill, it's mine. I'll make it up to you."

"I was just funnin' with old Gumps here, I didn't mean nuthin'. What you need me to do?"

Haynie pointed toward the woods, about where Caleb had come into the clearing. It was much closer than the gum tree where Junior's trail seemed to lead.

"Cut us some solid branches, to fit one of the blankets. Then make a litter for us to take him out of here. Meantime, Gumps and I'll backtrack this trail. See where it takes us."

Haynie led off, eyes on the ground following the trail of blood soaked, matted weeds leading away from the bodies.

"Gumps, watch the woods, while I study this trail for any signs."

The old man tightened the grip on his musket and stayed close to Haynie, straining to pick up any movement among the trees ahead. Night had begun its descent, the woods shadowy and obscure beyond the tree line.

As Haynie suspected, the trail of twisted and bloodstained weeds led them to the base of the massive sweet gum. He signaled a stop and bent his head, speaking close to Gumps' ear.

"Keep a sharp eye."

Gumps nodded.

Eyes fixed to the ground, Haynie slowly circled the tree about six feet out from the trunk. Numerous signs said that someone had spent a good deal of time here. The grass was well trampled for several feet out in all directions. The trunk was marred and worn where someone had rested against it and man-made objects had chipped the bark. Several feet up the trunk, a burl was positioned so that a tall man could rest a rifle barrel on it while he aimed at anything moving across the clearing where Caleb lay.

On the side of the tree facing the forest, where a killer would conceal himself, Haynie saw what looked like a spattering of blood at the base of the trunk. He signaled for Gumps and squatted for a closer look.

Haynie picked up a chunk of animal hide from the base of the tree. The brown hair was caked with blood, the ground around it spattered with more blood. The underside of the hide was smooth and dry. The piece had come from a tanned hide, not a live animal.

He handed it to Gumps then retrieved an empty, uncorked glass vial from the weeds nearby. He sniffed and said, "Laudanum," then put the bottle in his pocket.

Gumps cried out, "Look a here, Mister McKenna, this is the same as the hairs Caleb showed me the other day. I plumb forgot to tell you – I 'spect they're from a buffalo hide. Not many of them in these parts, but when I told Caleb, he got excited — said he'd seen one in town. Real recent, too."

Haynie nodded. "I figured as much. Caleb and I saw the same man. He carries a .72 caliber musket and drinks laudanum from little bottles like this one."

"How do you figure this here chunk of robe got tored off? And, got blood on it?"

Haynie stood close to the tree and scrutinized the landscape before him, certain he was standing where Caleb's killer had stood, visualizing what the killer had seen just before he shot Caleb.

Farther out, in the marsh, flecks of orange flame darted in and out of plumes of black smoke rising above the paddy shack.

Off to the left, where Caleb had emerged from the woods, Buster was busily lashing together young saplings. Anyone standing here would have seen a man running from those trees.

Haynie continued his study of the terrain. Pointing to the burning tower he said, "I figure the fella in the buffalo robe was paid to keep folks away from that prison. When he saw Caleb headed out that way, he just up and shot him. He's already killed Squire Towne. Maybe he learned to like killin' in the war.

"No matter. I believe Junior, sick as he was with rabies, was trackin' you and Caleb. When the killer fired, and Caleb went down, Junior was lurking around and attacked. That was the dog you heard. The killer was still holding that long gun so Junior bit him good before the back shooter could get his knife out and gut the dog. Junior, knowing he was dying, took all the strength he had left to drag himself out to Caleb."

Gumps nodded at the flaming prison hut. "You think he killed them boys, too, dontcha."

"Sure as we're standing here. He figured someone would come looking for Caleb and spot their prison shack. He didn't want them alive to tell what they knew. ...Mostly, he did it because he likes the feeling it gives him." Haynie took a last look around. "Let's get back."

Buster Maddox waited next to Caleb's body. Alongside, lay a litter fashioned from a blanket tied between long poles.

"I didn't touch him," Buster said. "Figured you should be the one to move him."

Haynie stopped at Caleb's head. Nodding to Buster, he said, "If you'll take his feet, we'll roll him onto the blanket."

Haynie closed his brother's eyes and gently brushed the dirt and grass from his face. Hesitating for only a moment, he covered Caleb with a second blanket.

Buster, head bowed said, “Your brother was a good looking boy, Mister McKenna.”

“Real smart, too.” Gumps said, eyes brimming, voice husky.

Haynie and Buster lifted the litter and stepped toward the boat.

Gumps spoke up, “We gonna leave him like that?” he asked, looking down at Junior’s lifeless form.

“Not carryin’ him up here, with Caleb,” Haynie said over his shoulder. “And, there’s no time to come back for him.”

“I know. I just hate the thought of varmints feedin’ on him, and him not bein’ able to fight back.”

Haynie stopped and looked back at the old man.

“I’m real sorry. I know he meant a lot to Caleb – and to you. Look, if you can carry him to the boat, we’ll take him out to the water. At least the varmints won’t have him.”

Haynie and Buster lashed Caleb’s litter to the deck and were growing impatient when Gumps clamored aboard, empty handed and shamefaced. When he spoke, it was directed at the blanketed litter.

“I’m real sorry,” he said, tears running from his nose.

“I tried as best I could. Toted him near half way, but he was a big dog and he — well he got to be too much for an old man. Had to leave him. Put him on a little piece of high ground and covered him best I could – with what I had.”

28

Little Deal Island
Tangier Sound
Saturday Evening, November 10, 1867

Landon Wallis avoided eye contact with Greeley and ate his supper in silence. The cramped cabin was warm and smoky, the blended smell of deer meat frying atop a wood fired cook stove. They were the last of the crew to eat. Biscuits, the cook, worked at the stove, the only other crewman in the cabin.

Landon assumed that at least two of the tongers attacked by the *Fish Hawk* had perished. He was sullen, taking his orders with a nod or shrug, keeping to himself as much as the confines of the boat would allow. With difficulty, he masked his emotions a mingling of fear, loathing and despair, which seethed endlessly.

Late Friday night he had a stern talk within himself, firm in the notion that he must avoid alarming Captain Jack and the other crewmembers while plotting a means of escape. Landon, desperate for someone to confide in, knew that he was most vulnerable around Nails; thus, avoided the boy as much as he dared.

Landon raised his eyes and took in the little room from a fresh perspective.

Anything in here I could use as a weapon?

He and Greeley sat at a square table that, jammed against a bulkhead, accommodated just two crewmen at a sitting. Room enough as the crew ate in shifts. Captain Jack was served first, the others came and went as work allowed, dishing their own food from pots on the cook stove.

At Landon's first meal aboard the *Fish Hawk*, he and Nails had eaten last. Since the run in with the tongers, Greeley was with him at every meal.

Greeley's with me, everywhere.

Above the table, a lighted coal oil lamp swayed dimly, the wick trimmed to provide minimum light. Along one bulkhead, cooking utensils, wooden matches, coffee, flour, and other foodstuffs sat on open shelves. Oilcloth rain slickers hung from wooden pegs next to extra coal lamps. Landon studied the area around the slickers, hoping to see a gaff or pike, something sharp he could use as a weapon.

I will kill somebody if that's what it takes to get home.

An enamel coffee pot, a fixture atop the stove, provided hot coffee at all hours. Bunk beds for Biscuits and Captain Jack were stacked along the rear bulkhead, opposite the entryway.

Greeley stood, wiped the grease from his mouth with a swipe of a sleeve, and said, "Finish 'er up. We got work." Landon nodded and Greeley left the cabin.

Landon raised his coffee mug, holding it close to his mouth with both hands. Over the rim, he watched Biscuits cleaning the tinware and stowing it on one of the shelves.

That door has a lock on this side, likely to protect Biscuits and Captain Jack from the crew after they turn in. I could pretend to be leaving, quick lock the door, so no one walks in on me, then grab up a heavy piece of that firewood next to the stove and thump Biscuits over the head. Serve the old bastard right for jabbin' me awake with the oyster rake — but, then what do I do?

"You deaf or somethin'," Biscuits called over his shoulder. "Mister Greeley told you to get, now hie your fat ass out on deck."

Landon ground his teeth, quelling an urge to attack Biscuits now. He drained his mug, stood quickly and walked onto the deck, shivering against the cold night air.

The *Fish Hawk* was anchored for the night and Landon maneuvered easily along the deck, the unbroken silhouette of Little Deal Island a few hundred yards off the stern. As he skirted the main mast, Nails appeared from the rigging, crossing the deck just behind him.

Nails slowed, "We'll be docking in Crisfield tomorra," he said. "They'll lock you below. Only Greeley will be aboard. I'll unlock the hatch, 'fore I go ashore. That's all I can do," then he continued to the starboard rail.

29

Great Fox Island
Tangier Sound
Sunday, November 10, 1867

The Drumm brothers' pungy rocked gently in a sheltered cove off Great Fox Island. Rodney leaned over the side, feigning interest in the oyster tongs he held in the water, his brother Roy concealed among the rigging. Jake Drumm, peering from behind the main mast, studied the lone waterman on the seventy-foot bugeye anchored some three hundred feet away.

"He's been pullin' 'em in by the bushel, ever since we dropped anchor," Jake hissed. "And see how low she rides, loaded with our pearls, I reckon. Looks like he's alone, boys. I 'spect our plan is about to come true."

"I, I, I don't know, Jake," Roy said, "t, t, that's —"

"'Course you don't *know*, Roy, that's why I'm the head of this family."

Roy tucked his head and mumbled into the canvass, "—I, I, I was only sayin'— t, t, that's a big boat for only one m, m, man."

"Damnit, Roy, damnit. You been against the plan from the start. That's a bugeye, they nearly sail themselves."

Furious now, Jake turned to Rodney, "Jesus, Rod, Jesus, your arms broke or somethin'. You ain't foolin' nobody. Pull them tongs out of the water ever now and again."

"Aw, fer Christ's sakes, Jake, theys heavy. 'Sides who'm I supposed to be foolin, anyways?" Rodney nodded toward the bugeye, "He ain't payin' us no mind. Doubt he knows we're over here."

"He'll know soon enough," Jake cackled. "We're goin' for it boys. Get ready to be rich." Jake slid to the deck and crawled toward Rodney.

Roy watched Jake moving along on all fours and scratched his head. "Y-y- you need help, Jake?" he asked.

Jake cocked his head and glared over his shoulder, "Damnit, Roy, damnit. Why was I cursed with two brothers — both dumb as dirt? 'Member, I told you to stay outta sight whilst I was hid behind the mast? Only Rod was to show his face. You remember that?"

"Y,Y, Yup."

"Why'd you think we was doin' that?"

Roy's gaze drifted around the deck, "You d-d-didn't tell me that part."

"It was so that tonger'd only see one man over here, doin' the same thing he was, and wouldn't get peevish about us."

"H-h-how long do I hafta hide in this sail, J-J- Jake?"

Rodney said, "Yeah, Jake, how long do I have to hold these here tongs?"

"Jesus, Rod, Jesus. Now both a you, listen up — but don't let on I'm down here talking. It's the last time I'm tellin' ya. When we're ready, me and Rod'll hide up at the bow. Roy'll come out from behind the sail and take up the anchor —"

"–B-b-but," Roy stammered, "I t-t-thought I was hidin and R-Rod was the one to show."

"Dammit Roy— when you show, Rod'll be hiding with me. There's still only one he can see over here – but now it'll be you and not Rod."

"B-b-but my face and Rod's face d, d, don't look the same."

"— Shut up, Roy, just shut up and listen. It's a damn good plan. Once you get the anchor up, you sail us right up to that bugeye – real quiet. Me and Rod'll climb on board. I'll keep my gun on that tonger – Rod, you bring somethin' heavy to hit him over the head with. Then we dump him over board and sail the bugeye up to the Big Annie – 'member Roy, you follow in this boat."

Still on his hands and knees, Jake looked from one brother to the other, neither spoke.

"Jesus Rod, Jesus, did you hear what I was tellin' ya?"

Rodney pulled the tongs on board and bent down, hands resting on his knees.

"You was talkin' real low, Jake, but I got most of it. Thing is, I don't know what to take aboard to hit him with. Never had to hit a man on his haid, before."

Rod straightened quickly and jumped away as Jake swung at him.

"You're damn lucky," Jake said, "that hiding down here is part of the plan, or I'd fer sure come up there, find something heavy and club you with it. Just grab a damn belaying pin, that'll do him."

Rodney stepped further from Jake's reach and said. "Is it part of the plan to drown this feller?'

Jake gritted his teeth, "Jesus, Rod, Jesus. It ain't our worry if he can't swim."

Roy had the Drumm brothers' pungy within thirty feet of the bugeye's starboard side at midship. The lone tonger was forward on the port bow, bent over the side, intent on working his tongs.

Jake and Rodney lay prone on the deck, head to head, concealed by the rail.

Jake gripping a revolver in his right hand, looked at his brother and grinned.

"The plan's working. You're about to be a rich man, Rod. You was smart to stick with me."

Rod looked at the belaying pin clutched in his right hand and grimaced.

Roy, at the wheel, noticed the aft deck of the bugeye was stacked with cords of firewood, but shrugged and said nothing.

The pungy struck the side of the bugeye and caromed several feet away. With the impact, Jake and Rodney jumped up, poised to leap over the gunwale and onto the other deck, but found too much water between the boats.

The tonger, jolted by the collision, turned to see Jake holding a pistol. The man bellowed and dove from sight.

"Damnit, Roy, damnit. Get us back to that boat, right now."

The boats bumped again and Rodney stumbled as he and Jake vaulted onto the bugeye's deck.

Gerhardt Stein burst through the cabin door waving a culling hammer in one hand. With a roar, he snatched up a slab of firewood and charged the Drumm brothers, swinging both weapons wildly around his head.

Jake whirled pointing his revolver as Stein swung the piece of oak with his considerable strength, smashing Jake's gun arm just below the shoulder. Jake screamed in pained as his gun clattered to the deck.

Clutching his crippled arm, he staggered backward and pitched over the side into the frigid water.

Rodney, struggling to right himself, recoiled from the culling hammer, as the pointed end narrowly missed tearing out a section of his cheek.

Stein made a backhanded swipe at Roy's head, when a shotgun roared from behind. Captain Mueller, master of the *Water Mule*, fired both barrels across his own deck and into the pungy.

Roy, at the pungy's helm, was beyond range, the shotgun pellets ripping harmlessly through the mainsail.

Rodney screamed as the pellets flew around him, lurched against the gunwale and disappeared over the side.

Jake thrashed about with one arm, in an effort to reach their pungy, as Rodney hit the water beside him.

Another shotgun blast cut the air overhead, with shot splattering the water like raindrops. The pungy turned away and Jake, spitting water, shrieked, "Damnit Roy, damnit. Don't you leave us. We're a comin'."

Roy, crouched at the wheel, did not look back as the boat's sails filled, pulling it toward open water.

Rod lunged at Jake from behind, wrapping both arms around his brother's head. "Help me, Jake." Jake clawed the air with his good arm as he went under.

Submerged, Jake worked his head free of Rod's grip and surfaced, gasping for breath and flailing at Rodney.

"Get off me, Rod. I only got one good arm. You're gonna drown us both."

"Help me, Jake, ah'm real scared. Help me. I cain't swim," Rodney screamed. With one hand he clutched at Jake's hair, as he wrapped the other arm tightly around his brother's neck.

Jake reached back, desperately digging his fingers at Rodney's eyes.

"Jesus Rod, Jesus."

30

Crisfield, Maryland
Sunday, November 10, 1867

Stick and Buckets shoved passed Landon and headed for the hatch, on their way topside and into town. Nails, trailing them, shot Landon a quick look as he too climbed the ladder.

Landon stared at the bulkhead, held his breath and listened. The hatch closed and the bolt was slid into place. A moment later, the bolt slid again and the *Fish Hawk* was quiet.

Nails kept his word, now it's up to me.

Landon dropped onto the nearest bunk, needing to give the crew time to leave the boat and, likely, arrive at the first bawdy house they encountered.

I have at least two hours. This is the only chance I'll get. It's got to work.

With a strategy in mind, Landon took a deep breath and headed for the ladder. He cracked the hatch cover enough to see that the deck aft to the captain's cabin was deserted.

Greeley's most likely in the cabin asleep or drinking coffee.

Landon gauged the distance across the open deck to the railing where the boat was tied off to the pier.

I'll stay low. I can keep the rigging between me and the cabin 'til the last few feet, then over the side and run as fast as I can into town and get help.

Landon eased the hatch cover back and crawled out onto the deck. Lying flat, he swung the cover closed and threw the bolt.

Give 'em something to think about.

Pulling himself up to a crouch, he started toward the rail.

"Where the hell you think yer goin'?"

Greeley was closing from the bowsprit. Landon stood and broke into a run for the pier. He quickly gauged that Greeley would reach the gangplank ahead of him and veered aft toward the captain's cabin.

Greeley, bigger and stronger, was gaining as they dashed past the main mast. He cursed and threatened Landon with grave consequences when he caught him.

"You got no place to go now, and, when I get ya I'm gonna break both yer damn legs. You won't run no more, damn you."

As they reached the cabin, Greeley lunged forward, making a grab for Landon's jacket collar. Landon dodged to his left and hit the cabin door, causing Greeley to miss and stumble past. Inside the windowless cabin, Landon slammed the door and threw the bolt, locking himself in.

Chest heaving, Landon leaned on the table while he sucked in air and waited for the pounding in his ears to ease.

Greeley cursed and kicked the door. "Hey, you dumb shit," he yelled, "how you gonna get outta there without me catchin' ya and poundin' the crap out of ya?"

Below deck Landon had speculated on whether, if it became necessary, he had the nerve to carry out this part of his plan. Now, he knew he could do it; he had no other choice.

He took down the coal oil lamp from over the table and splattered its fuel over the bunk beds. Next, he splashed the oil from the spare lamps and reserve can along the floor and bulkhead directly across from the locked door.

The pounding at the door ceased and Greeley's tone softened.

"What's goin' on in there?"

When there was no response, Greeley said, "Looky here, Captain Jack and the boys'll be back any minute. He finds you outta the hold, he's gonna skin botha us. Ya can't go nowhere and there's no sense in both us gettin' a whippin'. Open 'er up an come on out. I won't touch ya — I swear on Ma. You can go below like nothin' ever happened...What do ya say?"

Landon piled the few cloths and rags he could find in the far corner and shook the can out over them. Next, he took some wooden matches from over the stove and lit fires in four areas of the cabin, then waited for the flames to catch and began their destruction.

Greeley resumed pounding and kicking the door, “Godamnit,” he yelled. “I give you a chance, you can’t say I didn’t. Now, I’m coming in and whip yer ass good.”

Landon opened the wood stove and, with a ladle from the shelf, flung glowing embers around the room. Flames erupted along both bunk beds and he hurled the wooden chairs onto the burning bedclothes. Next, he upended the table into the flames.

Greeley cursed and yelled, “You better not be breakin’ anything in there. Captain Jack’ll take it outa your worthless hide — damnit, you hear me?”

Landon hefted a chunk of firewood from the woodbin and moved to the door. He stood flat against the doorjamb, with one hand on the door-bolt, the other poised to swing the wood chunk like a club. Flames consumed the bunk beds and raced across the deck and up the far bulkhead. Heavy, grey smoke curled into every corner.

This ought to keep him busy for a while.

The door handle rattled frantically, and as the kicking and pounding reached a crescendo, Landon threw back the bolt. The heavy door swung inward, pulling the mate in with it. As Greeley pitched forward into the room, Landon swung his club with both hands, striking his captor solidly across the shoulders, sending him sprawling onto the burning table.

Once outside the cabin, Landon hesitated, as Greeley labored to right himself.

“I wouldn’t lay in that fire.”

“If Captain Jack don’t kill ya, I will,” Greeley groaned, still struggling.

Landon raced to the gangplank. Once on the pier, he moved rapidly toward the center of town, stifling an urge to scream for help, lest he alert the crew of the *Fish Hawk* that he was free.

31

Somerset County, Maryland
Monday, November 11, 1867

"That coffee smells real good. I get a cup?"

Rat grabbed his long gun and jumped up, quickly turning toward the sound of the voice. An ivory tipped mahogany walking stick waggled at him from behind a nearby oak tree.

"You shoot me — you won't get paid."

Rat lowered his rifle. "Come on out and get yer own damn coffee. I ain't bringin' it to ya."

Mister Green emerged, dressed in a woolen greatcoat, matching grey wool hat, a fancy black scarf covering his shirtfront, and that elegant walking stick. Green led his horse across the clearing.

Rat said, "I only got the one cup," indicating the dented tin cup warming on a flat stone at the fire's edge. "How'd you find my camp, anyways?"

Green stopped next to the campfire.

"I know what I need to know," he said. "Why? Aren't I welcome," he said, eyes darting around the camp, "in your — home?"

Rat laid the great rifle on his bedroll. Turning to face the man again, he slid his right hand inside the buffalo robe.

"I reckon you was so anxious to tell me what a good job I done, and pay me up, ya couldn't wait for our regular get together. That suits me just dandy."

Green dropped his horse's reins and held the walking stick loosely in both hands. He eyed the end of a blood soaked rag poking from a rend in Jeremy's shirtsleeve.

"Looks like even though you back shot that boy, he was able to cut you."

"He did no such a thing. Whilst I was payin' attention to killin' him, some mangy dog snuck up and bit me. Sent him on his way, too — I might add."

"We need to discuss your compensation."

Rat held out his left hand. "If yer talkin' about how much you owe me," he said, "I got two words fer ya — pay up."

Green smiled. "You killed the wrong McKenna — Jeremy," he said, dragging out that hated first name.

Rat withdrew his hand, "Whatcha mean by that?"

"The boy you back shot up at Colbourne Creek on Saturday; that was Caleb McKenna. You were supposed to kill his brother, Haynie McKenna, the new bailiff in Crisfield. Looks like you've made still another error, making things decidedly worse for us."

Rat spat into the fire. "Now just a damn minute, Mister Fancy Britches. Don't know who it was I shot up there — don't care neither. I was guardin' that prison house of yers, that paddy shack, as you like to call it, just like I hired on to do. And don't get so uppity about back-shootin' neither. If you think I was gonna run out of them woods waving my arms and yellin' like a Comanche, just so's he'd turn around before I shot 'em, well yer crazy, that's what."

"Maybe you can explain why you killed all the inventory we had available. Then, in case your work went unnoticed, set fire to the shack."

Rat reacted as if he'd been slapped. "Hell, you talkin' about? The last thing I burned down was my own place, with my folks in it."

Green studied Jeremy closely, then shrugged. "No matter," he said. "Good thing you like back shooting people — Jeremy — 'because you're going to have to kill the right McKenna this time. He could be a problem for you, if you were to face him."

Coates's voice was a snarl. "You got my money, or aintcha?"

Green stepped closer. "Don't pretend to threaten me, you dung pile. You want your money, and without me you don't get it."

"I guess you figgered you was safe as long as you didn't turn yer back on me," Rat said, withdrawing his right hand from under the buffalo robe.

"Well, you figgered wrong," he declared, and fired all four barrels from Squire Towne's pepperbox into the man's chest.

"I want my money fer sure, but right now I want you dead more."

Green staggered backward, arms flailing wildly, hands clutching the air in vain, and then fell heavily to the ground, eyes staring at the sky.

Rat looked at the tiny gun in his hand. "Pretty good shootin' for a little fella," he laughed and jammed it back inside his robe.

Green's horse reared up at the sound of gunfire and charged into the woods, reins bouncing along the ground as he raced away. Rat looked over at his own scraggly mare, still hobbled and grazing nearby.

"Yer lucky day horse," he called out, "I woulda kept that one and shot you."

The animal paid no attention. Rat laughed, and yanked the ornate walking stick out of the dead man's hands.

"I gotcha now," he proclaimed.

Rat proceeded to strip the corpse of everything of value, alternately shouting and mumbling as he labored.

"Shame to tear up that nice coat, couldn't be helped. I'll have it just the same. Hat don't suit me though," he said and tossed the tailored woolen hat into the fire. Then he yanked the black scarf from the dead man's throat, unwound the bloody rag from his wrist and replaced it with the scarf.

"Blood won't show through this here cloth. Feels like silk, er somethin'. Goddamn dog. Wish he was here so I could cut him again."

Rat removed the suit jacket, cackling when he felt a money belt under the shirtwaist. He unbuckled the gun belt, wrapped it around a holstered six-gun, and laid it aside.

"Didn't do you any good now, did it."

Rat ignored the blood soaking into the vest and shirt, while he greedily tore the money belt from the man's waist.

"Well lookee here," he chortled as he removed a wad of bills from the pouch.

Rat leafed through the bills, ranging from five dollar to one hundred dollar denominations. Though unable to total the amount, he knew that it was far more money than he had ever seen.

"Sum bitch been holdin' out on me the whole time. He wasn't never gonna give me mine. Why, he was thinkin' on killin' me soon as I killed that McKenna, and keep that money too."

He bent close to Green's head and looked straight into the open eyes, searching for some sign of life. Hoping vehemently that the man could somehow hear what he was saying, could understand what was happening to him.

Rat worked himself into a rage, his face scarlet, veins throbbing.

"I never killed no man that deserved it more than you — bastard." He bellowed then settled back on his haunches grinning with genuine pleasure.

"You did good, Rat boy. You did real good with this one."

Digging his fingers into every corner of the money belt, Rat was angered when the effort produced only a small square of folded paper.

He started to toss it into the fire, then said aloud, "It's in a money belt must be worth somethin'. Maybe a map to buried treasure."

He unfolded the document with care and held it in both hands. Though finding no drawn landmarks or "X"s marking the location of hidden treasure, Rat continued to study the paper. It was all writing, and not block letters like he'd seen back in school but the scrawling, flowing words used by judges and generals and the like. The way they did to keep ever day folks like himself from knowing what they were saying to one another.

Acting on a hunch that the paper might someday be worth something, he re-folded it and returned it to a corner of the money belt. After covering the belt with his outer garments, Rat patted his mid-section and grinned.

"Sure feels good. A body don't even know he's got it on."

Next, he removed Green's boots and added them to the pile on the ground.

"If'n they don't fit me, they'll fit somebody who'll pay good money for 'em."

Rat unbuttoned the bloody vest to make sure the shirt beneath had no pockets containing any valuables.

"What the bejesus," he yelled.

Pinned to the shirt, partially obscured by blood, was a lawman's star. A bullet had torn away one the star points. Rat jumped to his feet, looking hard all around. For the first time since the man had appeared at his camp, he was concerned whether someone might have been with him.

He quickly calmed down, realizing that if the lawman had company, the shots would have brought them into camp.

He tore the star from the dead man's shirtfront. "Reckon I could use that little star," he said. "Maybe I'll be a lawman somewheres." He grinned and stuffed the badge behind the wad of bills inside *his* money belt. Rat quickly emptied his coffee cup into the fire and packed up his belongings.

"I ain't stickin' around here, that's fer damn sure," he said aloud.

32

Crisfield, Maryland
Wednesday, November 13, 1867

The white clapboard exterior of the First Methodist Church of Crisfield gleamed in the midday sun. Behind the church lay the sparsely occupied town graveyard. A freshly dug mound of dirt at the end of the first row marked Caleb McKenna's final resting place.

Haynie stood at the front door shaking hands and accepting the solace of the congregation, his mother across the walkway doing the same.

Lettie McKenna, her face pale and drawn, repeated by rote to each mourner as they passed.

"God has given Caleb a beautiful day to begin his journey."

With the church nearly filled to capacity, the Reverend Barclay Thomas appeared in the doorway and nodded that it was time. Haynie touched his mother's arm and escorted her inside where they joined Lila and Young Tench, already seated in the family pew alongside his sister, Mattie, and her husband Levin Tilghman.

Haynie, uncomfortable in an ill-fitting suit and tight collar, sat with arms folded, determined to get through the day without another clash with his mother. Pastor Thomas gave a brief opening prayer before yielding the pulpit to Josiah Muse.

Yesterday, at the Manor House, with Caleb reposed in the next room, Haynie grew incensed when his mother insisted that Josiah

Muse officiate Caleb's funeral. While they argued, Muse secluded himself in his second floor room, leaving Lettie to fight the battle alone.

In fleeting moments of reason, Haynie acknowledged that it would be ill-fated if Muse were to show himself.

"The Reverend Muse is the only hope for Caleb's salvation. I have to do what's best for my youngest. My oldest is clearly lost to the devil," Lettie had said, eyeing the holstered revolver at Haynie's waist. "You'll undoubtedly meet the men you kill, again — in hell."

"It's Reverend Thomas' church, Mother. He will be insulted to be asked to cede his pulpit to anyone, especially an outsider of Muse's ilk."

Lettie smiled weakly and shook her head, "I don't expect you to understand. Mister Thomas is a Christian, compassionate and forgiving. When I spoke to him, he readily understood and welcomed the opportunity to be in the company when Doctor Muse rendered his sermon."

Defeated, Haynie walked away from his mother and out the door, vowing to do one last thing for Caleb.

Now, as Muse strutted to the pulpit, Haynie's mind swirled. The emotional impact of Caleb's' death and funeral, becoming fused within a series of calamitous events. Haynie sensed that each event, though isolated, was linked to the others.

By suppertime on Sunday, Haynie had given Caleb into the care of Charlie Davidson, the town's undertaker, calmed his mother for the moment, and sat at home, prepared to eat to a hot meal, when Tawes Butler pounded on the front door. Haynie, scowling at the intrusion, jerked the door open.

"Sorry to be disturbin' ya Mister McKenna," the boy said. "Yer needed in town right quick. Young fella, stranger, has locked hisself in the storeroom behind John Burgess saloon and won't come out. He's yellin about being a kidnap, 'er some such. Says there's drudgers who'll kill him if he comes out."

The young messenger waved his arms toward town. "Oh, and there's a pungy a fire right at the dock. Folks are tore between staying at the shed, listenin' to that howlin' boy, or bein' down at the dock, watchin' the burnin boat."

Tawes stopped for breath then rushed on, "Some of the younger ones is running back and forth."

"Tell 'em I'm coming," Haynie said and rushed passed Lila seated at the table, Young Tench fussing in her lap.

"You heard?" he asked.

"I heard — and where are you running off to?"

He stopped and stared, "If you heard, then you know."

"I know you're not part of the fire brigade, thank God. And, nothing's gonna happen to that boy while you eat some hot food; you're clearly going to need it to see you through this night."

Lila had been right, of course. Landon Wallis was still locked in the storeroom behind Goodsell's Alley when Haynie arrived. He sent someone to fetch Wes Moore, then rushed a telegram to Fell's Point to be delivered that night to the Wallis family.

Later, in the bailiff's office, Landon huddled under a blanket, gripping a mug of brandy-laced coffee.

Haynie sat across from him, making notes as he probed for details of the boy's ordeal. When Landon described the other men held captive with him in the paddy shack, Haynie said simply that they had all been found – dead.

"I shouldn't have left them," Landon sniffed, tears filling his eyes.

"You had no choice. If you'd been there, you'd be dead as well."

Landon summoned the courage to ask, "Where are they now? I'd like to see them, if I could."

"I'm sorry, they're not here."

Landon shook his head. "None of 'em had much of a life," he said. "I expect they're, each one, in a better place."

Haynie resumed his questions, confirming that Landon had been aboard the *Fish Hawk* when the two tongers were drowned.

"It was Captain Jack and Greeley, the mate. They're bad, evil men. Nails, he's just a young boy, and the rest did what they were ordered to do. Too scared not to. I know Nails was."

Landon drank of the hot coffee while the bailiff scribbled down the names of the crew.

"Nails, Buckets, Stick, not much to go on. Should be able to track down Captain Jack and Greeley —"

Landon looked up. "Nails said if we didn't do what the captain said — no matter what — he could hang us. Is that true?"

Haynie nodded, "There's nothing to stop him — short of a mutiny."

"That's why Nails and the others are afraid." Landon's body tremored at the recollection of his time on the *Fish Hawk*. He set his mug down, lest he spill some, and pulled the blanket closer.

"Am I going to be in trouble for setting fire to the *Fish Hawk*?"

Haynie scanned the pages before him, "The official report says that a fire apparently broke out during your escape. I don't see any need for more details."

He looked at the boy quivering inside the blanket, "You think Captain Jack, or Greeley, are going to come forward with a different version?"

Landon looked sheepish. "Doubtful," he said. His head snapped up, "Was anyone burned in the fire?"

"You mean the mate, Greeley. The man who was keeping you a prisoner."

"Yes, sir."

"He was the only one on board when you fled, right?"

"Yes, sir."

"I've got a couple of men reporting to me about the fire. The first folks to the boat said they saw a man, with a beard and watch cap, come running off the deck and headed off up Main Street."

Landon nodded and reached for his coffee. "Too scared of Captain Jack to stick around."

"As soon as we finish here," Haynie said, "we'll get you a room for the night. Then, I'm going down to the boat. Fire should be out by now."

Landon nodded, suddenly exhausted.

"You didn't kill anybody." Haynie said. "You were being kept against your will and had every right to do whatever it took to free yourself."

Early Monday morning Haynie McKenna had only been home a few hours when Gumps appeared at the front door. He clutched Caleb's fiddle and bow in one hand, in the other a small sack containing the rest of Caleb's things.

Over breakfast, Gumps asked if he would be allowed to come to Caleb's funeral. He cried openly when Haynie said that the family would be honored to have him serve as a pallbearer.

As far as Haynie knew, his mother was unaware of Caleb's relationship with Gumps. He wondered if she would be curious about the odd little man helping to carry her son's coffin.

Later on Monday morning, in the bailiff's office, Haynie had listened to Gerhard Stein's account of the Drumm brothers' failed attempt at piracy. He shook his head in disbelief when it occurred to him that the Drumms had mistaken the scow, laden with firewood, for an oyster boat.

"Ja." Stein said, "Captain Mueller tong for only some bushel's to take home."

Now, Stein sat across the aisle, his massive frame dwarfing Gumps and the other pallbearers seated beside him. After agreeing to be a pallbearer, Stein told Haynie that he, alone, would carry Caleb. When Haynie explained that, it couldn't be done that way Stein shrugged. "Ja" was all he said.

A little before noon on Monday, Haynie accompanied Red Deal, a local progger, to a spot a few miles north of town where Deal had run across the body of dead man at a cold campsite.

"Big man, fancy dresser," Deal announced, standing in the doorway to the bailiff's office.

"Been shot. Little bitty holes in his chest. Big enough to do the job though; he's sure enough, dead."

Haynie sighed deeply, shaking his head as he buckled on his gun belt.

Is there no end to the killings?

As they neared the campsite, Deal said, "This happenin' out of town and all, you'll likely be calling in the high sheriff. I figured you can fetch 'em easier than me."

Haynie nodded.

"I for sure ain't shelling out the money for no telegram clear over to the county seat. Not ridin' over there neither."

Haynie dismounted at the edge of the clearing and motioned Deal to do the same. Through the leafless branches, they saw a man's body sprawled next to the stones of the cold campfire. Nearby, a saddled horse pushed the earth around with his nose in search of food, reins trailing to the ground.

"Careful we don't spook him," said Haynie.

Deal nodded. "We're going to need him to tote that body out of here."

"Let's go in slow and easy," Haynie cautioned.

"Nuthin' to be afeared of, Bailiff," he said. "The killer was gone when I come through, not likely he's come back."

"I need to get a good look at the ground all around here. No tellin' what we might find that could point to the killer."

"You mean like tracking deer, or signs, like what Indians used to hunt down their enemies?"

"Sort of."

As they neared the dead man, Haynie stopped abruptly, causing Red Deal to stumble into him from the rear.

"What the —" Deal yelled.

Haynie pointed to the body, "There's your high sheriff. Sheriff Gastineau."

"Mercy!" Red Deal bent down for a closer look.

"That for sure the sheriff? Don't see a badge."

Haynie pointed at the dead man's chest.

"See that ripped piece of his shirt," he said. "That's where he wore his star. Killer must have torn it off after he shot him."

Haynie scanned the area around the dead man, before squatting for a closer look.

"McKenna, you see any signs?"

"Right now, it's what I'm not seeing that's interesting."

"I ain't followin' ya?"

"When I saw him at my office, he carried around a fancy walking stick. Handled it like it was part of him. Probably always carried it. Expect the killer fancied it and took it with him."

Haynie indicated the man's shirttail, hanging out over his trousers. "That looks strange, doesn't it."

Deal shrugged. "Likely his shirt tail come out when the killer took his gun belt," he said, sure that he had identified the missing gun belt as a sign.

"Maybe, but he didn't need to pull out the man's shirt to get at the gun belt. Men who dress like this often wear a money belt concealed under their clothes."

Haynie lifted the shirt and studied the bare skin at the waistline.

"Could be the killer was looking for a belt or, he felt it when he took the gun rig. Either way," he said, pointing at several red scrape marks on the skin, "he got it."

Deal said, "I reckon the sheriff was camping here and the killer came upon him, not knowin' who he was. Figured he had money, the way he's dressed and all, and just up and shot him. That the way you see it, Bailiff?"

"That's one possibility. Another is, the killer was camped here and the sheriff came in, likely uninvited, and was killed for his trouble."

"So, you're sayin' the killer is a desperado that the sheriff was tracking, like we're a doin', and the killer got the drop on him."

Haynie picked up a stick and stirred the cold campfire. "No, I didn't say that."

Finding nothing of interest in the ashes or under the blackened stones, he dropped the stick and moved toward the base of the large hackberry tree whose branches overhung the campsite.

"If the sheriff was tracking a scoundrel, one who would think nothing of killing a law officer, it's unlikely he would come alone. And, he would not wander into camp with his gun holstered."

"I get it. You figger he just stumbled onto this scalawag's camp and got out drawed when he showed his star."

Haynie shook his head. "Doubtful. This camp is a good distance from the county seat and a ways from the road. Not someplace the sheriff would happen into by chance."

Red Deal grew impatient "What then? You think he came here a purpose. Unwelcome, like."

"I think there's a good chance that's what happened."

Deal chewed his lip. "That sounds like they knew one another, but wasn't real friendly."

Haynie moved around the big tree. "Look here," he said, holding a metal pail by its arched bail.

"That ole pail a sign of some kind?" Deal asked.

"I believe it is, but I have to show it to someone before I can be certain."

After tethering the stray horse, the two men scoured the vicinity of the campsite. At one point, Deal held up a small glass vial and yelled, "Don't know if it means anything, but it weren't left here by no wild animal."

"It means a great deal," Haynie said.

Deal beamed proudly.

Late on Monday afternoon, George Noch and the others of the Town Council called on Haynie. They fidgeted around his desk as Noch said, "We're sorry to intrude on your grief, but the whole town is frightened by all the killings; we need to tell them something to calm 'em."

Asbury Carter-Haines stepped forward, "We remembered what you said, for us not to go runnin' around sayin' anything until we all agreed on what it was we should say. I have to print something in this week's edition." He glanced at the others as if to be certain he had said his lines correctly, then stepped back.

Quentin Tyler spoke out, "Why, some are even sayin' it was you that burned down that prison place with seven or eight bodies in it. Some not yet dead, when you lit the torch."

Haynie fixed him with a stare and Tyler stepped back. His voice trailed off, "I'm just sayin'—"

Noch spoke out. "First, we had Squire Towne killed over here at the jail car."

He ticked off each incident on the fingers of one hand as he continued, "How many ever boys there was got killed up to that log prison; then those pirates got killed tryin' to steal Captain Mueller's boat – and for what – a load of firewood. Then —"

"Pearls," Luther Blades blurted out.

"What?" Noch asked, fingers poised in mid-count.

"Pearls," Blades repeated. "Stein was on the boat with Mueller and helped fight 'em off. He told me himself, that those pirates were yelling about getting their pearls."

"That makes no sense," Carter-Haines injected. "Mueller's not an oysterman; that boat was loaded with firewood. 'Sides everybody around here knows bay pearls are worthless. No luster to them. Stein must of misunderstood — him being a foreigner and all."

"Maybe the pirates weren't from around here," Tyler offered.

Haynie McKenna looked impatient.

Noch studied his fingers. "Damn it boys," he groused, "will you let me get through this list. I'll lose my place. Now where was I, oh yeah, the Bailiff's brother, Caleb, bless his soul, gets bushwacked. Last, but not be any stretch the least, the high sheriff of the whole dern county gets shot dead just up the road."

Noch looked up. "You can't blame the town for being scared — wonderin' who's the next to get their throat cut, or shot in the back."

"Bad for business, too," said Luther Blades.

Quentin Tyler nodded emphatically, adding, "The railroad opening up real opportunities, but who's gonna want to invest in a town with all these killins."

Haynie waved them silent. "You can tell them," he said evenly, "— and Asbury, you can put this in your paper, there won't be any more of these killings. We'll be going back to the regular Saturday night kind."

Carter-Haines shoved forward, pad in hand, pencil poised, "You got the killer, Bailiff? Where is he? He from around here? He —"

"He's not in jail, but I know who he is. He killed the sheriff at his own campsite and ran off. I'm getting a poster out on him."

"So, the sheriff was onto him and the scoundrel likely out drew him, or back shot him. Did you say the sheriff was shot in the back?" Carter-Haines said scribbling furiously.

Haynie spoke quickly, anxious to be done with it. "Can't say for sure what happened up there, but I can say that the man who killed Squire and my brother, along with the sheriff and those boys at the shack, has fled the area. He's on the run."

Haynie was relieved, though not surprised, when the town elders filed out the door with no further mention of the dead boys in the shack. Those boys were, after all, strangers. No one that the town fathers, or the voters who elected them, would be concerned about.

Today, George Noch, and the other members of the town council, were in the church seated several rows behind the McKenna family.

Haynie glanced at his mother who sat beside him, stone faced, without emotion. It seemed that she too was listening to a voice other than the one from the pulpit.

Muse words filled the little church. "....I did my best to lead Caleb McKenna along the path to find God and the glorious hereafter. His young soul hungered for salvation and I was able to feed this lamb of God. Oh, brothers and sisters, make no mistake, the devil had a hold of him first, but I prayed for strength and with the Lord's help I was able to rescue this lost lamb from the devil's clutches. I..."

Haynie had heard little of what was being said, but it was clear that the eulogy was meant to glorify Muse's ego, rather than celebrate Caleb's life.

Colonel Silas Wallis and his sons were seated in the last pew, nearest the door. Sterling Wallis and his father had debarked the Bay Princess at Crisfield wharf, yesterday afternoon.

Really? Haynie was flummoxed. *Was it only yesterday?* It seemed much longer.

At Haynie's request, Gerhard Stein met the Wallis men at the pier, and insisted on carrying their grips as he led them up Main Street, to the bailiff's office.

Silas Wallis resisted his son's embrace, keeping him at arm's length with a firm handshake. "Your mother is much better now that she knows you are well," he said. "Though still, too weak for such a trip."

The elder Wallis turned to Haynie. "I'm indebted to you for all you did for our family during this ordeal," he said, as they shook hands. "Please accept the condolences of the entire Wallis family on the death of your brother. I understand he was assisting in your search for Landon at the time."

Haynie nodded.

"When is the service?"

"Tomorrow, at the First United Methodist Church."

"The boys and I would be honored to attend."

"Thank you," was all Haynie could say.

Sterling Wallis listened intently to Landon's animated account of his ordeal.

Colonel Wallis turned to Haynie, "Let's step outside," he said, "there's something we need to speak about."

They walked across the hall to the empty conference room. Haynie closed the door and motioned to two nearby chairs.

Haynie declined the offer of a cigar and waited for the colonel to complete the lighting process.

Wallis, visibly pleased with the results, said, "I know we are of a like mind when I say that I want to see the men who took Landon caught and punished."

He rolled the cigar between his fingers and studied the bailiff through the curling smoke.

"I'm not suggesting that you kill them…" receiving no encouragement, he continued.

"Let them spend dark sleepless nights listening to the screams, endless days afraid to venture from the security of their cells. No sir, killin's too good for 'em. I'm saying this because —"

"They're dead."

The elder Wallis stopped, cigar smoke crawling over his face. "How? When?"

"It's certain that Landon was taken by the Drumm brothers; I wired you about them. They broke out of jail when our bailiff was killed. Sunday night, Jake and Rodney Drumm got themselves killed trying to pirate a bugeye."

"You sure about them being the same ones who took Landon?"

Haynie nodded. "My good friend, Gerhard Stein, was on the boat and helped repel them. 'Said he knocked Jake and Rodney into the water as they boarded. Seems Rodney Drumm couldn't swim and he took Jake down with him. Stein and Captain Mueller fished them out of the water and brought them in. Landon looked at the bodies. They're the ones."

"Two. That's all the gang doing the shanghaiing?"

"Landon knows of three. The third one left his kin to drown and headed out to sea. Soon as we sort him out, I'll be gettin' a poster."

Haynie started to lift himself from the chair, when Colonel Wallis motioned him to stay seated.

"Something else," Wallis said. "I realize it's a bad time, but I'm here, and it needs to be said."

Haynie waited.

"I'm of a mind that it we urgently need law and order on the Chesapeake. It's the California gold rush all over again. Tongers staking claims to rich beds, then claim jumpers – be they local drudgers, or oystermen from Virginia or New York, come sailing in and loot 'em. The side has the most guns carry the day."

Wallis waved his cigar at the room. "It's gettin' like a range war out there, with the most dangerous waters right here in Tangier Sound. And why not, the richest beds are here."

Haynie shrugged, "Not much we can do, unless the laws are changed."

Wallis nodded. "Until lately the state assembly has shown no interest in the problem. Baltimore city is where the voters are; not enough democrats down this way for them to bother about.

"But, there's a few of us, with money to do our talking, who are sick of all the killing and thieving. We're demanding that they do something. It's likely next session will see a law establishing a marine police, oyster navy, whatever label they give it. The big question is, how will they fund it? They can't take money from Baltimore City. Local bosses would raise hell. One answer is to have the scoundrels pay for it. State sell their boats, heavy fines."

Haynie experienced a glimmer of hope that law and order might come to the bay in his lifetime. "Be a god awful job," he said, "for whoever takes it on. There's thousands of streams, rivers and coves for them to hide in – they know them. Without money to pay experienced watermen, sound boats for pursuit and weapons —"

Wallis leaned forward. "Exciting news though, eh?"

Haynie nodded.

"It's a start," Wallis said. "The war showed that having the right leadership can make the difference."

Haynie rose to his feet. "Well thank you for letting me know about this, sir. Now, I —"

Wallis remained seated. "Another moment of your time, please," he said, motioning the bailiff back to his chair.

"This is a bad time for you and your family, and I don't like adding to your burden, but you would be a fine commander of the first state law enforcement effort on the Chesapeake Bay. I want your permission to submit your name to the legislative committee, and push you for the job."

"You want to ask them to name me to head up a marine police force?"

"Indeed. We need a man who knows the area, all of those coves and streams. One who's honest and not afraid to stand up to the rascals. You could make a difference.

"Others are pushing an ex-Reb officer, Hunter Davidson. Military experience is certainly an asset. In many ways, this will be more of a military action than peace officering. Your army record is good. One drawback though, you weren't an officer."

Haynie leaned forward, rested his forearms on his knees and rubbed his hands together. "I'm sorry, but I can't give you an answer. I've to bury my brother, then get this mess sorted out, before I can even think of leaving here."

Colonel Wallis removed the cigar from his mouth. "Didn't expect you to make a commitment now. Needed to get it said. Nothing's going to happen until next spring when the legislature meets. I trust you will not speak of this until they act."

Haynie nodded. "Of course."

"One more thing. Your father was killed on the bay and you want to find the man who did it. Probably not going to be able to do that. But, if you could have a say in keeping other watermen from being killed, well, it might help you some."

Wallis abruptly stood and extended his hand. "I'll get back to Landon. Again, sorry about your brother. My sons and I will be at tomorrow's service."

Haynie's brown study was interrupted by Young Tench fussing on his mother's lap. Lila looked at her husband then shifted the squirming youngster to his care and smoothed her dress front. When it was clear that Young Tench was not to be quieted, indeed, his discomfort was turning to sobs, Haynie stood and carried the boy up the aisle.

Outside the church, a doe and her fawn stood at the nearby tree line, frozen in place by his sudden presence.

The out of doors, glorified this day by sunshine, a splendid blue sky and crisp fall air, was Caleb's world. Haynie held his own son and felt closer to Caleb here than was possible inside the church, where he was strained to ignore Muse's bombast.

Haynie paced the churchyard and the deer darted to safety in the woods.

Caleb should be out here, in this glorious place, not indoors being spoken over by a scoundrel who neither knew, nor understood, him.

As he walked, Haynie recalled telling George Noch and the Town Council that he believed Sheriff Jonathan Gastineau had been shot by the same man who had killed Squire Towne, as well as his own brother and the boys in the prison hut. Now, with time for reflection, he was more certain that man was indeed responsible for the killings.

In mid-stride Haynie realized that Young Tench had stopped fussing and looked down to see his son fast asleep.

The congregation was standing and intoned an "Amen" as Haynie carried the baby down the center aisle. He took his place as the others sat and gently returned Young Tench to his mother's care.

Josiah Muse was clearly loath to surrender the pulpit as he reluctantly made way for Reverend Thomas. Abruptly, it seemed, the service was closed and the congregation stood waiting as the family filed passed them.

Once outside, Haynie left his mother with his sister Mattie and began edging back, through the crowd of mourners. Making his way down a side aisle, Haynie hurried to Caleb's bier where Stein and the other pallbearers were gathered.

Gumps, conspicuously uncomfortable, stood apart from the others, his eyes darting between the approaching Haynie and the door to the closet sized room that served the pastor and choir. The old man wore a stained hunting coat over a faded flannel shirt, buttoned at the throat.

"The bad preacher went into that little room with the good preacher," Gumps said. "What do ya want me to do?"

Haynie bent low, his mouth next to Gump's ear. "Sit tight. They have to come out soon and lead the others to the grave."

The door opened and the Reverend Thomas and Josiah Muse appeared, followed closely by Charley Davidson. Muse held back and gazed at the floor as Reverend Thomas approached Haynie.

Gerhard Stein eyed Muse, then glanced at Haynie who returned a slight nod.

Reverend Thomas said, "Doctor Muse and I will attend to the parishioners outside while Charley seals the casket."

Turning to Haynie he continued, "Soon as he's done, you lead the pall bears and your brother out the door; Doctor Muse and I'll head the procession that follows you to the grave site."

Charley Davidson, holding a handful of wood screws and a screwdriver, moved to the bier. Reverend Thomas nodded to Muse and the two men headed up the aisle toward the gathering of mourners.

Aided by the nearest pallbearer, Davidson positioned the coffin lid and prepared to insert the first screw. Haynie touched the undertaker's arm, then nodded to Gumps who hurried to the first row pew.

"One minute please, Charley," Haynie said.

Gumps returned, holding the fiddle that Caleb loved so much. The undertaker slid the coffin lid aside and stepped away. Gumps handed the fiddle to Haynie then moved to the coffin where, his eyes filled with tears, he gently laid the bow on Caleb's chest.

Haynie followed, placing the fiddle at his brother's right side, then stepped back and watched as the coffin closed, and his brother ceased to be.

33

Annapolis, Maryland
Tuesday, March 10, 1868

"Mister McKenna, I'm William J. Leonard, Comptroller for the State of Maryland. Thank you for coming all the way up here to meet with us."

Haynie shook hands and followed the state official into a vaulted anteroom adjacent to the chamber of the House of Delegates. Heavy drapes and dark wood paneling suffocated the small room.

"Is this your first visit to the state capitol?"

Haynie, succumbing to the room's somber character, spoke quietly. "Yes, sir. Thank you for inviting me."

Two men seated behind a long polished table, stood as Haynie approached. Leonard said, "Mister McKenna may I present Robert Fowler, the state's treasurer, and W. S. McPherson, Superintendent of Labor and Agriculture."

Haynie shook hands, aware that the three men, well attired and barbered, presented a cultured, mannered demeanor. They were clearly at ease in these formal surroundings. He was not.

Leonard moved behind the table and seated himself in the middle of three leather armchairs. He motioned Haynie to a bare wooden chair across the table; Fowler and McPherson flanked Leonard.

Leonard began, "Maryland's greatest natural resource, The Chesapeake Bay, and its environs, have become a battleground.

Killings, piracy, even kidnapping have become commonplace. The mad race to plunder the bay of oysters, and other treasures, matches, nay, surpasses, the gold fever in California a few years back. Action, swift and certain, is required to protect lives and property. We must prevent the devastation of oyster beds that, if left unchecked, will deny that delicacy to future generations. I don't believe I'm being overly dramatic when I say that the way of life chosen by many of our citizens is in peril."

Leonard paused as the two men alongside him nodded in vigorous agreement.

Haynie sat patiently. *Sounds like he's practicing a speech for the fall campaign.*

Leonard continued, "We are dedicated to bringing law and order to the Bay, nay, the entire Eastern Shore. At the urging, nay, the insistence, of this administration, the General Assembly is poised to enact legislation establishing a State Oyster Police Force. We expect that a five member Board of Commissioners will oversee this force. The governor and the Clerk of Court of Appeals, along with the three state offices represented at this table, will constitute that board.

"We consider the staffing and implementation of this law enforcement effort an urgent matter. The first step in the process is to select a qualified commander. You come to us highly recommended by Colonel Silas Wallis. By presenting yourself here, today, you are signifying a definite interest in the position. Is that not so?"

Haynie nodded. "Yes sir, it is."

"The purpose of this meeting is for us to get to know one another. Afford each party an opportunity to ask relevant questions of the other."

The men on either side of Leonard, shifted positions and murmured their assent.

Robert Fowler, the state treasurer, said, "If I may, Mister Chairman—"

Leonard yielded, "Of course," he said.

Fowler said, "Mister McKenna, I understand that you fought in the war, on the side of the North."

"Yes, sir."

"We know that Virginia watermen are crossing into Maryland to poach our oyster beds. It's only human nature that Maryland watermen fight back, often resulting in shootings, even killings."

"That has been a concern for several years," Haynie replied.

William Leonard touched Fowler's arm and leaned over, whispering briefly in the other man's ear. Fowler reddened and turned back to Haynie.

"I have just been made aware of the circumstances of your father's death, some years ago. Though unproven, it very likely occurred at the hands of poachers from Virginia."

Haynie nodded.

W. S. McPherson leaned forward. "Perhaps you could give us some insight into the tragedy," he said.

Haynie informed the officials that Tench McKenna had been gunned down fourteen years ago, maybe by Virginia poachers, maybe not; that the matter was never properly investigated by any authorities, and was long forgotten by all but his family; and that a state law enforcement presence on the Chesapeake Bay was long overdue.

Fowler followed up with a cautionary statement about using the state as an instrument for revenge.

W. S. McPherson emphasized the requirement that the Oyster Police guard against over reaction to Virginia poachers. "While poaching cannot be tolerated, armed incursions by Maryland officers into Virginia waters can be construed, in some quarters, as an invasion by the North and re-kindle the flames of civil war."

Fowler wagged a finger in the air. "Very sensitive," he said.

William Leonard cleared his throat and spoke, "You are from Somerset County, are you not, sir."

"Yes, I am."

"My brother-in-law is a waterman, down in Dorchester County. It surprised me to learn that many watermen, but especially those from Somerset County, are against the Oyster Force. They don't like the state coming in and telling them when and where they can fish, or crab, or dig oysters, — or whatever you do to catch 'em.

"As for poachers, and pirates, my brother-in-law says the watermen figure they can protect their own oyster bed. He says if they have a run in with poachers, and there's shootin', which is likely, by the time the oyster navy gets there they could all be dead and their oysters being served in some restaurant in Philadelphia."

Leonard chuckled, then hurried on when it was obvious that he alone was amused. "Point is, you could end up getting in a shoot up with one of your neighbors."

Leonard bent over the table, staring hard. "You prepared to do that?"

"Had neighbors wearing gray. That was war, so is this."

An hour later, after answering all of their questions, Haynie shook hands with each man and left the capitol building, certain in his own mind that he was not going to be the first commander of the Oyster Navy.

34

Crisfield, Maryland
Thursday, March 12, 1868

George Noch paused at the door to the bailiff's office. Seeing Haynie seated at his desk, Noch strolled in and dropped into the empty chair.

"Well," he said, "should we be looking for a new bailiff?"

"They're not going to ask me to take that job," Haynie replied. "I'm not sure I could handle it anyway."

"You'd do fine."

"It's not the work; it's the politics." He tilted his head in the direction of Tangier Sound. "They don't have any idea what's needed to do the job out there. What 's more, they don't really care.

"Oh, they'll give their speeches, say the right words. They'll spend as little money as they can get away with, while keeping up the guise of pushing for law and order on the water. Once our tax money gets to Annapolis, it's their money. They all got their list of gewgaws to spend it on and a proper Oyster Navy is pretty far down. Not even on some of those lists, I'd wager."

"They can't give these shanghaiers and pirates a free hand to plunder the bay at will."

Haynie shook his head. "It's not going to be about them. The way I see it, if this oyster navy does its job, it'll raise hell with our watermen and Virginia poachers. Both of 'em are gonna fight back, and I've not much stomach for killing a fisherman just out trying to make a living, even one from Virginia. Soon the politicians will be looking for somebody to blame; damn sure not going to be any of them. I figure they'll turn on this new commander, whoever he is, and he'll be gone within a year."

"Are you saying you're not takin' the job if they ask you?"

"Well, no, but I'm leaning that way."

Noch said, "The council is hoping you'll honor your promise to stay until Squire's killer is brought to justice. If you leave, who's gonna stand up to him, if he shows up here again. You any idea where he is?"

"About two weeks ago Gerhard was in Ellie's drinking with the crew off of a sloop out of Onancock. They were talking about a stranger who came through there, acting crazy. Could'a been Coates. Had the whole town upset."

Noch stiffened. "Onancock. That's just over the Virginia line."

Haynie nodded. "Just below Pocomoke Sound. Way Gerhard told it, the stranger was acting real peculiar."

"What'd he mean, peculiar?"

"Yelling and cursin' at folks, scaring the bejesus out of all the women and kids. Wore a ratty hide coat and waving a big rifle at them. Who else could it be?"

"Guess the law down there didn't catch him."

"I sent a wire to the sheriff soon's I heard about it. He wired back saying that by the time he'd got over there, the stranger was gone. 'Said he showed that poster I put out to some folks who got close to him. That poster only had a hand drawn picture of Coates, but they believed it was him. Sheriff says the fella only stopped in town long enough to get some laudanum and tobacco. Paid with money from a big wad of bills. Probably still wearin' that money belt he took off Gastineau. Man lives like he does, money's gonna last a good while. "

Noch stood to leave, his face pale, "You don't think he'll come back here — do you?"

Haynie chose not tell the councilman that it was his desperate hope that Caleb's killer would appear in Crisfield — and soon.

"Doubtful, but it sounds like he's gone mad. He might get it in his head to ride down Main Street, daring anyone to come out and face him."

Noch sighed, "We can only hope he gets caught before you leave."

Haynie looked up sharply, "I said —"

"I know what you said," Noch said on his way out the door.

With George Noch gone, Haynie put his feet up on his desk and tilted back in his chair. He needed to think.

George is scared. They're all scared. Haven't had but one killing since November — and that got the town all stirred up again.

It had been New Years night, two drunken watermen fighting over a bargirl. Still, it was a knifing and rumors flew around that the killer who slit throats was back.

This sighting was the first news of Coates since November. Then, after sending out the wanted posters, Haynie had scoured the area around Crisfield, vainly searching for a new campsite. Convinced that Coates was gone, he speculated that the killer had likely headed west to Missouri, or the Texas border. Somewhere that Southern sympathy was strong and the law weak.

This belief weighed on Haynie, often pressing him into a funk when mingled with his fear that Caleb's killer would forever go unpunished. He had failed his father, and now his brother. Haynie dismissed any notion that the stranger in Onancock was not Jeremy Coates. His gut told him that the man he hunted was close. *Just over the Virginia line, maybe headed this way.*

While that thought frightened the town folk, it cheered him immeasurably.

Truth is, I can't just go off to Annapolis with him on the loose, especially if he's nearby. Still, being head of the state oyster navy would give me a lot more authority to go looking for him than being a town bailiff. For one thing, the state of Virginia would have to pay some mind to what I say.

Last fall there had been talk of Haynie being named county sheriff, replacing the murdered Sheriff Gastineau. At least until the next election. He had liked the idea but quickly realized he did not have the political backing necessary to attain such a high office.

Just after Thanksgiving, a man had appeared in the bailiff's office and introduced himself as Deputy Estes McFaul of the Somerset County Sheriff's Department.

McFaul said he knew Haynie was interested in being sheriff, and had heard that the bailiff was an honest man. Deputy McFaul had come all the way to Crisfield because he wanted Haynie to know that he had put in for the job, and that even though he had worked for Gastineau, he too was an honest man. One that could not be bought off.

The deputy, though young, was well spoken and obviously possessed a quick mind. Haynie took an instant liking to him, believing that he would be a good lawman at any level.

Haynie looked across his desk. "You saying that Gastineau was crooked?"

"What I'm saying is, that no matter what you might have heard about Gastineau, and one or two other deputies, I'm not like them, and never would be. If you get the job, I hope you'll keep me on. If you decide not to take it, maybe you'll put in a good word for me."

The deputy was clearly reluctant to speak ill of the dead sheriff and Haynie chose his words carefully. "I'm real interested in anything you can tell me about Gastineau. His killing is connected to the murder of the bailiff here, and my brother. Maybe some others."

Deputy McFaul played his hat back forth between his hands. "I got to be careful here; Gastineau's got — had — powerful friends. If it got out that I was callin' him, and them, crooked..."

Haynie got up, crossed the room and closed the door. When he returned he said, "I had doubts about him myself, but he got killed before anything came of it. You said, I might have heard something; what did you think I might have heard?"

"If it comes to it, I'll deny sayin' it."

"It won't come to it."

"Mind you it's just guesswork — instinct. That's why I have to be careful."

Haynie nodded.

"Gastineau showed more money than a sheriff should have. You saw his clothes and that walking stick, cost plenty. You ever see his wife?"

Haynie shook his head.

"From Philadelphia. Fancy clothes, jewels — lots of jewels. They had that big house in Princess Anne, and a farm near Whitehaven. 'Nothing too good for Missus Gastineau,' he was always sayin'. Lots of visitors to that farm, mostly rich folks from Baltimore and Annapolis."

Haynie waited.

McFaul shrugged. "Might as well keep talking," he said. "One time, the sheriff came around saying that he had some folks comin' to his farm. Laughed and said his rich kinfolk were coming to visit. Said he needed a couple of deputies to tend to these folks durin' their visit. Pick 'em up from the train station in Princess Anne, or the wharf in Whitehaven if they came by boat. Haul their trunks and bags to the farm, get 'em drinks, stuff like that. It meant extra pay so a couple of us did it. During the day, we'd saddle a horse for them if they were going on a foxhunt, or just wanted to ride; the sheriff had a fine stable of horses, not a plug in the bunch – clean their long guns. You know, stuff like that.

"First thing that struck you when you met these folks was, they all spoke slow and drawly, like they were from the South. It's hard to figure how the sheriff, of Somerset County Maryland, was kin to all those Rebs."

"Not everyone with a southern drawl is a Reb."

"These were."

"How do you know that?"

"Once they got settled in, everybody got dressed up in Reb uniforms, like they were going to a costume ball, no music though. And that's not all. They talked like they were still in the army, siring each other and callin' each other major, or colonel and such."

Haynie interrupted. "For some folks," he said, "on both sides, the war is not over. The Yankee carpetbaggers are lootin' the South as much to punish them for killin' their son, or uncle, or whoever, as they are for the money. And, there's Rebs who can't bring themselves to admit they lost. For them, the saying 'The South shall rise again,' is not just a lot of talk."

McFaul shook his head. "Maybe so, but Reb army officers in Somerset County —"

"How many times did you see them in their uniforms?

"That's another funny thing. Couple of days after we were out there, I asked the other deputy, didn't he think all that soldier stuff was strange? He shook his head and wouldn't talk about it. I never got asked again. I know there was other times, I'd hear some talk and I'd have to work in the office for one of the men who was out there. The same two boys, who went every time, begun having considerable more money to spend."

"You hear any names you can recollect?" Haynie asked.

"Let me see...there was this one big fella. He seemed to be the headman they called him Colonel Mooney. The woman with him, blonde haired, name of Miss Grace, was quiet, but you could tell she was deep."

"What about Gastineau, he wear a uniform?"

McFaul nodded. "Called him Major Gastineau."

If Haynie's suspicions were correct, Gastineau, and maybe this pack of rich Rebs, were somehow involved with Coates and the Drumm brothers. Maybe running the whole thing.

If so, they were back of the shanghaiing and the killings.

What could he do about it? Probably nothing. It was likely neither he nor Deputy McFaul would be appointed county sheriff and who's going to listen to a small town bailiff? The truth is, that even if there was someone who would listen, Haynie didn't have any proof. Nothing but guesswork.

After Deputy McFaul left, Haynie wired Colonel Wallis, asking if the names, Grace and Mooney, meant anything. Wallis wired back that Grace Stringfellow was the widow of Isaiah Stringfellow and inherited his seafood processing business in Baltimore after he fell overboard and drowned. Soon after, Horace Mooney, who she introduced as her brother, moved in. They were from Virginia.

Though it proved nothing, Haynie was more convinced that Gastineau and Coates were in league with the Virginians, Colonel Mooney and Miss Grace. With Gastineau dead, Coates was the only living connection, he knew, to the people behind the killing of Squire Towne and Caleb.

Haynie told himself he needed more authority than he got from being the town bailiff to go after this gang.

Besides, what kind of future is there for Lila and Young Tench if I don't seize an opportunity when one comes along? I'd have to peddle a whole lot of dog licenses to get him in a good school.

Then, there was the situation with his mother.

Two days after Caleb's funeral she had been alone in her buggy, returning from town with provisions for the Manor House, when she was passed by a wagon heading toward town. Seated next to the driver, was Josiah Muse. 'That foreigner friend of Haynie's', as Lettie McKenna referred to Gerhard Stein, was driving the wagon loaded with Muse's belongings. Muse lowered his head, refusing to acknowledge her 'halloo's', while Stein tipped his hat and smiled as he drove on.

At home, Lettie was shocked to find all traces of Josiah Muse gone from the house. His room was bare of clothes and toiletries. Downstairs, the library was eerily empty, his books, desk and writing materials, gone. Everything gone. With not a letter of explanation to be found.

She slumped onto a settee and sat staring into the emptiness. Eventually, she roused herself and walked out onto the porch. There she stood, watching River Road until dark for Josiah Muse to return.

Later, she ate a cold supper in the shadowy light of one candle. For the first time since she had moved her boys there, her home was a cold and foreboding structure. She no longer thought of it as her Manor House. Ominous sounds wafting through the rooms on the lower floor frightened her. Was that a heavy footstep on the second floor? Was the place haunted?

Lettie slept little that night. Huddled under a blanket, downstairs on the settee, fully clothed, she listened as the house creaked and moaned.

Just after daylight, she threw back the cover and, without splashing water to her face or running a brush through her hair, marched straight to her son's home. She mounted the narrow porch and proceeded to pound on the front door.

Within moments, Haynie, fully dressed, opened the door, startled to see his mother standing before him, pale and in disarray. "What the — Mother — what's happened? You look awful; come in out of the weather."

Lettie McKenna folded her arms across her chest and stood firmly in place.

"If I look – awful, it's you who is to blame. And, I'll say what I have to say to you right here. Fie on you, Haynie McKenna. Fie on you. You have ruined my life...."

Haynie opened his mouth, but Lettie continued her tirade.

"Don't try to deny it. I saw that foreigner you brought back with you from the war, carrying my dear Josiah and every piece of his belongings away from me in that wagon."

She balled a fist and shook it under her son's chin. "And don't you dare try to tell me that you had nothing to do it. That foreigner and his wagon didn't just happen by and see Josiah standing alongside the road with all his belongings piled around him. That bully came here and threatened that good man. What did you have him say to the reverend? Must have scared him real bad for him to up and skedaddle like that — with nary a word."

Lila McKenna appeared at the door, a wool robe pulled close against the chill morning air. She looked sharply at Haynie and reached out for her mother-in-law. "Mother McKenna, do come in. What ever has happened let's talk about it in here."

Lettie shrank from Lila's touch and tears pooled in her eyes before spilling over both cheeks. Haynie, fearing his mother might collapse, moved to help her inside.

Lettie backed off the porch and, stiffened. "I have nothing more to say to either of you. I would never have believed that I'd say this to my own son — you are not welcome in my house." She turned and strode away, wiping tears on her coat sleeve as she went.

Haynie had honored his mother's wishes. It was now March and, except for a glimpse of her in passing the Manor House, he had not seen her since that day in early November.

Nor had Lila. At first, she and Haynie believed that Lettie would wait until he was not at home, and then beseech Lila to let her spend some time with Young Tench. But, such was not the case.

Early Christmas morning Haynie found a small box wrapped in brown paper, tied with a red ribbon, sitting on the front steps. It was covered with a dusting of the dry snow that had fallen over night. "Young Tench", printed neatly in Lettie's hand, was the only communication from Lettie McKenna in over four months.

Haynie opened the box to find the worn McKenna family bible, familiar to Haynie from his early home on Smith Island.

In mid-January, Lettie began taking in boarders and soon Haynie saw a procession of transient visitors around her house. Even as he searched the men for Josiah Muse, Haynie knew that, should Muse appear, he would do nothing.

Periodically, since that November morning, Lila McKenna had urged her husband to go to his mother, tell her he was sorry, and ask her to forgive him.

"After all," Lila said, "she says she's a Christian, and Christians are supposed to be forgiving of others."

But the most Haynie would do is promise Lila he would never again meddle in his mother's life. If he was to keep his word, he could do nothing, even if he saw the evil little man walking in her front door.

Haynie McKenna shook himself. He needed to clear his mind of the past and return his full attention to the present and the future.

Has all this pondering done me any good? Actually, it has. I am now certain that I am ready to move on, and equally certain I can't leave this job to someone else until Jeremy Coates is dead or in jail.

A breathless Tawes Butler appeared in the doorway, "Thank the Lord yer here, Mister McKenna. Mister Blades sent me fer ya. Says there's a crazy man in the store and you should come quick."

Haynie was immediately out of his chair. "Is Gerhardt Stein working there today?" he asked as he buckled on his gun belt.

The boy frowned. "I don't believe he is, sir."

"Find him, and tell him I said to stop whatever he's doing and get to Blade's as fast as he can. And Tawes," the lad hesitated, "tell him what's happened, and for him to come in quiet like, through the back door."

35

Crisfield, Maryland
Thursday, March 12, 1868

Haynie crossed Main Street, keeping in the shadows of the buildings, as he hurried toward Luther Blades's store. Coates, if indeed the crazy man was Coates, must not escape. He dried his sweating palms on his shirt, then patted the holster at his side, reassured by the bulk of the Colt .44 revolver.

Haynie was four buildings away when he abruptly stopped; his fingers tightened around the revolver handle. Tied to Blades's hitching rail, stood the same boney gray mare he and Caleb had seen Jeremy Coates riding out of town in early November.

He's here.

Haynie's mouth was chalky, his throat constricted. His heart thrashed violently and blood pounded in his ears relentlessly, making it difficult to think above the roar.

I might better walk right in there, gun out, and shoot him down where he stands. I'm no Texas Ranger, fast on the draw, and no sense giving him a chance to aim that big rifle. Still, he may not know I'm coming to take him in; if Gerhard shows up in time maybe I won't have to kill him. I'd sure like to ask him about how he came to kill the sheriff; maybe he knows some of those Reb army folks the sheriff was cozy with. Not likely, still...

Poised at the door, Haynie searched the empty street for Gerhard Stein, then took a breath and carefully opened the door.

Haynie hoped to be able to slip inside, locate Coates and decide quickly what to do. He forgot the front door was rigged with a small bell announcing the presence of a customer as the door opened.

Blades and Coates, standing together at the back of the store, turned to stare as Haynie closed the door.

Luther's weight was supported solely on the balls of his feet, his body swaying slightly as if he were about to swoon.

Coates appeared spare, wasted. The buffalo robe billowed away from his spindly frame. The grimy beaver hat fallen over his ears. The rest of his cadaverous face masked behind a tangled, motley beard.

Coates cowered, drawing back from the approaching figure. A boney hand clawed incessantly at a red, angry wrist, a piece of filthy black cloth unraveling as he dug at the wound.

The Prussian rifle leaned against the counter, forgotten as Coates backed away. The gun, Haynie noted, still gleamed, while the man had fallen further into despair.

"Thank God, you came, Bailiff," Luther Blades called out as he edged away from the counter.

"He's a opium-eater, been acting real crazy like. Shoot him now and be done with it. I'm a God fearing man, but it wouldn't be wrong to kill him – he's bad as any wild animal. This is my store and I say — kill him where he stands. "

Coates shifted a bewildered gaze from the intruder to Luther Blades. Not understanding the words, he was searching for the source of the latest noise in the room.

Coates blinked and swung his head back, again suspicious of Haynie. He opened his mouth to call out, his words a coarse whisper.

"That you, God?" he asked, withdrawing a large Bowie knife from beneath his buffalo robe.

Coates slashed the air in front of him, "I ain't goin' with ya."

Luther backed away from the thrashing arms. "Kill him, kill him," he shrieked, while throwing himself over the counter.

Haynie's revolver remained holstered. He was determined to kill Coates only as a last resort. The bailiff eyed a display of long handled shovels to his right and calculated the wisdom of grabbing one and swinging it at the man's head.

Gerhardt Stein appeared in the doorway directly behind Coates.

Haynie made eye contact with Stein and touched a forefinger to his lips.

Coates, detecting the movement, stopped his knife thrusts in mid-air and glowered at Haynie.

The bailiff circled his arms, lacing his fingers together in front of him, signaling to Stein that he was to wrap Coates tightly in a bear hug from behind.

Haynie's movement agitated Coates, who lunged forward, snarling and rending the air with the knife blade.

With two quick strides, Stein was on Coates, wrapping him in powerful arms and lifting him from the floor.

Coates, arms pinned to his sides, shook his head violently, flinging saliva from his mouth as he screamed curses and kicked out with both legs.

Haynie wrenched the knife from Coates's fingers, the man's spittle wet on his neck.

Gerhard yelled and Haynie jerked his head back as Coates's jaws snapped shut inches from his right ear.

Blades peered across the counter top, "Don't let him bite ya," he warned. "I seen a man with hydra-phobia before. He's got it for sure."

Coates struggled to free himself of Stein's grasp.

"Luther," Haynie called, "bring a length of rope — quick."

Blades's eyes and bald pate appeared over the counter top.

"I'm staying right here," he said. "Corralling crazy men is your job."

Coates kicked furiously, flinging his head about, eyes flashing wildly as he dug his heels into Stein's shins.

"I'm the devil," Coates screamed, "and you are going to burn in hell. Be warned! I'm comin' for ya. We're gonna fall into the fires of hell."

Haynie looked at Stein, "You got him?"

"Ja."

Tawes Butler appeared in the storage room doorway.

"Tawes," Haynie called, "go into that store room and cut a piece of heavy rope from the roll back there. Make it half-again as long as you are. Bring it to me and be quick about it."

Jeremy Coates was tiring. His eyes dulled, his breathing labored.

From under the counter, Luther Blades yelled, "Bailiff, shooting him is one thing, hangin' him in my store is quite another. No, sir. A man hanging above my counters is unseemly. Bad for business. Very bad. We're getting to the busy part of the day. Shoot him and be done with it."

Tawes Butler came through the doorway, a length of rope coiled around his shoulder. He made a wide path around the struggling Coates and tossed the coil to the bailiff.

"Now get over to Davidson's and tell him to hitch up his funeral wagon and load up one of those simple pine boxes he makes for Potter's Field. Bring the hearse to the back door, then tote the box in here. Quickly, now."

Tawes blinked, said, "Yes, sir," and rushed out the front door.

"Dammit, McKenna. If you're gonna hang him here, have the decency to lock that front door. It wouldn't do to have the wife of one of the town fathers come waltzing in here expecting to see the latest in yard goods and find that crazy man swinging from a beam. Lock it right now!"

Haynie tied the rope in a lasso. "I'm a little busy. You'll have to go yourself."

Stein, his forearms locked across Coates's chest, leaned back, allowing Haynie room to loop the rope over the prisoner's head, securing the struggling man's arms to his sides.

Coates curses became a mumbled whisper, his eyelids drooping as he went limp in Stein's grasp.

Luther Blades's eyes appeared over the counter, darting from side to side. "He dead?" Blades asked just as the bell over the front door jangled. A woman's form appeared in the doorway.

"Oh," she said, looking around. "I believe I'll come back another time," and rushed away leaving the door open behind her.

"Well?" the storekeeper challenged. "Is he dead?"

Before Haynie could answer, Luther waved a hand, "Don't really matter. Either way, you all get him out of here."

Coates, trussed within his buffalo robe, groaned as he was lowered roughly to the floor.

Haynie moved to the counter and grabbed up the Prussian long rifle. He extracted a live round from the chamber and dropped the cartridge in his coat pocket. The gun shook in his hands; a single bullet from this gun had killed his brother.

Haynie struggled with a strong urge to reload the gun and turn it on Coates when he heard a single, sharp report. Like the crack of a buggy whip.

Haynie whirled around as Luther Blades dove under the counter. Gerhard Stein grunted and kicked at Coates, catching his forearm. The bone snapped, just above the wrist, a jagged end splitting the emaciated skin. Coates squealed in pain and the Sharp's pepperbox clattered to the floor.

Haynie scooped up the tiny weapon and looked at Stein. "This is Squire's gun," he said.

Gerhard Stein examined the spot on his shirt where the blood oozed from the small hole in his right shoulder, soaking into the flannel material before it could splatter on the floor.

"Gerhard, my God, he shot you."

Stein looked up, dazed. "Ja", he said. His expression one of bewilderment, not pain.

"How in hell did he get to that gun?"

Gerhard Stein shrugged. "I looking at you, gun goes pop, I see *blut* on *hemd* – shirt."

Haynie bent down, grabbed Coates by his broken arm and rolled him over on his stomach. Ignoring the screams and curses, Haynie yanked Coates's hands behind his back, lashing them together with the belt from his own trousers.

"The rope had just enough play that he could move his right hand around inside that robe. Must have carried Squire's pistol right there."

Haynie reached under the buffalo robe and worked his hand in as far as he could reach. Looking at Stein as he worked, Haynie said, "I'm sorry, Gerhard, I'll never make that mistake again."

Luther Blades called out from his sanctuary. "What in blazes is going on out there? You boys sing out if he gets loose."

Tawes Butler appeared in the doorway to the storeroom, wide-eyed, breathing hard. Haynie could make out Charley Davidson, in the shadows, well behind the boy.

"Somebody get shot?" Tawes asked.

Davidson moved closer. On tiptoes, he was able to look over Tawes shoulder.

"We need that box in here," Haynie ordered.

Luther Blades's head popped up behind the counter, his eyes following Charley Davidson and Tawes Butler as they sat the pine box on the floor next to a moaning Jeremy Coates.

"Shoot him again, he's still movin," Luther said.

Haynie nodded toward Gerhard Stein. "Tawes," he said, "we're gonna need Doc Ward. Bring him to the rail jail."

Tawes shook his head in disbelief and charged out the back door.

Haynie McKenna stood at Coates's head. "Charley, with Gerhard shot, I'll need you to grab his legs and help me get him into the box."

Stein stepped in front of the undertaker. "*Nein. Ich* can do."

They lifted Coates's bound form and dropped him face up into the coffin. Though frail, the weight of his body landing on the broken arm was excruciating. Coates screamed in pain and glared up at the bailiff, his eyes suddenly clear, focused.

"Goddamn bastards," he cursed, "give me my damn knife and I'll gut ya. I know who you are you're the town law. If I hadn't got sick I'd have been back here long time ago and you'd be in this here box stead of me. Goddamn mutt hadn't bit me; I fixed him real good, yes sir."

Haynie moved closer, returning Coates's glare as he towered over the man in the box. The prisoner strained against the ropes and launched as much spittle as he could summon toward his captor. The sputum came out in a drool clinging to Coates's chin whiskers.

Haynie nodded to Stein. "Let's get him loaded on the wagon and up to the jail car where Doc can take a look at both of you."

Doc Ward and Tawes Butler were waiting when the funeral wagon stopped beside the jail car.

The procession of townsfolk trailing the wagon, as it rolled up Main Street, watched in curious silence as the coffin holding Jeremy Coates was unloaded.

Stein refused to lie down on one of the bunk beds, until he and Haynie, with Tawes Butler's help, had wrestled Coates's box into the first cell.

Charley Davidson wouldn't leave until Haynie assured him that he would be paid for the coffin.

"I couldn't really use it for no one else now that man has bled on it and all," Charley said.

Haynie nodded. "'Course."

"That price includes the lid." Davidson said, "I'll see that you get it."

Doc Ward finished his examination of Coates and walked over to Haynie.

"Make sure Charley gets you that lid, you're gonna need it by sunup."

"I need to talk to him about some of these killings he did. Will he know what I'm saying?"

Doc Ward removed his felt hat and ran his fingers through a thick grey head of hair.

"There'll be spells when he's lucid. 'Course he's in a lot of pain. Actually, his pain works for you; it'll help keep him conscious. No way to know when the spells will come, or how long they'll last. Before sunup, he'll be hurrying toward the light."

"So, there will be times he can understand my questions."

Doc Ward nodded. "He'll know. Can't say if he'll answer them or not. Oh, likely he's an opium eater. Kept begging me for laudanum. I got some in my bag."

"Got any paregoric with you, Doc?" Haynie asked.

Doc Ward looked puzzled. "Always have some for fussy kids. What're you thinking?"

"I remember from the war that the camphorated tincture has a lot less morphine in it than the laudanum."

"Ya don't think he'll know the difference?"

Haynie shrugged. "Worth a try. Better chance of keeping him alert."

"I better see to Stein's shoulder," Ward said. "I'll give you both of those bottles, before I go."

As Doc Ward entered the cell where Gerhard Stein rested, Tawes Butler stood and edged out, leaving room for the doctor to work.

"Tawes," Haynie called.

"Yes, sir?"

Haynie dug a two-dollar bill from his pocket and handed it to the boy.

"You were a big help to me today, to the whole town. I'll see the council knows about it and try to get you more than this. You deserve it."

Tawes grinned, rolled the bill tightly and secreted it in his pants pocket.

"If you don't think your mother will be looking for you, I need you to do a couple more things for me."

"Long as I'm home for supper. What do you need, Mister McKenna?"

"I need a hammer and a handful of ten penny nails, and a hacksaw." Haynie nodded toward the interior of the jail car, "Bring 'em back here and lay 'em over there, next to his long gun."

Tawes nodded and was gone.

Haynie loomed above the box, studying his prisoner's face. Coates had tilted his body to the left, taking some of the weight off of his broken arm. He licked his lips and moaned.

Haynie felt no pity for the man who had caused his family so much pain.

"I'm looking forward to spending some time with you," he said.

Coates looked about wildly, searching for the source of the words. "That you, God?" he called out.

Satisfied that Coates had been rendered harmless, Haynie left the cell and met Doc Ward leaving Stein's bedside.

"Gerhard's strong, hasn't lost much blood," the doctor said. "I dressed the wound and gave him something to make him sleep. He should sleep through whatever goes on in here tonight," Ward said. He glanced at Haynie. "Long as it doesn't get too loud."

The doctor dug in his bag and handed Haynie a vial of laudanum and a small bottle of paregoric.

"Thanks, Doc." Haynie called as Ward headed for the door.

"Don't let Stein run off 'til I can get back here in the morning," the doctor yelled over his shoulder. "By then I should be able to pronounce the other one."

The late afternoon air chilled considerably, Haynie draped a blanket over his sleeping friend. Then he moved to close the big sliding door against the cold. Tawes slipped inside as the door closed behind him.

"That was fast, boy."

Tawes shrugged and displayed a homemade hacksaw, rusty claw hammer and a handful of rough-cut nails. "I just went home and got 'em from the shed. I hope they'll do."

"They'll do fine, Tawes, thanks. I'll get them back to you."

The boy's smile was quick and sad. "No hurry. Without Pa around they don't get used much."

He brightened, pleased to say something good about his father. "Ya know, my pa made them tools with his own hands. Pretty good, huh, Mister McKenna?"

"First rate. Your father was a real craftsman."

Tawes smiled.

Haynie pulled a five-dollar bill from his pocket and said, "I need you to do two more things for me, you up to it?"

Tawes eyed the bill, straightened his arms at his sides. "I done all right so far," he said. "I can do whatever you want, sir."

Haynie patted the boy on the shoulder. "Take this money, hurry to the Main Street Café and get Mel to fix up two bowls of his soup. Tell him to put plenty of meat and vegetables in it, along with some coffee and a couple of biscuits. Get him to give it to you in something so you can carry them here without spilling it all over."

The boy nodded.

"With the rest of the money you get something for you and your ma, and run it home before bringing the soup back here."

"Yes, sir. Thanks."

Tawes was elated to earn enough money to let him treat his mother to a meal she did not have to cook.

"Er, Mister McKenna."

"Yes, Tawes,"

The lad fingered the rolled two-dollar bill in his pocket and said. "Would it be all right with you, if, instead of taking something home, I took ma to eat in the café?"

"Of course."

Tawes beamed again. "Is that all, sir?" he asked.

"Just one more thing. I need you to ride out to my house, don't tell Missus McKenna anything about what happened today, just tell her it's likely I wont be home 'til morning."

36

Rail Jail
Crisfield, Maryland
Thursday, March 12, 1868

Haynie McKenna started a fire in the pot-bellied stove situated between the two cells of the jail car. He checked on his prisoner, and left him, alternately groaning and begging for laudanum, to look in on the sleeping Gerhard Stein.

Charley Davidson had returned with the wooden lid for the pine box.

After leaving the food, Tawes Butler headed up River Road to the McKenna home.

"Unless Missus McKenna has an urgent message for me, you don't need to come back," Haynie had told him. "You and your mother go have a nice dinner."

Haynie quickly locked the door and set the food aside. The tools and the long rifle he laid on the floor alongside the pine box. Next, he rested the lid against the end of the box nearest Jeremy's head. Coates recognized the coffin lid, his look now of fear mixed with the loathing.

He licked dry lips. "Yer gonna bury me alive, ain'tcha," he rasped.

"Any reason I shouldn't? It was you killed my brother."

Haynie studied the man in the box. Rat was an apt name for Jeremy Coates. Feral, more animal than man, he lived most of his life like an animal; now he was dying like one.

As for vengeance, Haynie could ask no more than the lingering, painful death Rat was enduring.

His death, under these conditions, is not something I care to hasten.

Each cell boasted a cup and pewter pitcher that, on mornings he was able, Bozo replenished daily with fresh water pumped from a nearby well.

Haynie went to the pitcher and poured a cup of water, which he carried back.

"Soon as I can cut that rope away, we'll get you some of this water." He set the cup on the edge of the box. Drops of water sloshed onto Rat's face.

Rat flung his head from side to side, screaming. "Get it off me! No water. I don't want no water. Get that away from me, damn you."

Haynie now recalled that hydrophobia – fear of water – was another name for rabies. He smiled and set the tin cup on the floor, out of sight for the present.

Haynie tipped a wooden crate on end and sat glowering at his brother's killer. Rat watched with sullen indifference, believing he was about to be suffocated.

Normally, Rat was fearless, unlikely to be frightened into telling what he knew. But, the rabies raged within him creating additional terrors that Rat could not master. A man, who would otherwise sneer at anyone holding a gun or knife, was panicked by a few drops of water.

Haynie stood, pulled a hunting knife from its sheath, and cut away the rope binding his prisoner's wrists. He then raised Rat just enough to pull the rope from around him.

Rat cried out, his broken right arm at his side, hurting and useless.

Haynie knotted one end of the rope around Rat's left wrist, and then tied off the other end to the cell's iron cot.

Using his hunting knife, and working quickly, Haynie slit the filthy buffalo hide up the middle revealing grimy trousers and waistcoat cut from expensive cloth. A lawman's star inscribed "Sheriff Somerset County Maryland" was pinned high on the left side of the waistcoat.

"'Course. Yer gonna rob me before ya bury me alive, ain'tcha?"

Haynie tore the badge from Rat's chest and held it up for him to see.

"No doubt about who killed the sheriff."

Rat erupted in a rage. He flung his head violently from side to side and kicked air, like a child in tantrum. "Let me out of here," he screamed. "Billy Quantrill needs me. I got to kill the blue coats before they get Billy! Goddammit, I'm a comin', Billy – hang on – I'm a comin'."

Just as suddenly he was quiet, his eyelids drooped shut.

After determining that Rat was still breathing, Haynie slid the coffin lid over the bottom third of the box and partially drove a nail on each side. He covered the man's legs enough to prevent him from flailing out again, leaving sufficient nail exposed for easy removal when it came time to close the lid.

Haynie sliced away the remainder of the clothing.

"Let's make certain," he said, "that you don't have another gun or knife tucked away in here somewhere."

The contents of the pockets included a few coins, three stick matches and an empty laudanum vial.

"Figured you to have some cartridges handy in one of these pockets." Haynie shook his head, "Of course, they'd be in your bags or bed roll. I'll have to get Tawes to bring that broken down mare of yours up here tomorrow."

Haynie cut through the waistcoat and pleated bibs of the fancy dress shirt, revealing a money belt buckled at the waist.

"Likely something else you took from Gastineau," he said.

Rat opened his eyes to see the leather money belt dangling above his head.

"Here, that's mine. Gimme it back."

Haynie let the belt sway back and forth above the box. "You stole it from Sheriff Gastineau, the man you killed," he said. Seeing an opening, he continued, "From what I hear, he likely deserved it. I expect he did you a wrong and you did what any man would have done."

"Lord knows I done a lot of bad things, some real bad, but that man was a worse scoundrel than me. Truth is, I didn't know he was a lawman, no one would'a knowed the way he carried on, 'til I saw the star." Rat grew quiet his eyes closed again.

"How'd he wrong you?"

After a moment, Rat opened his eyes. The fear and loathing replaced by an impish light. "I guess you ain't gonna bury me anytime soon, and I know you got laudanum."

Haynie produced the laudanum vial, now filled with paregoric and held it where the prisoner could see it.

"Gimme a slug, damn you, I'm in a heap of pain."

Haynie shook his head.

"I know I'm dying," Rat said, "but I ain't out of my head, at least for now. I'm of a mind to tell you about that snake of a lawman – can't hurt me none – but you gotta hand over that laudanum, or so help me I'll close up right now and you can whistle for it. Now untie my good arm and gimme. "

Haynie uncorked the vial and held it over head.

"Here's how we're going to do it," he said. "I'll keep hold of it and pour some in your mouth, when I judge you need it, and if I can believe what you're telling me."

"Then I ain't talking. I'm already in 'bout as much pain as a man can stand, and I'm dying to boot. What more can ya do to me? "

"I saw what laudanum does to a man, in the war. You get a chance, you'll drink the whole vial and be on your way to hell without a word. You'll get what I think you need, or none."

"Nothin' you can do," Rat said, then shut his eyes and pressed his lips together.

Haynie picked up the cup of water and held it above the prisoner's head.

"How about a cool drink of water, instead," he said, letting a few drops splash over Rat's face.

"Get it off me. Get it off me," Rat screamed his eyes wide. "Ain't fair, damn you; doin' a man thata way with a cup of water. Goddamn dog. All right, get that water out of here, gimme some of that opium and I'll tell ya what I know."

Rat smacked his lips as the bailiff poured a few drops of paregoric through them, then shut his eyes and waited for the drug to act on his pain.

Haynie retrieved the money belt and opened the leather pouches. "How'd you meet up with Sheriff Gastineau?" he asked.

"If you mean the snake wearing that tin star, I never know'd his real name. 'Said he was Mister Green — Mister Green mah ass — he never said nuthin' to me about bein' a lawman." Rat closed his eyes, his breathing labored.

Haynie pulled a wad of bills from one of pouches and held it overhead.

"He likely carried this wad in the belt, so this isn't why you killed him. You didn't know it was there."

Rat's eyelids fluttered as he tried to focus on what the bailiff was holding in his hand.

"That was my money; bastard stole it from me. Stole my money— and him a sheriff."

"How did your money get into his money belt?"

Rat shifted and cried out. “That opium ain’t working. Hurts like hell.”

“I’ll give you some more after you answer the question. How was it the sheriff had your money?”

“It was money owed to me for — some work I done.”

“Was it pay for killing my brother?”

“Which one was he?”

“The one you back shot in the woods last November.”

Haynie pulled a tarnished gold pocket watch from one of the pouches and dangled it above Rat’s head. “The one whose body you stole this from as he lay bleeding to death in the marsh grass.”

It was his father’s watch. Haynie wiped his eyes as he read the inscription, “To Tench with love, Lettie – 1851".

Rat grunted. “Sayin’ a thing is somethin’ I stoled, don’t help me recollect. Ever thing I got I stole when someone wasn’t looking or was too dead to object. ’Cept that scraggly old mare. Found her in a old corn field grubbin’ for food, me on my hands and knees right next to her.”

“You’re the coldest bastard, I ever met,” Haynie said through clenched teeth. “You killed a lot of people and you’re not sorry about one of ’em.”

“You want to get any more from me; you best pour me another shot of that laudanum and get back to it. I can feel my time gettin’ close.”

Haynie shook off the urge to kill the man now, and dribbled a few drops into his mouth.

“Why’d you kill him – my brother?”

Jeremy savored the drops before saying, “They paid me to see that none of them boys got out of that log shack; the paddy shack, that sheriff called it, where they kept them shanghais before sellin’ them to an erster boat. They didn’t want nobody finding it, neither. Anyways, one day this fella breaks out of the trees headed straight for it, so I shot him. But Mister Green wouldn’t pay up, claimed I killed the wrong one. I was supposed to kill that boy’s brother – which I guess would be you.”

“Who was the money coming from? It wasn’t Gastineau’s.”

Rat shook his head. “Don’t know who they is exactly. Some rich Rebs living across the bay. Green told me one time that we had nuthin’ to worry about ’cause them and their friends was runnin’ the state.”

He snorted a laugh that triggered a coughing spasm. When the seizure eased he said, “Ole Green should’ve been worrying about Rat before he went ahead and stole my money.”

“You any idea who these friends are?”

“Maybe. A Reb captain I met up with in Kentucky tole me a name to go see, if I wanted to make some damn good money. The man he sent me to was livin' in a big house above the Potomac. Looks down on a little river town name of Popes Creek, on the Maryland side."

"You know the name of the man in that house?"

Rat nodded. "That coughin' spell was real painful. I'll be able to say out the name if I get me some more of that."

Haynie dribbled a few drops on Rat's lips and he greedily licked them dry.

"Goddamnit, that little bit don't do me no good. I need more."

"After I hear the name."

"Name of Mooney —"

"That his real name?"

"I believe it is. If you was making up a name for yourself, would you pick, Mooney? If'n you don't believe me, there's a scrap of paper in that belt, that captain in Kentucky wrote the name on. Mooney was mad as spit when I said out his name. Told me to forget it. 'Said things had changed and all of 'em had new names, to fool the Yankees.

"Anyways, I 'member this Mooney fella, 'cause he was such a damn fool. The war was over for some months before I got back here, and there he was struttin' around in the uniform of a Reb colonel. Acted like Lee hadn't give it up. Kept callin' me private. Made me salute and call him sir, or colonel. Now, how about some more from that little bottle?"

Haynie let a few drops fall. Rat smacked his lips and demanded more.

"How about a drink of water instead," Haynie said, and raised the tin cup above the coffin

Rat shut his eyes and cried out, "All right, all right. Put it away, you can't blame a man for tryin'." Then he gasped, his chest heaving, "What day is it?" he asked

"Thursday," Haynie said and looked at his own pocket watch. "Soon to be midnight."

"I'm gonna try and make it to Friday; but I figure you're gonna kill me soon as you got no more questions. That's what I'd do I was you. Be'ins I killed your brother and all."

"I believe this is not your first visit to our jail. Why'd you kill Squire Horsey Towne, the town bailiff, and break the two Drumm brothers out of here?"

Rat's laugh at the mention of Jake and Rodney Drumm quickly turned to a racking cough, the pain evident on his face. "I need me some more of that drug if I'm to recollect about that."

"You just got some, that'll have to do for now. First, you tell me about killing Squire."

Haynie held the sheriff's star where Coates could see it. "Did Gastineau tell you to do it?"

Rat licked at his parched lips and shook his head. "Truth is, he was mad as hell that I done it. Them Drumm brothers, the Dumb brothers I called 'em, would'a spilled for sure. Green said, all I did was stir up trouble; that his folks would have got them out without any fuss."

Thinking of Gerhard's account of the Drumm brothers' attack on the bugeye he was aboard, and how their pungy abandoned them, Haynie asked, "Was there a third Drumm?"

Jeremy nodded, his eyes closed.

"Just the three brothers?"

Getting no response, Haynie found a faint pulse.

He gets much more, even paregoric, he'll be asleep or dead; either way he can't tell me anything.

Haynie poured about half of the water from the tin cup over Rat's head. He gasped and howled at the vague form hovering above him.

"Damn you, Pa, you're dead as me, get yer own box, this 'uns mine. Get away ya hear, get away. My name's Rat, not Jeremy. Guess you know, it was me burned the house down. Figured you and ma gone to heaven; I'd never have to meet up with either of ya...." Coates words trailed off, his breathing labored.

Haynie reached down, picked up the Prussian rifle and laid it across the coffin directly above Rat's eyes. Next, he picked up the hacksaw and prodded him in the ribs cage.

"Open your eyes; I have more opium for you."

The man moaned and his eyelids fluttered open.

Haynie sawed furiously on the barrel of the gun, bits of iron drifting into Rat's eyes and mouth.

"HEY, you son-of-a-bitch, see what I'm doing to your beautiful gun,"

Haynie screamed into the box. "It was my brother's dog that bit you and it was Caleb McKenna that killed you. Now he's up there watching this and laughing."

A look of hate flickered across Coates's face as his eyes closed. Fleeting though it was, it signified that he had heard the words.

Haynie cut the rifle into three sections, and then hurled each piece into the box, praying his brother's killer felt pain from each separate piece of his cursed gun.

Disappointed at getting no response, Haynie returned his attention to the leather money belt. He removed two tightly folded pieces of paper, and spread them out on the coffin lid. The first, a stained sheet of white folio on which was neatly written,

Colonel Mooney
Popes Creek, Maryland

was of little value, other than serving as confirmation of what Rat had said.

The second, a telegram, had been tightly folded and concealed behind the wad of currency.

Port Tobacco, Maryland, November 9, 1867
Telegram
M. Green
Lest there any doubt, I fully support the orders issued to you by M. Brown.
It is imperative that you not fail.
C. White

Haynie re-read the telegram several times to fully comprehend the significance of his discovery. It showed that the Sheriff of Somerset County was in league with a militia of some sort. Whether the movement was as influential in the state as Gastineau claimed could not be determined. If true, they'll be well protected and very difficult to get to.

On the other hand, this Colonel Mooney, or White, could be a charlatan. Like Reverend Muse, a man preaching a cause to some gullible folks who worshiped him while he lined his own pockets. If so, Mooney will likely pack up and run at the first sign of trouble.

Rat's story was proving out and Brown's orders to Gastineau, endorsed by White, likely referred to Haynie's own killing. Rat had probably guessed right when he figured that, after he killed Haynie, Gastineau planned to kill him and keep the money.

Haynie folded both documents and put them in his shirt pocket, then satisfied himself that his brother's killer was dead.

Gerhard Stein stood in the cell doorway, his face ashen, but still, he appeared steady on his feet.

"What you do with big gun?" he asked.

"Making certain that nobody else gets killed with it."

"Is too bahd. I could like to hab it."

Haynie untied the rope securing Rat's left wrist to the cot frame and tossed it into the coffin. After removing the two nails holding the coffin lid, he waved off Gerhard's move to help and slid it closed.

He quickly nailed the lid down and turned to Stein. "Let's eat."

37

Popes Creek, Maryland
Monday, March 16, 1868

Dawn broke behind the small pungy as it maneuvered through the flotilla of fishing boats anchored in Somers Cove. Once in Tangier Sound, under full sail, Gerhard Stein made his way aft and settled on an upturned crate. Nearby, Haynie McKenna kept a light hand on the tiller.

Stein asked, "What we are doing *mit diese volks wenn* we get to Popes Creek?"

Haynie shrugged. "I'm not sure. We'll wait and see what happens."

"They is ones that *morder* Caleb, *ja*?"

"Jeremy Coates did the shooting, but it look like this fella Mooney and the woman Stringfellow were paying him."

Haynie watched as his friend processed the words. To ask about Gerhard's gunshot wound would be useless. He assumed Stein was experiencing some discomfort in the early morning chill. Later, the air, warmed by the mid-day sun, would alleviate some of the pain.

Stein said, "We find them, we kill them, *ja?*"

"No!" Haynie said. "I want to, but we're not murderers. We didn't bring guns because I don't want to be tempted. I need to know more about them — what they are hiding. If Coates worked for them, they are responsible for all the killings around here. Who else have they killed?"

Haynie shook away the vision of his brother lying in the weeds.

"For now, I need to look into the eyes of the man responsible for my brother's death."

With a strong following wind, they quickly crossed the open water from Crisfield to Point Lookout. Navigating the shoals up the Potomac River slowed them; still, they made good time to Popes Creek.

After mooring the pungy at the mouth of the creek, they set out along the left bank in an effort to locate the old logging trail, and thereafter, the area of the woods where they had lurked so many miserable hours, for naught.

Once on the trail, Haynie stopped and gestured toward the top of the bluff just across the creek. Through the stark tree limbs emerged the gabled roof and partial dormer of a clapboard house.

Haynie said, "I'm pretty sure that's Mooney's house. We'll ask at the post office before we go up."

Gerhard said, "So *wenn we ist hier....*"

Haynie nodded. "Someone up there was likely spying for the Rebs. They could look down on all our comings and goings along the Potomac and send word to the Rebs just across the river. We never had any hope of catching Wood and his men."

They followed the old wagon tracks further into the woods to the point they had waited in vain.

"Looks different without the leaves and weeds — and the bugs," said Haynie.

"*Ja.*"

Haynie pointed up the trail to the crest where the wagon hauling firewood had first appeared.

"That farmer was real lucky that day. All those green troops, laying there for hours with their fingers on the trigger; it's amazing one of them didn't stand up and start shooting."

Gerhard nodded, "*Ja, Ja.*"

Haynie continued his recollection as he tramped the area.

"That farmer wasn't scared though. He spoke out – 'how long you all been hidin' there,' he said. 'No wonder you Yanks are losing the war. Send all these men out for a whole day an all you got to show for it is one old farmer and a wagon load of firewood.' Set the sergeant into a rage. He would'a set fire to the wagon if the lieutenant hadn't stopped him."

Haynie halted next to a large maple tree, intently searching the ground at its roots.

"Looks like the spot where I was hiding. I'm sure of it." He rose up and pointed across the trail.

"You were right over there," he said.

Gerhard nodded but moved no closer. After a last look around, the two men doubled back and made their way along the creek bank to the main road. The handful of buildings comprising the village of Popes Creek was strewn along the bank of the Potomac, just ahead.

A quick stop at the post office confirmed that the house they had glimpsed atop the bluff was indeed the summer home of Grace Stringfellow and H. J. Mooney.

"Don't believe anyone's there right now," the postmaster volunteered. "Quiet around here 'til the end of June."

Haynie said, "Guess you've lived around Popes Creek for awhile."

"All my life. Didn't have to leave for the war on account of this job."

"I understand that Mister Mooney came here early in the war."

The postmaster nodded. "Likes to be called colonel. We sat out the war together, him up in that big house on the bluff, me down here in this post office."

"He wasn't in the war?"

"Nope. Claimed to be getting over a fit of malaria. Didn't look peaked to me. He'd come in for his mail and we'd joke about missing out on getting shot at. Every day the same – he'd say, real serious like, 'I didn't get killed today, how about you?' I'd pinch my arm and say 'guess not' and we'd both laugh."

The postmaster glanced at both men. "Guess it doesn't sound so funny, now."

Haynie said, "I was under the impression that he and his sister visited more frequently."

"Oh, no, not so much since the war. They used to be down here a lot during the fightin'.

"If he wasn't in the war, why do folks call him colonel?"

The postmaster shrugged and laughed. "Never asked, but he's from Virginia. Ever white man down there is at least a major. Guess ole Mooney isn't one to put on airs, or he'd be a general."

Haynie glanced at Gerhard standing stoically just inside the door. Turning back to the postmaster, he asked, "You ever see Mooney in a uniform?"

The postmaster was thoughtful. "Not with my own eyes, but Hoppy said he seen a bunch of folks up there," he pointed to the bluff, "all gussied up. The men was in Reb uniforms and the women wore them fancy gowns, like they was at a dress ball."

"Hoppy?"

"Jimmy Hopkins. There's a few houses along the river owned by rich folks from up north. Hoppy's kind of a caretaker for some of them. Looks after their places, closes 'em up in the fall, and gets 'em ready for the folks come summer. Can I ask why you're so interested in Colonel Mooney?"

Gerhard shifted his feet.

Haynie said, "I heard the Colonel might be thinking of selling his place and I wanted to take a look at it. Sounds like Hoppy is just the man to talk to. Where could I find him?"

The postmaster shook his head. "Funny," he said. "Hoppy never said nuthin' about them selling. Though, they've not been around for some while now. Anyways, Hoppy's usually up to the Colonel's place on a Monday. Probably find him around the grounds."

Haynie and Gerhard left the tiny post office, walked across the narrow wooden bridge spanning Popes Creek, then followed the steeply sloping road eighty feet to the top of the bluff.

Despite the cool March day, the shirts of both men clung when they reached the lane leading to the house.

The house set back a good hundred yards from the river, barely visible in a grove of lofty oak trees. The trim lawn was unadorned save for the cast iron figures of two Negro youths facing one another and displaying a large sign between them.

The sign, an oak board cut from a saw-log, was richly embossed with script lettering boasting:

Magnolia Bluff

They climbed the steps of a wide veranda whose roof served as the floor for an open balcony overhead. Floor to ceiling windows filled the walls on either side of the front door. Haynie looked through the glass to his right into a large room furnished as a parlor. A well-stoked fire blazed in the large, walk-in fireplace.

In answer to Haynie's knock, the front door opened a crack and a gruff voice said, "What 'cha want?"

Haynie stepped closer to the door, "We understand this property may be for sale and have come a long way hoping to talk to Colonel Mooney. I was very sorry to find out that the Colonel is not resident just now. The postmaster said that a Mister Hopkins might be able to help us, and that we might find him here."

"What'cha want?"

"Are you Mister Hopkins?"

"Mebbe, but you ain't answered the question."

"I was hoping you could take a few minutes to answer some questions about the property, so our trip won't be wasted."

The door opened mere inches more and Haynie could make out a man of about sixty, in work pants and a flannel shirt. A boney forehead sloped to a widow's peak, a lazy right eye wandered.

"Where'd you hear that Mooney wanted to sell this place?"

"We're from Somerset County across the bay, and as you may know, the Colonel and his sister frequently visited there. It was during a social occasion that we discussed the possibility of a sale."

Jimmy Hopkins studied the caller intently with his one good eye, finding it difficult to believe that a man wearing a thin cotton sack coat and unpressed jean trousers was a serious bidder for this estate.

Haynie gave an exaggerated shudder. "Could we come in and talk? It's quite chilly out here."

"I know who ya are," Jimmy Hopkins said and waved a dime novel in Haynie's face. Hopkins's right hand held the book open, marking his place.

"You ain't lookin' to buy this propity. I been readin' about you fellas in this book. You're government agents — Pinkerton's men. I 'spect yer down here to find out about Mooney and that Grace woman of his."

Hopkins paused and thumbed back a few pages. "I know yer tricks. It says right here — you fellas do 'shadowing' of folks and 'assuming a role'. That's what's goin' on here, yer pretending to be a rich man who's lookin' to buy this place, while trickin' me into telling you about them two. I got ya, better fess up."

Haynie, uncertain where the man's loyalty lay, remained noncommittal. "Can we talk inside?" he asked again.

Jimmy Hopkins shifted his right eye to the stoic Gerhard Stein. "Reckon he's one too."

"He's with me."

The caretaker stepped back and the door swung open. "Sure took you fellas long enough."

38

Magnolia Bluff
Popes Creek, Maryland
Monday, March 16, 1868

Jimmy Hopkins was obviously thrilled at being in the company of two of the legendary Allen Pinkerton's detectives. Haynie felt no need to disabuse him of the notion.

Haynie and Gerhard sat uneasily in a pair of wing chairs, waiting for Hopkins to return with mugs of coffee he had insisted upon preparing, over their demurral. The gaze of both men was immediately drawn to an oversized portrait, dominating the wall over the fireplace. The painting, displayed in a Victorian carved walnut frame, depicted a handsome couple, arm in arm, attired as if for a grand ball. She wore a floor length gown of pale orchid, he the full dress uniform of a Confederate colonel.

"They're full of themselves, ain't they," Hopkins said, and distributed the mugs of coffee. He seated himself between the two visitors on a high backed leather chesterfield facing the fire.

Haynie scrutinized the painting as he sipped the watery drink.

I had 'war coffee' tasted better than this.

He sat the cup on the table and said, "Seems an odd pose for brother and sister."

"Brother and sister, that's a good one." The caretaker filled the room with cackling laughter. "Besides the room in the back for their Negress,

Pearl, there's not but one bedroom bein' used in the whole place." He cackled again, "That's another odd thing for a brother and sister."

Haynie said, "Looks like Mooney gives you the run of the place, Mister Hopkins."

"Ever body calls me, Hoppy."

He looked around, as if checking for eavesdroppers, then said, "Well, Mooney don't so much give me the run of the place, as I take it. I don't hurt nuthin', and I never stole nuthin'. Mostly, it gets me away from the wife. She's become a real nag in her old age."

He grinned at Haynie, "You men ain't the only ones can look someone in the eye and lie to their face. I'm pretty good at it myself; course I've had a lot of practice. Been married to the same woman for over forty years."

Hoppy leaned forward, motioning them to do the same.

"I don't really have to be here ever Monday like I told her, especially not now. When I can get up here, I light a fire and read my books. Long as I get home before dark, she don't say nuthin'."

Nodding at the open book, he continued, "That there is the second book I've read about you Pinkerton fellas; pretty exciting what you do. Say, was you with Mister Pinkerton when he kept old Abe from getting shot up to Baltimore?"

Haynie shook his head, "I'm afraid neither one of us was there that day."

Jimmy Hopkins winked his good eye. "I gotcha," he said. "Can't talk about it. I know you fellas aren't supposed to tell about what you do. If'n Pinkerton hadn't saved him, there'd likely be two separate States of America today. Abe Lincoln's the only man could'a kept the Union together; yes, sir, the only man."

Haynie wished to steer the conversation away from the exploits of the Pinkertons.

"Hoppy," he said, "what did you mean when you said you wondered what took us so long?"

"Well I read where you boys go after smugglers and spies and such – and – well, this Mooney is sure enough one or the other. 'Course he's slacked off some since '65 – but they was going at it durin' the war."

"Doing what, exactly?"

Hoppy pointed through the window, toward the bluff.

"You may not know it, not bein' from these parts, but right there is where Maryland and Virginia is the closest of any point along the whole Potomac. During the war, lots of boats traveled back and forth across that little piece of water, mostly at night, which is peculiar right off 'cause folks from around here don't go on that water after dark. Makes no sense unless yer hidin' somethin or runnin' from the law, too risky."

"Any idea what they were doing?" Haynie asked.

"You name it," Hoppy said, with a sweeping motion. "This whole area was a nest of Reb lovers. I reckon you know that actor, Booth, went right through here after shootin' Abe."

Hoppy cackled again and slapped one knee, "Most folks don't know it, but Booth and another fella was put in a boat right out there," he said, and pointed toward the Virginia shore. "Somehow, they got turned around and came ashore back on the Maryland side, just up river at Nanjimoy Creek."

Hoppy shook his head. "Hard to believe anybody could be that dumb. Anyways, during the war, spy messages, guns, men goin' to join the Reb army and money, lots of money for the Rebs, all crossing right here."

"You're pretty certain Mooney was involved?"

"Ain't that why you're here?"

"What did you mean when you said, you weren't needed around here, 'especially not now'?"

"If I hadn't been reading that book," he nodded at Haynie, " and o'course them clothes yer wearin', I might a believed you had talked to Mooney about buying this place.

Haynie waited.

"They was coming around a lot. For a while, it seemed like they was down here more than they was up there — Baltimore. Since last November, they was only here onced or twiced. Last time he says he was takin' Miss Grace back home as her health was failing her."

"He say anything about coming back?"

Hoppy shrugged. "Handed me some money told me to keep an eye on the place whilst they was gone."

"You know where he meant by 'home'?"

"Somewhere in 'Ginia. Don't you fellas know?"

"You might know a place we haven't found yet. Happens some times."

Hoppy motioned to the table between them. "Coffee's gettin' cold."

"Sorry. So interested in what you have to say that I forgot about it."

Hoppy nodded. "Too strong fer ya, I reckon."

"It's fine. Tell me, what did you see that made you think Mooney was helping the South."

Hoppy walked to the fireplace, added a log and prodded the fading embers with a poker. He watched the fire rekindle and returned to his seat.

"Not too long after old man Stringfellow showed up with that young wife, Mooney moved in; told folks he was her brother. 'Said he'd been real sick, with malaria or something like, that's why he stayed here all the time.

"Well sir, it wasn't long and we was told that old Isaiah got drunk and fell off one of his big boats and drowned." Hoppy cackled, "Folks who knew him wouldn't been surprised if he'd been trying to get away from the first wife, but we all thought it mighty peculiar that he didn't get drunk enough to drown hisself until his new wife and this Mooney fella showed up."

"Do you know if Mooney was aboard that boat the night it happened?"

"Don't know it fer a fact, but when Mooney wasn't here, he was with her. And he wasn't here that night."

Haynie nodded.

"Well sir," Hoppy continued, "I looked after the place for Mister Isaiah and the first missus, had for years. Day or two after the mister drowned, Mooney come into town and told me he had his own man, and I shouldn't come 'round anymore. It was right after that folks started seein' the lights up here, and lots more boats on the river at night."

"What kind of lights?"

"There was many a night a man could look across to the 'Ginia shore and see lights flashing over there – on and off, like a signal. Some folks saw the same kind'a lights on this here bluff."

Hoppy paused and looked from Haynie to Gerhard, before continuing.

"Fall of '62 there was a transport boat anchored in the river just off Popes Creek. Carrying hay for Union cavalry horses. Well, that night Rebs swarmed all over her, took the crew prisoner and burned her to the water line."

Hoppy drew himself up, "How was it they come to know that boat was there? Mooney told'em, with them lights — that's how."

Hoppy sat back "How you fellas gonna remember all this? I got more; shouldn't you be writing it down?"

Haynie flashed what he hoped was a disarming smile and pointed to his head. "Everything is written down, right up here. We're taught to remember everything."

Hoppy let out another cackle. "I gotcha. Ya can't have nothing on paper in case ya get took by the enemy. Pretty smart."

"You catch on quick," Haynie said. "I can see you're going to be a big help to us."

Leaning closer, he spoke in what he trusted were conspiratorial tones. "Remember, there are other operatives working on this, too, so none of us can do anything unless we have a direct order. It could ruin everything."

Hoppy nodded and waved the open book. "Probably I should finish this, so I know how we do things."

Hoppy glanced at Gerhard, sitting stiff and silent in the wing back chair.

"Don't this fella ever talk?"

Haynie experimented with a casual laugh. "He's new on the job. With us, the senior man does all the talking. This is valuable information. Tell us, how is it that Mooney got you back up here to work for him?"

"Well, sir, when he and the widow Stringfellow set up housekeeping, they brought two Negras with 'em. Mooney struttin' around like the lord of the manor. The widow layin' around waiting to be served.

"The buck tended to the grounds and the woman, Pearl, kept the house. Well, sir, about a month after Lee give it up, it must have occurred to that buck – don't recollect a name for him – that he wasn't a slave no more and he up and run off."

"So, it was then he asked you to come back?"

Hoppy nodded. "There was no more boats going back and forth – no more lights winking in the night. I guess they figgered it was okay for me to be up here."

The caretaker stood and, with a cackle, signaled them to follow. "Sumthin' I want to show ya."

Hoppy led them up a richly carpeted stairway. They ascended past framed charcoal drawings of Virginia landscapes. A rococo banister of dark wood, perhaps mahogany or polished teak, separated them from the room below.

At the top of the stairs, Hoppy pointed to a closed door at the front of the house. "Wait'll you see this," he said.

The unlocked door opened into a cramped, windowless room that could easily be mistaken for the annex to a Confederate military museum.

Haynie's attention was drawn to a Confederate army officer's full dress uniform displayed on a tailor's mannequin in a corner of the room. Looking closer, he noted the upright collar of the frock coat bore the three gold stars of a full colonel. It was identical to the uniform in the painting over the fireplace. The yellow facing on the coat and the matching outer seam of the trousers represented that the wearer was an officer of the Confederate cavalry. Included was a one-piece leather carbine sling, with a buckle of polished brass, boldly displaying the letters—C S A.

An officer's saber was exhibited on the wall, immediately above the uniform. Unsheathed, the sword gleamed, and even in the dim light, the C.S.A. cannon and battle flags etched into the brilliant blade were readily discernable.

To the left, a McClellan saddle straddled a sawed section of oak log resting across wooden sawhorses. The cavalries of both armies used the lightweight McClellan saddle, this one carried the initials CSA stamped in gold on the pommel.

Haynie examined the saddle and the grey wool blanket upon which it rested, then moved to a pair of confederate issue, ankle high Jefferson boots. Though shiny and unscuffed, they paled next to the custom-made knee high dress boots alongside. The boots, of highly buffed black leather, were neatly arraigned in a military line. Across the dress, boots lay a pair of white leather gauntlets, embroidered with the cavalry insignia.

Hoppy stood to one side with a broad grin, as Haynie moved silently along the walls studying the array of weapons, news clippings, photos, and framed military correspondence before him.

Gerhard Stein stood in the open doorway continually scanning the corridor for any sign of trouble. He had no inkling what manner of trouble to expect, but he knew that Haynie relied on him, and no one would surprise them.

Mounted across the top of the wall were the long guns. A Sharps carbine, an Enfield two band musket, an Enfield Musketoon and, what Haynie knew from personal experience as the weapon of choice for many in the confederate cavalry, a double-barreled, sawed off shotgun.

Among the several framed news clippings was one reporting:

> On Tuesday last, September 17, 1861, A local man, Horace J. Mooney, run off to join up with General Joe Johnston and The Army of The Shenandoah. God Bless Virginia and the Confederate States of America.

No town was identified, but the smudged letters and rustic composition indicated a small town paper, likely a weekly. The remaining news accounts were more sophisticated, reporting of battles in which cavalry units received prominent mention. Mooney's name was not among those listed, but the presence of these accounts, in the room, clearly implied his participation in the battles.

The next item to catch Haynie's notice was a framed letter on the stationary of Brigadier General John Ewell Brown Stuart, dated November 12, 1861. The letter promoted H. J. Mooney to the rank of full Colonel in Stuart's cavalry. Haynie stepped back and re-read the item about Mooney leaving home to join up with Joe Johnston, and then he returned and again read the promotion letter. It seemed odd to him that Mooney could enlist in September under Johnston, and by November get promoted to full Colonel by Jeb Stuart. Such a transformation was unheard of, even in the Reb army.

Haynie had no way of knowing that, while the stationary itself was quite authentic, Grace had helped her self to several sheets while the guest of a junior officer in Stuart's headquarters; the promotion itself was counterfeit, written and signed by Mooney well after the war was over. Mooney and Grace, incensed over the failure of the Confederate Army to promote him, felt justified in correcting the oversight.

Haynie said aloud, "You notice anything strange about the uniform, the guns, the saddle, the boots and gloves?"

"I don't follow ya."

"Most folks keep a thing from the war 'cause it means a great deal to them. Maybe they had it through every battle, a good luck piece, or a bayonet that belonged to their best friend until he got killed right beside them. None of this ever saw a battlefield."

"I told ya, he was living right here during most of the war."

Haynie nodded. "Spying for the South. So, why is he play-acting that he was a cavalry officer? Who's he trying to fool – besides himself?"

Hoppy shrugged, then pointed to a device occupying a small shelf on the far wall. "What do you make of that?" he asked.

Haynie lifted it by the wire handle.

"It's a picket's lantern," he said, swinging the lens open.

"Hand held. The candle goes inside and the light is magnified through this lens. These shutters are operated to spell out the message," he said as he worked the shutters back and forth. Haynie replaced the lantern and studied the tri-pod mounted marine glasses next to it.

Looking at Hoppy he said, "I'd say that the lights the folks were seeing came from the picket's lantern. Mooney used these glasses to read messages from the other shore."

Hoppy gave short cackle, "Like I told ya."

Haynie said, “Be real easy to carry this gear out to the bluff. Only take a minute or two to send a short message, then fold ’er up and bring it back in here.”

“Looks like we’re gonna arrest us some spies,” Hoppy cackled again. “You gonna want me to watch them two, when they come back?”

Haynie shook his head. “If they show up here, you wire me right away. I’ll tell you how to get a hold of me, before I leave.”

Seeing Hoppy’s face shadowed with disappointment, Haynie said, “It’s likely that, by then, we’ll already have other agents tracking them. I have something else in mind for you.”

Hoppy brightened, “Like what?”

Haynie shook his head, “Later.”

The room was interesting, but it offered nothing to show that H. J. Mooney and Grace Stringfellow were in any way connected to Caleb’s murder, or the other murders in Somerset County.

Haynie shook his head. “This is only a part of what they’ve been doing. We need to find out everything.”

Hoppy nodded, but said nothing.

“There must be more,” Haynie muttered, then said, “Show me their bedroom.”

Hoppy stepped across the hall and swung open the door to a much larger room. “Doubt this will do ya any good. Just their bedroom; no war stuff.”

Haynie followed the caretaker into the room, while Gerhard stayed in the hall.

Crossing to the set of French doors, Haynie made no sound in the plush carpet. The doors opened onto the balcony.

Haynie visualized the Mooneys sitting here on a summer evening enjoying a mint julep while gazing across the Potomac to the Virginia shoreline.

Inside the room, a raised four-poster canopy bed provided it’s occupants a vista of the opposite shore without them bothering to get up.

Haynie turned from the French doors and headed for a small writing desk near the bed.

Hoppy said, “I never really been in this room before. Looked in once or twice, but it wouldn’t be right — this is where they do their personal business.”

Haynie understood the caretaker’s concern that they leave no sign that strangers had prowled here. Still, if he found something linking Mooney and Stringfellow to the killings, or the waterfront abductions...

Seated at the desk, Haynie went through each drawer, mindful of how its contents were arranged, returning any disturbed items to their original position after examination.

From the bottom drawer, he removed an embossed leather photo album and placed it on the desk. The book was ornate, with colorfully painted insets and the words – *Mooney Family Album* – stamped in gold leaf across the heavy cover. Haynie unfastened the brass latches.

The pages were of a heavy card stock with four oval shaped cutouts on each page, allowing viewing of a photograph tucked into a pocket on the backside of each cutout. A date and location where the photo was taken had been penned by a delicate hand under each oval.

The photos on the first few pages had been taken in and around Stanton, Virginia during the mid to late 1850s. Most of them showed a young Mooney with siblings and other family clustered about him. By turning the page, Haynie could see the names of those whose likenesses were depicted in that photograph — Horace J., Uncle Raymond and Aunt Bessie – Cousin Joe – Ma and Pa. The woman in the painting over the fireplace, Grace Stringfellow, was not present on these pages.

Grace's image first appeared as the bride in a wedding photo dated February 10th, 1861, Stanton, Virginia. The groom, surrounded by beaming relatives, was a smiling H.J. Mooney.

Haynie called Hoppy over. "In case there was any doubt about them being brother and sister," he said, pointing to the wedding photo.

Hoppy cackled, "Don't prove nuthin'. They're from Virginny."

Haynie laughed, "But, if she's his sister, why isn't she in any family photos before the wedding?"

As might be expected, there was a dearth of photographs during the years 1862 to 1865. In one, Mooney and Grace stood arm in arm, with backs to the camera, at the edge of Magnolia Bluff, obviously gazing across the Potomac toward Virginia. He was costumed in the colonel's uniform along with the custom dress boots, leather gauntlets, and officer's saber at his side. The photo was dated April 1863 – Magnolia Bluff, Virginia.

Hoppy stood at Haynie's shoulder following the turn of each page.

Haynie said, "Did you know that Mooney considers this property part of the state of Virginia?"

"No, sir. They musta really hated being in Maryland."

"Aha," Haynie said aloud as he turned a page and recognized Sheriff Gastineau, in the uniform of a major, Confederate States of America, in the midst of a group of other men all similarly outfitted. Haynie studied the faces of the others, of particular interest was another major standing between Gastineau and Mooney.

"Ya spot somethin'?" Hoppy asked.

Haynie tapped Gastineau's likeness with an index finger. "That's the county sheriff who was murdered over our w — over in Somerset County, last year." He hurriedly moved his finger to the other major. "And this one," he said, "looks real familiar, but I don't believe he had that beard when I saw him."

To himself, Haynie said*, I'll bet that's Coates's other contact, Mister Brown, standing next to Gastineau. If he's still alive, I've got a chance to learn a lot more about what this crowd is up to.*

Haynie turned the page and read the back of the photograph – Whitehaven, Maryland June 1866.

Hoppy bent lower to get a closer look, "Sounds crazy, but you reckon there's a whole gang of Rebs still aiming to free the South?"

"Maybe that's not so crazy," Haynie said.

"Look, Hoppy, I need to have my friend see a couple of these pages – for our report. Would you volunteer to stand lookout for a few minutes, while he comes in here?"

A grin spread across the caretaker's face. "Yes, sir. Fer damn sure you can count on ole Hoppy."

With Hopkins out of the room, Haynie slid the group photo from its pocket and tucked it inside his shirt. As Gerhard strode toward the desk, Haynie put a finger to his lips.

Finding nothing of interest in the album's remaining pages Haynie removed a picture from the second to last page and inserted it into the empty pocket of the photo he had removed. An empty oval in the back of the album was less likely to be noticed than one nearer the front. It wasn't much, but it was all he could think of.

Haynie shut the album and returned it to the drawer as he had found it, then motioned for Gerhard to watch the door for Hoppy's return.

Haynie opened the remaining door to find a large walk-in closet, barren except what appeared to be piece of carpet shoved into a far corner. He picked up the item that unfolded into a wooden handled carpetbag adorned in a brocade of bright red flowers.

Haynie was certain he held the bag described in the ransom letter Colonel Wallis had received. Folding the bag as tight as possible, he shoved it under his jacket and quickly closed the door.

He motioned Stein to follow him from the room.

39

Steamboat Wharf
Crisfield, Maryland
Monday, August 10, 1868

Haynie McKenna scanned the faces as the passengers shuffled up the gangplank of the steamboat, Bay Princess. The boat's stern paddle wheel churned idly at his back.

Without turning, he knew that Lila and the children were intently watching from the second deck. After seeing his family aboard, Haynie had returned to the wharf to await his mother's appearance to say goodbye.

She had not spoken to him since their confrontation on his front steps, last November, and refused to see him on the two occasions he had stopped by her house. Still, he believed she would come to say goodbye to her grandchildren.

Lettie McKenna had not seen Young Tench in that time and, equally perplexing, had shown no interest in her granddaughter, Ella May McKenna, in the four months since her birth.

After the mid-wife, Mrs. Whitford, assisted Lila with the delivery, she called at the Manor House to give Lettie the news. She later reported that Lettie stared at her for a full minute before closing the front door without a word.

Haynie waited, trusting that his mother would put aside her rancor long enough to see her grandchildren before they sailed for their new home in Annapolis.

He understood that the initial distress she felt at his refusal to embrace her Lord grew as she blamed him for Caleb's death, and blossomed into an unyielding rancor as she watched Gerhard Stein carting the Reverend Muse from her life.

Haynie relied heavily on the tenet that Christians were forgiving of the sins of others. Apparently, this was one of Christ's teachings his mother failed to embrace.

Haynie's several steamboat trips to Baltimore and Annapolis, over the past months, provided ample time to ponder – what had been and what was to be. He spent countless hours examining Lettie's relationship to her sons, and the Reverend Muse, as well as his own actions leading to the confidence man's forcible ejection from the Manor House.

He inevitably arrived at the same conclusions: he would never please his mother where religion was concerned; she would always blame him for Caleb's death; the Reverend Muse was a dyed in the wool rascal.

If Muse had not been driven away, in all likelihood he would possess the Manor House and whatever of Lettie's possessions he could convince her God wanted him to have. In the end, she would be just as heartbroken — and have nothing.

Haynie wondered if his mother was ever curious about what had become of Caleb's cursed fiddle. He had hoped that, once free of Muse's dominion, she might recover her senses. But, if anything, Muse's absence had driven her to become more radical in her devotion.

Two impatient blasts of the steam whistle signaled all passengers that the Bay Princess would shortly be getting underway. Haynie glanced to the upper deck to see Lila motioning him to come aboard while clutching Ella May. Young Tench mimicked his mother with a frantic wave.

A few stragglers made their way toward the boat. Haynie moved back a few steps and stopped with one foot resting on the gangway, as an assurance to Lila and Young Tench that he would not be left behind.

His pulsed raced as a woman approached, head bent, her face hidden. She was the same stature as his mother, but the clothing was unfamiliar. The woman looked up just as he realized that his mother, were she to come, would not be carrying a valise. He turned his attention to the terminal building and continued his vigil.

Surprisingly, perhaps, Haynie had not missed his mother's presence at Christmas. In recent years, she had shown little interest in the secular aspects of the holiday, celebrating the birth of Jesus Christ solely by attending church and prayer.

Haynie, on the other hand, reveled in all aspects of Christmas, taking particular pleasure in his Christmas Eve reading of the poem, *T'was The Night Before Christmas,* to Young Tench while Lila listened. The birth of his daughter meant having someone new to enthrall with his annual recitation.

Most of all, Haynie wished for the opportunity to sit with his mother, in her parlor, and share the events changing his life. A lot of thought had gone into deciding just what he would tell her, and what he must withhold.

Would she be comforted knowing that the man who killed Caleb was dead? Probably not. Haynie imagined his mother saying, "Revenge is mine, sayeth the Lord."

Haynie would argue, "Jeremy Coates's death was justice, not revenge."

Doubtful she would appreciate the irony that Caleb's dog, Junior, was the instrument of Coates's death.

Haynie would not tell her about the other men Coates had killed; or about the prison Coates was guarding; nor should she know about the bodies he found there, and how he had left them ablaze to retrieve Caleb's remains from the carrion eating wildlife.

He saw himself taking one of her hands and gently telling her, "I will not forget father's death, though my search is taking me along a far different road than I could ever have imagined before last November."

How his mother would respond, he could not be certain. She was a much different person than the woman who brought them from Smith Island over 10 years before. They were both different people.

Haynie would try to make her understand the compelling force behind his joining the Maryland Oyster Navy. He had, long ago, accepted that his father's killer would go unnamed, and now those responsible for Caleb's death had fled back to Virginia. Avoiding his reach – for the present.

So, Haynie was dedicating himself to help bring law and order to the Chesapeake. And, while there would be more killings, the families of those yet to be slain would know that someone was there for them to turn to. Someone who shared their hurt, and would not allow their loved one's death to be disregarded.

It would serve no purpose to relate to her how he and Gerhard had explored the Popes Creek home of H. J. Mooney, or the significance of the photograph he had taken.

"Haynie McKenna," she would say, "Thou shalt not steal. That's sinful. You return that man's property immediately."

He planned to mention a meeting he had at Colonel Wallis's Fell's Point office in March, though there was no need to burden her with the details.

When Haynie arrived at Wallis's office, he was surprised to learn that Major Hollins would not be attending. The three Wallis men were the only others present.

"I assumed that Major Hollins would be here," Haynie had said.

Getting no response, he pulled out the photograph taken from Mooney's album, and laid it on the desk.

Glancing at Landon, he said, "I think these people are connected to your kidnapping."

Landon quickly stood and leaned in for a closer look.

Haynie laid a finger in the center of the photograph and said, "I guess you know, H. J. Mooney."

The elder Wallis nodded

"Did you know he fancies himself a Colonel in the Confederate army?"

Silas grabbed up the photograph and held it close to his eyes. "Landon, fetch me that magnifying lens from the girl's desk."

Landon hurried back and handed the glass across the desk. Silas held it, and the photo, close as he studied the uniformed men.

Haynie said, "The bearded fella standing on Mooney's left looks familiar, but I can't place him. The man next in line is name of Gastineau, the county sheriff killed by Jeremy Coates, the man known as Rat. Coates took orders from Gastineau. It was him who killed Caleb and the others."

Silas Wallis lowered the glass. "The reason you didn't recognize this one," he said, his finger touching the unidentified man in the picture, "is he wasn't sporting a beard the last time you saw him. That's our good friend, Major Hollins."

Haynie unwrapped the cloth he carried and produced the decorated carpetbag. "That accounts for this being at Mooney's house on the Potomac."

The elder Wallis sagged into his chair. "Et tu," he mumbled.

"I'm sorry, sir."

Neither would Haynie tell her that H. J. Mooney and Grace Stringfellow had left Magnolia Bluff; fled, some say, after learning that two Pinkerton men came to Popes Creek looking for them. According to Colonel Wallis, the two were presently in Virginia and it was likely Hollins was with them.

She should know that he had not given up in his efforts to find all of those responsible for Caleb's death.

Colonel Wallis was instrumental in securing Haynie's appointment as a deputy commander in the newly formed State Oyster Police. Would she be pleased that a man of his position thought enough of her son to do that? The mother he knew on Smith Island would glow, as to the woman she had become, he could not say.

"You coming aboard, sir? We're taking up the gangway."

Haynie nodded. Though his mother may believe he failed her; of two things he was certain. He was doing the best he could for his father and brother; and now, finally, there was promise for the future.

He glanced quickly around the pier, and hurried aboard.

CPSIA information can be obtained at www.ICGtesting.com
Printed in the USA
BVOW071600180912

300411BV00001B/4/P